THE BOSS COURTED TROUBLE

THE BOSS COURTED TROUBLE

SHIRLEY JUMP

This is a work of fiction. All of the characters, organizations, and events portrayed in this novel are either products of the author's imagination or are used fictitiously.

eISBN: 978-1-937776-67-1
ISBN-13: 978-1-937776-84-8

CHAPTER ONE

Madison Worth knew she was in trouble the minute the manure hit her Prada heels.

Actually, the trouble had started months ago in New York, during the Fall Collection Show. One little incident with a chocolate cake and Kate Moss, and all of a sudden, Madison had been labeled as difficult. Temperamental.

And the unkindest cut of all—a diva.

That one hurt the worst. It wasn't like she went around insisting all the orange M&Ms be removed from the candy dish. Or pitched a fit because someone handed her a Dasani instead of Evian. Why, she rarely ever complained about having to smile and cavort in the ocean for a swimsuit shoot in February.

She was *not* a diva. Not even close. The cake throwing had been completely justified. Maybe not smart, but explainable.

It had merely been a bizarre twist of fate that Kate Moss's face had to come between Madison and winning an argument.

So now, because of that, Madison stood in the circular dirt driveway of the Pleeseman Dairy Farm, located in one of those no-name, blink-and-you'll-miss-it towns in the Berkshires of Massachusetts, trying to ignore the brown lump on her seven-hundred-dollar strappy sandals. The late July heat only intensified the odor, the experience. Madison forced herself not to turn her nose up in distaste, not to retch right there on the driveway. That wouldn't do, not when she desperately needed this job. If she'd had a choice, she'd have been out of here on the first private jet.

But those days were far behind Madison Worth. So she was forced to put up with the crud. Literally. She put a hand on her hip, the other shielding her eyes from the sunshine.

Ahead of her, the poop perpetrator—a massive green and black truck thing—a dump truck?—chugged along the curve, leaving a cow patty trail in its wake, several of which bounced off the dry, caked dirt and spattered in her direction. Ewww. She shuddered, resisted running as fast as she could back toward the sanity of New York, and instead raised her hand, waving, trying to catch the attention of the driver. Surely someone should be outside, ready to meet her, to show her to her dressing room and then escort her to her hotel suite.

To civilization and crisp, white sheets.

But the tractor, truck, whatever, kept right on chugging toward a barn and trio of silos on her left. A one-horned goat trotted along behind the machine, baaing and nipping at stray blades of grass along the path. The breeze picked up, whisking with it the heavy, distinct smell of manure, tinged with sour milk. Madison grimaced, swallowing the bile in her throat.

If she hadn't already looked at her calendar and seen Sunday on the little block for today, she'd have sworn it was a Monday, given the particularly crappy start to her day.

She'd put up with worse, hadn't she? That photo shoot in Greece, with the grabby photographer who had a habit of "making sure" her top was properly adjusted for the lens? The video she'd shot on the yacht, which had turned into a disaster when a storm whipped up, sending most of the crew and the models scrambling for the nearest bucket? Her agent had gotten an earful about that particular job, and as consolation had sent Madison a case of Dramamine and a hot-off-the-runway pair of Jimmy Choos.

This, too, was a job, like any other. And one she had to do without complaint, if she ever wanted to restore her career to its former beauty.

Now *there* was irony—modeling for a cheese company, steeped high in the scent of manure, as a way to get back into the pages of *Women's Wear Daily*.

Madison picked her way further up the drive and past the cow landmines, still waving futilely, and in between, waving her hand at her chest, trying to head off the perspiration before it started to show. Why had she worn a suit? Who was she trying to impress out here on *Green Acres*?

Anyone who wanted to hire her, that's who. She didn't care that Eileen Ford had dropped her from her model roster faster than Britney Spears could say "I do." That all the other top agencies in town had turned her down, refusing to see her, lest she darken the doorsteps of their Naomi Campbell built offices.

That she had had to go groveling back to Harry Blenkins, her agent from the early days, and listen to him chortle with glee, in between Marlboro hacks.

One—okay, maybe two or three—crying jags in front of the camera did *not* constitute a breakdown. She still had her looks, her body and most of all, her ability to model the pants off Cindy Crawford. And she was damned well going to prove it to the industry—

As the spokesmodel for the Cheese Pleese Company.

Behind her, her Benz made an odd clicking noise as it cooled, definitely a sign of owner neglect. It had sputtered to a stop halfway up the drive, leaving her to navigate on her own.

Surely, she had landed in hell, she thought, avoiding yet another dung disaster.

Around her, the scent of manure seemed to multiply, to take up residence in her nose. A bird swooped down, nearly decapitating her in its journey toward a nearby birdfeeder. And leaving her a nice surprise on the opposite Prada heel.

That was *it*.

Forget the whole damned thing. She couldn't do this. She wasn't *that* desperate.

Madison tugged her cell phone out of her purse, flipping open the cover. She had not driven all those hours along the crowded turnpike to be crapped on—literally. "I'm out of here," she muttered, holding one in-need-of-a-manicure finger over the first listed contact. In an instant, she could erase the manure, the cheese factory, that itty bitty nervous breakdown during Fashion Week.

All she had to do was push a single button. Well, that and maybe grovel a little. Okay, a *lot*.

One phone call would put her back into her Manhattan apartment, give her Benz some much-needed TLC, and send her on a shoe shopping spree that would make Imelda Marcos salivate.

She hesitated. One button. One call. And it would all go away.

And leave her right back where she'd started, except without any cake ammunition. Madison clicked the phone's flip top closed.

Aw, hell.

Somewhere along the way, Madison Worth had gotten the insane idea that she needed to grow up.

"Hey," Madison called to Mr. Green Jeans on the truck, making her wave bigger, using her phone to catch a glint of sunshine. "Hey!"

Farmer-guy put his foot on the brake, turned, cupped a hand over his ear and stared at her. If he was surprised to see a five-foot-eleven blonde in designer duds standing in the drive, he didn't show it. He just gave her a blank look, then one short nod. "Ma'am," was all he said.

"Do you know where I can find Jack Pleeseman?"

The engine of the tractor continued its low rumble. The guy lifted a shoulder, then dropped it, and shook his head. "Can't say that I do. He's a pesky one to keep track of. Always off on one idea or another."

Idiot, Madison thought. She hated dealing with anyone lower on the totem pole than the top. He was probably one of the worker bees, which meant he had no idea of the boss's whereabouts and wouldn't be a bit of help anyway. Madison waved a never-mind hand at him, squared her shoulders and marched the rest of the way to the front door.

She'd do it herself. It wasn't like she was completely incapable of self-care. Most days, anyway.

The tractor backfired, releasing an explosive boom and a plume of black smoke that surrounded Madison, surely turning her pink Chanel suit gray.

Okay, so, this wasn't the high profile runway work she was used to. It wasn't the cover of *Marie Claire* or hell, even an inside quarter-page ad. It was small town, hokie work, the kind the other models laughed at behind their thousand-watt mirrors.

But it was going to be Madison's saving grace, by God. If not, she'd have to find a real job and Lord knew she wasn't fit for anything more involved than returning a purse to Bloomingdale's.

She reached the porch and made her way up the steps. The wood was worn in places, the white paint peeling back to reveal a gray of years gone by. Each step let out an ominous squeak. And then, just when she reached the top, the spiky heel of her right shoe poked right through the landing.

And stayed there.

Madison yanked, but the porch still held her hostage. She had two choices—stay there and wait for rescue or bend over, undo the pain-in-the-ass buckle and take off the shoe.

Since her only chance for rescue seemed to be Hector the Tractor Guy, who had already chug-chugged away, backfiring like Patriots fans belched, she opted for the second choice. Madison bent over and tried to get her acrylic nails under the teeny buckle to slip it out of its brass tether. She nearly had it off and then—

The red tip on her index finger popped off, flying across the porch. It skittered across the wood, then slipped through a crack.

"Better watch out for our bull," a voice said behind her. "Big George sees that view and before you know it, you're having a calf."

She whirled around, her skirt whooshing against her bare legs, and faced the man behind her. It wasn't the tractor guy—it was someone far younger. He was taller than her, probably six foot two, and tan in a rugged sort of way that said he spent time outdoors, not at the Mist-N-Go booth. He had broad shoulders, easily defined by his pale blue cotton T-shirt and jeans that hugged along his thighs, tapering down to cowboy boots that were dusted with dirt. His hair was dark, with a slight wave, offset by even darker eyes, the same color as a good chocolate.

He may have been good-enough-for-the-runway gorgeous, but Madison hated him on sight. Because he was *grinning* at her. Like he found her predicament amusing.

"I'm stuck," Madison said. "In case you didn't notice. Could you find the boss or better yet, help me? Like the gentleman I presume you are?"

"That porch," the man said, ignoring her and rubbing his chin with one hand, that grin remaining on his face, "why, it's nabbed many a woman. My cousin Paul married the last one who got her foot caught."

"You're joking."

Still that smirk. "Only if you're already spoken for."

Madison let out a gust, gave her shoe a solid yank, pulling it from its wooden prison—

And sending her off balance, scrambling for purchase against the peeling wooden columns. Before she could fall to her humiliation on the cow patty drive, a pair of strong arms had scooped her up and carried her onto the middle of the porch.

"Put me down," Madison said. "Before I—"

"Sue me for saving you from falling on your ass?" The man tipped forward, dumped her onto the porch, then stepped back, crossing his arms over his chest. Madison teetered. Then, as only a woman who had spent her formative years in three-inch heels could, she regained her balance.

"You're pretty damned ungrateful," he said.

"And you're pretty damned touchy-feeling. You could have helped me without using your hands."

He quirked a brow at that. "Hmm…now there's a talent I haven't yet cultivated. Picking up a woman without using my hands." He thought a minute. "Can't say I want to learn to do that, either."

Madison bit back her first retort. And her second. She was here to work on her self control, with the bonus of earning a living. Lashing out at the hired help might make her feel better, but it wasn't working toward her goal. "I'm looking for Jack Pleeseman," she said, naming the man who had hired her, and who held the fate of her career in his hands. "Do you work for him?"

"Nope."

"Do you know him?"

The guy considered this. "Better than most."

"Can you point me in the direction of where I might find him?"

"Don't need to."

Madison took a step forward, pointing her naked nail at his chest. "Listen, buster. I have been spattered with cow crap, used as a Port-a-Potty by a low-flying bird, and suffocated by tractor exhaust. I am in no mood for your games."

"Too bad. Because you sure seem like you'd be fun to beat at checkers."

She bit back a shriek of frustration. Whoever this guy was, she was going to make sure Jack Pleeseman fired him for treating her so rudely. "If you won't tell me where your boss is, then I'll find him myself, wherever he is on this godforsaken hellhole farm." She pivoted on her heel and reached for the brass doorknocker.

"'Fraid you won't find him in there," the man said.

"And why is that?" Madison lowered the knocker hard against the door anyway.

"Because he's standing right here."

The manure had been nothing. This time, the shit really hit Madison. Square in the face.

Jack's The-Diva's-Got-Attitude Stuffed Jalapenos

1 pound bulk pork sausage
8 ounces cream cheese, softened
24 large jalapeno peppers

That woman has only been on your property for five minutes and already she's upped the heat factor a hundred times. The solution? Give back as good as you're getting.

Preheat the oven to 425 degrees. Trust me, you can operate an oven. Kitchen appliances aren't as hard as they look. Yeah, that's it, just turn the knob till you're looking at 4-2-5. Think of it as revving an engine to a certain RPM.

Cook the sausage in a skillet over medium heat, then drain. No whining allowed. We're men. We can cook some sausage and shove it in a jalapeno, for God's sake. Mix with the cream cheese and set aside. Meanwhile, put on some plastic gloves (hey, we're men, but we aren't nuts enough to handle hot peppers with our bare hands). Halve the jalapenos and remove the seeds. When you're done, spoon

11

about a tablespoon of the sausage mixture into each jalapeno half.

Place in a baking dish and bake, uncovered (meaning, with the top down, for all you men who speak car, not oven), for about 15-20 minutes, till the inside is as hot as the pepper.

When she makes you boil, pop one of these spicy snacks in your mouth—so you don't say something you'll regret later. And if you want to tone things down a notch, dip these hot puppies into some Ranch or blue cheese dressing.

But watch out—for the woman, not the jalapenos. It's the spice you *don't* see that can be the most dangerous.

CHAPTER TWO

Madison Worth was not what Jack Pleeseman had expected when he'd called the modeling agency, looking for someone who could work a long-term gig for short-term money. She was as ornery as Big George, as stubborn as Katydid the goat, and about as sweet as his great-grandma's cough elixir.

But she sure was a hell of a lot prettier than anything he'd ever seen on Pleeseman Dairy Farms.

She had vibrant blue eyes, sparkling like a lake under bright sun, high, defined cheekbones, with a tapered jaw. All fine and delicate features, perfect as porcelain. Her lips were full and red, yet the bottom one had a slightly pouty quality to it, as if it begged to be kissed. Her lush blond hair was long and straight, falling about her face in a shimmering curtain of silk, with the kind of smooth glimmer that other women paid hundreds of dollars to duplicate.

"You're…" she said, her voice trailing off, probably hoping he wasn't the man who'd hired her. "Him?"

"Jack Pleeseman," he said, extending his hand.

"Madison Worth," she said, recovering from the initial shock. "And I'm…I'm very sorry we got off on the wrong foot. Literally." She slipped her palm into his own. If he hadn't known better, he'd have sworn her skin was velvet. Her hair was definitely silk—long gold silk that he had seen spread out across the sands of Saint Kitts in last year's *Sports Illustrated* Swimsuit edition. The leopard print bikini she'd worn had told him she had the kind of body most men never got lucky enough to come within ten feet of.

He'd come that close and closer, by staring at her bikini picture for nearly a week before picking up the phone and hiring her.

Now, looking at her in the flesh, his mind mentally cladding her in itty-bitty leopard print, he had to swallow and remind himself—twice—that he had hired her for purely business reasons.

"I apologize for giving you such a hard time," he said. "I don't always remember to play well with others."

"Neither do I," she said. And then…she smiled at him. Not one of those measly little "I'm only being polite" kinds of smiles, but a real honest-to-God knock-you-in-the-gut smile. It spread across her face, illuminating her features with a radiant glow that he would have sold in a bottle, had he been able to replicate it. It electrified her cobalt blue eyes, erasing all comparisons between her and his more stubborn farm animals.

No wonder she was a model. A woman with a smile like that could make toothpicks look sexy.

He knew he was supposed to say something here. Tell her about his plan, about why he'd hired her. Jack opened his mouth. "Uh...," he said. "Uh..."

Damn, she was gorgeous. He'd clearly been spending too much time with the bovine species. The second Madison Worth had smiled at him, his brain cells deserted him, leaving him high and dry and without a single coherent thought he could latch onto so he didn't look like a complete idiot standing on his own damned porch.

It wasn't often—okay, never—that a pretty woman walked onto the Pleeseman property. Apparently, the shock had sent his gray matter scattering.

"You hired me," Madison supplied, releasing his palm from her own because he'd also become immobile, "to be a spokesmodel for your product line."

Oh yeah. That. "For the cheese," he said.

She swallowed and the smile lagged a bit. "Yes, the, ah, cheese."

"Well, come on in," Jack said, recovering his manners from somewhere around his size-eleven boots, "and we'll get acquainted."

"Great," she said, then took a step forward. But the old wood of the porch—another thing on his To Do list—cracked and splintered beneath her spiky heels, sending both of the points poking through the floorboards.

"Excuse me," Madison said, acting as if this were an everyday occurrence. She tugged and jerked, releasing her right foot, but the left shoe stubbornly stayed put. Madison bent over, working at the buckle again, her long tapered nails seeming to work against, not with her. She cursed, twice, while trying unsuccessfully to loosen the leather strap from its brass prison.

"Here, let me," Jack said. He bent down, intending only to do the gentlemanly thing and help her, but the instant his hands met her ankle, he knew he was a big fat liar. He'd wanted a close-up of her fabulous legs, of the pale bare skin that seemed to stretch twenty feet upward. He swallowed hard, remembered he was here to unbuckle her, not undress her, and worked the fastener free. She slipped her foot out—a perfect, delicate foot with red toenails—red, for God's sake, as scarlet as a cardinal—and placed it on the wooden floor.

"There," he said, yanking the shoe out and then handing it to her as he rose and before he gave in to the thoughts running through his now functioning brain cells. Apparently a little skin got them to start moving double-time, but they were still only traveling down one very dangerous path. "You're free."

"Thanks." Madison balanced on her left leg, then slipped the other shoe off. Jack did his best to keep his gaze on her face, not on her second bare foot. Or her legs. Or any of her other drop-dead gorgeous body parts. She stood before him, a couple inches shorter, but still nearly eye level with his six-foot-two frame. He knew, from the photo resume her agent had sent over, that Madison was five-foot-eleven. A hundred and fifteen pounds. And every ounce of her was flawless.

She gave him another one of those powerhouse smiles. "Thank you for helping me. Now, if we can get down to business?"

Oh *yeah.* A little *business.* His bedroom was just—

Oh. She'd meant the cheese thing. The *company.*

The company had to come before his own needs, however base they may be. Or however damned long it had been since anyone had met a single one of Jack Pleeseman's needs.

He backed up, opened the door and allowed her to pass by. The scent of wildflowers drifted off her skin, as sweet as daisies and as delicate as daylilies. It had been a long time since he'd smelled anything that nice.

"My office is down here," he said, leading the way down the long narrow central hall of the Greek Revival style farmhouse that had stood on Pleeseman land for a hundred and sixty years. The house was cool, shaded by big trees on either side and a cross breeze that negated the need for central air conditioning, something that would have been impossible to install anyway in the old plaster and lath walls. The hardwood floors creaked like a familiar song beneath his step. A hearty breeze carried in through the windows, releasing the scent of fresh-cut hay and the sound of cows lowing in the back field.

His office, which had been the dining room years ago when his mother had been alive and the Pleesemans had actually dined, not ate wherever they happened to be, was a mess. As usual. Jack hadn't spent enough time in here to do much more than keep adding to his To Do pile.

"Please, have a seat," he said, picking up a stack of newspapers and *Dairy Farmers Monthly* in the sole guest chair, one of the claw-footed relics from the room's former furniture. His mother may have lived and worked on a farm, but she'd always made sure that the home itself felt like something from another world.

Like the world she'd come from.

Madison sat down gingerly, probably wondering if something in the room might bite. "Thank you."

He swung around the desk and took a seat in a chair that was the twin to hers. Uncomfortable as hell and covered in a floral fabric that was too loud, too pink and definitely too feminine for his tastes. But it was there and it was functional, and for a man as busy as Jack, that was enough. "Now, what I'd like to do is go over the marketing plan with you and then, tomorrow, we can get started on working out the details of the ad campaign. The photographer is coming on Tuesday to shoot the pictures."

"First," she said, dispensing a bright, friendly smile, but not one that possessed the same wattage as her first smile, "I wanted to inquire about the accommodations. It was a long drive here and I was hoping to take a soak in the hotel's Jacuzzi before we started talking business."

He stared at her. "Hotel? Jacuzzi?"

"Of course, I prefer a hot tub in my room," she continued, slipping her shoes back on but leaving the buckles undone, "but if that's not possible, then perhaps you could call ahead and have housekeeping draw a hot bath before my arrival. I generally ask for unscented bath salts and heated towels."

He quirked a brow, bit the inside of his cheek to keep from laughing. "Housekeeping? *Heated* towels?"

"Yes." She brushed her hair back off her face and let out a sigh that said it had been a trying day. "Oh, and a cup of tea would be nice. Earl Grey. Any brand, I'm not picky. But please, not green tea, not at this time of day. And a plate of fresh fruit, definitely in season varieties only." She put a finger to her lips. "I think that's it. If you could arrange those items, I'll be ready to start fresh in the morning."

That's when he realized she was serious. She actually expected a hotel, a hot tub and a housekeeper? Of course, he remembered, she was a Worth. One of those multi-million dollar Worths at that, from the family that owned the worldwide hotel chain. She probably had a dozen housekeepers back on the estate or in the castle or wherever she lived, and hundreds of people at her Earl Grey beck and call.

"There's a tub here," Jack said, "but it's out back and used mainly to give the cows a drink. If you don't mind sharing with a few Holsteins, I could arrange that."

"You *are* kidding, right?"

"I don't kid, not about baths," he said.

Those blue eyes quickly turned to ice. "You were supposed to provide my accommodations for the duration of this project. It was part of the agreement."

"Yep, it sure was. And we have some mighty nice accommodations right here."

Silence covered the room, as thick and uncomfortable as those wool sweaters Aunt Harriet knitted every Christmas. "Stay...here? In this house?"

He nodded. "Third door on the right at the top of the stairs. And I even changed the sheets this morning."

"You changed the sheets?" Her jaw worked up and down, but the fire had yet to leave her gaze.

"Seems our housekeeper's on permanent leave."

"Permanent?" she repeated the word slowly, as if she hadn't heard him right.

"Yep. As in never had one, and not going to get one."

He saw her processing that tidbit, her jaw dropping more every second. Then, with a start, she rose, shaking her head, clutching her little pink purse with both hands. "I can't stay here."

He shrugged. "Okay. There's a bed and breakfast about five miles down the road. I wouldn't recommend eating Louisa's cooking, though. She's a little nearsighted and doesn't always catch those pesky expiration dates."

Now he really *had* horrified her. The perky, friendly look that had been on her face five minutes ago had been replaced by wide, shocked eyes and an indignant tip of her nose.

"I am *not* staying here," she repeated, grabbing her shoes from the floor. "You'll simply have to put me up at an Adams Mark or a Marriott or something."

He shook his head. "No can do. In case you didn't notice, we're out in the boonies so the only hotel you're going to get is probably Louisa's. Plus, my budget's tighter than a stray dog's grip on a hotdog. I'm giving you the accommodations I can afford. Anything more, and it's out of your pocket."

"You can't do that. We have a contract!"

Something he knew full well. "Did you read it?"

She flushed. "My agent does that."

Her agent had seemed damned glad to send her off to the boonies, if Jack recalled. The man had promised him Madison would be cooperative, happy to be "steeped in the environment" of her new gig. Apparently steeped and this willowy beauty went together about as well as peanut butter and eggs.

Or maybe, Jack mused, her agent had known about Madison Worth's prickly personality and uptown roots and decided to serve her a little humble pie. Well, Jack had a hell of a big pie server if that's what it took to wipe that "Earl Grey, not green tea" attitude away.

"There's a clause in our contract," Jack said, "that says you're to stay here, so you can really get a feel for the environment and how we work."

Her blue eyes shot arrows at him, the flush of anger deepening to scarlet. "I already *did* that."

He leaned back in his chair and put his hands behind his head. "Listen, from what I understand, you need a job. I need a spokesperson for my company. Now, you can either swipe that haughty little look off your face and we can get down to business or you can hop back into that overpriced piece of metal that died in my driveway and chug on back to New York."

He could literally see the steam coming out of her ears. She hadn't known how forthcoming her agent had been, explaining why one of the top models in the world had come at a bargain-basement price.

Apparently Miss Madison Worth had a temper—and had used it with a little dessert on another model, effectively blacklisting her in New York.

Just then, Jack saw a small furry face peek around the door. He thought of shooing the animal out. Nah. It might be nice for the uppity Madison to do a little barnyard meet and greet.

"I will *not* be treated this way," she said. That little nose of hers going up a few more centimeters.

"How do you want to be treated?" he asked. "Like a diva, or a part of this team?"

She went cold at the word "diva" and Jack knew he'd struck a chord. Madison Worth clearly didn't like the label.

She chewed it over in her mind for a second, then pasted a fake smile on her face. How many smiles did this woman have? "Fine. I'll *temporarily* accept your offer of acc—"

When the long, hard curved horn slid along her leg, Madison let out a shriek and clambered up into the chair, her shoes clattering to the floor. She drew in her legs, plastering herself to the floral fabric. "What the hell is *that?*"

"Katydid. Our goat. Our one-horned goat." One of those rejected orphans that Jack's dad had taken in and never had the heart to destroy, despite Katydid's tendency to get into trouble. A lot of trouble. The chewed piece of rope dangling off Katydid's neck said she'd pulled another Houdini.

"You *named* the goat?" If Madison could have sewn herself into the chair's padding, Jack had no doubt she would have. She looked about as happy to see Katydid as she would Joan Rivers' critical tongue on the red carpet.

"We name almost all our animals. Katydid here is named for her personality. She's harmless but mischievous. Tie her up, she chews through the rope. Pen her up, she climbs over the fence. Whenever we find anything missing or chewed, we can be pretty sure Katy did it. So I'd keep an eye on your shoes."

Madison's jaw dropped and she jerked her legs as far from Katydid's reach as possible. "These are seven-hundred dollar heels."

Jack shook his head. "Mighty expensive snack. You might want to consider sneakers."

Katydid leaned over, baaed, then started to nibble on Madison's skirt. That, apparently, was the last straw. Madison yanked the fabric out of the goat's mouth, climbed over the opposite side of the chair, grabbed her purse and shoes and barreled toward the door. The movement scared poor Katydid, who let out half a *baa*, then scrambled backward, her hooves knocking on the wood floor.

Jack didn't bother to tell Madison he never let the farm animals in the house. Someone must have left one of the doors open and Katydid's normal curiosity had driven her inside. He figured it served the model right, given the way she'd been treating him, to let Katydid take a taste of that uppity pink suit of hers.

Madison Worth turned back, giving Katydid a wary glance and Jack a heated glare. "I can not work like this. I did the catwalk in Paris, for God's sake. I have modeled Givenchy in Milan, Chanel in Athens. I've been all over the world and on nearly every magazine cover imaginable, but I am drawing the line here. I absolutely will *not* work with these disgusting, ill-mannered farm animals. And most especially not with you."

She pivoted—and ran smack-dab into a wall of resistance.

"Well, it's about time the new help showed up," said Jack's father, Joe. He thrust a pitchfork into Madison's free hand. "That manure isn't going to shovel itself, you know."

Madison's Should-Have-Packed-Slippers Easy Chicken Tettrazini

8 ounces spaghetti, cooked
8 ounces chicken, cooked
1 cup broccoli, cooked
1 10 3/4-ounce can cream of mushroom soup
3/4 cup water or milk
1/2 cup grated Parmesan cheese

You don't have time to be messing with a four-course meal—it's time to pamper those tired tootsies. Put yesterday's leftovers to work instead. Preheat the oven to 350 degrees. Layer the cooked spaghetti in the bottom of a 9 by 13-inch pan, then top it with the chicken and broccoli. Mix the soup with the water (or milk if you can stand the calories), and pour over the layers.

Get the foot massager plugged in, it'll only be a minute more. Sprinkle with the cheese, then place in the oven for 30 minutes. Just enough time for a good soak, a quick massage, and a little payback for that man who has disrupted your day.

CHAPTER THREE

Madison sat in her Benz, cursing the stupid luxury vehicle. Of course, it wasn't the Mercedes company's fault that the three-year-old roadster had broken down. It was hers. Skipping oil changes and transmission check-ups apparently took as bad a toll on a car's engine as going without sunscreen would on her complexion.

She'd put two miles between herself and the modeling job from hell before the Benz had given up on her. Frankly, she'd been surprised the car had started at all. It had to have been the transference of all her pent-up frustration that had given the engine the final impetus to turn over.

Either that, or it was afraid to defy her.

But now, the Benz had run its last mile. Assuming she could even find a qualified Mercedes mechanic in this godforsaken nowhere Massachusetts town, she knew she couldn't afford to pay for the repairs. Visa had apparently disowned her after she didn't pay the bill. Even the minimum, after a particularly costly pity shopping fest in France, had been too much when the jobs had dried up and the checks had suddenly stopped coming.

She pulled out her cell, looked at the list of names and numbers. The first name—Grandfather—stared back at her.

He'd been calling her a lot lately, but thanks to Caller ID, she'd been able to avoid answering and avoided his judgment over her Fashion Week breakdown.

Grandfather Worth, who had been her caretaker, and her parent, really, most of her life. He'd gladly pull her out of this mess, but he'd expect her to come around to his rules. Living by someone else's rules had never really been Madison's forte.

She'd been on her own since she was seventeen, heck, since she was born. And yet, there were days when she felt like she still had a lot of growing up to do. Going back to Grandfather Worth and asking for a handout wasn't exactly moving closer to being an adult. But at the same time, earning the money herself had become a chore, a job she dreaded going to, like the people she saw dashing into the subway tunnels to catch a train that led them further from their goals, instead of closer.

She wanted—

Aw, hell. Madison didn't know what she wanted anymore. A year ago, she wanted to be the new Revlon girl. She'd have killed for the job security of a five-year cosmetics company contract. But then one day, the flashing bulbs and glossy covers had stopped being so satisfying. It was as if she'd woken up in someone else's body.

Maybe that was because she'd never worked any other kind of job. Madison had fallen into modeling, almost literally. She'd been spotted at one of Grandfather's cocktail parties by Harry when she was seventeen and before she knew it, she was *on Seventeen*. The headiness of people telling her she was beautiful, she was perfect, she was going to make millions—it had all wrapped her in an intoxicating spell that sent her off on a career she never would have imagined otherwise.

In an instant, twelve years had zipped by. Any other path Madison might have taken was pretty much closed, considering she was kissing the underside of thirty years old. And she told herself that was just fine.

Madison wasn't bred, she knew, for much more than being a trophy wife or a model. She'd sampled the former and decided never again. So that left the latter.

This funk—she refused to call it anything else— would pass and she'd find the same satisfaction in her job as she always had. All she needed to do was get through the next few days.

And for that, she could get by without putting in a call to the family bankroll.

She scrolled past Grandfather's number to the third name on the list. When the call connected, she breathed a sigh of relief. "Cally, talk me down."

"Hey, Mad," Cally replied. "Don't tell me you're going head-first into the Godiva buffet again."

Madison shuddered. "No. Those days are behind me. I'm a carrots and fat-free dip girl from here on out."

Callista Wood's laughter echoed with empathy. She was *Cosmo*'s "It" girl this season and waged war with the same three pounds every day. "Okay, if it's not chocolate, it must be your grandfather. Is he trying to talk you into coming back into the family fold?"

"He would if I gave him a chance." Madison sighed, thinking of how close she'd come to dialing his number. "I don't want to rely on Grandfather to bail me out anymore. I don't know why, but I was all impressed by my cousin Daniel going the self-support route and now have this crazy urge to take care of myself. But..."

"But it's a lot harder than you thought to be a grown-up?"

"Yeah." She slid down against the leather seat, laying her head on the glass of the window, no longer cool now that the air conditioning was off, and beginning to heat up as the car baked beneath the sun.

How had Daniel done it? He'd walked away from the family fortune and was now making a decent living as a novelist and columnist for *Boston* magazine. Daniel, however, had a degree, some talent outside of getting into the *Herald*'s gossip pages. Madison did not. She had to be insane to think she could do the same.

"I know you want some Cally-girl advice or you wouldn't have dialed. So, here's what I think. Forget the whole renew your career thing. Forget working. Call Grandfather Bank for a withdrawal, come back to Manhattan, move in with me and spend a hell of a lot of time at the spa thinking over your future. It's amazing the kinds of decisions that can be made during a hot stone massage."

Madison laughed. The idea tempted her…more than she wanted to admit. How easy it would be to ditch the responsibilities, the cows, and especially Jack Pleeseman. She could be softening her skin beneath heated rocks instead of one-horned goat nibbles. She could say to hell with this job and hold out for *Vogue* to call, begging her to be the face of November.

But, deep down inside, she knew that offer wasn't going to come. The days when Madison Worth was a hot prospect on the modeling circuit had gone the way of the dinosaurs. They'd been declining ever since she moved into her twenties. Now, at twenty-nine, she was considered damned near ancient.

Pitching a fit in the frenzied dressing room of a top designer hadn't exactly helped either. In one fell swoop of calories and frosting, she'd lost all the control she'd worked so hard to cultivate over the years, lost her cool, lost her job…lost everything.

Truth was, that end had been coming for a long time. And what scared Madison the most was the days that lay around the corner. The days when she could no longer use her face to make her living.

She'd had a back-up plan—until it blew up in her face. Madison would be smart to stay right where she was, on the posing side of the camera lens.

"You still there, hon?" Cally asked.

"Yeah. Just considering my options." Madison glanced in the rearview mirror at the road that led back to Cheese Pleese. "Make that option *singular*."

"Does that mean you're coming to New York?"

"Nope," Madison said, feeling the decision take root in her chest. "I'm going to go back to work."

"You go, girl! Kick ass with that cheese thing and before you know it, you'll be the toast of the Big Apple again."

"Cally, that isn't going to happen. I'm never going to be the toast again, we both know that. At my age, I'm just crumbs."

"Now, don't you think of it that way. A little Botox and you'll be on your way, baby!" Cally chuckled, and in her mind, Madison could see her best friend tracing a line along her injection-smoothed forehead. "You gotta stay on top of the wrinkles, girl, before they stay on top of you!"

"That's why I packed my Retin-A," Madison replied. She inhaled, cradling the phone close to her ear. "I'm glad I called you."

"And I'm glad you didn't take my advice. I knew, soon as I said forget the career, you'd do the exact opposite."

Madison laughed. "A little reverse psychology, Dr. Phil?"

"Hey, whatever it takes to get you back in the saddle. I hate seeing you so down in the dumps, girlfriend. You're going to make it back, and show those people at *Vogue* they were insane for putting Claudia Schiffer on the cover. I mean, I don't even think she's a natural blonde. And you, my dear, are all that and more."

"You're the best."

"Nah, just your best friend." Cally's voice softened. "I'm rooting for you. Don't forget there's someone else starving on celery and thinking about you."

Madison smiled. "Thanks." She said goodbye, then replaced the phone inside the tiny Dooney & Bourke bag. She reached for the keys, turned them forward, and waited for the Benz to make the final decision.

It was as silent as the fading sunlight outside her window. Looked like she was going to be hoofing it.

Literally.

Joe's Fancy-Pants Bleu Cheese Burgers

1 1/2 pounds ground sirloin
1 teaspoon Worcestershire sauce
3 ounces bleu cheese
Salt and pepper

You wanna make something fancy enough for that New York princess? This should do the trick. First, light the grill, making sure your eyebrows survive. Then, mix the sirloin with the Worcestershire sauce, then form into four or five large patties.

Oh, all right, if you simply must have some for other people, then make smaller patties. But hoard as many of these as you can. They're too damned good to share.

Roll the bleu cheese into balls (the number depends on the number of burgers you made). Stuff one into each burger, seal it up, then season each of these with a little salt and pepper.

Grill until done. For me, that means until everything's pretty damned dead and black. If that uppity model is some kind of grapefruit-only freak, no problem. That leaves more for you.

Chapter Four

"You need better hiring policies," Joe Pleeseman said, plopping into the chair Madison Worth had just vacated. "You can't have the help taking off at the sight of a pitchfork, for God's sake."

"She's not here to work the farm, Dad."

"Then what the hell good is she? Especially with that silly little suit and ten-foot high shoes. Looks like a damned prima donna. The one thing we don't need around here is a pretty face."

"That's exactly what we do need. And why I hired her."

Joe scratched his bald spot. "You hired her to look pretty? That's about the dumbest damned thing I ever heard."

Jack swallowed back a sigh and willed himself to be more patient. He and his father had never really seen eye to eye on anything, much less the running of the farm. Once again, Jack wondered what on earth his mother had been thinking when she'd left half the business to her eldest son. "I told you, she's part of the new marketing strategy."

His father waved a hand in dismissal. "Marketing strategy. That's a bunch of two-dollar words those bankers throw at you. In my day, the only "marketing" we did was knocking on Edith Wilson's door to remind her she forgot to put out her milk bottles."

"Dad, this is the twenty-first century. Things are different now. We need to make the company more global. Reach further than just this corner of the Berkshires."

"Global? What the hell do you want to do that for? We do a damned good business right here in Massachusetts." He emphasized the point with a thump of the pitchfork handle. "Why do you always have to mess with things, change 'em up? Why can't you just do things the way I do 'em?"

Jack refused to run circles again with the same argument he and his father had had for the past three years, ever since Jack had returned to Pleeseman Dairy Farm to work with his father, and bring some of the lessons he'd learned in corporate America to the small, family-owned farm. Cheese Please was a goldmine waiting to be excavated—if only Jack could get his father to see the potential. The dairy business had been the family bread-and-butter, with the cheese serving as a sort of stepchild, left to flounder on its own. In an increasingly competitive market for the slim margin of profit on milk, Jack saw the potential in the cheese, and had been trying to make his father understand the same concept.

When Joe had announced he was stepping down as president of both parts of the business last year, Jack had been the one to step up and take the job. His younger brother David was happier in the barns than in front of the books, although Jack knew his father would have rather had David behind this desk than him. The two of them had always been closer, as if they shared a gene that Jack lacked.

"It's just called being proactive, Dad," Jack said. "Cheese Pleese could be huge, if we—"

"I don't want a huge business. I like things the way they are." Another pitchfork thump.

As much as his father might want things to stay the same, they weren't going to. When Nancy Pleeseman had died, she'd left Jack her half of the family business, and enough money to go to college so he'd have the business smarts to run it. His mother had probably had some crazy idea about forcing Jack and his father to work together—and work their differences out.

Jack had gone to college. But when he'd finished, he'd ignored his mother's legacy and gone to work as the marketing manager for Savory Corn Snacks. When the company was bought by Frito-Lay and the plant moved to Mexico, Jack had had a choice—brush up on his Spanish or take the early severance package and head on home.

And fulfill his mother's last request.

He'd gone back to the Berkshires, thinking his father might have mellowed. But if anything, as Joe Pleeseman delved further into his sixties, he had become more stubborn and more determined to waylay Jack's plans.

Still, Jack was the president now, which meant he could do what he wanted. He'd hired Madison and planned the Cheese Pleese appearance at the upcoming Berkshire County Wine Festival, all without consulting his father. He hoped to wow the wine drinkers and Joe, all at the same time, giving the company a new direction that didn't involve a daily butting of the heads.

Jack sighed and planted his hands on the worn desk. "Dad, we have more bills than income. We lost two grocery store accounts just this quarter alone. If we don't change the way we do things, we're going to lose the company. The farm. Everything."

Joe harrumphed. "We've lost business before and always found it again. So what if we're working hard? It's just family pitching in. Have a little faith, Jack, instead of these high-faluting New York ideas of yours. They're just like your mother's, God rest her soul, but she didn't know a damned thing about running a company." He rose, clutching the pitchfork, still as stubborn as ever. "And for God's sake, if you're going to keep that girl around here, get her some boots. Those pointy shoes aren't going to be a damned bit of good in the barn."

When his father left, Jack put his head on the desk and wondered for the thousandth time what his mother had been thinking. And more to the point, what he'd been thinking when he'd come back here, full of plans and a fairy-tale dream for the future of Cheese Pleese.

Whoever said walking was good for your health needed to be shot. Madison had been walking for what seemed like an entire day, heading back down the road to Cheese Pleese, going barefoot because she knew from experience that the high heels weren't good for much beyond making an entrance.

Now, her feet were calloused, she had a cut just below her right pinky toe from a rock with a mean streak, and she was pretty damned sure her legs were going to break right off and tumble into a ditch. Apparently a few Pilates and yoga classes here and there weren't enough to keep her in any kind of shape.

She was sweaty, dirty, wrinkled and annoyed.

And she was hungry. Damn, she hated feeling hungry. All that did was lead to eating—something Madison Worth avoided at all costs.

Her cell phone rang and she dug it out of her purse, praying for salvation, a fairy godmother, or at least, a miracle. "Hello?"

"Madison! How are you?" her mother's voice, shouting into the phone. Vivian Worth had this idea that cell phones were the equivalent of two Dixie cups and a string.

"Fine, Mother. How are you? And the natives?"

"Madison, they aren't natives. The people of Togo are just like you and me, just poorer."

Given the current state of her bank account, Madison wasn't so sure the comparison was all that accurate. Granted, she still had her apartment—for three more weeks—and her car, dead as it might be, but she'd been too cavalier with her money while it had been rolling in and now, there was nothing.

She'd always thought there'd be a job tomorrow. A check on its way. Eileen Ford had started talking Guess Jeans contracts and Madison thought her future was secure, so she'd kept spending.

Apparently, that wasn't the smartest way to operate a checking account.

"Anyway," her mother continued, "I called you for a reason."

Madison skirted the edge of the road to walk along the soft cushion of grass. "Mother, I'm broke right now so if you need funding to build some huts or something, I can't do it."

"I didn't call for money. I called to tell you I'm coming back to the States for a while."

"You're coming home? Why?" Though the word *home* was a misnomer. Madison knew her mother had never considered the United States anything more than a temporary stop in Capitalism Central. Vivian Worth was far happier digging wells in Haiti, building schools in rural China or hand-feeding orphans in Rwanda. Madison admired her mother's commitment to helping the starving, homeless and destitute in the world, but used to wish sometimes that Vivian had poured that same commitment into her own child. Vivian had barely taken enough time off from her philanthropic work to give birth to Madison, before jetting back to wherever someone else had needed her.

Though there'd been nannies aplenty to do the dirty work of raising Madison.

As if reading her mind, Vivian said, "I wanted to see my daughter."

Something in Vivian's voice told Madison there was more to the story. Madison shook it off, refusing to pursue the feeling. She also refused to feel joy at those words because more often than not, they wouldn't come to fruition. "Sorry to disappoint you, Mother, but I'm not in Manhattan; I'm out of town on a photo shoot. If you're in New York, you're welcome to use my apartment if you want." Madison doubted her mother would be there longer than a few days anyway, too short of a time to realize what a mess Madison's life had become.

Either way, before the first of the month rolled around, Madison would have the pay from the Cheese Please job and be able to eke another thirty days out of her landlord. By then, surely, she'd have a plan to restore her career.

And she'd have eradicated this weird feeling that she was in the wrong field altogether.

"Where are you?" Vivian shouted into the phone, over the sounds of a sputtering engine—a Jeep or a bus—roaring behind her. "I'll come to you. I haven't seen you in so long, honey."

No way. Vivian coming here, especially *here*, definitely wouldn't work. Her mother lived in worlds so remote, she'd never seen any of Madison's runway work, never picked up a *Vogue* with her daughter's picture on the cover. The last thing Madison wanted was for Vivian to find her modeling *cheese*, for God's sake.

In her mind, she had always dreamed of Vivian showing up unannounced at a photo shoot, then gasping with pride at her daughter, posing in Givenchy in front of the Arc de Triomphe in Paris or standing on the banks of the Nile in Bob Mackie. She'd bemoan the fact that she had ignored her daughter for all these years and beg for the chance to make it up to her.

Or at least, that's how it had worked out when Madison had been ten and Barbie had promised to be a better mother to Skipper.

"Mom, seriously, stay in Manhattan. I'll join you in a few days."

"And what am I supposed to do with myself in that city of excess?"

"Shop?" The first thing Madison was going to buy when she got back home was some of those massaging slippers. Her feet were going to need it after this grueling hike.

"Madison, I will not support child labor in Vietnam and the execution of perfectly happy minks."

Madison sighed, then winced as she stepped on another rock. "Then don't shop. Volunteer at a shelter or something."

"I can't. I need to tell—" Her mother's voice started to break up, and in the background, Madison could hear some calling Vi-Vi, the name most of the foreign people she cared for called her by. "I have to go. I'll see you in a couple days. Bye!"

And just like that, the line was dead. Madison shook her head, then put the cell back inside her purse. Most likely, her mother would get involved in harvesting wheat or something and forget all about her plan to visit Madison.

It had happened before. Enough that Madison had stopped counting on her mother for anything more than a Christmas card that usually arrived two weeks late, battered and worn by its airmail journey.

The hour-plus walk back to Cheese Pleese gave her plenty of time to rehash the conversation with her mother. In the end, Madison decided to dismiss it. The chances of her mother actually leaving the Third World to come here were slimmer than a Chihuahua's collar.

Jack's Keeping-the-Diva-in-Shoes Cheesy Spinach

2 10-ounce boxes frozen spinach
6 ounces cream cheese
1/4 cup half and half or heavy cream
2 tablespoons melted butter
1/2 teaspoon salt
Dash pepper
1/2 cup Parmesan cheese

This isn't one of those recipes for wimpy waistlines. It is, however, the perfect kind of artery clogging side dish to help you think about your stomach, instead of how distracting that woman has been.

First, defrost the spinach, then mix in the cream cheese, cream and butter. Stir in salt and pepper, then pour it all into a greased 9 by 13-inch pan. Top with Parmesan, then bake for 30 minutes.
In that time, if you still haven't been able to get your mind back on your work and off of her holy-cow legs, add a couple beers for personal garnish.

CHAPTER FIVE

When Madison Worth showed up on his doorstep a second time, Jack Pleeseman nearly choked on his roast beef sandwich. Sometime during the last hour and a half she had lost that pristine look, but none of the attitude.

He bit back a smile. Her hair was plastered to her head, her pink suit dusty with road dirt, and her ridiculous shoes were in her hand instead of on her feet. "I had to walk back," she said, scowling at him, as if it were all his fault. As if, in fact, everything that had ever gone wrong in her world should be parked at his feet.

"A walk in the country is good for you," Jack said, drawing in a deep breath that made his chest expand. "All that fresh air."

"Nothing about the air here is fresh." She made a face and pressed one of those slim hands beneath her nose.

Jack leaned against the porch column, his half-finished sandwich in one hand. "If being here is so distasteful to your delicate senses, why'd you come back?"

"I keep my promises." Her hand went down, her nose went up, daring him to disagree.

"I thought you didn't want to work with—let's see, how'd you put it?—those 'disgusting, ill-mannered farm animals' or with me." He dipped his head and eyed her. "Or was the disgusting and ill-mannered referring to me?"

He saw her swallow back a heaping serving of annoyance. Good thing she didn't choke. "I was simply out of sorts this morning. That drive down here from New York was overwhelming. All that..." she waved a hand, "exhaust."

"Uh-huh."

"Now, if someone would be so kind as to retrieve the luggage from my Benz, I'll be glad to," again, she swallowed, "take you up on your, ah, kind offer of accommodations."

He could have frozen a side of beef in her tone. But he gave her a grin, pretending she sounded as glad to be there as he was to have her. Regardless of her uppity attitude, he needed her, to help him pull his sinking business up by the bootstraps, and to help him prove to his father that introducing a few modern methods into the business was a Good Thing.

If he didn't turn things around—and do it quick—he'd lose everything that mattered to him. And that was a price Jack couldn't afford to pay.

All Madison Worth had to do was look pleasant on film and he'd be fine. Though he was beginning to rethink his plan of having her actually open her mouth at the wine festival. Maybe he'd do a ventriloquist act with her. Get his cousin A.J. to do the voice.

In her defense, a woman like Madison Worth probably had a right to expect more than a double bed on the second floor of a hundred-plus-year-old farmhouse, lacking in air conditioning, frills and maid service. She was the kind of woman men catered to, the kind they killed themselves to open a door for, to let her cut in front of them at the DMV.

And the exact kind of woman Jack had learned, from personal experience, wouldn't fit in around here or with him.

"I'm sorry," he said. "I thought your agent had explained our arrangement to you."

She blinked, clearly surprised by his apology. "No, he didn't. He never does. Harry isn't exactly the most communicative person on the planet. He's got this thing about watching the minutes on his cell. You know that clicking sound you hear in the background when you're talking to him? That's his stopwatch."

Jack chuckled. "Sounds like he needs a new calling plan." He tossed the rest of his sandwich to Buster, who had waited patiently at the foot of the porch stairs, knowing from experience that he was going to get lucky at some point. They'd been spoiling that dog ever since Dad had found the brown-and-white mutt on the roadside one day, as skinny as a fencepost and as beaten as a punching bag. "So, where's your car?" he asked.

"Down the road." She waved vaguely over her shoulder. "A bit." She smiled at him, the kind of smile that begged a favor. "Now, if you could go retrieve my luggage, while I rest, I would appreciate it."

"And you didn't think to carry it with you when you walked back?"

She blew a puff of hair out of her face. "Do you think I could possibly carry all those Louis Vuitton suitcases for *two* miles? Who do you think I am? Hercules?"

He let his gaze drift over her body, slim but slightly muscular, with a dusting of a tan. "Wrong build for that. I was thinking maybe Zena. But skinnier. And blonder."

She swallowed again, the frustration clear on her face. No wonder she was so thin. She was too busy eating her words to have any real food. "If you won't go," she said through gritted teeth, "then may I borrow your car?"

He thought of making it easy on her, just letting her go inside, cool off and grab something to eat while he played errand boy. The businessman in him said to cater to the talent. But the guy in him couldn't resist egging her on just a little bit more, if only to see that look on her face.

"Don't have a car," Jack said. "But you're welcome to my truck, long as you can handle a stick."

"A *what?*"

"Well, ma'am, we don't have those fancy automatic transmissions out here in the boonies," he said, affecting his best hillbilly accent. He took a step down, closer to her. "And I assume your driving expertise doesn't extend beyond luxury models made overseas?"

She put a hand on her hip. The skirt of the dusty pink suit hitched up a couple of inches on one side. "Maybe I just don't want to drive your stick."

He laughed. "Now that I believe." He eyed her, a standoff brewing between them. He could already see that dealing with Madison Worth was going to be a lot like butting heads with a bull.

Well, he knew exactly how to handle a bull. First lesson, teach it who was boss—but gently, so the bull didn't even know it was being led around by the ring in its nose. Until it was too late and it had already been tamed.

"All right," Jack said. "I'll go get your things. Truck's over there." He thumbed toward the side of the house.

She dangled a set of keys in front of him. "Thank you."

"Oh, I'm not going by myself. Your luggage, you come with me."

"*Excuse me?* Do I look like I'm in any condition to go back there?" She swept a hand over her rumpled clothes. "I need a hot bath, a cold glass of Evian, and a short, restful nap."

What was it about this woman that made him want to scream? *Evian?* Jack had half a mind to throw her in the cows' trough. "First, we already went over the bath thing. Second, you want a glass of water, follow your own damned nose to the kitchen. Third, nobody naps around here because there's too much work to do."

"But—but—" she sputtered, "I'm a guest."

"And in the Pleeseman house, all that means is that you get the good parking space. We're a team here, which means everyone," at this he let his gaze drift over her manicure and those delicate, callous-free hands, "pulls their own weight. So, if you want your luggage, Miss Worth, I advise you to come with me and help load it into the truck. Otherwise, I might just forget a few key items. By accident, on purpose."

She swallowed again, but this time couldn't keep the words down. "You are the most infuriating—"

"Aggravating," he supplied.

"Annoying—"

"Demanding—"

"Stubborn person I have ever met!"

He arched a brow. "And here I was thinking the same thing about you."

She threw up her hands, letting out a shriek. "This is not going to work. I don't know what my agent was thinking, booking me here. I can not possibly work with someone like you."

Katydid wandered by just then, letting out a *baa*. Madison started and jerked her pert little derriere forward, lest the goat get a hankering for rump roast.

"Read my mind again. I was standing here not five minutes ago, eating my sandwich and thinking there was no way I could work with someone like *you.*" He grinned. "Perhaps you should take up a second career in tarot."

Her glare answered that.

Jack checked his own aggravation and reminded himself that he needed her to help him. He'd hired her, therefore, he needed to work with her, not drive her off. No matter how tempting the latter might be. "Listen, let's call a truce, at least long enough to get your luggage. Then you can take your nap—today—and we'll get to work in the morning." He thrust out a hand. "Deal?"

She chewed that over for a long second. Finally, she put out her palm, slipped it into his and shook. "Deal."

He made a sweeping gesture in the direction of the battered 1995 blue Ford F-350. There was a dent in the passenger's side door—a gift from Big George the bull—and part of the bumper had been peeled off—thanks to Katydid's never-ending appetite. But it ran and it got him from A to B. That's all Jack cared about. "Then your carriage awaits, milady."

Madison glanced at the truck, then back at him. He was willing to bet this was one Cinderella who would have gladly traded in her pumpkin for a better squash.

Madison didn't say a single word on the ride back down the road she'd just walked. She was too busy working up a curse that would send Jack Pleeseman to Katmandu. Maybe Siberia. No, better yet...

Transylvania. He could use a few blood-sucking vampires to swipe that attitude right off his face.

Madison sighed. Instead of plotting revenge by the walking dead, she needed to buck up. Do the job. Like she had a hundred times before in the twelve years since her first photo shoot. If she blew this one, her agent would be done with her. Harry had made that damned clear—and in less than sixty seconds.

Then her career would definitely be over. She'd end up modeling granny pants in a Sears catalog. Or worse, *working* in the granny pants department. When it came to career options, Madison had exactly zero.

She had no education, no experience at anything other than smiling prettily. The few times she had tried to step out of the glossy pages and into something else, she'd failed. Miserably.

Going back to the Worth fortune was a last resort. She'd seen firsthand the price her cousin Daniel had paid all his life, living under Grandfather's thumb.

True, Grandfather had mellowed since Daniel had met and married the spunky Olivia Regan, who was now making a name for herself decorating cakes in Boston. Regardless of Grandfather's joy at seeing his namesake settled down, there were was one thing that still ran deep in Worth blood: high expectations. The last thing Madison wanted to do was to go crawling to her Grandfather and admit she had failed.

So she would tough it out, with the cows, the bull, the goat.

And Jack Pleeseman.

Jack parked the truck beside Madison's Benz. She got out, thumbed the remote and the trunk popped up, revealing stacks of perfectly matched red suitcases, in a variety of sizes, all monogrammed with her initials.

"Holy cow! How much did you pack?" Jack said, standing beside her trunk. "There's like a hundred cases in here."

"Only five," she said, her defenses pitching her tone a few decibels higher. "And...well, three more on the backseat."

"You're kidding me, right? You're only here for a week."

She parked a fist on her hips. "I like to have options."

He arched a brow at that, then reached inside, grabbed the smallest case, and put it in her hands. "Then go put your 'options' in the back of the truck. The day's not getting any longer and you could have a fashion crisis at any moment."

She bit her lip and did as she was told. For now. If she didn't play on the "team", she knew he'd make her regret it. Probably by dumping her on the side of the road and running over her makeup case for good measure.

Five minutes and a lot of male-muttered complaints about women and their options later, they had Madison's luggage stowed in the back of the truck. "What about my car?" she asked.

"You got triple A?"

"Uh…not at present." It was one of many things she had let go when her phone had stopped ringing. Living in Manhattan, she cabbed most of the places she needed to go, so AAA seemed like a waste.

Until today.

"I'll see if Coop can swing down and pick it up later today. He owns the only garage in town. Assuming he doesn't already have a six-pack in him, he should be able to get it hooked up to the tow truck and back to the shop."

"Assuming?"

Jack had to hold himself back from chuckling at her look of horror. He forgot sometimes what it was like for people who didn't live around here. "Coop doesn't much like working on cars. He's a frustrated artist. Even had a show once at one of those fancy Boston art galleries. But the *Globe* dissed his work and he ended up only selling one painting—to his grandma. So now, he dips into the bottle from time to time. Says it makes the grease easier to take."

She looked at the silent silver car, one hand pressed over her heart. "Let's just leave it here. I, ah, I'll have someone get it later."

"I wouldn't do that if I were you. Before you know it, some high schooler's souping it up for the Demolition Derby." Jack shut her trunk with a gentle push. "Listen, Coop's not so bad. And I'll make sure he's sober for the tow."

"It's not that. I'm just…between funds right now."

"Between funds?" Jack's gaze swept over her, taking in the suit, the expensive shoes, then went to the foreign car, the thousands of dollars of clothes stowed in the back of his truck. She was an heiress. How could she be between funds?

Maybe she'd been disowned. Or maybe…she was one of those one in a zillion wealthy kids who rejected the fortune, determined to make their own way. *That* surprised him, more than anything else he'd discovered since meeting Madison Worth.

"My pay is sometimes….sporadic." She looked away.

"This wouldn't have anything to do with you throwing a cake into Kate Moss's face, would it?" He knew, from talking to Harry, that the cake thing was the main reason she was modeling for Jack instead of Bill Blass.

That cobalt gaze whipped back to his. "How do you know about that?"

Jack didn't answer her. Not right away. He was too busy enjoying the look of surprise on the diva's face.

He walked away to tuck the keys for the Benz up inside the driver's side wheel well for Coop, then strode back to the truck and opened the door for Madison, giving her a helping boost. "Thank you," she said, sounding genuinely surprised that he had a chivalrous bone in his body.

"So why'd you do it?" he asked, once they were underway and heading back to the farm, Madison bouncing on the torn vinyl seat beside him, her designer luggage rattling in the bed, chattering complaints about the rough treatment.

"Do what?"

"Frost Kate Moss."

She laughed then, a sound so hearty, he couldn't believe it came from the pencil-thin blonde beside him. She had a rich laugh, the kind that said she appreciated a good joke and wasn't above a few of her own. "It was an accident. I was aiming for Janine Turner and ended up hitting Kate. Let's just say gym class was the only one I was guaranteed to fail." She shrugged. "No coordination."

To Jack, she appeared as graceful as a gazelle. Either way, he got the feeling the joke was a way to get him off the subject of the career-ruining food fight, because she'd only answered the how, not the why. "Oh come on, I bet you broke more than your share of windows playing catch in the yard."

"I never played catch in the yard," she said quietly. Madison turned, giving him a view of her long, elegant neck, gold-spun hair and nothing else. Her gaze remained on the dense woods lining the road.

"Never?" That was something Jack couldn't imagine. When he wasn't helping his dad, he'd spent every spare minute tossing a ball around. With the dog, with David, with one of the hands, with anyone who was willing and able. Well, anyone except his dad, who'd been pouring all his sweat equity into the farm. At nine, Jack had fancied himself the next Roger Clemens. Then he'd grown up and faced the reality—that a kid with a batting average of .300 wasn't going to get to the majors.

"I didn't exactly live in that kind of house," Madison said.

He wanted to ask what kind of house didn't have so much as a wiffleball, but he didn't. He wasn't here to get to know Madison Worth. All he wanted from her was her smiling image on his cheese.

That was his one and only priority. Then he could do his mother's memory proud, give everyone some financial security, and provide the stability the lawyer had said he needed if he wanted a chance in hell at getting Ginny.

The Pleeseman Dairy Farm came into view. Jack pulled into the driveway, parked in front of the house and shut off the truck. "Go on inside," he said, "and wash up. My Aunt Harriet is in the kitchen. She's a little odd, but you'll like her. It would make her day if you asked her to fix you something to eat. In the meantime, I'll bring your bags up to your room."

Surprise filled her features, then she hit him with another one of those killer smiles. "Thank you." Then she slipped out of the truck and headed inside.

Two words, two curved lips and bam, Jack was teetering on the edge of Lake Trouble.

Madison Worth wasn't just an ordinary beauty— she had the kind of beauty that drew a man in, made him wish he had endless hours to explore those curves, dip his lips into those peaches-and-cream valleys. And see exactly what road the path to her bed would take him down.

Whoa, boy. Jack shook his head and turned off the truck, hearing the engine give a few more coughs before finally settling down—a lot like the engine inside of him, which refused to turn off with a simple key. Either way, he had to forget the idea of him and the model.

Being attracted to a woman like Madison Worth was definitely a luxury a guy like him could afford.

Aunt Harriet's The-King-Speaks Macaroni and Cheese

16 ounces elbow macaroni

2 tablespoons butter

2 tablespoons flour

1 teaspoon dry mustard

3/4 teaspoon salt

1/4 teaspoon pepper

Dash cayenne pepper

3 cups milk

3 cups shredded sharp cheddar cheese

1/2 cup Parmesan cheese

1/2 cup breadcrumbs

2 tablespoons olive oil

Now, this might not be the real Elvis dish, but it's close enough to please the King and the man who might become king in your heart. Trust Aunt Harriet, this comfort food is the one to serve if you want to bring about the first stirrings of a hunk of burnin' love.

Preheat the oven to 375 degrees, then boil some water and cook the pasta. When it's done, drain really well—or you'll be staying at the Heartbreak

Hotel when your mac and cheese comes out too watery.

In a separate pan, melt the butter, then stir in the flour until you've made a thick paste. Add in the spices, doing a little shake, rattle and roll with a whisk to incorporate it all. Stir in the milk gradually, then allow it to boil and thicken for a minute or so.

Before you've lost that lovin' feeling, add the cheese. Pour macaroni into a greased 9 by 13-inch pan, then mix in the cheesy sauce. Toss the breadcrumbs with the oil, then sprinkle on top of the macaroni.

Make the world go away while you bake this for thirty minutes. When it's done, dig in and love that tender mac and cheese—and then share a plate with a brown-eyed handsome man, or a long-legged girl.

CHAPTER SIX

Jack's Aunt Harriet turned out to be a generously shaped gray-haired woman with a white apron emblazoned with the image of the young Elvis. As soon as Madison walked into the kitchen, Harriet rushed forward, an embrace ready. "Why come on in, sweetie," she said, giving Madison a quick squeeze before pulling back to look at her. "Goodness! You're all skin and bones! Let me get you something with sticking power."

"I'm fine, really," Madison said. "I just came in to ask if I could grab a piece of fruit. Or a bowl of lettuce. You don't need to make me anything big." Especially not as big as that sandwich that Jack had had earlier. Her mouth was still watering at the thought of it, sitting at the bottom of his stomach instead of hers.

"A piece of fruit? A plain salad? Oh dear. That's what we give the rabbits, not the guests." Harriet patted a stool beside the butcher block island in the center of the kitchen, then poured Madison a glass of ice water. "You sit right there and I'll make you a real meal. Why, when I was having tea with Elvis this morning, he told me the very same thing. He said, "Harriet, you be sure and stock that pantry with real food for your guest because you know darn well there wasn't any fruit in cotton candy land."

Elvis? Cotton candy land? *All right.* Madison slid a half step back from the stool instead of taking a seat. Jack had said his Aunt Harriet was a little odd, but he neglected to mention she saw dead people in her kitchen.

"Now, the King, he's the wisest of 'em all," Harriet said. "That's why he was the king."

"Um, I think I'll just grab an apple," Madison, hoping she could slip around Aunt Harriet and snag the fruit before she was sharing a pot of Earl Grey and singing "Love Me Tender."

"Oh, I see," Harriet said, wagging a finger at Madison. "You're one of them."

"One of who?"

"Those people who think Elvis is really gone. That he couldn't possibly be sitting in Harriet's kitchen, knocking back some orange pekoe."

"Well, he did *die*," Madison said.

Harriet shrugged. "That happens. It's made it damned hard for him to keep touring, so he stays here, has tea with me."

Uh-huh. "Is that because he likes cows or something?"

"Oh, it's not about the cows. Have you seen Graceland? The place is busier than the Bronx Zoo in the spring. Elvis likes a little peace and quiet. He doesn't want the tourists poking their heads in, looking at his jungle room. So, he comes here, gets his tea and his privacy."

"I'll, ah, keep an eye out for the white suit."

Harriet rolled her eyes. "He's *dead*, sweetie. You aren't going to *see* him. But if you get real quiet, you can hear him humming "Blue Suede Shoes" on his way out the door."

"Can I just get—" Madison reached for the bowl of fruit on the counter. She was going to grab it and run as fast as these ridiculous shoes would let her.

Harriet snatched the bowl away, setting it on the opposite end of the counter. "Listen to Aunt Harriet, dear. One decent meal won't kill you." She patted her wide hips. "That's what I should have done. Stopped at one." She winked. "'Course, my Lester wouldn't have liked that one bit. He always was a man who liked a little cushion for the pushin'."

Madison had to cough to keep from choking.

Harriet bent over the stove, opened the door, then pulled out a steaming pan. "Great timing. Ah... Smell that. Fresh baked macaroni and cheese. You ain't had mac and cheese till you've had mine. Why, even Elvis loved his mac and cheese. He *did*. His favorite recipe is even in that *Are You Hungry Tonight?* cookbook." She laid the pan on a tiled trivet shaped like a cow. One of them—the pan or the trivet—let out a tinny moo.

Cheese bubbled beneath the dish's crusty top, wafting its aroma toward Madison, teasing, tempting her. Sharp notes of cheddar were muted by the softer, sweeter harmony of Colby. A slight sheen glistened on the breadcrumb top. It looked gooey. Thick. Amazing.

Madison's mouth watered. Her stomach grumbled. Desire rose inside her, urging her to have one bite. Just one little bite.

If it was good enough for the King of Rock & Roll, then surely it was good enough for her.

No. One bite would lead to two, would lead to two hundred. If there was one thing Madison wasn't good at, it was pushing away from the table and saying, "Done."

She'd learned that lesson during her brief engagement to Renaldo. And heard about the consequences for months. She'd overindulged, both in the Parisian man and his French delicacies, figuring she'd finally found someone who would love her no matter what.

Until she'd returned early from a trip to L.A. and found him in her queen-sized bed with not one, not two, but three of the maids. He claimed they were doing a group dusting under the sheets. They were dusting all right, but the kind of bunnies Renaldo was finding weren't on any Pledge canister she'd ever seen.

"Here, let me get you a plate," Harriet said, reaching into a glass-front cabinet. "I'll even let you have Elvis's favorite. It's got a jungle print around the edge. See?"

"I can't," Madison said, scrambling away from the baking pan.

"Oh, don't worry about eating before everyone else. These men won't sit down for a family meal.

They're more like drive-through eaters." She shook her head and something sad seemed to fill her gaze. "Anyway, you have yourself a big ol' plate, and sit here with Aunt Harriet." She reached for a second plate in the cabinet, this one decorated with a scene of Vegas.

"I can't. Really. I, ah, don't eat cheese."

Harriet laughed. "Honey, that's blasphemy around this place. Try a bite. I've never met a person who didn't try my mac and cheese and come running right on back for seconds."

"That's what I'm afraid of," Madison said. She knew from experience that the only way to avoid temptation was to run. So she yanked an apple out of the Blue Willow porcelain bowl on the counter, then ran from the room before she could sink her teeth into another mistake.

Even it was endorsed by The Other Side.

"*That's* who you hired to save our bacon?" David Pleeseman said, striding into Jack's office and making himself damned comfortable in one of the dining room chairs, putting his feet up on the corner of the desk. "I hope you know what you're doing."

Jack let out a sigh. "I hope I do too."

He and his brother had always been close, especially since they were only a year apart in age. "Trouble in pairs," is what their mother had called them when they were younger and had gotten into the tar bucket wearing their Easter suits or when they had let the cows out of their pens, determined to set the beasts free—and right into crabby Edgar MacDowell's prize cabbage garden.

Since Jack had returned to the farm three years ago, David had become his one ally. Even if he didn't always agree with Jack's ideas, or his plans, he supported his older brother.

"I mean, don't get me wrong," David said. "She's hot. But in general, hot and the Cheese Pleese Company haven't gone together."

"I'm trying to change that. The company image could use an overhaul, something that gets people talking about us."

"Well, in that case, you picked exactly the right spokesmodel." David leaned forward, dropping his boots to the floor and propping his elbows on the desk. His face turned from teasing to serious. "You all right, big brother? 'Cause you look like shit."

"Gee, thanks. Can always count on you to boost my spirits."

"I'm serious, Jack. You haven't been the same since—"

"Don't say it."

David leaned back, hands up. "All right, I won't. But that doesn't change the fact that you look like a Mack truck parked on your face last night."

Jack shrugged, like it was no big deal. He picked up a pencil, toyed with it. "So I don't sleep much. Who does?"

"People who don't worry."

Jack let out a laugh that sounded more like a bark. "You know any of those folks?"

David shook his head. "Nope. Not in these parts." He rose, holding his cowboy hat into his hands and running his fingers along the brim. "You just watch yourself. It's all going to work out, so don't worry yourself into an early grave. Alyssa is going to come around."

The pencil in Jack's hand snapped in two. "She's made those promises before. I can't count on her. This time, if she—" Jack shook his head, unable to go down that road. Those were the what if's that kept him up at night. He didn't need to drag them out in broad daylight, too. "Dave, just shut up about it, okay? Please."

David nodded. Point taken. He thumbed toward the door. "That woman out there—"

"Madison."

"She might be good for you."

Jack let out a laugh. "She's going to kill me, that's what she's going to do. Or drive me insane. Have you heard her? 'I like tea, not coffee. Evian, not tap...'" Jack rolled his eyes. "I have some freakin' Evian for her."

"I meant she might be good for help. Give her some hip waders, toss her into the whey, let her stir things up."

Jack thought of the testosterone engine that had started in his gut the second she'd gotten stuck in his front porch. "She's already stirred up plenty, believe me."

David rose, then paused in the doorway. "If there's one thing you could use in your life, my friend, it's a woman who stirs things up, gets you back to your life."

David was wrong. That was the *last* thing Jack needed. He had one goal and one goal only—to get Cheese Pleese profitable again—so he could bring one very special girl back into his life.

This time for good.

Jack's Get-Her-Out-Of-Bed Egg Bake

6 eggs, well beaten
3 cups milk
1 teaspoon salt
1 teaspoon dry mustard
6 slices bread, cubed
1 1/2 cups cheddar cheese, grated
1 pound ham, chopped
1 4-ounce can mushrooms, drained and chopped

You have two options with this dish—either mix all the ingredients together and dump it on that sleepy model's head or try a little honey in your approach and by assembling this the night before to give her a nice morning surprise.

Preheat the oven to 350 degrees. Beat the eggs, then add remaining ingredients. It's so easy, a guy could do it. Pour into a 9 by 13-inch glass baking dish, cover and refrigerate overnight.

I know, I know, delayed gratification. Waiting overnight isn't such a big deal—you aren't sleeping anyway. In the morning, bake this for 45-55 minutes, till firm and as set as your resolution to stay away from her. Let it sit for ten minutes before serving.

Just enough time for her to finish curling her eyelashes or whatever it is she's up there doing while she's also intentionally driving you crazy with waiting.

CHAPTER SEVEN

Madison's first morning in the Pleeseman household offered all the comforts and amenities of a half-star hotel.

There was no wake-up call, no soft beginning to her Monday, with the maid gently drawing the blinds back an inch or two until Madison was ready for her bath. No coffee waiting on her nightstand, the scented steam drifting over to tickle her nostrils awake.

Just Jack yelling up the stairs asking if she was ever going to get the hell out of bed so they could get to work.

So she made him wait. Forty-five minutes. While she showered, combed, make-uped and dressed. Then sat on her bed for ten minutes more, just to make him suffer.

Since she was going without caffeine, he sure as hell could go without her for a while.

"Finally. Let's get down to business," Jack said when she came down to his office, striding in as if she wasn't a moment late.

Madison looked around before taking a seat, making sure there were no pitchforks or goats waiting to get her. She had put on a crimson DKNY wrap dress for their ungodly eight a.m. appointment, hoping that the bright red color would detract his attention from the bags under her eyes.

Harriet came into the office, a kind smile on her face. "Thought you could use this, honey." She deposited a tray with two mugs of coffee, creamer and sugar on the desk.

"Bless you," Madison said, lunging for one of the mugs, as desperate as a drug seeker. She cupped her hands around the image of Elvis in *Blue Hawaii*, gyrating beside waves, hula dancers and surf boards. Madison didn't care if the java was in a fine china cup or a Made in China memento mug. All she wanted was that jolt of energy, and an excuse to avoid Jack Pleeseman's annoyed face.

She had finally fallen asleep around one in the morning, after telling her stomach for the ten thousandth time that an apple was a perfectly filling meal. Between the rumble in her stomach and the sounds of everything from cows to crickets outside her window, sleep had been hard to come by.

Who was she kidding? It didn't matter if she was in Paris or Manhattan, sleep had never been something Madison did well. Especially not when she slept alone.

But then, once she'd finally succumbed to exhaustion and closed her eyes, she slept better than she ever had in her life. The six-thousand-dollar queen mattress in her Manhattan apartment had nothing over the soft guest room bed she sank into when she'd finally been able to stop pacing and climb under the covers. The bed had let out a soft squeak-squeak, then seemed to envelope her in comfort. Normally, Madison tossed and turned for a half hour, sometimes an hour, sometimes much more. But last night, she'd fallen into that cloud and been out in seconds. It seemed like only a minute had passed before her travel alarm was bleeting its morning call.

"Are you ready to get to work now?" Jack asked drolly, taking the second mug from the tray.

"Of course." She gave him a sweet smile. Winning the fly over with honey, instead of vinegar.

"Good. Let's start with your experience with cheese. Do you have any?"

Experience with cheese? She'd been asked a lot of questions over the course of her career, but that one definitely ranked at the top for uniqueness. "I've never modeled anything cheese related, if that's what you're asking," Madison said. "There's not a lot of call for American Cheese dresses on the runway."

Jack steepled his fingers and leaned back in his chair. Now that her vision had cleared with the ingestion of the coffee, she took some time to notice him. He wore a button-down denim shirt that was open at the collar, revealing just enough of his chest to make her wonder what the rest looked like. Unlike hers, his eyes were bright, alert. Interested. She dropped her attention to the hula dancers welcoming Elvis to the Aloha State, suddenly much, much too aware of the dark brown intensity of Jack's gaze.

"I didn't mean modeling it," he said. "I meant eating it."

"Oh, I don't eat cheese," she said quickly. Too late, she realized she'd made a mistake—the model was always supposed to rave about the client's product, to make him think his was the only shampoo brand she used, the only socks she'd ever wear. Admitting the truth would mean he'd find someone else, someone who was better suited to stroke the company ego and then display a hell of fake smile.

"You *never* eat cheese?"

"Well…" Madison stalled. How could she extract herself from this one? Once again, she'd opened her mouth and inserted a size eight. "Not never. Exactly."

"Then when was the last time?"

The last time?

Her gaze went back to him, to the way he filled out the cotton shirt with definition that didn't come from a Nautilus machine, but from honest hard work. His face was smooth, clean shaven, almost begging for her to stroke a hand along his cheek. His chocolate eyes watched her, their attention so concentrated, she forgot he was talking about cheese and went straight to the true last time—

The last time she'd been with a man.

Six months ago. Six, long, agonizing months, with no one in her bed to fill the empty quiet of her apartment. No coat to see draped over the back of the sofa, no shoes by the door, no second wineglass in the sink, letting her fool herself for one night that she had someone in her life. That she wasn't navigating choppy waters alone.

That she was, indeed, fine enough to love. For just one night.

She looked at Jack and wondered, for a fleeting, insane second, what it would be like to see *his* coat on her sofa. *His* shoes by her door.

His body in her bed. Against hers. On hers. In hers.

"Miss Worth?" he asked.

"Huh?"

"I asked you when was the last time you had cheese," Jack said. "I was hoping to incorporate some of your emotions about that experience into the ad campaign."

Oh yeah, the damned dairy product. She'd been thinking all-afternoon sex and he'd been thinking business. Clearly, she had gotten up way too early and hadn't met her caffeine quota.

She took another sip, then a second, before speaking. "It's actually been a while," Madison said, scrambling to recall some memory. She really stunk at lying, and though she had practiced the craft most of her life—with makeup, with advertising—she had yet to master it. Something on her face always betrayed her, so her usual plan of action was to look away and utter whatever the person across from her wanted to hear.

Now, she dipped her head and watched the toes on her right foot swing her slingback back and forth.

"Last month, I think," she said. "I had some spinach au gratin."

Actually, she always ate her spinach plain, dry and in a salad bowl. Never, ever with anything remotely fattening on top.

"And how was it?"

She made a circle with her toe. "Absolutely divine. I had seconds."

Madison hadn't gone back for seconds since she was fourteen years old. But her foot already knew that, so lying to it didn't seem so bad.

"Bullshit," Jack said. "I know a cheese lover when I see one and you're not it." He let out a gust. "This isn't going to work. I'll call the agency and have them send someone else."

She jerked her head up. He couldn't fire her. The Cheese Pleese campaign was her last hope, her only hope, for redemption. Sure, she'd behaved badly with him over the last twenty-four hours— maybe even a teeny bit diva-ish—but who wouldn't, given the pressure she was under? With that career guillotine looming over her head?

Harry had made the consequences clear: if she screwed up something as simple as a few print ads and a half day spokesmodel gig, he'd forget her name and erase her from his cell's phone book.

She couldn't let that happen. There weren't any doors left for Madison to open, not at her age, and not with her looks fading as fast as a cheap pair of jeans.

"It doesn't matter if I've eaten it or not," Madison said, her gaze locking on his, making her case, "all that matters is if I can make people believe I love cheese."

Jack snorted. "People can see a lie. Even through a camera."

"Oh yeah? Let me prove it to you." Madison slipped into modeling mode, feeling the persona settle into her veins, straightening her posture ever so slightly, adding that coquettish smile to her lips, opening her eyes into doe range. "Bring Cheese Please to your next party," she said, her voice husky and dark, "and you'll have a damned good time."

Across from her, Jack swallowed, then he recovered and shook his head. "Nope, don't believe you." He laid his hand on the desktop phone.

One more shot, Madison. Make it the money shot.

She rose, skirted his desk, then lifted one hip and rested it on the corner of the dark wood surface. When she did, her skirt hiked upward, exposing her bare legs, her thighs, nearly everything to his gaze. She let one slingback dangle against his jeans, the tiny leather shoe whispering along the denim. Madison drew in a breath, held it long enough to expand her chest, tilting to the right, allowing her breasts spill forward, straining against the confines of her dress. Her cleavage beckoned with each inhale, exhale, up and down. She watched Jack's eyes widen, his breath beginning to flow in and out faster—

And knew she had him.

Moving slowly, one agonizing inch at a time, Madison reached forward, her eyes never leaving his. The simmering tension increased inside her, infusing her veins with a heat she hadn't felt in a long, long time.

With two fingers, she latched onto the edge of his shirt and slowly drew her grasp downward, the soft cotton slipping between her touch, at the same time pulling him ever so closer, wrapping him in her spell. "Bring Cheese Pleese to your next party," she said again, moving in, placing her face within inches of his, near enough to kiss, to taste, "and I promise you'll have a damned good time."

"Holy shit," Jack whispered, his voice hoarse. "You're hired."

Madison sat back, triumph soaring through her. "Like I said, as long as you believe me, the camera will, too."

"I, uh, don't know if we need quite that much sex appeal," he said, his gaze going to her exposed thigh, then he jerked it back up to her face. "I want people to want the cheese—"

"Not me?"

"Yes. Especially considering you aren't for sale."

She smiled. "You bought me."

"Only to photograph, not to eat."

The innuendo filled the heartbeat between them with a coiling, tensing heat. Her eyes locked with his, and she opened her mouth, certain she'd have a witty reply, as always.

Nothing.

All she could picture was his mouth on her body, devouring her skin like a man who'd starved himself of her touch for far too long. She nearly arched her back with want, and fought the urge to spread herself on his desk and have him see which he wanted more—the cheddar or her—right now.

Her body kept pushing the gas pedal, but her mind wisely braked. She was here for the job, not the man.

Redeem the career, remember?

Otherwise, she might as well sign on for pitchfork duty.

"So," she said, forcing a bright tone into her voice and returning to her seat as if she hadn't been affected at all by the last few seconds, "what kind of campaign were you planning? My agent didn't tell me very much about it." In his fifty-nine second conversation, Harry hadn't said much more than "screw up and you're modeling Depends next week."

"It's a two-pronged campaign," Jack replied, seeming relieved to return to business mode. "First, we have a wine festival this weekend."

"Harry mentioned that. I'm supposed to be the spokesmodel, helping to sell your product at the festival."

"Exactly. It's the first time the vintners are allowing outside products into the festival. Wine, cheese, it's a good combination. We need to make a big splash there, really attract the attention of the gourmet shops and the wineries. I'm hoping to work out some partnerships from this."

She nodded, making mental notes of his goals, as she always did when she went into a preliminary client meeting. It helped to know what the client wanted to accomplish, who they wanted to reach. Madison had learned to adapt her look, her approach, even her smile, to match different campaign objectives. "That's a lot to expect out of one weekend."

Jack ran a hand through his hair, displacing the dark brown locks. On any other man, the move would have looked unkempt, messy. But on Jack, it gave him a look of vulnerability. His shoulders seemed weighed down, as if there were two tons of worries sitting on them. For a second, Madison wanted to cross the room and tell him it would all work out okay.

Which was completely insane. She didn't know that and couldn't promise him something she had zero control over. She could barely work her own life, never mind someone else's.

Besides, doing so would break her number-one cardinal rule: never, ever get involved with the client.

"To be honest," Jack said, "Cheese Pleese needs the business. Our biggest local competitor, Dandy Dairy, has taken more and more market share every year. So, we've got some ground to gain, and fast." His gaze connected with hers. "I need you, Madison, to help me make that happen."

"Don't worry. I'll sell those wine people on Cheese Pleese." She felt the charge of a goal coursing through her, a feeling Madison hadn't had in years. How long had it been since a client had said they actually needed her? For years, she'd just been another face in the glossy pages crowd, an interchangeable pair of eyes and lips on a magazine cover. To the media she was another heiress with too much money and too little purpose. But to Jack Pleeseman…

She was more.

"What about wardrobe?" she asked.

"I hadn't thought much about that," he said, a slight flush filling his face. Suddenly, she saw Jack Pleeseman in a whole new light, as a man who was new to her world. This was another novelty for Madison—being the one with more experience, more knowledge. "I have no idea what women need for clothes and I—" He threw up his hands.

"Don't worry, I have it covered. I brought options, remember?"

He grinned. "Almost makes me glad I carried all those suitcases up to the second floor." They stared at each other for a long second, the sexual tension of earlier still in the air, waiting to be dealt with. Then Jack cleared his throat. "I also have a whole print ad campaign worked out for Christmas, sort of a 'this is a great gift' idea kind of thing. Gift baskets are our biggest sellers, and so I want to really capitalize on that. I have a stack of magazines for you to look at, to see where I'm going with this, as well as some thumbnail sketches of the ads."

Madison nodded, assimilating the information, concentrating on that instead of Jack and the too-brief peek she'd had at his muscular chest when she'd had his shirt in her hand a few minutes ago. "Gift baskets? I'd have thought you'd be doing a lot of sales in grocery stores."

He shook his head. "It's too competitive. Grocery stores receive incentives, sort of like cash bonuses, to display your product in a certain area, within a certain square footage of shelf space. We're a small operation and we don't have pockets deep enough to compete with the Krafts of the world."

"Wow. I had no idea it worked that way."

"It's pretty much the law in all of retail. Didn't you ever wonder why some stores have lots of one brand and none of another?"

She shook her head. "I really don't shop much—at least not for food. Now, shoes, I'm really good at buying those." She grinned.

"Well then, I think we should make a field trip. We made cheese yesterday so I have some time this afternoon. I'll take you down to the SuperSaver, give you an idea of what we're up against consumer wise. Maybe we'll brainstorm some other marketing ideas, too."

"In addition to the gift baskets? The wine festival?"

He nodded. "I believe in aiming high."

"You'd have a lot in common with my grandfather. He says aiming high means you either crash and die, or punch through the clouds. Grandfather's more a cloud kind of guy, lucky for him—and his investors."

"And you? What do you believe in?"

"Me?" Madison blinked at him.

"Do you see anyone else in the room?" He grinned. "Tell me, what do you believe about which way to aim?"

No one ever asked Madison what she thought. She was the pretty face, the sexy body, the mannequin for the clothes. No one cared about her brain, just her measurements. "I...well, I...I've never thought about it."

He sat back in his chair, surprised. "Never thought about it? But you have a career, surely you must have had a business plan, a five-year plan or something."

She laughed. "I'm a model because it's the only thing I know how to do. There is no five-year plan. There's only working as much as I can while I can. Because in five years, all this," she drew a circle around her face, "could be gone."

"In five years, you'll only be more beautiful," he said quietly.

"See how many magazines want me for their cover then," Madison replied, dismissing his words before they got too close, treaded on the parts of her that she kept hidden. She needed to remember that her clock was ticking—not her biological one, Lord knew she had no idea how to take care of herself, much less a child—but her physical one. The tag team of wrinkles and cellulite were just waiting to tackle her. One more slip-up, and she'd be jiggling herself out of a job.

Jack's eyes met hers again, the intensity as hot as a poker. A long moment passed, the silence broken only by the sounds of the farm outside the open window. The tractor running. The cows mooing. The goat baaing. It was like a preschooler's Old McDonald Had a Farm book.

"Well," he said, clearing his throat. "Either way, you're perfect for what I want right now. Assuming, that is, that you can behave." One corner of his mouth turned up.

"Yesterday was a difficult day." She felt a mirroring grin on her own face. "Made more difficult by certain frustration factors."

"Meaning me, I assume?"

"If the one-horned goat fits."

He tipped his head back and roared with laughter. She decided she liked his laugh, the richness of it, the depth of it, as if it came from somewhere far inside him. "Okay, I admit, I was partly at fault, too. I might have exacerbated the situation."

She grinned. "Might have?"

"Truce." He put up his hands. "Now, give me a few minutes to finish some paperwork and then we'll check on your Benz over at Coop's place before we head to the SuperSaver. I'd like to see what kind of vibes you get from the shelves."

Madison Worth was getting some vibes all right—but not a one of them had to do with cheese. And everything to do with the cheesemaker.

Coop's Work-of-Art
Cheese-Stuffed Chicken in Phyllo

1 1/2 pounds boneless chicken breasts (eight pieces total)
Salt and pepper
2 tablespoons olive oil
4 cups fresh spinach
1 medium onion, minced
4 ounces cream cheese, softened
1 cup mozzarella cheese, shredded
2 ounces feta cheese
1/2 cup cheddar cheese, shredded
1 egg yolk
1 tablespoon flour
1/2 teaspoon nutmeg
1/2 teaspoon cumin
16 sheets phyllo dough
2/3 cup melted butter

Looks like a lot of ingredients, doesn't it? What the hell do you think art is? A whole lot of ingredients blended together to make a statement, that's what. Those graduates from idiot school (i.e., the art critics) wouldn't know a decent piece of art even if it was shoved under their upturned noses.

Start by preheating your oven to 350 degrees, then pounding out the chicken breasts until they're nice and flat. Sprinkle with salt and pepper, set aside.

Cook the spinach and onion in the oil, add the cheeses, egg, flour and spices. Ah, it's gorgeous isn't it? A true blending of color and scents. If I could, I'd slap it on a canvas. Wouldn't sell the damned thing, because those critics would be all over it, claiming a misuse of dinner or something.

Divide the mixture evenly between the chicken breasts, then roll them up. Take two sheets of phyllo per breast, brush them with margarine, then wrap the chicken in them, sealing the edges. Brush with more margarine before putting on a jelly roll pan (or a cookie sheet) and baking for 30 to 35 minutes.

That gives you just enough time to get working on your next masterpiece: *Model and Farmer in Lust.*

CHAPTER EIGHT

Coop's garage looked like something out of a Jackson Pollack painting—either that or a preschool's finger paint haven. Every square inch of the metal pre-fab building was covered with colored streaks and dots, in a random, screaming riotous kaleidoscope.

"It's early," Jack said. "So Coop should still be in a fairly good mood. Catch him after noon and he's like Hemingway with a wrench."

They entered the garage, which was even more colorful inside than out. Two walls were red, a third bright blue and the fourth was white, with half a painting started on one side. The smell of oil colors hung heavy in the air, mixing with the scent of grease and motor oil. Frank Sinatra boomed from the stereo on the counter, the volume up so loud, the speakers were vibrating in protest.

"Coop!" Jack called. "Hey, Coop!"

There was the sound of metal wheels on concrete, then a skinny, bespectacled man slid out from under the body of a Toyota. "Who the hell is bugging me this early in the morning?" He got to his feet, brushing grease along his paint-stained coveralls, the name Coop embroidered in a rainbow of colors over his heart. "Oh, it's you. Jesus, Jack, can't you leave a man to his misery?"

"Sorry, Coop. I heard the juried art show rejected your work again—"

"Bastards," he growled. "They spit on it. Might as well have been dog crap, the way those people shoveled it back into my hands." He scowled, then pulled off his cap and tossed it onto a workbench littered with tools. "Art critics. The bane of my existence." He crossed to a sink and started washing his hands with an orange-scented cleanser.

"*This* is a *good* mood?" Madison whispered.

"Actually, he seems pretty damned chipper today. It's always a good sign when he's not punching anything."

Madison cast a wary glance at her SL500, waiting in the next bay. No new dents. Once again, she considered finding another garage—any garage.

"He's the best there is," Jack said, as if reading her mind. "You won't even recognize your car when he's done with it."

Madison looked around the garage, taking in the paint party dancing its way through the walls. "That's what I'm afraid of."

"You the one with the Benz?" Coop said, returning to them.

"Yes," Madison said, introducing herself. "It's a very expensive car, most of the time it's been babied and—"

"Don't worry. I know how to treat a car. A lot like you treat a woman, 'cept without the roses. You talk sweet to her, give her what she needs to purr and then shine her up all pretty before you send her out the door."

Shine her up all pretty? Dread sank to the pit of Madison's stomach as she thought of the florid shop. "You aren't going to *paint* the car, right?"

"Well, hell, that's a good idea," Coop said. He squared his index fingers together, turning to frame the Benz in his view. "*Mercedes in Repose.* Can't you just see it?" Coop raised his digit viewfinder toward Madison.

"Uh...I like the silver."

He shrugged. "A lady like you, you should have a car that screams personality. Silver is for conformists." He eyed her. "And there's nothing I hate more in the world than a goddammed conformist."

"I brought along something to inspire you," Jack said, reaching into his back pocket and pulling out a long metal tube, effectively changing the subject. "Burnt Sienna."

Coop took the gift, then, still clutching it, swiped at his eyes. "Damn you, Jack. Why do you gotta keep bringing me paint?"

"Because I know what it's like to have your dreams shot down." Jack clapped the mechanic on the shoulder. "Just promise me you'll fix Madison's car before you start your next masterpiece."

Coop nodded. "It'll be my pleasure. People's idea of buying foreign around here is a Maxima.

Now a Benz, that's a car I can sink a wrench into. You leave your baby in my hands and she'll be up and running in no time."

Coop told them he estimated two days or so, to take care of the wide variety of maintenance issues that Madison had let slip. He said something about a blown gasket or some such thing. She just nodded, hoping all the while that she could call Visa and beg them to give her back her charging privileges.

A moment later, they were back in Jack's pick-up, heading a couple of blocks down the road. There wasn't much to the town—a combination fire station, police station and library, a two-pump gas station and a coin-operated Laundromat advertising its quarter dryer special.

She'd seen more retail space in the first floor of Macy's. And yet, something about the sparseness was refreshing, clean, like newly washed towels. The buildings were old, their architecture a mismatch of years of ownership and individuality. The Worth decorator would have been horrified by the downtown scene and rushed to paint it all the same upscale cream.

For some reason, though, it seemed perfect just as it was. Homey.

And a hundred worlds apart from the one Madison knew.

That homey feeling disappeared when they pulled up in front of the supermarket—if it could be called that. The cement block building was small and nondescript, sporting only a sign that read "Bunch's

SuperSaver". She didn't know if that meant it was owned by a guy named Bunch or if someone had made a typo in the sign and put the bunch before the super savings.

Three cars total were parked haphazardly between nearly invisible yellow lines. The unlandscaped parking lot looked like it had been created by a carpet bomb. Big chunks of tar were missing in some places, other areas were simply reduced to gravel. A battered grocery cart had been upended and left to rust by the side of the building. It sported only a single wheel, spinning lazily in the breeze.

If this had been a store in Manhattan, there would have been bankruptcy declarations going out already.

"This should be an adventure," she said under her breath.

Jack turned off the truck. "Shopping here? Why?"

"I've...well, I've never been in a supermarket before." Madison eyed the tiny store. Did this even qualify as a supermarket? There didn't seem to be anything super about it. In fact, it looked more like a prison for rotten eggplants.

"Are you kidding me? Who's never been in a supermarket?"

She bristled. "Well, some people, obviously."

He pocketed the keys, then leaned an arm over the bench seat, genuinely surprised. "How on earth do you function? Eat? Get toilet paper?"

"All of that is taken care of for me. It's just there when I need it." It always had been, since birth. She never questioned it, never wondered if there'd be food in the refrigerator when she returned from Cannes or Venice. Without fail, someone—the maid, the butler, the shoemaker's elves—took care of those details.

"That would be weird. I can't imagine someone else making my toilet paper decisions."

She blinked. "There are choices?"

He laughed, then opened his door. "Let's go inside, Madison, and I'll show you the advantages of quilted over two-ply."

A few minutes later, Madison was walking beside Jack, who had insisted on grabbing a rickety metal shopping cart, to give them the "entire shopping experience." One wheel squeaked, another had an annoying habit of turning in, and the handle flipped back and forth between the red "keep your child buckled" message and the bare metal side. "Are you sure you don't want another one?" Madison asked as he wrestled the thing around a corner.

"What, and miss all the fun? If you're going to do this, you've got to do it right. In fact…" Jack let go of the handle and stepped away from the cart. It jerked to a stop. "She'll all yours."

"You want me to push that…thing?"

"Get behind the wheel, Miss Worth, and start shopping."

Madison hesitated, then did as he told her, trying to be at least somewhat cooperative. She was going to prove to him, once and for all, that labeling her as a diva had been unfair.

Mostly.

Madison knew she acted like a spoiled brat from time to time. The problem was, she was, indeed, a spoiled brat. With an absent mother, no father to speak of, and raised by a wealthy grandfather and a team of nannies, she'd had her every whim indulged for her entire life. As a model, people had only sucked up to her even more.

To the point where she couldn't tell who her real friends were and who was being nice to her because someone had paid them to act that way.

Madison shook off the thought. For God's sake, she wasn't here to do a maudlin *This is Your Life*. She was a wealthy heiress who could have anything she wanted, *if* she decided to go back to the family fortune. No one was going to cry over that spilled milk. So Madison better damned well not either.

The stainless steel handle felt cold and hard beneath her palm, foreign, weird. She paused, reading the instructions about strapping a child into the hard plastic seat, knowing she was stalling.

Wait. This was shopping. If there was one thing Madison Worth excelled at, it was shopping. She'd just pretend this was Bloomingdale's and she was scoping out the latest couture offerings.

With that, she stepped forward, high heels clicking on the hard lime green linoleum, trying not to notice the way people in the store stared at them—the fancy-clad New York princess and the jeans-and-button-down shirt local guy.

As she walked by, a stockboy replenishing the banana supply stopped and gaped, dropping a pile of fruit to the floor. Another man pushing a cart of his own filled with one liter of soda, one pizza, one loaf of bread—no left hand ring, no big hunks of meat, definitely single, a part of Madison noted—stepped aside and with a gracious wave and a wink, allowed her to pass by.

"You could stand in the twelve items or less line with three thousand packages of ramen soup and not a man would complain," Jack whispered in her ear.

"Oh, I doubt that."

"Are you kidding me? A woman like you, with a sexy body, long legs and blonde hair walks by, and every man in a twenty-mile radius is reduced to senseless drooling." He grinned.

"Even you?"

Where had that come from?

She knew exactly where. From that well inside her that never seemed to be filled, not with food, not with men, not with gushing compliments.

"Even me," Jack said quietly, turning to investigate the lettuce.

Oh, boy. This was treading on some very dangerous ground. Taking a direction she never intended.

Business only. Because she needed to fill up her bank account before she thought of filling anything else.

With Jack trailing behind her, she skirted a display of Hunt's canned tomatoes, twenty-eight ounces on sale for fifty-eight cents. Was that a good buy? And what did someone do with twenty-eight ounces of tomatoes anyway? She wanted to ask Jack but knew she'd be exposing herself as the poor little rich girl who'd never experienced real life—and who couldn't find a can opener in her seventy-thousand-dollar designer kitchen if her life depended on it.

Canned green beans, low salt, three for a dollar. Loaves of bread, white, enriched, seventy-nine cents. Ho-Hos, one-ninety-nine.

She stopped suddenly, one wheel on the cart screeching.

"Oh my, Ho-Hos," Madison said, the words a breath.

"And they're on sale. Fifty cents off," Jack said, tapping a little yellow sign beside the stack of boxes.

She glanced up at him. "Is that a good price?"

He chuckled. "I'd say so. If you want them, toss them in the basket."

She reached out, brushed her fingertips across the chocolate and icing filled image, then withdrew. "No. I can't."

"Sure you can. It's not that hard."

"You don't understand," Madison said, pushing the cart past the treats before she changed her mind, the taste of them already spiraling in her stomach, pinging off her nerve endings, igniting feelings of want that she was having a lot of trouble tamping down. "If I have one, I'll want another. And another. And another. There'll be no stopping me."

Jack chuckled. "An over-Ho-Ho'er, is that it?"

"My whole living is made off my body. One too many Ho Hos will ruin it."

He paused in the aisle, his hand on her arm, his dark eyes meeting hers. Heat brewed within them, a heat that had nothing to do with tiny chocolate cakes, and more to do with a whole other kind of desire.

Adding a new complication to their business relationship. A complication Madison hadn't counted on.

"An indulgence or two won't hurt you," he said.

Madison knew, as surely as she knew her own name, that Jack Pleeseman wasn't just talking about a bunch of Hostess products. The small grocery store seemed to shrink, the crowded, buy-one-get-one-free filled aisles closing in, the canned goods and boxes tightening the circle around the two of them.

Her gaze traveled over his face, down his shoulders, following the bulging curves of his biceps, the firm planes of his chest and his tight, trim waist.

She swallowed, the Ho Hos forgotten. How long had it been since she'd met a real man? Not the kind manufactured by *GQ* and Abercrombie & Fitche catalogs, but a real, honest to God man who worked hard and earned his looks with his own two hands?

The answer came easily, swiftly.

Never.

And that made her want him. To taste him, to touch him, to have him do the same to her, over and over again. The need pulsed within her, beating its own drum, whispering its native call. She glanced down, at the strong, thick fingers on his hands, the wide grip of his palms, the dark tan that tinted his arms. She opened her mouth, imagining his fingers dancing along her neck, up her jaw, to her lips, where she could suck one digit in and—

"Madison?"

She jerked her gaze back up to his. Fantasizing about the boss was definitely not a good idea. Those kinds of things only led to trouble.

And the last thing Madison Worth needed in her life was more of that.

"My goodness, is that you, Jack Pleeseman?" said a female voice from behind them.

Madison had heard that tone a hundred times— on the catwalk, which got its name not from the peril of walking in high heels down a narrow path as wordsmiths would have people believe—but from the claws that came out regularly behind the scenes.

"Oh, shit," Jack muttered, a scowl darkening his brow. "Not now."

"What?" Madison asked. "Who is it?"

As she turned, Madison saw a husky brunette who seemed built like a prize mare, striding down the aisle toward them. She had that air of ownership about her, the kind that said she had dibs on Jack and any female in a fifty-mile radius better damned well back off.

"Just someone who'd rather see me under a truck than in one," he said, whispering into her ear, slipping in beside her. "Kitty Dandy, the owner of Dandy Dairy and the one person who would do anything to get her hands on my marketing secret. And every inch of my business." He turned and put on the fake smile people gave the neighbors they hated but put up with for the sake of fence peace.

"What a surprise to see you here," Kitty said. "Checking out the competition in the dairy aisle?"

"Just doing some shopping, Kitty," Jack said. In his face, Madison could see the barely restrained tolerance. He had one foot moved back, ready to make a break for it.

Kitty laughed. "Shopping? Right. Don't tell me you're thinking you'll be able to get the SuperSaver contract, Jack. Dandy has that all wrapped up. Oh yes, along with Stop & Shop and Shaw's. No room at any of those for your little operation. Sorry. Though if you'll reconsider selling, I'd be glad to absorb Pleeseman into the Dandy family."

Madison hated the woman on sight. She didn't know Jack well, had barely spent twenty-four hours on the Pleeseman farm, but already she felt like she was a part of the company, if only because this was her job and this evil woman was dissing it—and trying to steal it.

"And who is this?" Kitty said, shooting Madison an air of disdain. "Don't tell me you've hired a maid? Or is she here to milk the cows?"

Maid? She thought Madison was the maid? And in a DKNY dress that was hot off the runway, too?

That was the last straw. First she dissed the job, then she dissed Madison herself. Madison's fist curled into a ball behind her back.

"No," Jack said to Kitty. "This is Madison Worth, my—"

"Fiancé," Madison finished. No way was she going to let Jack let the marketing plan out of the proverbial bag. So she'd gone and blurted out the first word that had come to mind.

And then, it hit her. Fiancé? Of all the words in the English language, what had made her pick *that* one?

She already knew. It had spilled from the same impetuous mouth that had gotten into the cat fight during Fashion Week. The same one that had told off the senior editor of *Marie Claire* when he had pronounced her a fat moose with all the appeal of used chewing gum. When Madison's dander was up, the governor on her mouth seemed to run for the hills. About anything was liable to come out.

Including the last word she'd ever associate with herself again—fiancé.

Beside her, she heard Jack choke.

"Fiancé?" Kitty asked, laughter in her voice. She turned to Jack, pencil-drawn eyebrows raised. "Since when did you get engaged?"

"Just recently," Jack said, recovering his wits. "It was a surprise."

Kitty looked to Jack, then to Madison. "You wouldn't be doing this to make anyone in particular jealous, now would you, Jack?"

"Hell, no, Kitty," he said, slipping his arm around Madison's waist. It felt warm, protective. Oddly right. "It's a publicity stunt."

Then, with Madison securely against him, he pivoted and headed off, leaving Kitty gasping like a mackerel left flopping on a boat deck.

Jack waited until the cereal aisle before spinning to face Madison, his face as hard as stone and unreadable as Sanskrit. A sinking feeling gathered in her stomach. She knew immediately.

She'd done it again. And this time, with less calories.

Jack gripped the cart, halting it with a protesting squeak of the wheels. "What the hell was that?" he said, the words harsh and hard under his breath.

"I don't know. Honestly. I was just trying to help."

"By claiming to be my *fiancé*? That doesn't help a damned thing. Do you have any idea what Kitty will do to me? Who she'll tell about my 'engagement?'" His eyes flashed fire, the set of his jaw as stiff and cold as the rest of him. "You're like a train wreck, you know that? Just rolling in, screwing up my life."

"Hey, I was only trying to help," Madison said, stepping forward and pointing a finger at his chest, the one that had sacrificed a nail to his nasty front porch. "And I haven't even known you long enough to screw up your life. If you have some history with the evil kitty cat woman back there, that's your problem. I was just trying to keep your marketing project under wraps."

He scowled. "You could have come up with a better plan."

"I don't exactly think well on my feet."

"Must be the shoes," he said, eyeing her Manolos. "Those pointy toes probably cut off the circulation to your brain."

Madison's first instinct was to grab a box of Fruit Loops—on sale for three-ninety-nine—and beat him with them until his head was the same rainbow color as the cereal.

But that wouldn't be a good choice for a woman whose entire financial future was hinging on this one job. So Madison sucked up her anger and glared at Jack instead. "Then call off the wedding," she said. "I'm sure no one would blame you for dumping me."

"I'm sure they wouldn't. You—" He had a finger pointed at her, then cut himself off at the sound of a familiar pair of high heels clicking up the aisle, warning of the approach of the evil cat.

Jack looked at Madison, she looked at him, both recognizing the sound at the same time in the nearly empty store. They had two choices—either try to hide behind the Cocoa Puffs or go for an Oscar.

"She's coming," Madison whispered. "You'd better pretend to love me, at least for now."

He glared at her. "I'd rather go bankrupt."

"Men," she muttered. "Stubborn as walls." Then, before Jack could lose his shirt, she reached forward, drew his mouth toward her own, and kissed him.

Once again, Madison hadn't thought—she'd reacted. That had always been one of her greatest faults, and one of her greatest strengths. Most of the time, acting without thinking had led her to leap off cliffs she never would have tried.

And other times, it had caused her to run face-first into a concrete wall of stupidity.

She hoped kissing Jack Pleeseman wasn't in the second category.

Startled, he didn't kiss her back at first, and it seemed as if the whole impetuous plan was going to backfire. She kept on, lifting her fingers into his hair, curving into his body, asking him without words to go along with her. Out of the corner of her eye, she saw Kitty round the corner and stop, gaping at them.

A monkey could have seen that there was zero carnal knowledge between Madison and Jack—and even less sexual attraction.

But then, something within him melted and the icy wall of anger washed away, replaced by the heat that had simmered in his office earlier. The game she'd begun, the act she'd put on, had suddenly become something real, tangible.

Instead of her kissing him, things shifted and he began to take the lead, his powerful mouth claiming hers, guiding her in a heated dance that urged her to open to him, to allow him access she hadn't allowed anyone in a long, long time. She forgot about the store, Kitty, the marketing ploy. All she felt, all she knew, was this man and the magic touch of his lips, his fingers and the whisper of his breath against hers.

She arched against him, softening into his chest like butter on toast, her fingers tangling in his hair, her tongue sliding into his mouth, tangoing with his, teasing, tasting, trying each other out, learning the curves, the valleys.

After a moment, Madison vaguely heard the distant sound of heels clicking angrily away, growing distant. Leaving. She heard a man clear his throat. Someone call for a price check on Spaghetti-O's. The coast was clear.

And then, just like that, the magic dissipated and the kiss was over.

Jack drew back, a look of soft surprise on his face. "What did you do that for?"

"Kitty was coming. You needed…" Her voice trailed off, her gaze locked on his lips. She knew she had a reason for kissing him but she couldn't quite think of it right now.

"Yeah. I did." His chocolate brown eyes dropped to her mouth, watching her inhale, exhale. "It's, ah, probably not a good idea for us to be doing that. Again."

"Probably not."

And why not? Her mind asked. It sure felt good. Tingled in some places. Okay, every place. Reminded her it had been quite a while since anyone had made her tingle.

"We're working together," Jack continued, as if he'd read her mind, or, maybe, as if he were trying to make a case for himself, "and my priorities need to be on the business." He cleared his throat, put more distance between them. "Now, let me show you the dairy aisle."

And just like that, Jack Pleeseman went back to being all business. Before Madison knew it, she was being treated to a lecture about the many varieties of cheddar and Colby, the benefits and drawbacks of soft and hard cheeses—

And she didn't hear a single damned word.

Five minutes ago, Madison had told herself she didn't need any more trouble in her life. Now she'd gone and whipped up a hornet's nest of it all on her own. The best thing she could do was put on her model face, smile pretty for the cameras, then get the hell out of town before someone else ended up with cake on their face.

Someone like her.

Jack's Things-Are-Spicing-Up Taco Dip

8 ounces cream cheese, softened
8 ounces sour cream
1 teaspoon cumin
8 ounces salsa, choose your heat
1 1/2 cups cheddar cheese, shredded
1 cup lettuce, shredded
2 tomatoes, pulp and seeds removed, diced
3 scallions, diced
1/2 cup sliced green or black olives
Tortilla chips

After that grocery store encounter, you definitely need something fiery to take your mind off the hot number in the upstairs bedroom. Start by beating the cream cheese with the sour cream and cumin. Smooth it over the bottom of a 7 by 11-inch pan or a 10-inch pie plate. Refrigerate for one hour. If necessary, refrigerate your entire body to cool it off after kissing her.

Now you're ready to get down to business. On top of the cream cheese base, layer the salsa, cheese and vegetables. Get those chips out and start dipping—

Before you think of dipping into her lips again. A woman like that, whose not just from the other side of the tracks, but from the family that owns the whole damned railroad, is definitely bad for your heart.

CHAPTER NINE

"**D**id a hornet fly up your ass again?" Joe said, entering the plant. Jack had returned from the store and headed straight to the production floor. Madison had dashed out of his truck the second he'd parked it, heading into the house and far from him. He'd gone in the opposite direction—to work out some frustrations on the cheese. "Because you're as grumpy as a Siamese in a hot tub."

Despite his mood, Jack paused in his work and laughed. "Got a lot on my mind, Dad, that's all." Like the way Madison Worth had grabbed him in the SuperSaver and turned his world, his hormones and his entire plan to keep it impersonal upside down.

Not to mention added a complication that he didn't need to his personal life.

"What's to worry about? We milk the cows, we make the cheese, we sell it, then we get up in the morning and do it all over again. Been doing it like that for going on more than a hundred years now at Pleeseman Dairy Farms. It was good enough for your grandfather, and his grandfather." Joe shrugged out of his light brown Carhartt jacket, draped it on a hook on the wall, then slipped a Cheese Pleese emblazoned apron over his denim coveralls. "Why you want to change all that with that high-falutin' New York girl, I'll never know. We got along just fine before without advertising and marketing." He said the words like he was spitting out tobacco, in two distasteful chunks.

Jack sighed, turning the last of the molds in the row, filled with curds from that week's production. Holes at the bottom ensured final draining of every ounce of whey. As his father had said, it was the same process they'd used for decades, and while he had no argument over the production process, he knew, from his years of experience in corporate America, that everything else within the business could be improved. He removed the latex gloves on his hands, then turned to face his father. "Dad—"

"I know, I know," Joe said, putting up his hands to stop the argument before it started. "Your mother gave you her fifty percent, and I handed over the reins to you last year—"

"Because you said you wanted to retire. Take up golf."

Joe waved a hand in dismissal. "Golf's for old men who look good in plaid. I don't know any of those. Either way, smacking a little white ball around the lawn isn't my cup of Joe. Like it or not, you're stuck with me butting my nose into the business. Telling you what I think."

"I don't mind, Dad." And Jack didn't, not really. As much as he and his father knocked heads, he kept hoping one day, they'd find the kind of rapport he saw between David and their father, built from years of working side-by-side. "I just wish you'd trust me."

His father picked up an antique oak mold, used back when Joe had pressed his first horn of Colby, as the official beginning of the Cheese Pleese division of the company. Since those early days, it had stood on the production floor, still ready to be called into service, but more as a reminder of how far the company had come. "And I wish you'd see that sometimes doing things the old way doesn't mean you're acting like your old man." Then he left for the cooling room, leaving their argument still simmering on the production floor.

The workers at Pleeseman wisely kept their own counsel, staying out of Jack's way as he worked out some of his frustrations with a mop, scrubbing the floor of the plant until it was as clean as the stainless steel surfaces of the prep areas. When he was finished there, he headed out to the barn, hefting a pitchfork for the better part of the afternoon.

Sometime after four, Jack left the barn. He'd skipped lunch, knocking off long after the rest of the staff. His muscles ached from the day of hard labor, but he finally felt as if he'd worked Madison Worth's kiss out of his system.

More or less.

He'd needed to pitch a hell of a lot of hay to forget the way her lips had felt on his. The surprise of her taking the lead, hauling him to her, falling into the act of being in love with a gusto that would have put Julia Roberts to shame.

How long had it been since a woman had kissed him like that? Since he'd returned a kiss?

He knew the answer. Felt it in his bones every lonely night he spent, restless and sleepless, wishing hard work was enough to make a man forget.

To forget that the woman he had married had betrayed him for a limo and an unlimited bank account. Forget that the dreams he'd thought they'd shared had all been one-sided. Forget that he had sworn off relationships until he had all his ducks in a row—

And one duck in particular back where she belonged.

As soon as he hit the yard and strode toward the porch, he saw Madison, sitting on the porch swing, reading some of the dairy industry magazines he'd given her, an icy glass of lemonade sitting on the small wicker table beside her.

With any other woman, the scene would have been ordinary. Homespun even. But with a woman who looked like Madison Worth, it became worthy of fine art. He halted in the middle of the drive, shading his eyes from the hot sun, and allowed himself one sweet second to stare at her.

Her legs, those long, creamy legs, were propped up on the porch railing, the peachy smooth skin seeming to go on forever before disappearing beneath khaki shorts. Her feet were bare, the toes painted bright red. Gone was the straight lines of the business-like suit of the day before, as well as the slinky red dress from the morning, replaced instead by a soft white T-shirt that skimmed her curves and set off a barely there tan that told him Madison wasn't the type to spend hours worshipping the sun.

In one hand, she held a straw, which she was worrying between her lips, unaware that he was watching her as she read. With an easy movement, Madison tucked a strand of blond hair behind her ear. Jack nearly groaned at the innocence of the gesture, and the way it exposed her graceful, delicate neck to his view.

A sparrow fluttered past the porch to dip its beak into one of Aunt Harriet's many Graceland-shaped birdfeeders ringing the house. The sudden movement startled Madison and she looked up. Her gaze caught Jack's and she smiled.

Holy cow.

This smile was the kind that was unaware, friendly in its simplicity. Given too quickly to have added airs or meanings. It was real and true and it socked him in the gut with a tidal wave force that told Jack he was in deep trouble.

Really deep trouble.

He had other priorities—the farm, the business, his family—and bringing this citified woman, or any woman, into that mix would be crazy. Hadn't he learned that lesson with Alyssa? When he'd married the younger Dandy sister, he'd thought what they'd had was real.

Until it turned out to be as fake as No-Moo Milk, the chemical equivalent of a dairy drink some company in Boston had created.

"Are you thinking what I'm thinking?"

Jack turned to find David beside him, grinning at the sight of Madison on the porch. She'd dropped her gaze back to the magazines. For that, he should be grateful. But a very big part of him—the part that operated solely on testosterone—missed that smile.

"That dating the help is a bad idea?" Jack said. "A *really* bad idea."

"Hey, I'm not the boss. She doesn't work for me." David straightened his collar and made as if he was going to walk toward the porch.

"Don't you dare. Besides, little brother, you're part owner. Close enough to the boss that I think it's a good policy to stay away."

Yeah, like Jack had done a good job of keeping his own distance. Kissing her in Aisle Seven was setting a whole new kind of company policy. If he kept that up, he'd need to rewrite the employee handbook.

David gave Jack an elbow in the ribs. "Getting jealous?"

"No, not at all."

His younger brother chuckled, knowing him far too well. "Uh-huh. Let's grab a beer and then you can lie to me about how uninterested you are."

They circled to the left, away from the porch, heading into the house through the back door. It opened with the same familiar creak that had announced the presence of everyone from Uncle Lester to Tommy Williams, one of those neighborhood kids who'd never knocked. Every ounce of this house was as well known to Jack as the back of his hand. He saw his mother in the tiles on the backsplash, in the spindly spider plants that still hung in the kitchen window, persistently hanging on despite intermittent waterings.

So much of the house had fallen by the wayside, paint peeling, fabric fading, wood cracking. But every time either Jack or David brought up the idea of repairing something, their father resisted. He'd been like that for nearly fifteen years, refusing to move on since the loss of his wife, wanting only to continue every day the same as the last.

As Jack entered the kitchen, he half expected his aunt to come hurrying up, chiding him about his absence at lunch, latching onto him until she had him in a chair at the kitchen table and seated before a heaping plate of fried peanut butter and banana sandwiches.

But the room was empty, save for a stew or something simmering on the stove. Jack grabbed two beers out of the fridge, then he and David headed out to the Adirondack chairs beneath the big maple in the backyard. Like everything else in the Pleeseman household, they needed a coat of paint. But they were still good enough to hold a man and his beer.

"Mom would have never stood for this," David said, indicating the flaking white paint. "Seems ever since she died—"

"Yeah," Jack finished, then twisted the top off his Coors, done with that conversation. It was one that hadn't gone anywhere since he was a teenager.

"You know, you are damned good at one thing," David said, settling into the opposite chair.

"What's that?"

"Not talking."

"I talk."

"Bull." David twisted the cap off his beer, flinging it toward a milk pail sitting against the tree with a flick of his thumb. It pinged against the edge and landed on top of hundreds of other caps with a plunk. "I can understand not talking to me. I mean, I'm your brother. But for Pete's sake, Jack, you have a hot, sexy woman sitting on your porch and you don't talk to her."

"I talk to her." Jack did the same with his bottle cap but it fell short, landing on the grass just beside the pail. He rose and retrieved it, avoiding David.

"About business." His brother let out a snort. "What kind of guy talks *business* with a supermodel?"

"The guy who hired her."

"Well, there is that." David took a swig, then sat back, propping his legs up on a stool. "Are you going to tell me there's nothing going on between you two? Because something sure as hell has changed since yesterday. When she first arrived here, she was all piss and vinegar. But what I just saw in that smile a minute ago was something a lot closer to honey."

Jack held the metal cover between his thumb and forefinger, squeezing it until it bent together. From somewhere behind the barn, he heard an exasperated shout of "Katydid!" Undoubtedly the curious goat had gotten into something new. "Hey! Not the tractor!" one of the hands shouted. Jack chuckled, then turned to his brother. "She kissed me today. But it was more like a...favor."

David let out a low, appreciative whistle. "Now that's the kind of friend I need."

Jack crossed to his chair. "Whoa, little brother. Before you fill your head with lewd ideas—"

"What do you mean, *before*? I was already there five minutes ago."

Jack chuckled, took a sip, then settled into the Adirondack. Despite its condition, the chair, handmade by his grandfather two decades ago, still offered the same comfort as always. He tried to concentrate on that, not on the memory of Madison kissing him, of his own personal lewd images video that had been playing in his mind ever since that moment in the grocery store. "It was all because we ran into Kitty."

"Uh-oh. Were her claws out?"

"Of course. She seems determined to make me pay for the divorce, like it was my fault, not her sister's." He swore, then shook his head. "Madison thought she was helping me out by pretending to be my fiancé."

David choked back a laugh. "That should make things interesting at the wine festival."

"Tell me about it." Jack ran a hand through his hair, not wanting to think about the implications an instant fiancé was going to have on the event next Saturday. He wanted the attention on Cheese Pleese, not on his love life—or lack thereof. And not to mention what would happen when Alyssa heard about his new "bride-to-be". "I'm not sure how I'm going to fix this mess."

"Why bother? Unless you're blind, my brother, you have a totally hot supermodel posing as your fiancé. I could find at least fifty—no, a thousand— men who'd pay to trade places with you."

On any other day, he might have agreed with David. But not now, not with so much at stake. "Have you forgotten who's arriving next Sunday, immediately after the wine festival?"

David lowered his beer before taking the next sip. His features instantly sobered and the testosterone teasing disappeared. "Alyssa."

"And she could just as easily get in a snit because she thinks I'm happy," at that Jack let out a snort, thinking of his ex-wife, who had done nearly everything in her power to make his life miserable, "and take Ginny to Europe."

"You could fight her in court."

Jack shook his head, twirling the dark amber bottle between his palms. Wishing again he could go back and fix the mistakes he'd made in his life, but knowing most of them weren't repairable. "With what? Alyssa's married to Daddy Warbucks. I'll lose before I even pick up the phone and dial 1-800-Cheap-Lawyer. I've tried battling Alyssa and I always lose."

"You know she doesn't really want Ginny with her."

"She does if she thinks it'll make me suffer." Jack steeled his jaw and tried very hard not to hate the woman who had made his life a living hell but had also gifted him with the most precious human he'd ever met. "She promised to sign over permanent custody on Sunday, David. I can't screw that up."

"So, what, you're going to keep pursuing this monk thing until then? Or are you going to come up with some other reason for not moving on?"

Jack shrugged and leaned back in his chair, taking another swig of Coors. Blocking the images of Madison Worth—and those ten-mile long legs—from his mind once again. "If that's what it takes to keep Ginny, yeah."

"And if Madison Worth kisses you again?"

"I'll tell her to keep her hands to herself."

David roared with laughter, then rose and tipped his beer in Jack's direction. "You're one hell of a bad liar. You might want to use that business brain and put it to work on the rest of your life."

"Why?"

David leaned in, lowering his voice. "Because there's got to be a way to get your cake and have second servings, too." He pulled back, nodding his head in the direction of the house. Then he left, leaving Jack alone in the yard.

Before Jack could think about cake—or going back for seconds—he saw Madison, bare feet on the grass, long legs stretching toward the sky, the white shirt skimming her curves and outlining breasts that were more than generous.

The afternoon sun shone behind her, glinting off her hair, casting her in an almost angelic light. If he hadn't known better, he'd have thought this pared down version of Madison Worth was the girl next door—

Granted, every guy's totally hot XXX fantasy dream girl next door.

She scowled. "I won't do it."

He stopped smiling. In his fantasies, the girl next door never started with that opening line. "What did you say?"

She tossed half of the magazines onto the Adirondack chair. The pile fanned outward in a blur of colors and images: cows, dairy products, people, factories. "I'm not going to shoot that ad campaign. It's not going to sell cheese. You need another strategy."

He bristled, getting to his feet. Why did everyone have to argue with his ideas? Didn't his degree in business, his years of experience, count for anything? "Are you trying to tell me how to run my business?"

She took a step forward. "I'm not saying you don't know what you're doing. The whole approach to selling the cheese with a pretty face beside it, with that "more please" concept is great. But—" at this, she held up the remaining magazines, all consumer ones, Jack saw, the kind that women snatched up off of checkout stands to find out how to get thin thighs and still have dinner on the table by six. "I think it could be so much more."

"More? What do you mean, more?" He crossed his arms over his chest.

"Your ideas look good on paper," she pointed to the thumbnail sketches he'd given her, detailing his ideas for the ad campaign, "but they won't work in reality. They—"

"And what do you know about it?" he said, cutting her off, immediately annoyed that one more person had to disagree with him, as if he didn't know a damned thing about business. "You're just the—" he bit off the words.

Her blue eyes flashed, the temper evident in them, an instant storm behind the irises. "Just the what? The pretty face? No brains, merely a body, right?"

"I didn't say that." He wanted to take those words back, to retrieve them out of the air and shove them down his throat again, where they belonged.

"You were about to."

Hell. He'd gone and screwed up, offending her and acting like a Cro-Magnon Man, all at the same time. Jack cleared his throat, then relaxed his posture to take the edge off his anger. "So," he said, not offering an apology, but at least a truce, "what are your ideas?"

Madison pointed at the first concept, the one Jack had labored over for at least a week, fine-tuning until he was sure it was the one to use for his launch. He had a lot of money tied up in that one—money committed to *Boston* magazine, the local papers, his brochures, the website he planned to launch, even a ¼-pager in American Airlines's magazine. Big bucks for what he saw as a big idea. "This will never work. It's the kind of ad everyone does, the safe ad that says hey, here we are, please buy us."

"And what the hell is wrong with that?"

She threw up her hands, the paper fluttering. "Where's the risk? Where's the thing that's going to make people sit up, take notice, rush off and buy Cheese Pleese over Dandy?"

He strode forward, his own temper ignited now. "It's right there." He tapped at the page, nearly slapping at the bullet points in the pencil sketch. "Our quality ingredients. Family ownership. Product—"

Madison cupped a hand over her mouth and feigned a yawn. "Everyone says that, Jack. Give me something I don't know."

That was the last straw. This was *his* damned business. He was the one with president after his name, not her. No model from New York was going to come marching in here and tell Jack Pleeseman how to run his company. "I'll tell you what you don't know. You don't know anything about business. You're on the other side of the lens, not on the side with the general ledger." He snatched the paper out of her hand. "So don't go telling me how to run my company. Or my ad campaign."

She parked a fist on her hip. "Then don't expect me to model for such a lame concept."

"Are you quitting?"

"Are you insisting on throwing your money away on this?" She flicked a manicured finger at the paper.

He stood his ground, glaring at her. "Yes."

"Then I refuse to have my image associated with your product. I have to worry about my reputation." Up went that perky little nose.

"I think that went out the window a long time ago. From what I hear, no one is beating down your door." He moved forward, leaning in to hammer the last point home. "Or is Walmart doing runway work now?"

He could practically see the steam coming out of her ears, the fire in her eyes. "I can't stand you."

"Good. The feeling's mutual."

"I should have never agreed to this job. Cheese farm." She let out a very unmodel-like snort. "I must have been out of my mind."

"Or incredibly stupid."

Her hand came up, fast as a whip, but his was faster, catching her before she connected with his jaw. "A fist, Madison? And here I thought you were the slap kind of girl."

She glared at him. "You're the kind of man who needs more than a slap."

"Tsk-tsk," he said, moving in closer, his breath whispering against hers, both their chests heaving with barely controlled anger, the twin emotions of want and hate churning in the air. "Is that any way to speak to the man you intend to marry?"

"Oh, I have intentions for you, Jack Pleeseman, and they have nothing to do with pretending to be your fiancé." The final words came out on a hiss, her wrist tense in his grip.

"And I—"

"Daddy!" a familiar four-year-old voice squealed, before launching herself across the yard and against his legs.

And with that, the trouble in Jack Pleeseman's life quadrupled.

Madison's More-Trouble-Than-You-Need Fettuccini with Artichokes

2 tablespoons olive oil
1 pound mushrooms, sliced
3 cloves garlic, minced
1 teaspoon thyme
1 red pepper, chopped
1 9-ounce can artichoke hearts
1 cup heavy cream
1/2 cup milk
1/2 cup Parmesan cheese
1 pound fettuccini, cooked

The best way to take your mind off a man is to get busy doing something else. If your funds are a little… low right now, and the mall is out of the question, use food for your heartbreak-avoidance therapy.

Sauté the mushrooms, garlic and thyme in the oil until softened, about six minutes. Add the pepper, cook another three minutes. Then add the artichoke hearts, trying not to make that heart-heart connection. Your heart needs to be kept to yourself—giving it to a man will only leave you crying in your Manolos later.

Add the cream, milk and Parmesan cheese, stirring with each addition. Toss with the fettuccini and serve—to everyone else, since you're busy avoiding the dinner table and the gorgeous guy who comes with it.

CHAPTER TEN

Madison took several steps back, as far away from the little person as possible without making it look obvious that she was trying to avoid her. Everything Madison knew about children could be written on a grain of rice.

With room left over for the Gettysburg Address.

She didn't want one for herself, had no desire to be a godmother—fairy or otherwise—and wouldn't babysit even if Ralph Lauren himself begged her to take his grandkids on the Tilt-a-Whirl.

"Daddy, daddy, daddy!" The little girl was climbing up Jack's legs and into his arms, latching onto his neck like a starfish going after a minnow. "I missed you so much!"

"I missed you too, pumpkin," he said, ruffling her hair before leaning back to look her over. "Boy, you've grown. What are you, ten feet tall now?"

She giggled, her ebony ringlets bouncing when she did. "Nu-uh. Daddy, you're silly."

Daddy. Jack Pleeseman had a child?

She didn't know why it hit with her such surprise. After all, she barely knew the man. Hadn't exchanged much more than a few hundred words—

—and one amazing kiss—

—with him. He was, virtually, a stranger. She hadn't paid much attention to the inside of the house, either, but now that she thought about it, she realized she *had* seen photos of this little girl all over the place. Stuck on the refrigerator with little blue suede shoe magnets. Hung in frames on the living room wall. A trio of them, facing Jack on his desk.

Now, looking at the miniature, Jack-besotted person, with her curly black locks and green eyes as big as saucers, she could see, indeed, he was a father, if only by the look in his eyes. It added an entirely new dimension to the man.

And a whole other reason to swear off getting involved with him.

"Genevieve! How many times have I told you not to run off on Mummy? You simply must—" A woman, small and delicate, with dark hair and China doll features, rounded the corner off the house and stopped when she saw Jack. She wore a black Jackie O style suit and a pair of pumps that Madison recognized from Prada's latest collection. "Oh. She's with *you.*"

"Yep. All safe and sound."

"You shouldn't reward her like that. She broke a rule." The woman brushed invisible dirt off the pristine black and white jacket, then pressed a hand to a flawless pageboy. "There should always be consequences."

"Yeah and if there's one thing you're good at, Alyssa, it's consequences," Jack grumbled.

"Don't start, Jack. I haven't the patience for it. Nor the time. For God's sake, I've been so busy traveling with George that I haven't even had time to talk to my family. My own sister called today and I had to have the maid take a message. The *maid*, Jack. If I don't have time to talk to my blood relatives, I certainly don't have time to argue the same old points with you again."

"Don't worry, Alyssa, I'm being a good boy."

She flicked out her wrist, reading the time on the elaborate Rolex on her wrist. "Anyway, I'm off to Wales. George has an opportunity to dine with Prince Charles tomorrow night."

"Gee, wouldn't want to miss that." Jack's voice was droll.

"You have no idea how important it is to be invited by the royal family," Alyssa said. "Daddy says—"

Jack lowered his daughter to the ground and pointed her to a swing set fifty yards away. He waited until she was out of earshot before continuing. "I don't care what your father says, or George says or frankly, even what you say. The only good thing that ever came out of our marriage is Ginny. So go off to dinner with the Queen—"

"The prince."

"—and leave me the hell alone."

Alyssa narrowed her gaze and crossed her arms, clearly not happy at his lack of enthusiasm for her moment of royal glory. Then, for the first time, her gaze traveled past Jack and over to Madison. The light of recognition dawned immediately. "You're that model," she said, wagging a finger in Madison's direction. "I saw you in *Lucky* magazine last month. What on earth are you doing *here*?" She said the last word as if Madison had dropped into a vat of cockroaches.

Madison opened her mouth to supply the same answer she'd given the Dandy Dairy woman, then remembered how angry Jack had gotten. She thought of telling the truth, then realized how quickly that would get around. Madison Worth was slumming it—working a cheese farm instead of the Betsey Johnson collection. "I'm—"

From behind them, a horn beeped. Alyssa turned. "Oh, dear. That's George. We're late for the private jet."

"About Ginny…" Jack began.

Alyssa waved a hand vaguely. "Keep her for a couple days, will you, Jack? It really wouldn't do to bring a child to the Prince and Camilla's home."

"What about the custody agreement? I thought you were going to sign over full custody. We talked about this, Alyssa."

The horn beeped again, twice in rapid succession. "I'm not so sure I like the idea of my precious darling growing up with cows, Jack, you know that. However will she learn anything?"

"I managed." The words were a growl. "So did you, if you remember."

Alyssa ignored him. "Ginny! Be a dear and give Mummy a kiss!"

The little girl stopped the swing, clambered down and ran over, planting a quick kiss on Alyssa's cheek before dashing back to play. Her starched pink dress had already become wrinkled, the matching patent leather shoes scuffed from the dirt patch beneath the swing. Madison saw Alyssa make a face at her daughter's appearance, then let out a sigh of resignation.

"What's with the Mummy thing?" Jack said. "I thought you wanted to be called Mother or Mommy Dearest or something like that."

"If Ginny lives in England, she'll have to learn to talk like the other children. She has to speak the Queen's English and the Queen called her mother Mummy."

"What do you mean, *live in England?* We had an agreement, Alyssa."

Alyssa shrugged, suddenly interested in studying her French manicure. "George is rethinking his no-children plan. We may keep her after all."

From her position on the sidelines, Madison watched the volcano of Jack's temper hit near to bursting. Crimson raced up his neck, lines standing out like a roadmap. "Ginny isn't a goddamned vase you can put on the shelf or throw in the attic because it doesn't match the décor!" he said. "She's a little girl, Alyssa. A little girl who needs a parent, not a nanny."

"She has *two* nannies, Jack."

"Who the hell *are* you?" he said, the words a barely controlled shout. "This isn't the Alyssa who grew up next door to me; this isn't the woman I married."

"No, it isn't. Thank God." She turned on her heel, then gave Madison a smile that seemed altogether too friendly after what had just happened. She took a step, then paused and laid a hand on Madison's arm. "I don't know why you're here, but get out quick because this place is hell on earth. Before you know it, this life will suck you in and keep you in Nowhereville."

Then she was gone, speeding away in the limo, escaping to the world Madison knew, the one filled with ballrooms and chandeliers and caviar. Across the yard of Nowhereville, Katydid wandered over to a tree and began to chew on the bark. Someone started the tractor, releasing a cough of smoke and gasoline fumes into the air.

Ginny returned to her father's side, then tipped her head to look up at Madison, clearly not recognizing her or seeing her as out of place on the dairy farm. "Wanna go catch frogs? We can squish in the mud and get all dirty and stuff."

Madison turned, watching the dust cloud kicked up by the limo. Maybe, if she ran, there was still a chance she could hitch a ride.

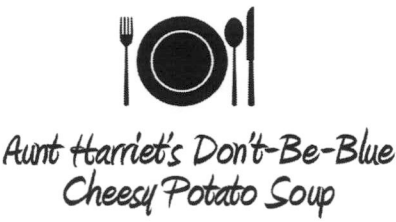

Aunt Harriet's Don't-Be-Blue
Cheesy Potato Soup

1/2 pound bacon
1 small onion, diced
4 russet potatoes, chopped
Salt and pepper
4 cups heavy cream
2 cups cheddar cheese, grated
1 teaspoon all-purpose flour

While you might be tempted to return that man to sender, trust me when I tell you he's worth all the aggravation. Sit down with a bowl of soup; it'll help you make better decisions, like whether it's now or never.

Start by cooking the bacon in a large pot until it's crispy. Remove the bacon, leaving some of the drippings in the pan because they still got a lot of living to do. Add the onions and potatoes, seasoning them with salt and pepper and then cooking until they're love-me-tender.

I know that man's sending your senses into a frenzy, but add a little heavy cream and you'll be just fine.

Stir in the cream, taste, then after loving the taste, season if needed. Toss the cheese in flour and add it slowly but surely, until it's melted. Crumble the bacon, then stir it in.

Dish up two bowls—one for you and one for him. When you do, you'll see that Aunt Harriet was right—

You can't help falling in love.

CHAPTER ELEVEN

"Don't you worry about Jack," Harriet said, bustling around the kitchen as she cleaned up from dinner. Madison had avoided the meal by claiming she needed to make a phone call. And she'd been avoiding Jack, who still seemed pretty ticked about the whole fiancé slip. "He's got a lot on his mind. You know men, they get as grumpy as circus bears when they have to think about more than one thing at a time."

Madison laughed, warming to this woman who seemed part mother and part home manager. "You know him well."

Harriet turned, a soapy wooden spoon in one hand. "Why I should, dear. I've lived here for going on thirty years, ever since my Lester passed, God rest his soul. I was changing Jack and David's diapers and burping them from the day they were born. My sister-in-law, their mother, was never very good with that kind of thing, poor woman. She tried, bless her heart, but babies just weren't her specialty."

Madison ran a finger along the rim of her tea cup—her version of supper. "I have a mother like that."

Harriet paused in running a sponge over a plate, the scent of the dishwashing liquid adding a lemony hint to the kitchen air. "You poor thing. No wonder you're so thin. Why, you're lacking in love and home-cooked meals."

"I turned out fine. And I'm thin because people pay me to be thin."

"Well, if you ask me, those people are crazy. You'd look even prettier with another ten, twenty pounds." Harriet turned back to the plate, rinsing it under running water, then putting it in the plastic dish drainer to dry. "'Course no one asks us old people what we think. Now do they, Elvis?"

Harriet turned to her right, conversing with the dead rock-n-roller about the merits of Madison adding a dress size or two. Apparently, Mr. Presley agreed because Harriet mm-hmmed and nodded.

For a second, the delicious thought of allowing herself the luxury of gaining that much weight rumbled in Madison's stomach. How fun it would be, she thought, picturing the chocolate frappes, the fettuccini, the cheesecakes she'd denied herself all these years, that could be sitting right before her. What would it be like to live, for just a little while, without worrying about her looks, what people might think if she dove headfirst into a platter of gnocchi?

Yeah, like that was ever going to happen. Madison knew better, especially after Janine Turner's betrayal, which had ended Madison's attempts to step outside the modeling world. It was just too damned bad her cake had missed its target. At least then, Madison might have had something to show for her wasted efforts.

She sighed, picked up her teacup and took a sip of the orange pekoe. This would have to do. For a long, long time. Until she found a career that didn't rely on the size of her waistline.

"I have my theories about food," Harriet said, loading a stack of bowls into the soapy water. "Elvis does, too, but his are all about deep frying."

"There are *theories* about food?" Madison tried to give the subject of food as little thought as possible.

Also a good policy to maintain with men. If she never thought about them, it would keep them from intruding on her heart, thus leaving it as impenetrable as Fort Knox.

Her cousin Daniel might have found happiness with Olivia Regan, but that didn't mean happy endings were being doled out to the rest of the Worth relatives like horns at a New Year's Eve party. In fact, Madison knew for a fact that her other cousin, Roger, was in the midst of his fourth divorce. Aunt Deidre had just been dumped by a man who'd found the love of his life—at a family reunion. Apparently marrying a cousin was a lesser evil than staying connected to a Worth.

Hadn't Madison seen the transparency of relationships often enough in the modeling industry? Love came and went as quickly as the flavor of the month. Today's hot affair cooled as soon as another pair of long legs and big eyes came along.

Love, it seemed, only ran skin-deep. Madison had learned that firsthand with Renaldo and a host of other men who never saw beyond her face.

The real theory about love? It was as much an illusion as a David Copperfield show.

"Food, my dear, is all about the senses. It's about emotion." Harriet took a large spoon, ladled a scoop of that night's potato soup into a bowl, then pivoted and handed the stoneware container to Madison. The heady aroma wafted upward, teasing at Madison's senses, awakening a stomach that had sat dormant far too long.

"Food is about love," Harriet continued, laying a spoon beside Madison's bowl. "We cook it to show people we love them, eat it to fill the spots that need love. We give it at Christmas, serve it for birthdays. Heck, even the Egyptians sent it along in the after-life. Food is *everything*."

Madison pushed the bowl aside, resisting it—but with some effort. "For some people, maybe."

"Oh, honey, around here, it *is* everything. Especially if that food contains cheese." She leaned in close, smiling. "Between you and me, the way to Jack's heart is definitely through his stomach."

"Oh, I don't want to get to Jack's heart." She didn't even want to ping a sonar off it.

"That's not what I heard when I was picking up a rump roast at the Bunch's SuperSaver this after-noon. Charlie, the checkout guy, told me he heard you tell that evil Kitty Dandy that you and Jack were engaged." Harriet laughed. "Won't that just frost Alyssa's socks?"

Oh, God. She'd hoped her impetuous little act had been forgotten, that Kitty had believed Jack when he told her it was a publicity stunt.

Yeah, just like Kate Moss had believed the cake in her face was all due to a weak pitching arm. "The fiancé thing, it was—"

"A slip of the tongue."

Madison spun around at the sound of Jack's voice, the deep timbre sending a shiver down her spine that she refused to acknowledge. He was a man, just a man. A client she needed to work with for the next couple of days.

And yet a part of her remembered that kiss from the grocery store and wondered what might happen if...

If he wasn't a client. If she wasn't Madison Worth. And if she had the luxury of living a normal life, like the women she had seen pushing carts in the grocery store, babies in tow, TV dinners tucked into their carts beside roaster chickens.

"A slip of the tongue or a sign of the future?" Harriet said, a knowing smile on her face. "Seems to me Dr. Freud might have a comment or two about that."

"Good thing he's dead," Jack said, scowling, "and not here to put in his two cents."

"You never mind him," Harriet said, giving Madison a pat on the arm. "He's taken one rotten banana and lumped all the others into the same bunch."

"Aunt Harriet…" Jack said, his voice a warning.

"I'm sorry, Jack," she said, her voice softening. "At least one good thing came out of that mess." She crossed to him and laid a soft hand on his shoulder. "Our Ginny is the most precious thing on God's green earth."

Madison saw the two exchange a glance, the kind shared by family members who were bonded by a common history. She could feel the thread of emotion between the two generations, and an odd new feeling that an heiress, of all people, shouldn't feel—

Envy.

Madison Worth, who had grown up in the most privileged of environments, surrounded by the finest that money could buy, had never known that kind of tender touch.

She may have had the Ming vases and Chanel suits, but she had never had anyone to cup her cheek and tell her she was more precious than all the Swarovski crystal in the world.

Jack gave his aunt a smile, then cleared his throat and turned to Madison. "The wine festival is a few days away. If you have a moment, Miss Worth, I'd like to discuss your duties."

All business-like. Just the way she liked it.

Or at least that's what Madison told herself as she followed Jack Pleeseman's very pleasing rear profile out of the kitchen.

Jack's Send-Your-Thoughts-Down-Spicy-Lane Loaded Nachos

4 cups tortilla chips
1 cup shredded cheddar cheese
1/2 cup salsa
Sour cream, amount up to you
Sliced olives, black or green, your choice
Sliced jalapenos, as many as you can stand
Optional: sliced scallions, chopped tomatoes, shredded lettuce, heated refried beans

All she has to do is enter the kitchen and your internal temperature raises twenty degrees. Impress her with your bachelor-worthy cooking skills and make these to keep your mouth busy—with food, not her.

Layer the chips in a microwave safe plate, top with cheese and salsa. Pop into the microwave for 1-2 minutes, until the cheese is melted and hot. To avoid rubber cheese, try lowering the power level to 70%. It might take a little longer to cook, but the way the cheese melts will be worth it. Or, if you have time to kill and don't mind waiting on the oven, bake the chips at 400 degrees for 8-10 minutes.

Add the other toppings, then serve. The smile of gratitude you receive will be well worth every ounce of effort. Just be sure you keep your hands on the snack...and off of her. Tangling with a woman this spicy can only lead to disaster.

Chapter Twelve

Jack paced the floors of the silent house, his only company the antique grandfather's clock in the hallway ticking its way from midnight to one.

What the hell was he going to do now?

Ginny was here—joy incarnate. But she was also a distraction he couldn't afford. He needed to make the cheese side of the business work. And work really well—and really quickly.

The dairy farm provided a steady living, and always had, but it wasn't enough. In order to take things to the next level, to make Cheese Please all he knew it could be, and all his mother had dreamed, Jack had to do more.

Then, when Alyssa returned, he'd have a little ammunition to throw back at her. Some money to show he could damned well provide a good life for his daughter.

Because as much as he wanted it, love wasn't enough. It cost a lot to raise a kid. Half a million dollars by some estimates, several million by others. He guessed it depended on whether you were dressing your kid at K-Mart or Gap. Alyssa had money by the millions, now that she had married George Thurgood. She lavished ponies and parties on Ginny like tinsel on a Christmas tree.

How could he compete with that?

Alyssa had held that axe over Jack's head for three years, using Ginny as a weapon to make him suffer, though what for, he had no damned idea. Ever since the divorce, Alyssa had decided that Jack was Public Enemy Number One—

Even though he hadn't been the one caught wearing thigh-high red boots and playing pony with George at a Holiday Inn.

Alyssa was enough of a worry. Plus, with Kitty running around out there, looking for any opportunity to discredit him, he knew it was only a matter of time before Kitty reached her sister and told her about Jack's bride-to-be.

Madison. From the first moment he'd met her, Jack had never been more aware of being alone with a woman. It wasn't simply because Madison was a model. Wasn't that the fantasy every man dreamed of? Being alone with the leopard print bikini girl from *Sports Illustrated* Swimsuit issue?

He'd only been looking at that issue in the name of research, of course.

The problem with research, though, was that it seemed to have this annoying habit of coming to mind— in the middle of the night, at odd moments throughout the day, and right now, when Madison was one flight of stairs away and every hormone in his body was demanding he continue what they'd started in Aisle Seven.

When they'd been arguing, he'd wanted nothing more than to grab her by the hand and take her off to the nearest flat surface and settle things without words. She got his dander up—and a whole lot more than that. He hadn't had this much interest in a woman in…

Years. And to make matters worse, she had him questioning his business thinking.

Could she be right? Could his ad ideas be trite? Boring?

If there was one thing Madison Worth possessed in abundance, it was sizzle. Maybe it wouldn't kill him to listen to what she had to say. If anything, it would allow him to argue with her some more, which had the bonus effect of raising the temperature between them a few degrees.

And in doing so, hopefully he could persuade her to do the ads. She hadn't left yet, so there was still some hope. And now, with Ginny's custody at stake, he needed it all to work even more than ever.

He stopped at the front door, peering through the bevel of antique oval glass, at the buildings lit by moonlight, the acreage curving away from the house. They were all depending on him—his father, brother, aunt, the staff, Ginny. As the president of Cheese Pleese and Pleeseman Dairy Farms, the buck stopped with him.

He better damned well have a plan for making those bucks. There wasn't much call for a washed up dairy farmer with a background in snack foods and a way with cheddar.

"Thinking of ways to bribe Coop to tamper with my engine?"

Jack turned at the sound of Madison's voice. She stood in the hallway, clad in a pair of pink drawstring pants and a plain pink T-shirt, her feet bare. Those women in the Victoria's Secret catalogs had nothing over how sexy Madison looked right now, all soft and curvy, ready to be led off to bed. "Hey, what are you doing up?"

"Couldn't sleep." She smiled, this one a softer, sweeter smile of understanding. "Apparently I'm not the only one."

"Lot on my mind."

"I know the feeling," she said, gliding toward him, crossing the wood floor on bare feet, quiet as a cat.

It made him think of the Carl Sandburg poem about fog, something he'd read in one of those required literature classes in college, and never forgotten. He watched her approach, intrigued by her, wanting to know what was ticking behind that beautiful countenance. "And what worries you, Madison Worth?"

She shrugged. "Not nearly as much as is worrying you, I'm sure. For me, it's little things. Like whether I'll ever be on a cover again, how I'm going to pay my rent next month. Whether I want to go crawling back to the family fortune for a bailout."

"Sounds like big stuff to me." He gave her a grin.

Madison halted mid-step when Jack smiled. Every inch of his face spelled camaraderie, friendship.

Connection. In that smile, she knew staying downstairs with him would mean crossing a bridge that Madison had vowed never to traverse. Connections meant opening her heart, exposing it like a quadruple bypass.

She'd do less cardiac damage chaining herself to an all-you-can-eat buffet. At least an intimate relationship with Ponderosa could be worked off with a few thousand hours of Pilates.

An intimate relationship with a man like Jack needed a lot more than yoga to erase those memories. She should go right back to bed, sleepless night or not. In the moonlight, everything between her and Jack—every word, every look, intensified a hundredfold. His words took on a huskier, more intimate tone. The inflections in his voice seemed to say he understood what she was feeling.

And more.

Whoa. She should *definitely* head back to bed. Alone.

Jack Pleeseman was like the Ho-Ho's. Off limits. If she had him once, she would undoubtedly want him again. And again. A man like him, who poured passion into his business, his family, his relationship with his daughter, would pour passion into everything he did.

Including her.

Madison didn't need that complication right now, not when she was trying to get her career back on its feet and come up with another back-up plan, one she wouldn't fail this time.

But that didn't stop her from wanting everything that Jack had, from craving it like a chocoholic peeking in the windows of Ghiradelli Square.

Even as she told herself to back away, to hurry up the stairs and slam the door on the heat building between them, she stayed. Watching him, the shimmer of moonlight in his deep brown eyes.

"So," she said, taking a step back, putting the distance between them, but not feeling it at all, not in this silent, dark house, the quiet wrapping around them like a blanket, "what's worrying you?"

He let out a short, dry laugh. "What isn't? The business, my daughter. My ex-wife. The cow that's going to give birth any day now, the tractor that's acting up, the silo that needs to be replaced." He shrugged. "Don't know why I'm pacing the floors, though. It doesn't seem to solve anything."

She laughed. "I tell myself that every night and yet, I end up pacing all the same. Sleep is something I seem to be able to do without."

He moved away from the door, approaching her. "And meals? Did you decide you didn't need those, either? An apple, a plate of dry lettuce—that isn't a dinner, Madison."

Something warm infused her, shooting through her veins, straight to her heart. He'd noticed what she'd eaten. And he'd worried about her. When was the last time anyone had done that?

"In my line of work, that's dinner *and* dessert." She grinned, trying to make light of it, ignoring the continual rumble in her stomach that reminded her there was a refrigerator jammed with food just a few feet down the hall.

And a man who would gladly feed her, one delectable bite after another, if only she asked.

"No, it isn't." He reached out, took her hand, and before she could protest, led her into the kitchen, reading her mind. Here, the moonlight cascaded through the large windows, painting the countertops, the floor, the cabinets, in muted shades of white.

It glinted off the nooks and crannies, reflecting wear and tear, the kind that came from a busy family—nicks on the countertop edges from children rushing by with toys, knife marks in the butcher block top, signifying years of cutting roasts, slicing vegetables. There was a scuff here and there on the vinyl flooring, made by boots or shoes...from all the someones who had walked through and left evidence of their presence.

In the Worth household, and in Madison's apartment, there was none of that. A crumb fell and a maid was there within an instant to whisk it way. Something got dented, it was replaced. Nothing ever had a chance to wear out, fade or break. Every day, every single thing was as pristine and beautiful as her airbrushed face in a Lancôme spread.

And just about as real.

Jack clicked on the small light over the sink. Madison hesitated in the doorway, her hand running down the woodwork, waiting...

For Jack to make the move, to call the shots, to make the decision for her. Then she could plead temporary hormonal insanity.

She wasn't on her home turf. She wasn't in her usual clothes. And she felt unsure, out of her element. Not the same confident, can-walk-the-runway-and-not-fall-off Madison.

"What's this?" she asked, when her fingers rolled along a series of ridges in the molding.

"Growth charts." Jack grinned, then his gaze softened, and Madison swore she saw his eyes glistened. He took two steps forward, then traced the lines with his fingertips, his gaze going to some far off place. "My mother...she used to mark our progress. Dave grew a half inch this month, I grew a quarter inch. There's a mark here for every birthday, every milestone, until—"

He cut himself off, the silence extending long and empty in the moonlight space.

"Until what?"

"Until she died. Then those kinds of things stopped." He drew in a breath. "A lot of things stopped that day."

She wanted to reach out to him, to draw him into her arms, and erase the pain in his eyes. Instead, she remained where she was, maintaining her distance. "How old were you when she died?"

He stepped away from the wall, returning to the sink, grabbing two glasses out of the cabinet. "Fifteen."

"That must have been—"

"Yeah, it was." He lifted a glass toward her. "Ice water?"

"Yes, please."

He filled the glasses, added some ice cubes from the freezer, then handed her one of the glasses. The subject had been closed as firmly as a door. "So what about your mother?" he said. "Did she carve heights into the wall, too?"

Madison spun the glass between her hands, the ice clinking a watery melody. "In my house, there wasn't any carving allowed. It would have reduced the property value or destroyed some antique molding or some such thing. Either way, she was never there to measure my growth." Madison took a sip, waited for the cool liquid to soothe her throat. "My mother is what you call a philanthropist."

"Meaning?"

"Meaning she has dedicated her life to caring for the poor, the hungry and the needy all over the world."

His gaze, always sharp and direct, zeroed in on hers. "Leaving her daughter to fend for herself?"

She shrugged, then looked away, tracing the rim of the juice glass with her finger. "I did fine. I lived with my grandfather and my cousin Daniel, then went off to boarding school. I grew up a Worth and that means I didn't want for anything."

Except love.

Where had that thought come from? Madison hadn't thought about her childhood in a million years. That was one of those topics she put aside, moved past and left where it was—over and done. She was a grown-up, a functioning, well adjusted adult. There was no point in crying over the poor little rich girl who had been surrounded by money and not a Mummy. There were millions of people in the world who would have gladly traded places with her.

"What about your dad?" Jack asked.

"I never knew him. He died before I was born, which is about all I know, considering how little my mother has told me. Even if he had lived, though, he wouldn't have lasted long in the Worth family. Grandfather would have never given his Grade-A stamp to a guy from the Peace Corps who knocked up his sister."

"So your mother was a rebel, huh? Going for the bad boy?"

Madison tipped her head, considering that. "I never thought of it that way."

In fact, she hardly ever thought of her origins. Her mother—had Vivian Worth been the forthcoming type—had never been home long enough to question. And Grandfather, well, he wouldn't discuss anything that didn't fit the family mold.

The thought of her mother being the rebel, loving the black sheep, put a whole other spin on things. One Madison refused to consider, because it meant she and her mother shared more than just some DNA strands.

"Anyway," she said, taking a seat at the kitchen table, "since we're both up, why don't we talk about the print ad campaign? I probably didn't handle that right earlier," she swallowed back the effort of the apology, "and want to apologize."

He shook his head. "If we're going to talk, then we need to eat. I don't know about you, but I can't concentrate on an empty stomach."

"I'm fine. I'm not—" Her stomach let out a rumble, belying her words. What was it about this place? Ever since she'd arrived at the Pleeseman Dairy Farm, she'd had this continual hunger, as if she hadn't eaten in a year.

Maybe Katydid's ravenous appetite was starting to rub off on her.

"A snack won't kill you. Trust me. I know that from years of late-night fridge-raiding." He opened the refrigerator, peeked inside, then opened the bread-box, and turned to her. "Well, I'm not much of a cook, but I do have one specialty and we have all the ingredients, so you're in luck. How about loaded nachos?"

"*Loaded* nachos?" She'd never had them. All she knew was that they were a sinful treat she should avoid at all costs. Particularly with the photo shoot tomorrow and the wine festival a few days away. The clothes Madison Worth owned didn't allow for die-tary slip-ups. She put up her hands. "Thanks for the offer, but no. I should—"

He grabbed her palms, slowly lowered them to her sides. "Let me make them and quit arguing."

When he did that, surrender coursed through her. Maybe it was because someone was taking care of her—someone who wasn't being paid to do so.

Maybe she was weakened by her lack of sleep or the unfamiliar environment.

Or maybe she was doing a damned good job of lying to herself and she just wanted to spend a few more minutes with this intriguing man, even if it cost her a few calories.

He moved about the kitchen, clearly at home here, loading tortilla chips on a plate, sprinkling them with freshly shredded cheese, then adding dollops of salsa before popping them in the microwave. A minute or so later, he pulled the stoneware plate out, then topped the dish with scoops of sour cream, sliced olives and jalapenos.

Madison watched him work, mentally adding up the calories. When she passed five thousand, she gave up. Even with Jenny Craig and an abacus, Madison had no hope of configuring the caloric impact of something as loaded as this snack. Still, the smell of the melted cheese and the heated salsa wafted through the room, teasing at her nostrils.

It had to be the late night, the dark room, because she was more ravenous than she'd ever been in her entire life. "Well, maybe one bite…" she said, reaching forward when he placed the plate on the table before her. She'd have just one.

And then she could stop. Really.

"Uh-huh, just one. That's what they all say." He waited, allowing her to choose the first cheesy chip.

She pulled one out, tipping it to let the extra toppings slip off, leaving the bonus calories on the plate.

"Oh, no, no. You can't do that. You have to try the whole enchilada, so to speak." He took the chip from her, loaded it all up again, then held it toward her lips. "The chips are great, but the cheese...that makes the whole snack."

She inhaled. "It's yours?"

"Of course. You don't think I'd have any of that Dandy Dairy crap in here, now do you?"

She laughed. "No. I guess not."

The nacho waited mere inches away, ready for her to open her mouth, take it in, and answer the rumbling call of hunger. Just one bite...and she could stop. Truly.

Right. Maybe if she told herself that often enough, she'd believe it, too.

"Come on, you know you want to try it," Jack said, his voice as teasing as the loaded treat. He wiggled it back and forth, brushing it against her lips, then pulling it back. As tempting as Lucifer himself with that apple.

Oh, she wanted to try it all right. Try it, and him, and everything in this kitchen. In the moonlight, he looked sexier, rumpled, but in a cozy, comfortable way that spoke of going to bed and lazing there all day.

Her gaze drifted down, to the powerful hands holding the delicate chip. She'd always been a sucker for a man with powerful hands. Especially ones like Jack's, with long, strong fingers, defined by wide palms that seemed capable of holding half the city of New York. Palms that could cup her breasts easily, then slide down to her waist, her hips. She imagined his hands, tightening their grasp before lifting her up and bringing her against his pelvis, thrusting—

Whoa. She needed to fill her mind with something else. Something like…the nachos. Better to pay for a waistline mistake than a relationship one. Or at least, that's what Madison told herself as she opened her mouth, inhaling the delicious fragrance at the same time she did the food.

She bit down, and her taste buds exploded in a crunchy mixture of soft and sharp, spicy and smooth. The coolness of the sour cream was the perfect marriage for the spicy notes of the salsa, the bite of the peppers.

But it was the cheese that did it. Perfectly melted, it glided across her palate, instantly making her want more. A lot more.

"This is good. I mean, not good. *Amazing.* I've never tasted cheese like this."

He chuckled. "That's because you haven't tasted *our* cheese. There's a reason we're called Cheese Pleese."

She swallowed, then leaned forward, her mouth already anticipating another bite. Wanting it. Needing it. Stop at one bite. Ha! Who was she fooling? "Because everyone says please give me more?"

"Exactly."

"Then please give me more, Jack," she whispered, her eyes on his, not on the chip.

Jack lifted another chip toward her, then paused, his gaze sweeping over her makeup-free face, lingering on her open mouth, her unadorned lips. She watched his Adam's apple work up, down.

'What?" She closed her mouth again, suddenly feel self-conscious, exposed in her lack of make-up, plain PJ's, flat hair.

"If you, ah, look like that in our ads, I won't have any trouble pitching my cheddar."

She swallowed, the desire for everything in front of her multiplying by the second. "Right now, Jack Pleeseman, you wouldn't have any trouble pitching anything about you to me."

The words were out before she could stop them, wrapped up in the sensory overload of the food, the moonlight, the nearness of him, the spicy under-tones of his cologne, the soft comfort imbued in his T-shirt and the simple cotton shorts he wore.

He watched her for a long, silent, heated moment, then seemed to shake himself back to his senses, and redirect his attention to the nacho still in his fingers. "Another?"

Another. And then one more. And more after that, until the entire plate had been consumed and she was ordering seconds.

She didn't want just the damned chips, either. She wanted him. He was the first man she'd met who seemed genuinely interested in her—in what she thought, what she ate, whether she slept.

If Johnson & Johnson could find a way to bottle that, they'd have a hell of an aphrodisiac.

Uh-oh.

Hadn't she just vowed not to complicate her life with a connection? Madison pushed back her chair, rose and crossed to the sink, staring out the window at the inky dark. This was going down the path she'd vowed to avoid. Not only was she indulging in a high-calorie sack, but she was also indulging some very high-heat plans for Jack Pleeseman's body. Plus, not to mention breaking every single one of her cardinal rules.

This was going way beyond calorie overload.

"I can't."

He crossed to her, the food forgotten. "Because it's bad for you?" He reached out a gentle hand, spinning her toward him, brown eyes seeking the truth in the blue of hers. "Or because we're bad for each other?"

She swallowed. "Both."

"You're right," he said, the words a hoarse, nearly groaned whisper. Then he reached past her, brushing against her shoulder as he did, to shut off the light over the sink. The touch, so innocent, so everyday, nevertheless set off fireworks in her belly, igniting the smoldering embers that had started burning nearly the minute she met him. "We should get to bed."

"Mmm," she murmured, picturing Jack in her bed, naked, with her. "We should…"

She saw him watch her mouth form the words, as cognizant of her every move as she was of his. She grasped the cool stainless steel edge of the sink for support, hoping it would give her the strength she needed to back away, to head to her room, to forget the nachos and Jack and the building, tensing heat in this kitchen.

He hesitated only a second, then reached up and cupped her jaw, his grip easy yet sure, allowing her to leave if she wanted. Regardless of her best intentions, Madison stayed exactly where she was.

"Yes, we should," Jack said. "But we won't. Not yet." Then he leaned forward and kissed her.

The Fourth of July exploded inside Madison's body, with a blast of desire so hot, she knew why people spontaneously combusted. From this. From kisses that surprised you with that intense, I-need-you, I-want-you rush.

She opened her mouth to him, darting her tongue in against his, the desire rushing hard and fast within her, as if a floodgate of denied wants had been opened with his touch. Her arms wrapped around his back, fingers pressing against him, drawing him closer, hard chest to her softness, wanting more contact, more kissing, more everything.

His fingers tangled in her hair, tilting her head to one side, so he could nip and taste along her jaw. She nearly cried at the sensation of those quick, nibbling kisses. Heat gushed between her legs, and Madison inhaled sharply, her breasts rising against his chest. "Jack," she said, asking with his name for an end to the feverish agony building inside her.

He groaned her name in response and lifted her onto the sink, fitting himself into the space between her legs. She wrapped them tightly around his waist, pressing her pelvis against his erection, the hardness giving her little relief from the fiery need to have him inside her.

She reached a hand between them, cupping him through his shorts, stroking his length, no longer thinking, no longer caring if she shouldn't be involved or should be looking for something more comfortable than the kitchen sink, only thinking that if someone didn't get some damned sex right now, that someone was going to die.

"Oh, God," Jack whispered against Madison's lips, then his hands went up, under her T-shirt, cupping her naked breasts, cradling the fullness there with his palms. In an instant, he went from just being hard to tempered steel, every ounce of his body electrified by hers. She gasped, her hand clutching at him, tight—oh so tight, enough to nearly push him over the edge—her body arching toward his, asking, needing. Still kissing her, he teased the nipples between his thumbs and forefingers in sweet, agonizing ecstasy, then rolled his touch over the sensitive tips, wishing it were his tongue tasting her sweet flesh, and that they were in a bed with nothing but lazy, sex-filled hours ahead of them.

He knew it was wrong, knew he should back away, forget this woman—forget any woman—until he had his life, his daughter, straightened out. But rational thought had lost him somewhere between when she came downstairs and when she'd slid her tongue into his mouth.

He wanted Madison, God help him, he wanted her more than it seemed he'd ever wanted anything in his life. He didn't care if she came from Mars or wealth, if she was leaving in a few days or staying forever, all he knew, all he was aware of, was that she was in his arms, her breasts warm beneath his touch, and he'd be a fool to let her go.

Madison moaned beneath the incredible torture of Jack's hands on her breasts. Fire raced through her as he pressed his pelvis to hers, his fingers creating magic on her nipples. The sensations launched rockets within her veins, propelling a tidal rush that seemed to have been waiting there all along, waiting for that one final push into ecstasy. "Yes," she whispered to him, reaching up to grab his head, to make him understand, "yes, yes."

He ground into her pelvis, his kisses more heated, more demanding, his tongue playing a game that mirrored exactly what would happen if they'd gone to bed—together.

And then, the orgasm was rolling over her, waves crashing into her mind, obliterating everything but this man, this touch, this moment. She raised up into him, crying out, breaking away only long enough to release one long, shuddering breath. "Oh my God," she whispered. "Is that a bonus when you buy the cheese?"

"No, but I bet we'd do one hell of a gift basket business if it was." His voice was shaking, still laced with desire. He took one last, long look at her, then slid his hands down, replacing her T-shirt over her waist, withdrawing a few respectable inches.

She laughed, the first genuine laughter she'd felt come out of her body in months. Years, maybe. It felt rich and full, as satisfying as the climax a moment before. "Too bad. That'd be a hell of a marketing campaign."

He grinned. "I'll keep that in mind for next year's advertising budget."

"You know, I can't be the only one here," she said, reaching again for him, but he moved back even further, away from her.

"Please don't think I don't want to continue this," Jack said, his gaze telling her he did, very much, want more. "Because right now, I can barely see straight. But the business has to come first. I can't let myself get sidetracked."

"I think you already did that," she said.

"No, I think you were the sidetracked one." He grinned.

Then the easy mood between them slid away as the reality of what they'd just been doing hit both of them at the same time. Jack reached out a hand, helped her hop down off the sink, then backed up even further.

"Jack, I didn't intend—"

"Neither did I. So let's leave it at that, before you tell me that you didn't want me or don't ever want to see me again." He pressed a hand to his heart, his tone joking, but nothing in his eyes a joke. "My ego doesn't need the slam."

"I wasn't going to say that. I just...I don't get involved with clients."

"And I don't get involved with my spokesmodels."

She grinned, thankful he was making light of it, allowing both of them an easy way out. As if they could forget the whole thing, move on and get back to work. Like it had been a lunch break bonus.

"Now, do you want to finish our snack?" he asked. "And this time, I think it's a good idea to talk business while we eat."

She looked at the plate of nachos, still warm and releasing a slight curl of steam. She wanted them. But the bigger trouble was, despite everything she'd said and told herself, she wanted Jack even more now than she had before.

If anything, the orgasm had made things worse. Not better. "Thank you, but no. I'm...full." Then Madison turned away, before Jack could see another lie in her eyes.

Madison's Going-Back-For-A-Double-Dip Artichoke Dip

2 12-ounce jars artichoke hearts, chopped
1/2 teaspoon salt
1/4 teaspoon pepper
1 cup mayonnaise
1/2 cup sour cream
1/2 cup shredded Parmesan cheese
1/2 cup pimiento, chopped
Shredded cheddar cheese for topping

You've gone and made a mess of things, so the only solution is to eat—or at least make something amazing to eat and then avoid it as penance for kissing the boss. Okay, not just kissing the boss, but climaxing in his kitchen.

Probably not the best way to ask for a raise.

Preheat the oven to 350 degrees then stir all ingredients together, spread in a greased pie plate and top with shredded cheddar. Back for 20-25 minutes, which should be enough time for you to get your priorities—and your pajamas—straight again.

CHAPTER THIRTEEN

C *offee.*

Madison inhaled, her eyes still closed, sure that she was dreaming. The scent of the morning brew remained, however, real and strong.

She peeked an eye open, expecting a blast of the Tuesday morning sunlight to hit her square in the face. But no, the blinds in her room were still drawn, with only one corner pulled back, letting in enough light for her to see two things: Jack Pleeseman and the steaming mug in his hand.

If last night had been a fantasy come true, this was definitely its twin.

She raised herself onto her elbows. "You brought me *coffee?*"

"That and an apology. For shooting down your ideas before I even listened to them." He handed her the coffee, then looked around, seeming uncomfortable now that his mission was accomplished.

Careful not to slosh, Madison slid to the side, then patted the empty space on the hand-quilted comforter. The white cover had connected blue rings running up and down the blanket, a pattern

Madison was sure had a name. "Have a seat. I promise, I won't bite."

He did as she asked, settling himself on such a small slice of the bed, she was sure he'd fall off.

"Last night..." she began, suddenly very aware of him, the bed, her state of near undress. And everything that had happened in that kitchen.

"Was last night," he said, clearing his throat, wiping any trace of flirting away. "Today, we're back to all business."

It sounded like he was reminding himself more than her.

"Except you're sitting on my bed—"

"And you're wearing something that would bring a lesser man to his knees."

She glanced at her pajama pants, draped over the chair because it had been hot in her room last night. And hot in the kitchen, but she wasn't going to think about that. Not right now. Nope, nothing sexually inflammatory in the PJ pants. Then she looked down at the plain pink T-shirt covering her chest. It was nothing more than a regular cotton blend, Old Navy issue, with a V neck that dipped between her breasts, giving a barely-there peek of what lay beneath. And yet, when she glanced back up at Jack, she could see Old Navy could go toe-to-toe with Frederick's of Hollywood in the secret to sex appeal department. "I can put on a robe—"

"And I can leave." He rose, taking a few steps back. "I, ah, just wanted to make amends before we got to the photo shoot later this morning. And to offer you a deal."

She took a sip, watching him over the top of the stoneware mug. "A deal?"

"We shoot half the day my way, then half the day your way. Then, at the end, we'll see which works better."

"You're...trusting me?" She blinked, surprised.

"Well, yeah. I'd probably be a fool not to." He toed at the braided rug on her floor, as if he meant to straighten it. "Listen, what I said about you being the pretty face—"

"Is true, Jack. I'm no marketing guru. I just smile and wear the clothes." How many times had that point been hammered home? The few times she had tried to become something other than the living mannequin—

Had been a complete disaster. She'd been shot down like a Mallard duck on the opening of hunting season.

"You've done this a lot longer than me. You probably have instincts I'll never cultivate." He reached over, grabbing her hand. The gesture, she was sure, was meant to be friendly, but it sent a heat of a whole other kind soaring up her arm. She was very aware of the lack of anything more than panties below her waist and wondered if he was, too. If as if he thought of her as more than a piece in his marketing puzzle, but as a woman. A smart woman.

Fear raced through Madison. What if she was wrong? What if Jack put his faith in her and the business went south? What if the ideas she'd had yesterday were just a fluke?

He smiled at her. "Show me what you've got, Madison Worth."

Then he was gone, leaving her with her coffee and a challenge that Madison wasn't so sure she could handle. At least, not without a really killer pair of high heels.

Where the hell was a mall when a girl really needed one?

"So," Cally said when Madison called her a few minutes later, "how's it going? You making nice with the cows?"

"You could say that."

"Ooh, sounds like you've met a man. You do mean a man, right, not something from the bovine species?"

Madison laughed and lowered her mascara wand, replacing it in the bright pink tube. She sat back in the chair in her bedroom, drawing her knees to her chest. "Yes. A man. A...client."

Cally swore under her breath. "You broke your cardinal rule?"

"I'm not going to do it again, though."

"Uh-huh. Isn't that the same thing Bill told Hillary?"

"Ha ha. Very funny." Madison picked up the bottle of OPI she'd just used to re-polish her nails, put it in her makeup bag, then zipped it shut and stowed it under the vanity table. She took another look in the mirror. Not bad, considering she'd slept even less last night than the night before. Too many dreams about Jack—and the many ways the president of Pleeseman Dairy Farms could please her.

In the kitchen. In the barn. In the bedroom.

"Well, make it a happy ending, will you? One of us deserves one," Cally said. In the background, Madison could hear the sounds of an airport, announcements for boarding, the rustle of hundreds of people hurrying to their destinations. "I'm sick of my love life. It's depressing as hell."

"What's Robert done now?" Cally had been dating Robert Witt for three years off and on, more off than on because he was one of those charming-as-hell men who had a bad habit of breaking promises.

"Nothing. And that's the whole problem. The man has a serious commitment problem."

"Cally, he's already committed. *That's* the problem."

"Yeah." She let out a sigh. "Why did I have to go and fall for a married man? Do I have "stupid" branded on my forehead?"

"If you did, *Cosmo* wouldn't be putting you on the cover."

Cally laughed. In the background, Madison heard a monotone voice announce first class boarding for a flight to L.A. "Damn. My plane's boarding. Oh, wait! I forgot to tell you. Word's out about this new job of yours. You...well, you merited a mention in the Insider column in this week's *People.* "

"You're kidding me. It's not like I'm Cindy Crawford or anything. Why do they care what I'm doing?"

"Honey, you're rich and you're famous. That alone makes you paparazzi kibble. Plus, I hate to remind you of this, but you pitched a fit during Fashion Week, complete with dessert toppings, bumping you off the pages of *Vogue* and in with the cheddar chunks. Even in Timbuktu, that's a news story."

Madison dropped her head into her hands. "My career is toast."

"You haven't been all that happy with your career for a long time, hon. Maybe it's time for a new plan." Cally's voice was soft, filled with the concern of a ten-year friendship, built out of being another passenger on this crazy modeling roller coaster.

"I never said—"

"I'm your best friend. You never had to." Across the miles and cell connection, Madison could practically feel the telepathic hug from Callista. "Whatever happened to that back-up plan of yours? Those college courses you were taking?"

Madison toyed with the brush on her vanity table, spinning the hard plastic in a circle. "I'm not cut out for college," she said. The familiar doubts crowded into her stomach, reminding her that she had been a fool for ever thinking she could be anything more. "I'm a one-trick pony, Cally. I know how to smile, strike a pose and make bell bottoms look attractive."

"That's bullshit," Cally said. "Hang up with me and then call NYU. Sign up for the fall semester. You still have time."

"Maybe," Madison said, fully intending not to do it. One humiliating educational experience was enough for a lifetime.

"No maybes, Madison. You *have* to do this. *People* is predicting that you'll be modeling for the Pork Association next."

Madison laughed. "I draw the line at pigs and bacon. No, I'm going to come up with another plan B. There's got to be something I can do besides look pretty."

"Yeah," Cally said, laughing. "Marry well."

Jack's Concentration-Gone-To-Hell Ravioli Lasagna

1 26-ounce jar spaghetti sauce
1/3 cup water
1 32-ounce package frozen ravioli
1 egg
16 ounces ricotta
1/4 cup Parmesan cheese
1/4 cup mozzarella, shredded
10 ounces frozen spinach, thawed

What is it about her? Ten minutes against a kitchen sink and you might as well just donate your brain to research. All you can think about is finding a way to finish what you two started.
And doing *that* more than once.

The best solution is to keep your hands busy cooking something. Start by bringing the water and spaghetti sauce to a boil. Add the ravioli and cook for five minutes.

Meanwhile, stir the remaining ingredients together in a separate bowl, trying not to picture her beneath you, eating the shredded mozzarella one teeny piece at a time, sending your libido down some very dangerous paths.

Put the cheese mixture on top of the ravioli, cook for ten minutes. Dish up a plate for yourself...and then dish up something else altogether with the woman you've invested your future in.

CHAPTER FOURTEEN

If he didn't stop this pacing, Jack was sure he'd be digging a path to China, just like he and David had tried to do a dozen times when they were boys. The ground outside of the small Cheese Please gift shop was packed tight, grass worn into a circular path. Madison was ten minutes late, and to Jack Pleeseman, every one of those minutes was one more annoyance.

It wasn't that he was annoyed with *her* so much. It was himself. He knew better than to fool around with her. Knew better than to stay up all night, fantasizing about what might have happened, had she invited him up to her bedroom. Knew better than to jeopardize the future of the family business, but most importantly, his custody of Ginny.

But that didn't stop him from wanting her with a desire so palpable it exploded in his gut the second she rounded the corner of the house and strode toward him, a plastic garment bag over one shoulder. She wore an above-the-knee black skirt that made her legs seem longer, barer, sexier. It drew his gaze to her thighs, then upward, past her waist, along the shimmery teal fabric of her blouse, to those vibrant blue eyes. Her golden hair framed her face, then settled around her shoulders in tousled waves.

If there'd ever been any hope of Jack winning the war against his testosterone, it was lost the second she smiled at him.

"You're late," he barked, more out of sexual frustration than business impatience. "The photographer has been here for half an hour."

"I'm sorry." The words came out simply, heartfelt. She'd done the exact opposite of what he'd expected—instead of fighting back, arguing the point, she'd gone and apologized.

Damn, she was a contradiction. Just when Jack thought he could predict her, Madison went and turned the tables on him, making it that much harder for him to maintain his exasperation level—the only thing keeping him from demonstrating a re-run of last night, this time with an ending that worked to his advantage, too. As much as he'd thought he could walk away after the sink incident, he'd realized pretty quickly that the worst part hadn't been not finding relief with her that night—it had been the continual thinking about her afterwards.

"Let's get to work," he said. "I don't have time for chit-chat." Of course, she hadn't done a bit of chit-chat, but his frustration level was peaking at the sight of her legs so he'd gone and cut her off at the pass, before she had a chance to say a word to him, like, *Hello, last night was nice, what are you doing in the kitchen after midnight?*

She raised a brow, but didn't argue. "Sounds good. I brought several changes of clothes so each ad is a bit different. I thought this," she swept a hand over her frame, "might be a good starting point because it picks up the colors in your logo."

"Great idea. I hadn't thought of that."

She shrugged off the praise. "It was nothing more than planning what I was going to wear."

A distracted part of him wondered what she was planning to wear tonight, after their business was concluded.

Behind him, Neal, the photographer Jack had hired from Boston, cleared his throat. "We might want to get started before we lose the morning light."

"Of course," Madison said, slipping into business mode as easily as changing an outfit. Her face grew serious, her back straightened.

She hung up her garment bag inside the store and then, seconds later, she was in place, posing for the first ad he'd sketched, the one where she was supposed to hold up a block of cheddar and look ravenous. The rolling acreage of the farm spread out behind her in a lush, green tableau that Jack hoped would embody the message of natural, home-grown products.

"Perfect," Neal said, eyeing Madison through the lens and taking one picture after another, as rapid-fire as a machine gun. "Now, smile a little. Exactly. Gorgeous, sweetie. Totally gorgeous."

Jack moved behind Neal, seeing her as the camera did. Her cobalt blue eyes connected with the lens, establishing a relationship, an intimacy. His pulse quickened, thudding through his veins. Madison cupped the cheddar block, her newly polished fingers seeming to caress the aged cheese.

"Let's try sexy now," Neal said.

Madison's glossed lips parted slightly and she inhaled, drawing her breasts upward, Jack's gaze traveling with them. A breeze whispered through, catching a tendril of her hair, brushing it against the soft pink hue of her cheek.

Holy cow. With her looking like that, he could have put her face on any product and sold a million. Hell, Madison could sell Reeboks to orangutans.

"Marvelous, sweetie." Neal clicked the digital camera, moving in, then back, getting to one knee, shooting upward, from the side, virtually from every possible angle. Throughout it all, Madison kept that concentrated gaze on the lens. Every ounce of her attention was zeroed in on that one spot, like a Madison laser, shooting straight at his gut.

The whole thing was so damned hot, Jack was surprised the camera didn't dissolve in Neal's hands.

"Great. Let's move on. I got what I wanted on that shot," Neal said.

"Let me change," Madison said. "That'll give us a different look for the next set."

Neal nodded, non-plussed, apparently nowhere near as affected by Madison as Jack. Watching her walk away, hips swaying with her high-heeled strides, Jack's pulse banked hard around an interior Nascar track.

As she slipped inside the closed store, Jack was half tempted to ask if she needed help doing up her zipper. Or undoing it, for that matter.

When he'd hired the heiress model to put her image on his product, he'd hoped the woman he'd seen in the *Globe*'s society pages and staring back at him from the SuperSaver checkout stand would give his products something to help them differentiate themselves on the crowded dairy shelves.

What he hadn't expected was how damned good she was at her job. And how it was making him insane with a hunger that had nothing to do with Colby-Jack.

Thirty minutes and three fast outfit changes later, they'd run through the entire list of Jack's ad concepts. "I don't work with too many like her," Neal said, coming up beside Jack. "Barely had to do a retake on anything. She nailed them all, first time out. Let me show you."

Jack watched as the photographer scrolled through the digital images, each one better than the last—at least when it came to the way Madison looked. She'd done her job, and done it well, but she'd been right.

His ideas were as boring as Supreme Court appointment hearings.

"All right, Madison," he said, striding into the shop, where she'd gone to slip out of the denim skirt she'd donned for the last shots, half-hoping she was still dressed. And half-hoping she wasn't. "You're on."

She paused in undoing the last button of her denim jacket. "On?"

"I just saw the preliminary shots." He gestured outside, in Neal's direction. "And while I'm sure I could sell used sweat socks with your image on the package, I also know an ad that isn't packing the punch it should when I see it."

"Jack, I could be wrong—"

"No. We'll use your ideas. I'm turning the photo shoot over to you." Then he turned, calling over his shoulder to Neal. "Madison's in charge now, so go with whatever she wants."

Neal let out a little snort of disbelief. "You're making the *model* the boss? Models don't call the shots. They just stand there while I take the pictures. They're not always the brightest bulbs on the Christmas tree."

Beside him, Madison had turned away, busying herself with hanging up the jacket. It surprised him, because ever since he'd met her, Madison had been the kind of woman who fought back. Why wasn't she defending herself now?

"She's in charge," Jack repeated, making his point clear to Neal. "Whatever Madison says, goes."

"Uh, Jack," she said, laying a soft touch on his arm. "I'm really, ah…hungry. Can we break for lunch first?"

"Sure, whatever you want." But as he looked in her eyes, he didn't think she was hungry at all. She seemed to be…stalling.

For the sake of his business and his family, he hoped it was only a touch of stage fright—easily curable with what he'd put in the cooler waiting on the table: a hefty slice of Aunt Harriet's Hound Dog Cake.

Madison heard her cell ringing, the vibration of the call making her tiny purse dance on the wooden picnic table.

"Madison, you have a shot at the Maybelline contract," Harry barked into the phone, a familiar tick-tick-tick sound in the background. His stopwatch, timing every cell second. "This is your comeback, baby."

Joy flooded her chest, making her feel as buoyant as a balloon. *Maybelline.* "Are you serious? They want me?"

"Yep. New line of Retin-A stuff. They needed a more, ah, mature face."

Mature? If ever there was a death knell for Madison's career, that word was it. Still, there was a chance she could be with Maybelline for a few years. Build up her bank account, her reputation, get back on her feet, and *stay* on them this time.

It was the call she had waited all her career for, the one that validated her as an asset to a company, not just a pretty face. The one that gave her security and status, elevating her beyond a cover girl.

"But…" Harry paused. "There's a catch."

"A catch?"

"They want you in New York on Friday; some big honcho meeting. If all goes well, and I'm sure it will, they're going to have you at one of those big store makeover things at the downtown Macy's on Saturday. They're planning on revealing the new face for Maybelline." Harry drew in a breath that Madison was sure had a Marlboro attached to it. "Which is gonna be you, baby."

"Friday? *This* Friday?" She shook her head, glancing across the yard at Jack, who was talking to his father, probably working out some issue with production. "I can't possibly go then. I'm supposed to be the spokesmodel for Cheese Pleese at the wine festival this Saturday. It's their big shot—"

"Madison, are you hearing me? This is *Maybelline*. The big time. They're talking multi-year contract." He drew in another lungful of smoke. "Oh, shit. My minutes are almost up. I gotta go. I already gave you two, which is more than I give most of my clients."

"Harry, I—"

"Just be there Friday, Madison. Screw the cheese farm. I'll send someone else. It's just freakin' cheese. You were always too good for that anyway." Before she could get another word out, the line went dead and Harry was gone.

Madison sat back on the wooden bench seat, staring at the phone in her hands. A cosmetics contract. That was the kind of job stability most models would give their two front teeth to have. It meant continual work, often for three or four years at a time.

A year ago, six months ago, she would have ditched the cheese in a heartbeat for this chance. It should have had her burning with excitement, thrilled that they *wanted* her.

But when Madison closed her eyes, picturing herself as the face of Maybelline, hawking everything from Great Lash mascara to toning masks, the images refused to stay put. Every time she inserted her face into a Maybelline inspired photo shoot, it disappeared. The excitement that had surged inside her when Harry first mentioned the deal had already subsided, like a wave that petered out once it got closer to shore.

What was wrong with her? This was *it*, the zenith she'd been trying to reach ever since she'd left high school in the middle of junior year, because Harry had seen her and thought she'd be perfect for *Seventeen.*

Madison refused to entertain the thought that she didn't want to be the face of Maybelline. That she would turn down something so lucrative and steady as a cosmetics deal. That would require an entire rethinking of the Madison Worth future, one where she revisited crazy ideas like going to college and becoming a brain instead of a beauty.

That hadn't worked when she'd tried it, and she was fooling herself if she thought a high school dropout whose area of expertise was kissing up to a camera had a shot at anything but this. She had no other future options. Either she nabbed the Maybelline contract this coming Friday, or she became intimately acquainted with the granny pants department.

Finally, every one of her dreams, everything she'd worked for, was within her grasp.

All she had to do was disappoint the one man who was counting on her.

Jack's Uptown-Girl Bleu Cheese Tenderloin Steaks

4 beef tenderloin steaks
1 tablespoon olive oil
1 garlic clove, minced
2 tablespoons cream cheese, softened
4 tablespoons bleu cheese, crumbled
4 tablespoons plain yogurt
2 teaspoons onion, minced

She's done an amazing job, she deserves an equally amazing meal. Start by firing up the grill, then rub the oil and garlic over the steaks. While they're sizzling—and okay, admit, your thoughts are still sizzling after seeing her slip in and out of clothing as easy as a gymnast on the parallel bars—mix the remaining ingredients together. When the steaks are done, top each with some of the cheese mixture and cook for one or two minutes.

Just long enough to make everything melt in your mouth. Especially the way she looks at you.

CHAPTER FIFTEEN

"These are great," Jack said later Tuesday afternoon, looking over the preliminary digital images, uploaded by the photographer onto Jack's Dell. There was Madison, leaning her chin on her hands amid a display of gaily wrapped gift baskets filled with a variety of cheeses. Blowing a kiss at a stack of cheese balls, piled like a yellow and white Christmas tree and topped with a single red bow. Holding one of Cheese Pleese's Colby-molded birds, part of their animal-shaped collection, mocking a look of surprise with a sexy little O on her mouth. Her idea—the twelve days of Christmas featuring twelve different items from their product line—had translated into images a hundred times better than he'd expected. "I have to say, you had the right idea."

"Really?"

The unexpected praise infused Madison with something she had never found on the runway. Or in front of lens. Despite the years of being told she was beautiful and thin, there'd always been one little chink left out, as if her self worth was a jigsaw puzzle that had been missing a few pieces.

Jack shook his head, clicking and moving through the different images. "You're definitely on the wrong side of the lens." He glanced up at her, smiling. "You want a job?"

She laughed, suddenly feeling more self-conscious than she ever had before, even more than in sixth grade when she'd gotten braces, and in eighth grade when she'd gotten breasts. "A job? Doing what?"

"Being my marketing guru, of course. Heck, I have a degree in business and I never thought of pulling something like this together. You're really great at this."

"It was nothing, really." The thought that Jack— or anyone—would put the entire sales fate of a company into her hands was terrifying. She'd tried that in those college marketing classes, until Janine had come along and caused the entire thing to explode in Madison's face, proving to Madison that she should stick to what she knew—looking pretty.

"Madison, this was huge. I can't wait to see what ideas you have for the wine festival." He leaned forward, his eyes wide with excitement, churning with ideas. "I don't want you to just head up my marketing, I want you to be *the* face of Cheese Pleese. I know I can't offer you the money New York does, but I hope you'll at least consider it." He glanced again at the photos. "I can't imagine anyone else representing my company."

Oh, no, no. That was *not* the plan. Harry was supposed to send another girl so she could leave and Jack could still sell his products at the festival.

Jack putting his faith—his dollars—into her was a huge mistake. Especially when she was planning on trading him for some wrinkle-smoothing foundation. "It was just an idea," she said, letting out a nervous laugh. "I don't get a lot of those."

He paused, his gaze connecting with hers. "Don't sell yourself short, Madison. This is incredible. In fact, I'd really like to get your ideas about how we can capitalize on this theme at the wine festival. I'm sure you could come up with—"

"I have to go," she said, scrambling to her feet and dashing for the door before Jack could finish the sentence and she would have to tell him a lie to his face. "Jack, don't rely on me. You'd be betting on a Grade-B cow."

She left the room, closing the door. Guilt tossed and turned in her stomach. The wine festival. The event she wouldn't be at because she'd be too busy saving her own skin.

She hesitated, her hand on the doorknob. *Tell him,* her conscience urged. *Tell him you're ditching him, breaking a promise.*

Disappoint him, like she'd been disappointed so many times. Like during Parents Day at boarding school, when she'd been the only one walking around alone because her mother had gotten distracted building boats in Indonesia and forgotten her promise to fly home. Or the time she'd sent a copy of her first cover to her mother, and had it come back, marked "Return to Sender, Addressee

Not Known." Vivian had moved on, to another country, another cause, and forgotten to tell her own daughter where she went.

Madison had vowed she would never break a promise, would never be the cause of someone else's disappointment.

And yet, she couldn't turn around and tell Jack the truth. Especially not now, not with him thinking he could turn over the entire marketing end of his business to someone like her. Not when she was about to become an advertising Benedict Arnold.

Madison leaned against the wall, inhaling and exhaling, working hard to bring her churning stomach under control.

She didn't know what had possessed her to fight him on the ad concept in the first place. She'd never done that before, no matter how dumb she'd thought dressing as one of the faces on Mount Rushmore had been for an insurance company ad, or how idiotic it felt to sport galoshes and umbrellas in that condom piece.

"I should leave," she muttered to herself, if only to vocalize the words and thus, make it happen.

Maybelline wanted her. There was no reason for her to stay here any longer, to feel guilty about what her leaving might do to Jack's business. Harry would make it up to him, send another blonde. She could walk away, without an ounce of guilt.

But her conscience wasn't listening. It weighed on her like a semi full of Keebler cookies.

What had gotten into her lately? She seemed destined to ruin her life, her livelihood...and drag down Jack Pleeseman with it.

The guilt washed over her. Today was Tuesday. She'd stay till late Thursday night, working with him on the print ads and maybe tossing out a few ideas. That much she could do.

Yeah, she was staying solely because she wanted to *help* Jack. Not to see where they could go if they journeyed past Aisle Seven, not because he was the first man she'd ever met who noticed she had a brain beneath the blondeness.

Madison Worth, who had learned the art of subterfuge with her first tube of cover-up, was doing a damned good job of fooling herself.

David's Stuffing-The-Truth-Down-Deep Sausage Mushrooms

1 pound country-style sausage
8 ounces cream cheese
2 pounds mushrooms, cleaned, stems removed
1/2 cup Parmesan cheese

You can't ignore the truth forever—you're interested in her, no matter how much you try to deny it. And why shouldn't you be? She's gorgeous, available and your heart's still beating—what more does a guy need?

Preheat the oven to 325 degrees. Fry up the sausage till fully cooked, then drained. Hey, I'm a guy. I think everything's better with meat in it. Mix the sausage with the cream cheese, then stuff the mushrooms with the mixture. Sprinkle Parmesan on top, then bake for 45 minutes.

While you're waiting, make some plans to move forward—with one particular woman helping you do the movin'.

Chapter Sixteen

"Every time I see you, your mood just gets better and better," Dave said early on Wednesday morning, taking a stance against one of the hundred-year-old maples on the back of the property. "Makes me glad I'm heading to the feed store instead of hanging out here. Especially when you're holding an axe."

"Thanks," Jack said. He brushed the back of his hand against his brow, wiping off the sweat built up over an hour of chopping wood he didn't need.

"Where's Ginny?"

"Still sleeping. I let her O'D on Cartoon Network last night."

David chuckled. "So, you're out here, working a certain woman out of your system?"

"No." Jack glanced down at the growing pile of split logs. "Yeah."

"Just go to bed with her and get it over, will you? Watching you moon over her is making my chest hurt."

"I am not mooning over her. And besides, she'll be gone in a few days anyway. After Saturday, her work here is done."

"And you're going to let her go?"

After yesterday's encounter in his office, Madison seemed pretty intent on getting the hell out of here. She didn't want a job with him, didn't want to spend one more second on the farm than she needed to.

He knew better than to try to make her stay. Look at how that had backfired with Alyssa. Madison Worth lived in the same uptown world as Alyssa now did—and an entire planet away from Pleeseman Dairy Farms.

"She doesn't belong here, Dave. She'd not the kind of woman who'd be happy living with a bunch of cows and a hungry goat."

Or with him.

The thought slammed into Jack's chest, proving that no amount of chopping wood was going to help him eradicate the disappointment building inside him. What had he been thinking? That the heiress model would ditch the five-thousand-a-day work to come separate the whey from the curds?

David shrugged, then took a sip from a mug of coffee in his hands. "Mom was."

"And Alyssa wasn't. Not every woman is like mom."

David nodded. "Ain't that the truth. She was one of a kind." He didn't say anything for a long while, just sipped at his coffee, looking out over the land where both of them had spent most of their lives. "What do you think she was doing in San Francisco that day?"

It was the same question David and Jack had tossed around for over a decade, like Monday morning quarterbacks trying to figure out the sense of the last play. Their mother had left the farm, returning to her native San Francisco, to the mon-eyed family she'd given up when she'd fallen for Joe Pleeseman.

And been hit by a speeding taxi driver crossing the street in front of her mother's house.

Nancy had never reached the house, never made a phone call home that would have explained why she was there. Her head had hit the concrete on Nob Hill and the light of the Pleeseman farm went out.

"If you ask me," Jack said, heaving a sigh, facing a truth he'd kept to himself for the better part of his life. "I think she was running away."

"From us?" David shook his head. "Never."

"If you were Mom, wouldn't you run away? From all of this?"

"Are you saying that just because you did?"

Jack didn't reply. Instead, he grabbed David's coffee mug and took a long, searing gulp. On any other morning, the java would have done its job, filling the cobwebbed spots in his mind with a few hours of energy.

Nothing, however, filled the cavern in his chest, a cavern that had existed for a long, long time.

"Why are you doing all this?" David asked. "Working so damned hard to change the business? I know you, Jack, and it's not about money."

Jack paused for a long, long time. Finally, he laid the axe on the chopping stump and let out a breath. "Because that's what Mom would have wanted."

"And would Mom have wanted you to work yourself into the ground instead of having a life? This farm is not everything, Jack. You need to—"

"I have to bring the wood in," Jack said, knowing he didn't have to do any such damned thing. It was the middle of summer, for God's sake. No one would be lighting a fire.

"Quit fooling yourself," David continued, watching Jack load a pile of chopped logs into his arms. "You like the woman, go after her. You deserve a little happiness, brother."

"I'm afraid—" He cut himself off, looking out over the property that had come to mean more to him than he'd ever thought possible.

"That's your whole problem, Jack. Quit being afraid and just go for it." He gave his older brother a good-natured jab. "What's the worst that can happen? You get to brag to the boys at the Bar & Grille that you slept with a model?"

Jack knew, as surely as he knew not a single damned stick of this wood would be burned for another two months, that sleeping with Madison Worth wasn't the worst that could happen.

No, the worst would be falling for her and having his heart trampled by the Budweiser Clydesdales again.

But still, the guy side of him said, going to bed with her would be a hell of a job perk.

On Wednesday morning, Madison woke up to a quiet house and a carafe of coffee on her nightstand with a note from Jack tucked under the mug. "Join us for breakfast. Keep that brilliant mind well fed."

If only he knew. A stack of pancakes wasn't going to give her Einstein genius, that was for sure. She wasn't the marketing savant he wanted. She poured herself a cup of the coffee, wrapping one hand around the now familiar image of Elvis with a hula girl.

Madison was a model. Not a marketing director or an ad designer. A model. She would do well to remember to stick to the things she knew and leave the rest to others with far more education than her.

She glanced again at the note and felt guilt tighten her stomach, better than four hundred crunches with Lars, the trainer from hell who worked at the gym near her apartment in Manhattan. Lars was half the reason she'd switched to Pilates and yoga. No one yelled and made her sweat in yoga.

Madison sighed. She'd avoided Jack for as long as possible. At some point, she had to get up the guts to tell him she wasn't going to be at the wine festival. That she was trading his business needs for some collagen-enhanced foundation.

She got up, threw on some sleep pants, then left the room, pausing at the bottom of the stairs to look out the small round window, centered by a stained glass image of a newly-opened rose. Outside, the life of the farm went on, a constant hum of activity, like ants in a colony. Only these ants were a mixture of humans and smelly, black-and-white cows. Across the yard, Katydid was protesting her new confinement behind a six-foot chainlink fence. The goat dipped her head and began to gnaw at one of the fence posts. Madison laughed. Clearly, it would only be a matter of time before Katydid the Wonder Goat escaped.

Oh, hell. She *was* going to miss this place. She was going to miss the quiet nights, the serene landscape, even the old house that was as far from her normal life as Venus was from Mars.

Maybelline, her mind whispered.

A couple of days and she'd be on her way, back to her career, back on the top of the mountain. Her stay here would be forgotten, Madison told herself, as soon as the camera began to click.

The sounds of merriment caused her to turn and look in the kitchen. Jack was laughing at something Ginny had said while he stirred a yellow mixture in a bowl then poured it into a pan. The scene was so ordinary, so *Father Knows Best*.

It was the kind of scene Madison would have given the entire Worth fortune to see when she'd been a child. A father, a mother—people who were there in a sunny, cluttered kitchen because they loved her—not because they were on the Worth payroll.

But this wasn't her family. Those weren't her memories being created over a sizzling pan and an old chrome and laminate table.

She considered avoiding the kitchen altogether. Then she inhaled. Caffeine whispered its siren call. She'd already finished off the carafe in her room and had yet to fill the morning emptiness in her stomach. Another cup and a couple of slices of dry toast and she'd be fine.

Madison followed the scent of Maxwell House instead of following her original plan of avoiding Jack. If the cops ever needed a bloodhound to find a stolen shipment of coffee, she was their girl.

"Join us," Jack said when she entered the kitchen, hoisting a spatula her way. "I made too many eggs."

Ginny giggled. "Daddy always makes too many."

"Oh no, really." Madison waved off the offer. "Thanks, but I'm just going to have—"

"Sorry, I won't take no for an answer," Jack said. "You're my investment and I'm going to take care of you." The investment word signaled a return to business as usual, but it was counteracted by the words *take care of you*. Madison told herself she didn't need to be taken care of, but stayed where she was all the same, riveted by the sight of Jack doing exactly that.

He tipped the pan, sliding a pile of fluffy scrambled eggs onto one of Harriet's jungle plates. He sprinkled a little shredded cheese on top of the eggs, then crossed the room and thrust the plate into her hands. "You need to eat."

Damn. They looked good. The yoga studio seemed a million miles away. When Madison tried to recall downward facing dog, she got only an image of Buster and her in a cheddar tug of war. "I do eat."

"Yeah, things that have all the calories of a glass of water. Celery? Lettuce? Apples? That not food. They're plate decorations."

"Eww, celery," Ginny said. She stabbed her fork into a big hunk of cheesy eggs, then shoved the whole bite into her mouth. "I like eggs. Daddy makes the best."

"I'm sure he does," Madison said, trying to work up a smile she hoped was friendly. Truth was, close proximity to a child made her uncomfortable as hell. The only children she'd ever been around had been child models, given to pitching tantrums, screaming when they didn't get their way, and generally competing for the title of Biggest Prima Donna.

It hadn't been their fault, of course. Child models were often indulged, by everyone from the stylist to the photographer, who would all give up a right arm, or a Hershey bar, to buy some peace and get the shot.

The plate of eggs sat before her, steaming hot, the scent of cheddar rising off them. That led to thinking of the nachos, and then, unbidden, her gaze went to the kitchen sink. Heat filled her face when she realized Jack had caught her visually returning to the scene of their midnight rendezvous. He smiled at her, a secret, hot smile that spoke of what they had shared...and what they could share again.

So much for being all business. Apparently she wasn't the only one having a hard time keeping her focus on the bottom line—

The business's, not Jack's.

"Mommy says I always have to try one bite," Ginny said, interrupting Madison's thoughts with a little G-rated reality. "Doesn't your mommy make you try one bite?"

How was Madison supposed to answer that? The whole story of her absentee mother was way too complicated for a child who hadn't even learned her ABCs. "Uh, my mommy doesn't worry about what I eat."

"But I do," Jack said, leaning down to whisper in her ear. "Now be a good girl and take one bite."

The words *good girl* sent a thrill running down her spine. Particularly with that sink a mere six feet away. There were a lot of really awesome memories associated with that particular area of countertop—

Memories that didn't have a damned thing to do with breakfast. More like dessert.

"Remember," Jack said, "'I'm paying you to prove to the customer demographics that you are totally, completely in love with my *products*.'"

The unspoken words: not with him. He needn't worry. Madison didn't fall totally in love with anything or anyone. Especially not with foods that were bad for her waistline—and men who were as bad for her heart as a truckload of French fries.

Her stomach grumbled in disagreement. She took a quick gulp of coffee, but it didn't fill the empty, yawning space inside her gut. Jack was right. A few pieces of lettuce didn't constitute a meal, not unless your name was Thumper.

She looked down at the plate, ran through a hundred reasons why she shouldn't eat a single bite. The devil on her shoulder reminded her that the

Atkins and South Beach people had made millions convincing people that eggs and cheese were the secret to slim hips.

Maybe there was some truth to their assertions. And maybe letting a rumbling tummy make decisions was insane.

Either way, it sure was easier than telling Jack the truth about where she was going to be this weekend and how she was going to be letting him down.

"Okay, just a little." Madison dipped her fork into the eggs. They were as fluffy as a cloud. Back in the days when Madison had eaten eggs—and just about anything that came within biting range of her mouth—this had been exactly how she'd liked her scrambled eggs, soft and airy.

For some reason, perfectly scrambled eggs were an art form few of the Worth cooks ever mastered. One made them too hard, another too runny.

Then again, none of the Worth cooks had looked as sexy as Jack Pleeseman, standing barefoot in his kitchen in khaki shorts and a T-shirt that said Everything is better with cheese on top.

Everything? Including him?

She reined in those thoughts. No matter how Madison felt about Jack Pleeseman, with or without cheese, she had to remember she was here for a job. Paying rent was far more important than how his lips had felt on hers and whether she was going to spend tonight dreaming about what he looked like beneath that button-down shirt and jeans.

Dreaming about him was one thing. Acting on it was another entirely.

She inhaled, drawing in the scent of the food before she took the bite and let it hit her tongue. And then, like a memory too long denied, the eggs and cheese slammed into her taste buds in a whoosh of flavor.

Holy cow. No…holy chicken and cow.

This was what she had been missing. What she had been denying herself.

And why exactly was that? When had she started thinking a slice of cantaloupe was a suitable breakfast? That skipping meals was a good policy?

With the taste of the eggs still on her tongue, her brain couldn't come up with a single reason. The cover of *Vogue* had never seemed as distant as it did right now.

"These are incredible," she said, diving in for a second bite, and then a third, before she could worry about the consequences.

Ginny nodded agreement. "That's 'cuz Daddy made them. He's the best cooker ever."

Jack had fixed himself a plate and slid into the seat between herself and Ginny. "I'm flattered. Growing up as a Worth, you've probably dined at the best tables in the city of Boston."

"Five stars don't always guarantee a good meal," Madison replied. "Neither does a pedigree," she added, thinking of all the men she'd met in her circle who were as self-centered as a mirror, who would have called the maid to make the eggs, figuring that impressed the girl more than standing over the stove and insisting she eat because he worried about her.

"I think my cows might disagree," Jack said, laughing.

"What's a ped-a-gee?" Ginny asked.

Jack opened his mouth to answer her, then shut it again when the house phone rang. He rose, answered it, then immediately started frowning. "Yeah. I'll be right there." He hung up, then turned to Madison. "I gotta go. An emergency in the barn. One of the pregnant cows is having a difficult delivery and I need to go help out. Aunt Harriet's at the grocery store, my dad is who knows where, and David went to pick up a load of feed. Do you mind...?" He gestured at Ginny.

"Oh, of course," Madison lied. "No problem. You go help the heifer."

"Thanks." He told Ginny where he was going, then slipped on a pair of boots and left. The screen door shut with a squeak and a bang, leaving Madison and Ginny alone.

The clock in the hallway ticked its slow journey from eight fifty-five to nine. Ginny continued eating her eggs, her eyes on Madison, watching her with the keen interest of an owl watching a field mouse.

If only to avoid the girl's inquisitive gaze, Madison went to work on her own breakfast, finishing off the food, then pushing the plate to the side. She drummed her fingers on the table, sipped her coffee, drummed some more.

Where the hell was Jack? How long did it take to birth a calf anyway?"

"So, are you gonna marry my Daddy?" Ginny asked. "'Cuz he's lonesomes."

"Oh, no, I'm not marrying him." Madison choked back the coffee in her throat. "No, not at all. I…just work for him."

Ginny nodded, took a bite, swallowed. "Why?"

"Why do I work for him?" Madison repeated, stalling. Damn. Where did this kid come from? Five minutes into it and she was already throwing out questions like Geraldo Rivera. "Uh, because that's my job."

"What is?" Ginny asked, crossing her arms on the table. "Do you make the cheese, too? Daddy's the best at that. I know, 'cuz I love his cheese."

Oh yes, he was the best, Madison agreed. At cheese and at—

"No, I don't help on the farm," she said quickly, cutting off her own thoughts before they traveled down an R-rated path. "I'm a model."

"A model?" Ginny frowned, thinking. "Like the plastic ladies my Mommy looks at when she buys clothes?"

It took a second, but then Madison realized Ginny meant mannequins. "No, not…" She paused. What were the real differences between what she did and the "plastic ladies" did? Except for the amount of silicone? "Yeah, pretty much like that."

Ginny sipped at her orange juice. "That's not very fun. It's like playing Freeze. I think Freeze is boring."

"Sorry." Madison started banging out her table tempo again. What was Jack doing? Birthing quadruplets?

"My Daddy likes fun people. Him and me, we have lots of fun."

"I'm…" Madison stopped. She'd never been fun, not really. She'd grown up in a houses filled with antiques, rules and nannies who had governed her every move. Even though the nannies had done their damndest, several of them ended up throwing up their hands and quitting when Madison's obstinate nature got to be too much. And yet, as much as Madison had tried to buck the rules, for the most part, it had been a life as rigid and as boring as the mannequins in Nordstrom's.

The only time she truly broke away from the Worth expectations was when she stepped in front of a camera lens. Then she felt like she could loosen up, become someone else—a sexy siren in Armani, a serious businesswoman in Chanel, a glamorous actress in Givenchy, even a bride for Vera Wang.

There, she pretended, had fun. But in her real life, rarely.

For a second, she envied the four-year-old, her life, her family, her "fun." Maybe Madison had been playing Freeze too long.

She leaned in toward the little girl. "What do you do for fun?"

"With Daddy?" Ginny shrugged. "I play catch and stuff. He likes catch." She lowered her voice to a whisper, cupping her hand around her mouth. "Don't tell Daddy, but I really like playing dolls."

Now there was something Madison could get behind. "Dressing them up? Setting up little houses out of boxes and things like that?" She had done a ton of that as a child, all those hours alone in her room, acting out exciting lives for Barbie and Ken.

Ginny nodded, smiling, then just as quickly, she sobered. "But I don't have any dolls at Daddy's house 'cuz he likes balls and bats and things. My dolls are at mommy's house and she forgot to pack them. We left kinda quick. She was eating with the king."

Madison didn't bother to correct Ginny's royal connection. She looked down at this miniature woman-to-be and realized how much they had in common, even if Madison wasn't sure she could bridge the gap of twenty-five years to reach that common ground. They were both the children of distant, distracted mothers and jet-setting, object-filled lives.

But there was one difference, one thing Ginny had that Madison had always lacked—

A father who clearly adored her.

Just as the perfect scrambled eggs had filled one yearning, Madison wanted to fill another. To do that would mean getting closer to Ginny. She'd already had a conversation with the child. Surely doing more wouldn't be all that hard.

"I have a doll with me," Madison said. "She's very old and I don't really have any clothes or anything extra for her, but if you want to play with her—"

Ginny had already scraped her chair back, and dashed over to Madison's side, her eyes bright. "Could I? Really?"

"Sure." She rose, putting her plate in the sink and running some water over it. Outside the kitchen window, she caught a glimpse of Katydid, clambering over the railings of the pasture as easily as stairs, then pausing, four hooves on the thick log. She darted her gaze one way, then the other, then, with a joyous baa, leapt off the post and into freedom. "Katydid! Get back in there!" called one of the men, taking off after her. The goat cantered away, in a goat's version of tag.

Madison chuckled, then added a squirt of dishwashing detergent to the water, like she'd seen the maids do a hundred times. Anything beyond that—meaning actually *washing* the dishes—Madison wasn't about to attempt, not without some adult backup. "Let's go up to my room and I'll introduce you to Ella Mae."

Aunt Harriet's Stuck-On-You Three-Cheese Ziti

12 ounces ziti, cooked
2 tablespoons olive oil
1 onion, diced
2 cloves garlic, minced
1 teaspoon ground fennel
1/3 cup tomato paste
1 8-ounce can tomato sauce
1 cup water
1 teaspoon oregano
1/2 teaspoon sage
1/2 cup Parmesan cheese, divided
15 ounces Ricotta cheese
1 egg
8 ounces mozzarella cheese, shredded, divided

It's now or never—you need to start opening up your heart and let someone in, or before you know it, you'll be crying in the chapel all by your lone-somes. Preheat the oven to 350 degrees. Saute the onion, garlic and fennel in the olive oil, add the tomato paste and cook for one minute. Add sauce, water and spices, then cook for ten minutes. Stir in half of the Parmesan, all the while singing your top picks from the "Live from Hawaii" album.

In a separate bowl, combine the remaining cheeses and egg, reserving 1/4 cup of mozzarella. Don't be thinking about suspicious minds—instead, in a 9 by 13-inch pan, layer the sauce, pasta and cheese, topping with sauce and remaining mozzarella. Get a little burning love going by popping this casserole into the oven for 40 minutes.

Serve to a hard headed woman even if she makes you feel like the devil in disguise.

CHAPTER SEVENTEEN

J ack paused outside the door to Madison's room and just listened.

To the sound of his daughter laughing, enjoying herself. It was such a magical sound, so filled with joy that it seemed to overflow, spilling into the empty nooks and crannies of the house that had gone too long without laughter. If it hadn't been for Ginny…

Jack wasn't sure where he'd be. Or whether he'd be half as sane as he was right now.

"Why'd you name her Ella Mee?" Ginny asked. Jack peeked around the corner and saw his daughter holding a life-like baby doll.

It was porcelain, with a face so realistic, it could have been on a Gerber jar. The doll was just a bit bigger than a real baby, dressed in a soft white dress and matching little shoes, all trimmed with lace and pearl buttons. It looked antique—and breakable. For a second, he wanted to dash in there and tell Madison to watch for a four-year-old's clumsy grip.

"Ella Mae," Madison corrected, her tone gentle. "Well, Ginny, that's a long story."

Ginny settled back on her knees. "That's good," she said. "'Cuz I love long stories. Daddy says that's 'cuz I got big ears."

Madison laughed. "All right, I'll tell you. And Ella Mae." She took the doll from Ginny, and held it in her lap, facing it out, as if the toy was listening, too. "Ella Mae was the name of my grandmother."

"My grandma's name was Nancy," Ginny said, then frowned. "She died."

"Ella Mae died, too, when I was a little girl. I don't even remember her."

"Then how's come you named your doll after her?"

"Because Ella Mae was her gift to me. She gave it to my father to give to me when I was born. She wanted her first grandchild to have something special."

"Did your daddy like your doll?" Ginny leaned forward, lowering her voice. "Daddy said he doesn't like to play dolls."

Jack bit back a laugh at Ginny's words. He definitely wasn't a doll playing kind of dad. Give him a catcher's mitt and a softball, and he was out there with his kid, bonding in the way only a dad could bond. But when it came to setting up imaginary worlds and taking Barbie out on the town—well, there were some things Jack sucked at doing.

Madison fingered the doll's strawberry blond curls. "I don't know. I never met him either."

"You never met your daddy? Didn't he come to your house or anything?"

Madison gave Ginny a small smile, then tucked the doll back into the little girl's arms, giving it a final pat. Ginny beamed, snuggling the baby closer. "No, he died before I was born. He was in an accident. But," Madison added, putting on a bright smile, "I had Ella Mae, so I made her my friend."

Jack was glad Madison had left off the details and changed the subject. Knowing Ginny's insatiable curiosity, Madison would have ended up giving a full Discovery Channel worthy play-by-play of how her father had died.

"I have a bear," Ginny said, clutching Ella Mae to her chest. "He's my friend, too. I named him Bear-Bear."

Madison chuckled. "That's a wonderful name."

"Wanna see him? He's in my room. I can go get him."

"Sure," Madison said. "I love bears."

Ginny scrambled to her feet, tucking Ella Mae under one arm, causing Jack to cringe with worry. But Madison only smiled, clearly not worried about the fate of that porcelain face. As Ginny hurried across the room toward him, Jack stepped back, then moved forward, as if he'd just come upstairs. "Daddy!" Ginny beamed. "Was it a boy? Or a girl?"

"A boy…?"

"The cow, Daddy." She giggled. "You're so silly."

He'd gotten so distracted by the scene in Madison's room that he'd completely forgotten about the calf. "A girl. Guess you're going to have to put on your thinking cap, Ginny. That baby's gonna need a name."

"Okay, I will. But first, I gotta get Bear-Bear. Madison wants to meet him." She hurried off down the hall, disappearing inside the small room that Jack and his father had turned into a bedroom for her three years ago, when Jack had moved away from Boston and back home. It had been his mother's sewing room and still sported the pink walls and fabric-covered window seat that his mother had loved. He couldn't help thinking his mother was looking down from heaven, pleased to see her first grandchild giving new life to the space.

"Jack," Madison said, rising and approaching the door. Her face was free of makeup, her hair tousled around her shoulders, her blue T-shirt and pajama pants still wrinkled from sleeping in them last night. He'd never seen anything more sexy in his life. "I didn't know you were back."

"You were great," he said, clearing his throat and reminding himself—twice—that his daughter was just down the hall. "Especially with all those questions. I swear Ginny took out a patent on the word "why," she uses it so much. She can be a handful when she gets on a roll."

"Oh, she was fine."

"She really likes you."

Madison blinked at him. "Really? You think so?"

"She's introducing you to Bear-Bear. That's Ginny's big seal of approval."

Madison laughed, clearly pleased. "Well then, I'll have to make sure he is appropriately fawned over."

He chuckled, then tipped his head, studying her. "I didn't take you for the kids type."

She threw up her hands, stopping any more maternal thoughts. "Trust me, I'm not. I wouldn't know which end was up on a baby."

"That's easy. Keep the stinky one as far from you as possible." He leaned against the door jam, enjoying the melody of her laugh. Jack considered signing up for comedy lessons, just to hear that sound more often. "Seriously, you were great."

"Well, Ginny made it easy. She's an adorable, sweet kid."

The praise for his daughter filled him with joy. He, of course, thought the sun rose and set on her cherubic face, but to hear someone else say she was sweet...well, that topped the cake for him.

"Madison!" Ginny called, hurrying back down the hall, her bare feet slapping against the old wood finish, "here he is!"

As promised, Madison made a big deal out of Bear-Bear, sending Ginny over the moon. Then, Madison went into her room, withdrew a thick blue ribbon from one of the sweaters draped over her chair, and handed it to Ginny. "Here. This is for when he wants to go someplace fancy."

"A tie!" Ginny gasped and clutched the thin fabric. "Now he can look just like George."

A knife sliced through Jack's heart. George was Ginny's stepfather; it was only natural for her to think of him. But it hurt Jack all the same.

He didn't know why the thought of Bear-Bear mirroring George should bother Jack—George was the tie wearing type, and Jack no longer was. In the days when he'd been riding the Ambition Train, though, Jack had had more suits than jeans in his closet.

But ever since he'd come back to Pleeseman Dairy Farm, the suits had grown dusty and the jeans had multiplied like bunnies.

Ginny skipped away, Ella Mae under one arm, Bear-Bear under the other, off to plan a threesome tea party. When her bedroom door shut, Jack turned back to Madison. "Are you sure you want to let her handle that doll? She's four and still doesn't under-stand what the word careful means."

"She's fine," Madison said, her gaze still on the hall, a slight smile crossing her lips. "I'd rather see the doll played with than stuck in my suitcase." Then she turned away, stepping inside her room, reaching for the blue shirt and putting it on a hanger before moving to the closet.

Jack followed, not waiting for an invitation. He turned out the dainty chair that sat in front of the vanity before settling his large frame onto the small seat. "Do you always bring your own toys on a photo shoot?" he said, grinning, but really wondering about this new and surprising side of Madison.

"Ella Mae has gone with me everywhere." She shrugged. "I guess it just got to be a habit. When I was a kid, I was always going between my mom's apartment and my Grandfather's house, like a ping-pong ball. Then I went to boarding school, and Ella Mae came along. The poor thing has been in more suitcases than rooms. It's the only thing I have that connects me to my father."

"All that back and forth living—it must have been hard. On you, not the doll."

"You get used to it." Madison smoothed a hand over the blue shirt, whisking away a wrinkle that didn't exist. "When you're a kid, you get used to most anything."

He got the feeling her life hadn't been all luxury yachts and private schools. That there had been something missing in Madison Worth's youth, something all that money couldn't buy. Jack realized how lucky he had been, to have had two parents for most of his life, to have grown up with his aunt, his brother, the family of staff on the farm. He could count on one hand the number of times he'd used a suitcase, traveled to another city or been more than a couple hours from the people who knew him best. In more ways than one, his formative years had been radically different from those of the woman before him.

For that reason, he wanted to share some of the magic he remembered with her.

He rose. "Want to meet the newest addition to the farm?"

"The newest... Oh, the calf." Her eyes brightened and a smile of excitement took over her face. "Sure. If nothing else, it'll be something to talk about during Fashion Week this spring. Not many supermodels have cozied up to a newborn calf."

The mention of Fashion Week reminded him that she was leaving, returning to her world. For a minute there, he'd imagined Madison staying.

Becoming a part of his life, Ginny's.

Insane thoughts. Madison Worth wasn't meant for his world, no matter how much he tried to tempt her with baby animals. But that didn't stop him from taking her to meet the calf anyway.

There was, after all, such a thing as getting lucky.

A moment later, they had left the house, going out to the barn, Ginny in tow. Madison had slipped on a sweatshirt and a pair of flip-flops. As they walked, Ginny ran through an assortment of potential names for the newborn calf, ranging from Rapunzel to Annie and several jumbles of vowels and consonants in between.

When they reached the stall where Betty was standing with her new calf, Madison let out a gasp. "It's so...big. *That* came out of *her*? Just now?"

He chuckled. "Be glad you're a woman. At least your babies won't come with four hooves."

Ginny marched up to the stall, draped her arms over the railing, took one look at the calf and pronounced her "Ellie." She turned to Madison. "'Cuz Ella Mae doesn't have a cow named after her."

Another of Madison's thousand different smiles stole across her face. This one was soft, vulnerable. She looked as young as Ginny, as if the inclusion of Ella Mae within the farm had given her a priceless gift. "That sounds perfect to me."

"Ellie it is," Jack pronounced. "I'll get it on her tag tomorrow."

Ginny squealed with delight, then shoved a hand through the railings, waiting for Ellie to amble over, the calf's steps tentative and stumbling. Ginny stroked the animal's nose, laughing at its cold wetness.

"It walks already?" Madison took two steps forward, nearly touching the railing, as if she wanted to do what Ginny was doing, but was afraid to.

"Oh yeah. About from the minute they're born, calves are walking. And if they don't, their mom gives them some incentive." He turned to her, grinning. "Cows apparently don't have the patience human moms do."

"Can I..." Madison took another step forward, her fingers outstretched. "Can I touch her?"

"Sure." Jack gestured to Ginny to move over, then stepped back himself, allowing Madison to slip in against the railing. She slid her fingers below the wooden post, then turned, a look of surprise on her face, when she touched the calf's cheek. The animal moved closer, sticking her nose through the railing.

Madison shook her head. "I've never had a pet. Especially not a friendly pet cow."

"Never had a pet?" He couldn't imagine that. The Pleeseman farm had never been without some kind of pet, from a dog to a goat—and sometimes all of the above. "We should do something about that."

Too late, he realized his words implied a future. Something permanent.

Something that wasn't going to happen.

"She's adorable." Madison continued petting the calf, ignoring what Jack had just said. He should have been grateful, but half of him wanted a response.

What he got was a hungry calf, who decided Madison's hand was a good place to look for a meal. Ellie swiped her long, thick tongue across Madison's palm, eliciting a double female giggle.

"Look at Ellie, Daddy," Ginny said. "She's eating Madison."

Madison drew her hand back, still laughing. The youthful sound of her merriment seemed to lighten the air in the barn, infusing it with a spirit that had been lacking for so long. "I do believe it's her mom's job to feed her."

Once Ellie realized nothing was going to come from a human, she toddled over to Becky and found what she was looking for. Katydid trotted through the barn, stuck a nose in to investigate Ellie, apparently decided she wasn't worth a nibble, then trotted off. Jack shook his head, then waved off going after the goat. Later, there'd be time to pen Katydid again. For now, he was enjoying the moment.

As the three of them left the barn, Jack looked over at Madison and saw a contented smile on her face.

"This place agrees with you," he said.

She chuckled. "I am *so* not a farm girl."

"You could become one," he said, voicing his fantasy from moments before, caught up in the magic of the new life, the quiet peace of the barn, and the magnetic pull of her gaze.

Madison paused and turned to him. Ginny skipped ahead, toward the swing set in the yard. From behind them, Becky let out a moo, with Ellie trying to copy. "I live in Manhattan, Jack. I work all over the world. My place is there, not here. I'm not a farm kind of woman. And I never will be."

Then Madison walked away, slipping, perhaps without knowing it, into the model she really was. Her back straightened, her strides lengthened, and despite the sweats and flip-flops, she looked as regal as a princess.

And, as she'd just reminded him, a million miles from the kind of woman Jack Pleeseman wanted.

Madison's Keep-Your-Priorities-Straight
Seafood Linguine

2 tablespoons butter
2 cloves garlic, minced
1 teaspoon oregano
1 tomato, chopped
1/2 cup scallions, sliced
1/2 cup whipping cream
1/2 cup Swiss cheese, shredded
1/2 cup Parmesan cheese
8 ounces crab meat
8 ounces linguini, cooked

When you're mind is wandering, yank it back on track with something to keep you busy (something besides shopping; I know those Jimmy Choos are calling to you, but you have to earn the money before you can spend it...unless you can buddy up to the folks at Visa). Start with sautéing the garlic and oregano in butter until as tender as new skin after a facial. Add the tomato and scallions, cook for three to five minutes.

Stir in the whipping cream and cheeses. Yes, I know how many calories are in that—you don't have to eat it, just cook it. The whole point is to get your mind off the disappointment you're just about to wreak on your new friends, human and bovine.

Add the seafood, then toss sauce with the linguini. Take a look at those long, straight noodles and tell yourself that the only choice is the one already in line with the ones you made before.

CHAPTER EIGHTEEN

As soon as Madison got back to the house, she called Coop. She needed to leave here in forty-eight hours—sooner, if she could—before she started to consider what Jack had proposed back in the barn. Having Madison Worth permanently working on the farm was akin to having Sylvester Stallone star in a remake of "Tootsie."

In other words, no one would believe it—and it would be a huge flop.

"Your baby will be ready tomorrow," Coop said when he answered the phone, Michael Bublé's "Home" playing in the background. The sound was both melancholy and tender, making Madison think of the very thing the Canadian singer was crooning about.

"She's running like a Rembrandt," Coop said.

"Great." The word came out of Madison's throat, but seemed to get stuck, like a hairball in a cat. She should be overjoyed that she had a way out of here, that she wasn't going to be tied to the cows and the bugs and the manure one second longer than she had to be.

She finally had her transportation to the Maybelline meeting. All she needed to do was tell Jack she was leaving.

And figure out a way to pay Coop. "Uh, how much is this going to cost?" she asked.

He laughed. "A little less than a Picasso knock-off but more than a Thomas Kinkaide." He went on about the reasons why, a blur of words involving things like carburetors and radiator hoses. Damn. Visa definitely wasn't going to pony up that much credit, not with her payment history. There was only one choice left.

Call for a familial donation.

"I was wondering…" Coop began. "How would you feel about a new paint job on the Benz? A little something to jazz her up."

"Jazz her up?"

"Yeah, make her more like her owner. You're way more than a run-of-the-mill, straight-from-the-factory silver. I'll even knock twenty percent off the bill, to have the chance at a foreign canvas."

"Twenty percent?" That brought the number down to a manageable amount. Still, the idea of one of Coop's frenzied Jackson Pollock impressions on her car left her feeling uneasy. "What exactly are you going to do to this canvas?"

"Don't worry. Just embrace your individuality, let it show on your Benz. Make it more fun."

The final word was the one that did it. The last thing she wanted was to prove a four-year-old right. She was fun, dammit, and she was going to prove it, starting with the Benz. "All right," she said, then felt caution grip her intestines. "Just don't make it too… jazzed."

Coop chuckled. "Just enough to help this butterfly come out of her cocoon."

Jack sat in the chair behind his desk later that morning, trying like hell to be businesslike. It was a losing battle, considering Madison was seated across from him in a sundress that might as well have been a slip. The pale yellow fabric glided over her curves, the scalloped edge along her chest an innocent tease for what lay beneath.

Business. Keep his mind on business. Madison had made it clear she wasn't the kind of woman he wanted.

Yeah, well someone needed to get that message through to his body. Because it sure as hell was thinking she was perfect.

"I had an idea," he said.

She nodded, listening. Unconsciously, she slipped one leg on top of the other, her skirt rising a couple of inches, exposing more of that long, creamy, delicious skin.

Jack cleared his throat, tightened his grip on his pencil. "Since I'm paying you for the week and things went faster yesterday than I expected, I was thinking we should add a photo shoot for the dairy farm."

"I thought your emphasis was on the cheese end of the operation."

"It is. But I believe in having my eggs in more than one basket." He pulled a sheaf of papers from his back pocket and spread them over the wood surface of the desk. "I was up last night—"

"Couldn't sleep again?" she said, a soft smile on her face, a smile that spoke of shared experiences.

"I can't sleep ever," Jack said, the words slipping out before he could stop them. He pressed on, pointing to the first drawing. "I'm no Picasso, so ignore the stick figures."

Madison leaned forward, her hair swooping past her shoulders, the scalloped edge of her dress taking a tantalizing dip. "I take it I'm the happy face with the straight line hair?"

"Hey, I put you in a triangle skirt. And gave you long legs." Long, long legs, nowhere near as sexy as the ones a few feet away.

She paused, studying the thumbnails, the pictures he'd sketched of her, beaming beside a cow, as if Pleeseman Milk was her favorite food. "I like this."

"You do?"

"What, you think I'm going to fight you at every turn?"

He grinned. "I thought it might be a hobby of yours."

"I like how you capitalized on the Got Milk concept, but with one of your own. The whole idea of Be Pleesed, with me as the customer who is clearly pleased with the product, is really neat. Different."

"Well, thanks."

"You're welcome." Her attention went to his face, and a long, heated second passed before she looked away. "So, ah, are we shooting this today?"

And then, Jack decided to hell with what Madison had said earlier. Maybe, if she just had a little time to enjoy it, she'd feel differently about the farm. And him.

"Tomorrow," he said, knowing he was playing with fire for what he was about to say next. He should stay here. Work. Fill out some forms for the IRS or something—anything to keep him from the woman who alternately drove him crazy and made him crazy with want. "Today, we're playing hooky."

Smile number four hundred and three crossed her face. "I thought farmers never did that."

"That's why I have employees, as my brother reminds me on a daily basis." His brother had also told him to sleep with her and get her out of his system, but Jack wasn't going to do that. He was simply taking a personal day. "I haven't taken a day off in years."

"I recognize that A-type," she said, a hint of laughter in her voice. Then her eyes brightened, excitement giving a new light to the deep blue hue. "So, where are we going?"

He tick-tocked a finger at her. "It's a surprise."

"You have to give a girl some hint," she said. "Like what to wear?"

Nothing, he wanted to say. Absolutely nothing at all. Or better yet, that leopard print bikini, so he could indulge his own personal *Sports Illustrated* fantasies. "Uh…wear something comfortable. And bring a swimsuit."

If there was a God in heaven, Madison had packed that particular bikini and would gift him with wearing it today.

"Okay. Any more hints?" she asked.

"Just that it'll be fun. I promise," he said.

"Fun," she mused. "I've been looking for some of that." She popped out of her seat. The sundress settled back into place again.

Bummer.

"Give me ten minutes to change into some shorts and grab my swimsuit."

"Ten minutes?" Jack said. "What happened to the forty-five minutes it took you the other day?"

She grinned. "That was just to make you suffer." She leaned over his desk and tipped a finger under his chin, smile number four hundred and four taking over her face, giving her a teasing, happy look. "But you earned beaucoup brownie points this morning when you left that carafe of coffee on my nightstand. Bring me caffeine and I'll love you forever."

Then she was gone, hurrying out of his office and upstairs. He watched her go, wondering how she felt about espresso in the afternoon. Because if Madison Worth was that pleased by a cup of morning Joe, he'd buy a damned Mr. Coffee factory and keep her in coffee twenty-four-seven.

Jack's Don't-Get-Too-Involved Cheese and Crackers

Variety of cheeses, sliced
Wine, anything that tastes good with the cheese
Grapes, for temptation only

Pack all for a picnic, telling yourself all the while that you're just going to eat, maybe take a swim...and definitely not finish what you started in the kitchen.

Definitely not.

Maybe.

CHAPTER NINETEEN

The day of Madison's ninth birthday, she had gone to an amusement park with her cousin Daniel and two of the nannies. Her mother had left the day before for Haiti; Daniel's parents had been on their annual trip to Europe.

Maybe because it was her birthday, maybe because she had been inconsolable, or maybe simply because they pitied her, the nannies had opted for a trip to Nantasket Beach instead of the usual round of private lessons in arithmetic and decorum.

She and Daniel had ditched the nannies and slipped into the line for the giant wooden roller coaster. Daniel, nearly two years older, had just squeaked by on the height requirement. But Madison, already gaining the inches that would predetermine her career path, had passed the marker easily.

Her bravado had left her the minute the roller coaster began clicking its way up the track. Click-click-click, each turn of the wheel bringing them closer to the top—and the terrifying plummet down.

It was pretty much the same feeling, she thought now as she slipped onto an ATV behind Jack. He started the engine, every rumble telling her she was about to go on a ride like no other.

"You okay back there?" he asked.

She nodded and tightened the strap on the heavy helmet, hoping to keep her gray matter from ending up as fertilizer. "Just fine."

"Hold on tight," he said, gripping her hand and planting it on his waist. "And enjoy the ride."

The ATV lurched forward in a plume of smoke and fuel fumes. Madison wrapped her arms around Jack's waist, pressing her cheek to his back. On the roller coaster, she'd been scared.

But here, she felt safe, even as the four-wheeler zipped across the Pleeseman property, tackling the grassy hills with ease. Exhilaration raced through her, coupled with the heat of Jack's body against hers, sending Madison on a thrill ride Disney would be hard pressed to reproduce.

They bumped along on the off-road vehicle for what seemed like miles, driving along something that passed for a road, if one considered a swath of flattened grass a path. After about ten minutes, he turned off suddenly, driving straight into the woods, scrawny branches inches away from scratching the ATV and them. "Are you sure you know where you're going?" she said, ducking to avoid a low-hanging limb.

"Know it like the back of my hand. Now, close your eyes."

"Close my—"

He turned and grinned at her over his shoulder. "I didn't think it would be long before you were arguing with me again. Just close your eyes. I promise, it'll be worth it."

She did as he asked, shutting her eyes *and* her mouth. A moment later, he slowed the four-wheeler to a complete stop.

"Okay, open now."

Madison drew back, opened her eyes, and looked around. "Wow."

She had been on the beaches of the Caribbean, the rugged coastline of Greece, the safari grasslands of Africa. But none of those exotic locales compared to the simple, serene hideaway Jack had brought her to.

They were stopped in the middle of a cozy copse of trees. Meandering through them was a lush green path of grass, tapering down to a glistening lake. Giant flat rocks skirted the edge, inviting someone to sit a while and fish or think or just be.

She slipped off her helmet, getting off the back of the ATV as she did, and was immediately hit by the quiet. Except for the occasional call of a bird and a splash here and there from a jumping fish, the lake was unspoiled, tranquil.

A thick forest of evergreens populated the opposite side, mirrored by the deep blue water. The sun glinted off the water, reflecting in the ripples like tiny diamonds.

"This is…incredible," she said, when he came around the vehicle to join her. "Where are we?"

"Still on Pleeseman land. We don't own the lake but we do own about a mile of the frontage."

She inhaled, drawing in the scent of fresh, unspoiled air and nature at her best. For a moment, living in the Berkshires didn't seem like such a crazy idea. "Why didn't you ever build a house here? If I owned this, I'd just sit on my porch and look at that view every day of my life." Grandfather's house—estate, really—sat on a beautiful piece of land in Brookline. But it was nothing compared to the exquisite view before her.

"It's a bit far from the farm operation and the cheese factory," Jack said. "For a while, my dad was going to build a house. If you look way down that way," he pointed to the left, to an area hidden behind lush foliage, "you might be able to see the concrete foundation he had poured back then. It was supposed to be a surprise for my mother, for their twentieth wedding anniversary."

Madison caught the sudden shadow in Jack's eyes and knew why construction had stopped. "But then she died—"

"And so did the plans for a house." He drew in a breath, his gaze sweeping over the sparkling water before them. "My father has never returned to this spot. Far as he's concerned, this lake doesn't even exist."

"Well, maybe for him, without her, it doesn't. If that makes sense."

"I never thought of it that way, but yeah, I guess you're right. The house was their dream, and without her, the dream vanished." He cleared his throat, then went to the back of the ATV, unhooking a yellow bungee cord and pulling out a cooler, then a blanket he had packed beneath it. "Anyway, I'm not here to resurrect old ghosts, just picnic."

"Is Ginny coming along?" Madison asked.

"Not this time. Harriet has her in the kitchen, baking cookies. I thought it might be nice for us two workaholics to have some…quiet time."

Alone time. No kids, no other adults, not even a cow to interrupt them. Oh boy.

A couple of minutes later, Jack had spread the red plaid blanket out on the grass, then set up an afternoon tableau of wine, cheese, crackers and grapes. "I'm impressed," Madison said. "You thought of everything."

"I had some help. Aunt Harriet made sure I didn't leave without utensils." He held up a set of silverware, all topped by dancing Elvises.

She laughed. "Harriet's the kind of aunt everyone wishes they had." There was more truth in Madison's words than Jack could know. She'd never had a relative who worried so much, expressing her concern for her loved ones in everything from casseroles to spoons. Madison wouldn't have minded having an Aunt Harriet, even if it would have meant dining daily with the dead King of Rock and Roll.

Jack pulled a corkscrew out of the basket, removed the cork, then poured them each a glass of wine, handing her one. She swirled the pale liquid, inhaling its sweet, fruity flavor. "Do I smell pears?"

He nodded. "It's a new blend from one of the local vintners. And we created this," at that, he opened a container to reveal slices of cheese, "to go with it. This is our Apple Cinnamon Jack."

"Named for you?" she asked.

He laughed. "No, the real credit goes to a landowner named David Jacks, who was smart enough to stamp the cheese he made with his own name. He owned 60,000 acres and fourteen dairy farms in Monterey, California back in the 19th century. He took a recipe that had been made by Franciscan monks since the 1700s and made it global, hence the creation of Colby-Jack."

"Smart man," Madison said. "And you have similar plans?"

"Well, not for having a cheese named after me, but to take the family company up a few notches, yeah."

For a second, Madison considered resisting the cheese, the wine. The man. But then she sat back on one elbow and allowed the peacefulness of the location to sweep over her. What would it hurt, to indulge for one day? To forget it all and give in to the thoughts that had nudged her ever since she'd arrived on Pleeseman land.

She withdrew a slice of cheese, taking a bite, savoring it for a moment before drinking from the wine glass. A burst of flavors hit her tongue, from the muted apple of the cheese to the sweet nectar of the wine. "You were right. This is perfect together."

"Did I hear you correctly?" Jack cupped a hand over his ear, teasing her. "Did you just tell me I was right?"

"Hey, don't push your luck, buster. That's a once in a lifetime occurrence."

"Sort of like a solar eclipse, huh?" Jack chuckled and took a piece of cheese, pairing it with a cracker before popping it into his mouth.

They sat there like that for a long while, drinking, eating, laughing and talking about nothing.

It was as if aliens had picked her up and transported Madison to an entirely different world. As the alcohol and the warm sun slipped into her veins, she felt herself relaxing, sinking into the blanket, into him. She stretched out, languid and sated. "Thank you," she said, resting her head in the crook of her arm and looking up at him. The position felt right, perfect.

He smiled down at her, clearly not minding Madison's closeness. "For what?"

"For giving me this." She swept out a hand, indicating the lake, the picnic, all of it. "I've never just... been someplace."

Jack picked up the pile of grapes, dangling the cluster over her lips. "You haven't enjoyed the best part yet."

"Mmmm. What's that?"

"Letting me feed you." His eyes had darkened with desire and Madison felt an immediate twin quickening in her own veins.

She'd tried lingerie, oysters, even a couple of toys from the Lovers Palace store on 42nd Street, but never, ever, had Madison thought of using food as an aphrodisiac.

Until Jack.

"Good timing, because I'm starving," she said, her voice low and husky.

The heavy, fat grapes whispered over her mouth. "Really starving?"

"Ravenous." Madison caught Jack's gaze with her own. Then she opened her mouth, tipped her jaw upward and caught a grape with her teeth, tugging it off the stem.

He watched her every move, still as a statue. When she finished that one, he plucked a second off the vine, then teased it up her chin, along her bottom lip. She opened to the treat, but he danced it away. Madison smiled, then lunged forward, capturing the grape with her mouth, sucking it out of his grasp and taking his fingers into her mouth with a gentle pull.

He swallowed hard, then groaned when she nipped the end of his finger, playing with him as he had played with her. He pulled away only long enough for her to digest the grape and then, his mouth was on hers, hot and frenzied—

And feeding the truly hungry, needy parts of Madison.

He devoured her, as tenderly as he had the grape, but with no mistaking the appetite that lurked inside. This kiss was as heated as the one in the kitchen, but with an edge of something more, something almost…

Reverent. As if this time, he wanted to give her a little dessert with dinner.

She rolled to her side, molding her body to his. Jack went hard, sending an answering tingle through Madison's body. All traces of tranquility disappeared, replaced by a screaming, fiery need to have him.

Madison reached between them, tugging his shirt upward, wanting her hands on his hard chest, to feel the muscles she'd only glimpsed. As she'd dreamed, he was just as hard beneath his shirt, with a physique built from real life, not sculpted by some fascist personal trainer at the 24-hour gym.

She broke away from him, sliding down the length of his body, peppering her kisses along his neck, curving over his shoulder, and then tracing the midline that traveled down his torso. His hands caught in her hair, his breath coming hot and fast. "Madison—"

"Yes," she answered, knowing the question without him even asking it.

He moved over her, planting his legs on either side of hers. Beneath her, the ground was hard, firm. Perfect leverage for what Madison hoped—no, knew—was coming next.

Between them, Jack was working at the buttons of her shirt, but his big hands were no match for the tiny fasteners. "Here, let me," she said, slipping the fasteners apart.

When she was done, she let the shirt fall to the side, exposing her torso to his gaze. He smiled and something warm rushed through Madison's veins. "You wore it," he said.

"Wore what?"

"The *Sports Illustrated* suit."

A heated flush bloomed in her cheeks. "I had no idea you saw that."

"Saw it? I memorized it. When I'm on my deathbed, that'll be the last image I see." He grinned, then dipped his head to kiss the valley between her breasts, his hands going to the silky fabric of the swimsuit, sliding across the sensitive tips of her nipples.

Oh, God. Madison nearly screamed with desire. "Take it off," she begged, wanting only to have his hands on her breasts again, to let him perform an encore of the midnight kitchen meeting.

"Patience, Madison, patience. One piece at a time." In less time than it took to say "zipper," Jack had her shorts undone and had tipped her hips upward, sliding the denim down, revealing the other leopard-printed half.

He drew back, allowing his gaze to rest on her. Madison had been stared at nearly all her life—by the paparazzi, by modeling agencies, by photographers, by strangers on the street.

But none had ever looked at her quite like that, with a mixture of wonder and desire. "You are beautiful," he said.

For the first time in Madison's life, she believed those words. In fact, she felt beautiful, lying there beneath him while he looked at her with that gentle, pleased smile on his face. *This* was the feeling other people had talked about, the same emotion she saw reflected in Daniel's eyes when he looked at his wife.

The kind of feeling she'd been sure didn't exist, at least not for her. As she drank in what she saw in his gaze, it swelled within her heart, quadrupling her desire for this man, this feeling.

"I want you," she whispered. She slipped her hands into the waistband of Jack's shorts, sliding her fingers along his hips, until she reached the snap and zipper that stood between them. With the nimble movements of a woman who spent her days slipping in and out of clothes, she undid his shorts, slid them down his waist. With one hand, Jack removed them the rest of the way, dipping his head to kiss her again, the touch sending her senses into a spiraling, needy frenzy.

Madison slid out from under Jack, tearing off the bikini bottom and tossing it aside. Jack grinned, the light in his eyes dancing with merriment and want. "A woman who goes after what she wants," he said. "I like that."

"And I like this," Madison whispered, dipping her head to kiss him this time, sliding along his body like a cat, stretching the length of him.

"Give me one second," he said, tearing his mouth away from hers long enough to grind the words out. He patted the ground blindly until he hit the cotton fabric of his discarded shorts. He wrestled his wallet out of the back pocket, then flipped open the tri-fold, digging into a small side pocket and coming up with a condom that had clearly been in there for a while.

She grinned. "You do remember how to do this, don't you?"

"If I don't, I'm counting on you to be my tutor."

She laughed, then grabbed his briefs, yanking them down, marveling at the sight of him, full and ready for her. It seemed an interminable wait for him to sheath himself.

And then, she was straddling him, his hands gripping her hips, guiding her and yet, at the same time, allowing her to set the pace, the tone.

Hard and fast was what Madison wanted. Hard and fast helped her forget, for just a moment, that as soon as this was over, she'd go back to being alone. That none of this was really about love.

But Jack had other plans. He groaned, sliding his hands beneath the bikini top, kneading at her breasts, his touch igniting nerve endings, electricity raging through every ounce of her.

"Madison," he said, lifting his head to kiss one breast, taking the nipple into his mouth, sucking gently and sending her spiraling over the edge.

The sun beat down against her back, adding heat where none was needed. The quiet woods surrounded them, forming a private grotto. The rest of the world disappeared, leaving them stranded together on an intimate island.

She'd modeled swimsuits and shot ads in parks and on beaches, but never had Madison done *this* in the outdoors. The sense of doing something illicit only fueled her desire, adding kerosene to an already blazing inferno.

Jack tipped his head back, Madison's name a whisper on his lips, his chest nearly exploding with need for this woman. Above him, she felt perfect, as if someone had taken a model of him and carved this woman to fit exactly against his body. Intuitively, she read his every move, adjusting her position, her touch, to make every movement as powerful as the last.

It wasn't that she was beautiful. It wasn't that she was a famous model, an heiress from a wealthy family. It wasn't even the swimsuit—though that had been a hell of a bonus. It was the way she made him feel as they made love—

As if he mattered.

He caught her by her hips, then reversed their positions, putting himself in the driving seat. He looked down at her, at the priceless sight of ecstasy in her features, then increased his strokes as the desire within him climbed, reaching for the sky, the moon—wherever Madison was going and he was going with her.

"Madison, oh, God, I—" Before the sentence escaped him, the two of them hit the same crescendo, their lovemaking reaching a feverish, heated pitch. A second later, the wave of an orgasm was crashing over him, sweeping Madison up into a dual rush.

At the last second, Jack brought her lips to his; the touch less a kiss and more an intimate joining that deepened the impact of their climax.

It was only after the sensations had ebbed and Madison had slid into the cozy comfort of Jack's arm that Madison knew she was fooling herself if she thought this was just a temporary way to ease the loneliness.

Making love to Jack had been more. So much more.

Adding a complication to Madison's plans to do the job, leave fast and get back to her normal life.

Because already she was craving seconds. Of the wine, the grapes, and most of all, the man.

If Jack had been smart, he would have packed up the picnic, rolled up the blanket and headed back to work. Away from Madison and the brewing connection between them.

Instead, he laid there, with her curved against his body, desire for her already stirring again, and wished the day would never end, that he could stay here forever with this beautiful woman in his arms... and see where else they could go, given enough time alone.

He was playing a very dangerous game. If Alyssa found out he was involved with Madison, she would surely change her mind about Ginny's custody, if only out of spite. If there was one thing his ex-wife didn't want to see, it was Jack happy.

He attributed it to some twisted guilt on Alyssa's part, the same guilt that had made her turn her repeated affairs into something that was his fault, rather than her own doing. As if his choosing to save the family business was enough to drive her into another man's arms, rather than her own ambition for the big house, the big car and the big life.

Ever since the divorce, Alyssa had continued her emotional assault on Jack, maybe because she thought that by making him unhappy she could justify her choices, or anger him enough that she could leave without a backwards glance.

Jack pushed the thoughts of Alyssa aside and turned again to Madison, placing a soft kiss on top of her golden hair.

For now, for just an hour more, he didn't want to think about what would happen after he returned to the farm. He had one of the most beautiful women in the world in his arms and he was damned well going to savor every last second.

He'd deal with the topsy-turvy confusion running through his heart later.

"You sure know how to pack a picnic," she said, her voice lazy and quiet. "That was…incredible."

"Wait till you see what I do for a cross-country road trip."

She laughed, the sound as full-bodied as the wine. Then she sighed, snuggling against him and touching a part of his heart he thought he'd lost when his marriage had gone south. "It's beautiful here." She drew in a breath, closing her eyes. "'On either side the river lie long fields of barley and of rye that clothe the world and meet the sky.'" Madison tipped her head back and looked up at the blueness that peeked between the canopy of trees. "That's what it seems like here, like the world is clothed in those fields."

"I've heard those lines before," he said. "In college. It's..." he paused. "Tennyson, right?"

"Yes." She smiled. "You surprise me, Jack."

"Hey, I'm more than just milking cows and pressing cheese. And you, you're not just about make-up and clothes," he said, turning to look at her, bringing their bodies together, front to front. The position, ironically, seemed even more intimate than their lovemaking had been. It seemed to call for the sharing of secrets, the baring of souls.

She shook her head. "I don't know about that. A lot of times, I feel more like The Lady of Shalott."

"The woman in that poem," he added, remembering now the gist of the Tennyson tale. "Wasn't she cursed or something? To weave instead of being able to see the world?"

"Worse," Madison said. "She was only allowed to glimpse Camelot through a mirror."

"Is that how you feel?" he asked, studying the woman who had made her living from her flawless image. "That you're trapped in a mirror?"

There was a glimmer of something in her eyes that told Jack he'd come close to the truth about Madison Worth. A truth she clearly didn't want to discuss. She rolled over, turning away. "Sometimes."

"Camelot is right here, Madison," Jack said, leaning over her, making a sweeping gesture toward the lake, wishing he could package this, give it to her.

Or better yet, share it with her today, tomorrow and all the tomorrows to come. Because she'd opened up a part of him he'd thought was dead. Because of the tender way she'd played with his daughter. But most of all, because he wanted to hold onto this afternoon for as long as he could. "Leave the mirror behind and stay here. With me."

"I can't." She shook her head, avoiding his gaze.

"Why not?" Jack clasped her hand, drew in a breath and took an even bigger chance. "Stay here, Madison. Not because you're working for me, but because you want to be with me."

She pulled her hand out of his and got to her feet suddenly, stepping over him to retrieve her swimsuit and pull it back on. "It's hot. I'm going for a swim in the lake." Before he could say a word, she was heading down the grassy path to the water.

He retrieved his own shorts, then hurried to catch up with her. "Not so fast. I may be a guy, but even I can tell when someone is avoiding the subject."

She ignored him, continuing until she reached the water's edge, the lake lapping gently against her toes. In the distance, Jack heard the high pitched whine of a saw slicing through wood. He glanced at the woods, but the thick green foliage didn't show any activity. He shrugged it off.

"I can't stay, Jack," Madison said. "I have to—" She cut herself off, biting her lip. "Today was beautiful, wonderful," for a second, her face grew wistful, "but I don't think I should be with you in anything other than a professional sense. That's good for your business, and for mine."

Then Madison strode into the lake, dipping her body underwater, the leopard print bikini disappearing in the darkness of the lake, along with the woman who'd starred in his fantasies, brought one to life, and then jerked it all away.

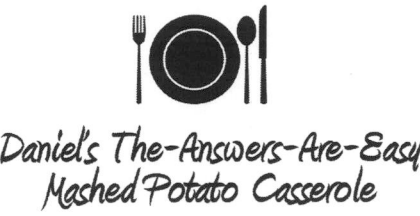

Daniel's The-Answers-Are-Easy Mashed Potato Casserole

1 28-ounce bag frozen mashed potatoes, cooked
3/4 cup sour cream
2 eggs
1/2 cup scallions, sliced
1/2 teaspoon salt
1/4 teaspoon pepper
1 cup cheddar, shredded, divided

I know from experience that sometimes, the perfect person for you is standing right there—but you're making it all too hard. Think of it like making this casserole. Don't take the hard route when the easy one gets you to the same destination.

Preheat your oven to 375 degrees. Mix all the ingredients together, reserving 1/2 cup of cheddar cheese. Pour into a greased casserole dish and bake 30 minutes, uncovered. Add the rest of the cheddar on top and bake until the cheese is melted and gooey, pretty much like the sticky mess you've made of things so far.

Serve to Mr. Right and if you need a little love inspiration, take a peek at the cake decorator who captured my heart.

CHAPTER TWENTY

The leopard print swimsuit sat in a puddle on the floor, looking like roadkill gone horribly awry.

Madison stared into the mirror at her vanity table and knew she was in serious trouble, way more trouble than when she'd thrown the cake in Kate Moss's face. The uproar over that had been a minor tremor compared to the personal earthquake she'd just launched today.

By starting to fall in love with Jack Pleeseman.

Her heart had lost the battle long before they'd made love. It started the day he took her seriously.

Never before had anyone—especially a man—listened to her. Those with testosterone usually didn't see past the breasts and blond hair to realize she had something more to offer than a pair of 36Cs. But Jack...Jack had looked at her and he hadn't seen just a model—he'd seen a smart, capable woman.

The kind of woman Madison had dreamed of being, way back before she'd ever stood in front of a camera lens. Then she'd realized pretty quickly at NYU that she had about the same chances of making it in college as a duck living in the desert.

Jack, however, saw her differently. She'd felt it in the way he kissed her, the touch of his hands on her body, but especially in the way he talked to her, like an intellectual equal.

In love. The thought sent a thrill of discovery, then a lurching, constricting fear through her veins.

She was playing with fire. This was no Campfire Girl s'mores blaze, it was an all out, run-for-the-hills volcano, ready to spew lava all over her efforts to reconstruct her life, her career. The last thing Madison needed was a mess like that.

So she'd do the next best thing—run. Leave him before he could leave her, and disappoint her like so many others had done. Tomorrow, she'd be gone, heading back to New York. Unfortunately, it was a few days too late to save her heart.

Madison stared at her reflection in the vanity table mirror, made a goofy face, stuck out her tongue, then shook her head. "Who are you?" she whispered to the image.

The mirror didn't have any answers. Neither did she. A week ago, she'd thought she knew what she wanted—to restore her career as quickly as possible, leaving everything bovine far behind. And now it was possible. All she'd ever wanted was within her grasp, a mere three hours away in New York, waiting for her to show up.

The trouble was, Madison didn't want to leave. Some insane part of her was itching to stay right here. Clearly, she'd been using too much hairspray.

Her styling products weren't just eating away the ozone layer—they were sucking up her brain cells.

She was a *Worth*. A model—the "super" prepend had gone flying with the cake—but still, a model. She could have the entire world at her fingertips—

And all she could think about was this tiny corner of the Berkshires.

Madison dug her cell phone out of her purse. On the missed calls list, she saw two from her Grandfather. She sighed, delaying that return call, and instead punched in Daniel's number. He answered on the third ring, caught in the middle of a laugh as he said "hello." Not for the first time, Madison marveled at the change in her cousin since he'd married Olivia Regan. "Hey, Daniel."

"Well, what do you know, it's my long-lost cousin."

"Ha, ha, very funny. I go, what, a week without talking to you and you already have an APB out?"

In the background, she heard Olivia call out, "Hello, Madison!" Olivia's sister, Josie, shouted the same, telling Madison that Daniel was inside Pastries with Panache, Olivia's Boston pastry shop. He retreated there often to write—and keep his new bride company.

"I worry about you, Mad," Daniel said, his voice sober with concern. "You've pretty much dropped out of sight since that cake thing."

She clutched the slim silver cell phone to her ear. It had always been like this—her and Daniel, as close as a brother and sister. Their lives had been nearly twin reflections, both lacking in parental involvement and normalcy. Over the years, it had drawn them into a kinship based on shared disappointments and broken promises. "I'm okay," she said.

"You sound anything but. What happened, did you run out of cake? Dipping into a brownie stash for ammunition?"

She rolled her eyes. Daniel was the only one in the world who could tease her about the Kate Moss incident—and live to laugh at his own jokes. "Remind me again why I call you."

He chuckled. "Because I'm the only person in the world who understands how you can be wealthy and totally screwed up."

"Believe me, I've got the screwed up part down." She sighed, toying with the hairbrush on her table. "I think I might have fallen in love."

He let out a low whistle. "It's about damned time. It's lonely being the only Worth registered at Nordstrom's."

The tension in Madison's stomach quadrupled at the word *registered*. "Whoa, don't be marrying me off. You know how I feel about marriage. It's a hobby for other people."

"Marriage is not a hobby, Mad."

"I know." She sighed. "It's also not for me. Could you see me, wearing an apron, cooking bacon for some guy, then sitting back on the sofa with him every night to watch *Jeopardy!*?"

"Actually, I could," he said softly, then chuckled. "Although, I've tasted your pretty pathetic attempts at cooking, so in my mind, your husband is about as well fed as Niles Crane."

She laughed. "You're mean. But I still love you."

"Seriously, Madison, falling in love isn't so bad. I did it. Got married. And now, I'm even reproducing."

Madison gasped. "Olivia's pregnant? Oh wow, Daniel, congratulations!" For just a second, an insane twitch of jealousy ran through Madison. She was definitely inhaling too many CFCs. Madison was far, far from wife and mother material.

"Yep. She's due right before Christmas." The pride and excitement was clear in Daniel's every syllable.

"How'd Grandfather take the news?"

"Are you kidding me? He's turned into SuperGrandpa. Stopped going to his weekly poker game with the buddies just to have time to visit us. He's already sent us enough gifts to outfit an entire nursery three times over, calls Olivia almost every day to be sure she's eating right and taking good care of his grandbaby. You'd think this was his kid." Daniel laughed. "He's even talking about changing diapers."

Madison couldn't imagine her stern, standoffish grandfather handling the Pampers and Huggies wipes. "It's scary to see what happens when old men get senile."

"No, that's the weirdest part. Ever since he had his heart attack and cut back on his working hours, he seems determined to get involved with me, with Olivia, with every family member within a two-hundred mile radius." Daniel paused, drew in a breath. "He's asking about you."

"I'm fine." Talking to Grandfather would mean telling him what had happened during Fashion Week, and where she was working now—assuming the *People* magazine report hadn't already reached him—but most of all, it would mean admitting she had failed.

That was a conversation Madison would save for another day. In 2038.

"You already told me that," Daniel said. "So fine that you fell in love? Broke your cardinal rule?"

The trouble with making cardinal rules was that everyone liked to remind you about them just when you were trying to forget you broke them. More than once.

Madison was done with the discussion of love. It wasn't a topic she wanted to visit, not now. A smart woman would stick to the subject of work. Work never let her down. Work never broke her heart. "How'd you do it?" she asked her cousin.

"Do what?"

"Go out on your own and be successful. Not to mention, manage to escape the family expectations?"

"Madison, I hate to be the one to tell you this, but the real expectations in this family come from yourself."

"That's not true. You know Grandfather."

"If there's anything this past year has taught me," he said, "it's that Grandfather respects people who go after what they're meant to do, what they feel passionate about."

Madison sat back in the small chair and looked at the stranger facing her in the mirror. "That's the whole trouble," she said. "I'm not so sure what I want anymore."

"Sure you do. You want to be happy, healthy and loved."

Yeah, well, she'd thought she'd had that with Renaldo and learned that happy and love didn't go together. "What about wealthy?"

He paused, and through the phone line, Madison could almost see him looking at his wife and the burgeoning life inside her. From cell tower to cell tower, Madison could feel Daniel's contentment, happiness. "Wealth is overrated," he said softly. "Love is all you need."

She laughed. "You sound like a bad country song."

"Yeah, I probably do," Daniel replied, chuckling. "But it's a tune I bet you'll be singing soon."

"Daddy?"

Jack looked up at the sound of Ginny's voice, a double-purple square card in his hands. "Yeah?"

"I don't wanna go to England." Ginny plopped her chin into her hands and stared glumly at the Candyland board.

"Why not?"

"I don't like tea." Her face scrunched with a non-verbal eww. "Or crumples."

"Crumpets," he corrected gently. "That's okay, kiddo, neither do I." Not that he even knew what crumpets were, but anything that far from home sounded awful to his ears, especially when he pictured Ginny across the world, sipping real tea instead of hosting pretend tea parties just down the hall.

"Yeah, but you get to stay here. With Grandpa and Aunt Harriet and Uncle David and Madison and Katydid and even Ellie."

Jack gave Ginny a smile, but inside, a painful ache tightened in his chest. "I don't want you to go to England either, sweetie. If you do, who's going to name all the new calves?"

"That's what I told Mommy...Mummy," Ginny added, correcting herself.

Jack held his breath, afraid to ask the next question. "And what did Mommy say?"

Ginny shrugged. "She said 'we'd see.' That's like maybe, isn't it?"

"Yeah, pretty much."

"I don't like maybe." Ginny's shoulders sagged. "It always means no."

"Not always, kiddo," Jack said, reaching out and drawing Ginny into his lap. Inhaling her sweet goodness, committing every ounce of her to memory. "Sometimes it turns into yes."

Jack prayed that this time, Alyssa's answer would be yes, and that she would give Jack custody of this four-year-old half of his heart.

Ginny looked up, her cherubic face seeming wiser than it should be. "Can I live here, Daddy? Can you tell Mommy I can't go live with the queen?"

Jack drew his daughter into a tight hug, burying his nose in her Johnson & Johnson scented curls. "I want you here every day, every minute, Ginny. If you move to England, I don't know what I'll do."

"Will you cry?"

He already felt a catch in his throat, just thinking about the prospect of his daughter on the other side of the world. "Yes, Ginny, I'd cry. A lot."

"Will you talk to Mommy? Tell her I hate tea and I have to stay here so all the baby cows get names?"

"You betcha," he said, the words far lighter than the heaviness weighing on his shoulders, lumping in his throat. "But you have to remember, Mommy is your mother and she gets to have a say, too. She and I have to make this decision together."

Ginny nodded the nod of a child who doesn't like the answer she's getting. She sighed. "I wish you were married to Madison."

That was a path even Jack hadn't traveled down. "Why's that?"

"Because then she could be my mommy and I could live here with both of you. And Madison could help me name the cow babies. And we'd play with Ella Mae and I'd show her my dolls and we could play house and—"

"Whoa there, partner. Madison isn't staying. She has to go back to New York."

Ginny's eyes met his. "Why?"

"Because that's where she lives."

"Why?"

"Because that's where she works."

"Nuh-uh. She works here."

"That's only for a little while. Most of her work is in New York." He needed to keep that in mind, before he got too wrapped up in Madison's piercing blue eyes.

"Why can't it be here?" Ginny asked.

"Because..." Jack's voice trailed off. Why couldn't it be here? Why couldn't Madison stay here? New York was only a few hours away, the airport even closer, why couldn't she maintain her career and stay with him? For a second, it seemed possible, even plausible, and then Jack remembered the biggest roadblock had nothing to do with distance. "Because she'd have to want to stay."

Ginny scrambled off his lap and got to her feet, grabbing Bear-Bear out of his place as the third Candyland competitor. Bear-Bear, sadly, was winning. "That's easy."

"What's easy?"

"Making Madison want to stay. All she has to do is love us."

Then Ginny was dashing out of her room, presumably off to convince Madison that a dairy farm was the perfect home for a Manhattan model/Boston heiress.

Jack leaned against Ginny's bed. "Yeah, Gin. If only it were that easy."

Aunt Harriet's Everyone-Needs-Family Fettuccini Alfredo

1 pound fettuccini noodles, cooked
1 pint heavy cream
1/2 cup unsalted butter, softened
1 cup freshly grated Parmigiano-Reggiano
1/8 teaspoon nutmeg
Freshly cracked black pepper

Put on your blue suede shoes and start dancing because mood is everything when you cook. If you're in a happy mood, you'll undoubtedly add a little of that to your sauce, making that family dinner a success. A good way to deal with a certain grumpy brother.

Start by heating the heavy cream over low to medium heat—but don't let it boil or this will all be ruined. A gentle, loving heat is all you need. Use a deep sauté pan so you have lots of room for the lovin' feeling of cheese. Add the butter, whisk it (being sure not to rattle and roll your pan) until melted. Now add the miracle of the cheese, stirring until it's well mixed.

You're almost ready to rock and roll, and get the family singing around the table. Add the nutmeg and just the right touch of pepper, then toss your noodles in the sauce. You'll have Girls! Girls! Girls! scrambling for the dinner table in no time. Now, if those guys could just fall in love with what's right in front of their eyes, you'd be all set.

CHAPTER TWENTY-ONE

Aunt Harriet was putting her foot down and holding the fettuccini hostage. "Joseph, we need to sit down at the table like an ordinary family."

"Give me my damned dinner, Harriet. And let me eat in peace. In the living room. Alone." Joe lunged for the plate in his sister's hands.

"No." She swung the dish behind her back and out of his grasp.

From his station by the doorway—and out of the fray—Jack stifled a chuckle. Beside him, David bit his lip, keeping back a laugh of his own. Aunt Harriet and their father had this argument at least quarterly. Never before, however, had she used his favorite meal as leverage.

"We have a guest," Aunt Harriet said, "and it's not right for us to scatter like roaches the minute the oven timer goes off. For God's sake, Joe, Nancy would have never stood for this."

"Nancy isn't here to argue," Joe said, going for the plate again, feinting to the right, then reaching on the left.

But his sister was faster. "Your boys need to eat like a family."

"My boys are all grown up and don't need a damned thing."

"Joseph Pleeseman, I have half a mind to dump this plate on your head." She raised it, the threat clear in her eyes. "Now you either sit down here with all of us, like a real family, or you'll be dining on Buster's kibble."

From under the table, the dog let out a yip of objection.

"Women," Joe muttered. He turned to his sons. "Come on, you two. I'm not doing this alone."

"One of you go get Madison," Aunt Harriet said. "I'll call Ginny in and we can all eat together, like one big happy family." She got up, went to the back door to yell Ginny's name. A second later, Ginny had come inside and went to wash her hands.

"I'll go get Madison," David volunteered. "Unless Jack wants to claim dibs first." He sent a teasing grin his brother's way.

"She's my employee, not my girlfriend," Jack replied, shrugging as if he didn't give a damn who went upstairs to tell Madison dinner was on the table. He plopped down into one of the kitchen chairs, preventing his feet from making his mouth a liar. David loped off, taking what seemed like an hour to go upstairs and bring Madison back.

Jack should have been glad. Earlier that day at the lake, Madison had effectively ended the personal relationship, leaving everything all business between them. Despite Ginny's mission to make Madison fall in love with the farm and them, Jack knew the worst possible match for him was a woman whose life was wrapped up in Tiffany chandeliers and Faberge eggs. The only thing he'd wanted was a woman who saw support and marriage as a two-way street, one where they each believed in the other's dreams and stood by in times of need.

He'd thought Alyssa was that woman, but from the moment he slipped the gold band on her finger, she had proved the opposite.

Madison seemed different, but Jack was the kind of guy who only had to burn his hand once to know touching the hot stove was a stupid move.

If that was the case, then why had he started falling for her? Somewhere between the kitchen sink and the picnic blanket, something in Jack's scorched heart had begun to come back to life, like a forest recovering from a campfire gone wrong.

It wasn't her looks that had tipped him over the edge, it had been her feisty determination, coupled with the tender way she had connected with his daughter. He looked over at Ginny, who had just come back from the restroom and scrambled into one of the chairs, her fork at the ready, and smiled.

If there was a way to Jack's heart, it was definitely through Ginny.

Nevertheless, he wasn't going to trust these feelings, to let himself get wrapped up in thoughts of building a life with another woman whose own life existed in another stratosphere. Because Jack knew, as surely as he knew the ghost of Elvis would be here for his cuppa at three, that falling in love again would only lead to disaster.

But then, the moment Madison appeared in the doorway, all long legs, knee-length teal capris and sleeveless, silky black shirt, he forgot all those fancy resolutions he'd just made. Instead, he concentrated on staying in his chair, instead of lunging for her like she was his own personal plate of fettuccini.

Madison entered the room, slipping into the empty chair across from Jack and Ginny. "Thank you for calling me down for dinner," she said to Aunt Harriet.

"Anytime, dear," Aunt Harriet said, patting Madison's hand. "Even if those big lugs are as rude as bulls at a watering trough." She shook her head. "They'd never fit in at Graceland."

Jack didn't ask if his aunt was talking about the bulls or the male Pleeseman members.

Watching his father and David dishing up their dinner from the stove—ignoring Aunt Harriet's suggestion that they eat family style instead—Jack had to agree. It had been so long since any of them had dined together in a group that their manners seemed to have fallen by the wayside. There was no saying of grace, no waiting for all to be served before digging in, just a help-yourself-and-don't-bother-with-conversation foodfest.

"Grandpa," Ginny said while trying to wrangle a fettuccini noodle onto her fork, "how come you don't like to eat with Daddy? Does he burp too much?"

"I like to eat while I'm watching the news, that's all."

Aunt Harriet harrumphed. "From now on, we're all eating together. CNN will repeat the news every thirty minutes." She cast a warning glance at Joe. "At least one meal a day, we can pretend to be a family."

"Why do we have to pretend?" Ginny asked. "Aren't we already a real family?"

Joe laughed, then reached out to ruffle his granddaughter's hair. "Yeah, pumpkin, we are. And I'll try harder to remember that."

Jack and David began ribbing each other, joking about the pick-up truck. "Don't you think, big brother, that when the front bumper runs away, it's time to spring for a new vehicle?" David said.

"Hey, that truck is just fine. And I know right where the bumper is. Somewhere off of Wheeler Road."

David laughed. "You and that truck. The thing is an eyesore. Go test drive a new Sierra and then see if you want to get back inside that thing."

"I like my truck. It's like a pair of jeans. Breaking in a new one is way too much work."

David grinned. "Then buy the new one for me. I'll break it in for you."

Madison twirled several fettuccini noodles onto her fork, then popped the bite into her mouth. The creamy Alfredo sauce sent smooth comfort through her body, into the parts that seemed perpetually empty. She took another bite, and then a third, the thought of calories a million miles away as she listened to the Pleeseman family tease each other with the good nature of people who had spent most of their lives in close proximity.

"So, Madison, tell us about your family," Harriet said, clearly determined to draw her silent guest into the conversation.

"There's really not much to tell," Madison said, opting for another bite instead of sharing more information.

"There's always something to tell," Harriet said, taking the bowl of peas and dishing up a heaping portion on her own plate before passing the bowl to Madison. "Did you all eat together every night? Or did your father," at this, she gestured toward Joe, "try to avoid the table at all costs?"

"I...I never knew my father," she said. All eyes swiveled toward her, a human spotlight far brighter than any that had shone on the catwalk.

"That's 'cuz he died," Ginny added.

"Oh, you poor thing," Harriet said. "Did your mother ever remarry?"

"Will you leave her alone?" Joe said. "For God's sake, Harriet, you're giving me indigestion. Can't we just eat without talking?"

"That's what the cows do. I'd like to think we're a little further along the evolution scale." She eyed her brother. "But maybe not." Harriet turned toward David, a friendly smile on her face. "Tell me, David, how was your day?"

"Not nearly as fun as Jack's." He gave his brother a teasing grin, then oomphed when Jack kicked him under the table. David had seen them returning on the ATV and clearly added two and two.

"Oh! I nearly forgot," Harriet said, turning her attention to the other Pleeseman son. "You and Madison went on a picnic. Did you have a nice time?"

Madison felt her face heat up. A nice time. Oh yeah, they'd had a nice time. Some of that niceness was still tingling inside her whenever she looked at Jack. Her body wanted an instant replay—

But her mind kept hitting the Stop button.

"We had…fun," Jack said, turning toward her. "Didn't we, Madison?"

"Oh, yeah. The…swimming was great."

"You were out at the lake today?" Joe asked. "Why didn't you tell me you were going out there?"

"I thought I was old enough not to need permission." Jack grinned.

Joe stood abruptly, throwing his napkin onto the table. "This is what I hate about this family. Too damned much meddling." He directed his attention to his eldest son. "You have a business to run. You don't have time to be playing in the water. If you can't run the company, then I'll damned well do it for you."

Then he grabbed his plate and stomped off, heading into the den. A second later, Madison could hear the muted sounds of the news coming from the TV.

"Well," Harriet said, giving Madison a smile that wobbled with disappointment. "I think we all need a little practice at this eating together thing."

"Do you think Grandpa knows he can't have any pie if he didn't say 'xcuse me?" Ginny said, her little brow furrowed with concern.

Everyone laughed. "If he doesn't know it now, he will by Thanksgiving," Harriet muttered. "Because I'll deliver his pumpkin pie, straight onto his La-Z-Boy cushions."

Jack's The-Cheese-Hits-The-Fan Bacon and Cheese Quiche

1 pound bacon
1/2 small onion, diced
10 eggs
2 cups milk
1/2 teaspoon salt
1/4 teaspoon pepper
1/8 teaspoon ground nutmeg
3 cups Swiss cheese, shredded
1/4 pound ham, cooked and diced

The other shoe has dropped. Before you take it out on that new woman in your house, try a little meat and cheese. Preheat the oven to 350 degrees. Cook the bacon until crisp, drain on paper towels, then crumble, taking out your frustrations on the pork instead of other people.

In two tablespoons of the bacon drippings (a sure way to make a guy meal is to use bacon grease), cook the onions until translucent. Using a separate bowl (I know, there's two dishes already to wash. But a man's gotta eat and he's gotta keep his mind off that phone call bombshell), beat the eggs, then add milk, nutmeg, salt and pepper.

Add in all but 1/4 cup each of the bacon and cheese and pour into a greased two-quart baking dish. If you have trouble figuring out which one is the two-quart, don't worry. Just pick something ovenproof and big enough to fit the eggs. Good enough, I say. Sprinkle the reserved cheese and bacon on top.

Now that's a meal for a man. Bake it for 35-40 minutes, until you can slip a knife into the center and it comes out clean. Or until your stomach says it's done. For best non-jiggle results, let it sit for ten minutes before eating. Gives you time to curb that temper before it lashes out at the one you kissed in Aisle Seven.

CHAPTER TWENTY-TWO

Kitty Dandy hadn't wasted any time. Jack hung up the phone, the remains of his dinner churning in his gut. Alyssa was on the rampage—and Jack knew exactly who to blame.

He headed into the kitchen, where Madison was helping Aunt Harriet finish drying the last of the dishes. "I need to talk to you, Madison," he said.

"Sure." She tossed the towel onto the counter, then went to pull out a chair at the table, but Jack stopped her.

"This isn't a conversation I want to have in the house," Jack said.

Aunt Harriet took one look at him and instantly read his face. "I'll go see if Ginny wants to beat me at checkers, keep her occupied for a bit."

"Thanks." Jack didn't want his daughter overhearing this conversation, nor did he want to let his family in on the latest of Alyssa's stunts. They had enough on their plate without him adding this.

He pulled his keys out of the pocket of his jeans, then headed out of the house and toward the truck, moving so fast, Madison practically had to run to keep up with him.

"What is your problem?" she said, grabbing his arm when they were outside. "Why are you so mad at me all of a sudden?"

"I just got a phone call from my lawyer. My ex has heard about my 'new fiancé' and has rethought custody." He cursed, then glared at Madison, blaming her even though he knew he really wanted to be shouting at Alyssa. "That little supermarket stunt is going to cost me everything."

"Excuse me, but what does my telling Kitty Dandy we're engaged have anything to do with your ex-wife?"

"Kitty is Alyssa's sister."

"She's her…" Madison paused as those words sank in. "Really?"

"Yeah. Trust me, Alyssa got the hell out of *that* gene pool as fast she could. Wouldn't want any of her socialite friends to know she's just a dairy farmer's daughter. Or the farmer's ex-wife." He cursed and walked away, determined not to have this conversation. Talking about his ex-wife was like igniting a bad case of acid reflux. There wasn't a Tums big enough to handle the burning in his gut.

"Will you quit walking away from me?" Madison said, catching up with him again. "In case you haven't noticed, I'm wearing high heels."

He glanced back, saw the ridiculous shoes she was teetering along in and stopped. "Sorry. I'm angry as hell and taking it out on you." He slowed his pace, keeping his mouth shut until they reached the truck.

"Why does your ex hate you so much?" Madison said when they were both settled inside.

"Don't worry about it." He inserted the key into the ignition and turned it on. The truck sputtered a bit, before the engine finally caught. Another thing that was wearing out on the Pleeseman farm. His shoulders hunched, weighed down by the responsibility and worries sitting on them. "It's my problem, not yours."

"Yeah, but I obviously stirred up a hornet's nest at the supermarket. Jack, I never meant to hurt you or your daughter. When I said it, I didn't even know you had a daughter, that you were battling custody, that Kitty was your ex-sister-in-law." She turned toward him. "You haven't exactly been the most forthcoming guy in the world."

"Do you want me to be?" He didn't know what he wanted anymore—if his plan to stay away was smart, or if he'd be smarter to dive right in and take his chances at love again. Madison wasn't helping things by sending out contradictory messages. "At the lake, you made it clear we were just working together from here on out, nothing more. What was all that about in the kitchen, Madison? And at the lake? What, was I just a temporary distraction for you?"

"I, ah, lost track," she said.

Jack swung the truck out of the driveway and onto the main road. "Track of what?"

"Of my goals. It won't happen again."

And so had he. He was supposed to be focused on the business, on his daughter. He'd fooled himself this afternoon into thinking a love affair between a farmer and a model could be something of substance, that it could last beyond the assignment.

Yet, a very big part of him did, indeed, want the two of them to share something more than just sex. Wanted to believe that what had happened back at the lake had meant far more than just quenching a thirst.

Even if it had, it didn't change the basic facts: they came from not only two different worlds, but two radically opposite planets. He was never going to live in New York, she would never settle in on a farm, no matter how much Ginny tried to convince them both that happily ever after was a possibility.

Beside him, Madison reached up to brush her hair out of her face. The movement caused her sleeveless shirt to peek open, giving him an all-too-brief peek at a black lace bra. Jack swerved, then jerked his attention back to the road instead of her.

What he needed was a pair of blinders. Because whenever Madison was around, he was distracted as a mustang running in a field of available mares. His testosterone was staging a coup against his mind. He needed, especially now, to keep his focus on the business, on Ginny.

Madison averted her gaze, staring instead out the window at the road. "So, what's your plan, Jack?"

The truck chugged along, bouncing and dipping in the rough road. "Undoubtedly, the entire county has been told by the Kitty bullhorn that you're my 'fiancé,'" he said. "Since Dandy Diary will have a strong presence at the wine festival, I suppose the best thing to do is—"

"Continue the charade?" she finished for him.

"I was going to say tell the truth. I'm not a man given to lying."

"And what will telling the truth accomplish?" Madison put up a finger to cut off Jack's protest. "Don't get me wrong, I'm not a pathological liar myself, but one thing you learn pretty quickly in the modeling world is that everything is about deception. The clothes don't really fit that well—they're pinned and clipped and taped. The faces are airbrushed, the cellulite scrubbed away by a computer. Breasts are enhanced, eyes made bluer to match a shirt. It's all a matter of illusion."

"David Copperfield for advertising?"

"In a way, yes. And maybe..." she began, thinking, "maybe our engagement could work out, if you played along."

He shook his head. "I don't need a pretend wife."

"Oh, I wouldn't actually marry you," Madison said, and something in Jack's chest panged hard. If he hadn't known better, he would have said it was disappointment that she shot that answer back so quickly. "But I think you can use this to your advantage."

He took a right, not driving anywhere in particular, trying only to escape the stress and worry. "Meaning?"

"Do you know who I am?" she asked.

"Of course I do. I hired you."

"Yes, but, do you know what being involved with someone like me, someone with my last name, could mean to your business?" Madison turned in the seat to face him, drawing one leg up beneath her, apparently unaware of what such a move could do to a man's blood pressure. "Wealth, fame. It's like an *E True Hollywood Story* waiting to happen."

He scowled. "I don't use people for their last name."

"For God's sake, Jack, you damned well better start." She threw up her hands, clearly frustrated with him. "Listen, the way I see it, Kitty Dandy would love to eat you alive and have Cheese Pleese for dessert."

"Yeah."

"And from what I gathered after meeting Alyssa, she'd be all over the entrails."

"Thanks for the image of my demise, but yeah, you're right."

She reached out a hand, laying a light, concerned touch on his arm. "Then why are you letting them manipulate you? Why not do a little of the manipulating back?"

"You've forgotten one important detail," Jack said, feeling every fiber of his being begin to shred at the mere thought of losing Ginny, "my daughter. Alyssa would do anything to take her away."

"Even if she could brag to her society friends that her daughter is part of the Worth family? I know George Thurgood's father and if there's one thing he'd love more than anything, it's a link to old money, no matter how tenuous the connection. Particularly my grandfather's fortune since the two of them are big on dollars and cents one-upmanship."

Madison had read Alyssa and her financial motives perfectly. Yet, Jack also knew, his ex's reactions were often unpredictable. "It could just as easily go the other way. Alyssa is determined to see me suffer."

"Because you did it to her?" Madison's question cut through the quiet of the truck's interior.

He swallowed hard, the taste of bile thick in his throat. Weariness filled him. He had driven enough, the miles he'd put on the truck finally expending his anger and frustration. He turned into an empty lot, parked the truck and shut off the ignition. "The only way I made her suffer was by marrying her. All the rest she brought on herself." He shook his head, then went on, his voice lowering into the quiet range of a man sharing details he'd kept to himself for too many years. "She was the one who was cheating. She was the one who broke all the promises." He draped his arms over the steering wheel. "Except one."

Madison didn't say anything. She merely waited, sitting in the truck.

He sighed, not wanting to go on, to open this wound. But when he glanced at Madison, he saw true concern in her cobalt eyes. For the first time in a long time, Jack felt like he had an ally outside of his family. "When I married Alyssa, I promised her that we'd get the hell out of this town. That we'd never come back to the dairy business ever again. And when I broke that promise, she thought it was okay to break all of hers, too."

"Because you didn't maintain the life she envisioned," Madison said quietly, as if someone had done that to her, too.

"Yeah." It hadn't been the life *he'd* envisioned, either, when he'd blown out of this town, thinking he was leaving the Berkshires behind for the career-driven hubbub of Boston.

"What changed your mind?" she asked.

"Ginny."

When Jack said the name of his daughter, a soft smile stole over his face, a smile of true adoration. Madison swallowed back her envy for a four-year-old girl who had a parent who loved her with such power, for a father who looked like that at the mere vocalization of his daughter's name.

"When she was born," he went on, "it changed everything for me. I'd been resisting my mother's legacy—she left her half of the business to me but I hadn't done anything about it up until then. But when Ginny was born, my priorities shifted. I wanted to bring her up here, surrounded by family, and work a job that allowed me to duck out early for school pageants and soccer games."

What would it have been like to grow up with a father like that? Or a mother who had made it a priority to attend even half her school events? Madison looked at Jack and saw the man before her with new eyes. A powerful feeling began to take root in her heart. "Ginny's lucky to have a dad like you."

He shook his head. "I don't know about that. Every time I try to do the right thing, it backfires."

"There are few men," Madison said, "who would do what you did."

"Well, none of it's going to matter, if I don't have Ginny." He leaned back against the seat, resting his head on the worn vinyl, and let out a heavy breath. "Which is why being successful at the wine festival is so important." He turned to face Madison. "I need to make this company strong. First, so Alyssa will see that Ginny can grow up here, with security, something Alyssa didn't have when she was a kid. Dandy Dairy struggled for many years and I think that's what has made Alyssa so resistant to being in the business. Second, if the company is making money, and if, God forbid, I have to go to court and fight Alyssa, I'll be able to afford the battle."

Madison didn't want to tell him how much he'd need to fight a dynasty like the Thurgoods. If George Thurgood decided to back his wife's court fight, there wasn't enough cheese in the world to fund Jack's battle.

"That's where you come in," Jack said, laying a hand on Madison's. "I don't need you to be my fiancé," at that, the ghost of a smile crossed his face, as if the mere thought of them being engaged was amusing, "but to be a hell of a spokesmodel. The cheese will speak for itself once people taste it, but I need *you* to be the face that draws them in."

She swallowed hard. She had to say it. She couldn't let him go on thinking that she would be there for him, for Cheese Pleese. "Jack, I need to tell you something."

"First, let me say this," He said, putting up a hand to stop her. He drew in a breath, released it. "I'm sorry for snapping at you earlier. I'm just worried as hell about this whole thing with Ginny. But with you helping me, I know this business is going to succeed and Ginny will be able to grow up here, surrounded by my family, as weird as they sometimes are, and not have to spend her childhood trotting around the world. Or worse, with a nanny who barely knows her, who wouldn't love her even a hundredth of how much I do."

Oh, hell, why did he have to say that? Why did he have to paint such a perfect picture of the childhood Madison had lived through—and hated. She closed her eyes, the words *I'm leaving tomorrow* lodging in her throat like an orange. She opened her mouth, tried to vocalize them, but nothing came out.

If she left, she wouldn't just be letting down Jack. She'd also be disappointing Ginny.

"I can count on you, right?" Jack said, giving her hand a squeeze.

What could she say? She turned her gaze away, studying the word "Ford" on the dash so he wouldn't see the lie in her eyes. Two words escaped her lips. "Of course."

Joe's The-Surprise-Is-Inside Sausage and Cheese Bread

1 tablespoon olive oil

1 1/3 pounds raw Italian sweet sausage, casing removed

2 cups ricotta cheese

1/4 cup parsley, chopped

2 cloves garlic, chopped

1 cup Parmesan cheese

1/4 teaspoon ground nutmeg

1/4 teaspoon pepper

2 tablespoons pimento, chopped

2 (10-ounce) tubes prepared pizza dough

2 cups mozzarella, shredded

2 cups tomato sauce

This is the kind of meal you can eat by yourself, sitting in front of the news with your TV tray. No need for company you didn't ask for. Start by preheating the oven to 425 degrees, or, if you're oven challenged, asking someone else to do it for you.

Brown the sausage in the olive oil, then drain on a paper towel. Don't start thinking you know what's coming next because believe me, if there's one thing I've learned, it's that women have more tricks up their sleeves than David Copperfield.

In a bowl, mix the sausage with the cheese, parsley, garlic, nutmeg, pepper and pimiento. So far, so easy. Since making bread from scratch isn't one of my strong suits, I vote for those Pillsbury godsends in a can. Roll out the pizza doughs, cutting each into two rectangles. Put 'em on a nonstick cookie sheet to avoid as much time doing dishes as possible. Add the filling, then fold these puppies up like a triangular pocket. Pinch the edges so nothing runs out the sides (mess avoidance, remember).

Toss 'em in the oven and leave 'em alone for 15 minutes. Cool long enough so they don't burn your tongue off, then use the tomato sauce as a dip.

And while you're at it, don't be a human dip. Pay attention to what's happening because that city girl is about to drop a few surprises into your lap.

Chapter Twenty-Three

If Jack had been a betting man, he would have taken fifty to one odds that Madison would have run out of here before dawn. All to avoid the scene currently before him.

Madison stood in a field on Thursday morning, bevied up to a couple of his best Jersey cows and pretended to be delighted to be in the bovine huddle. Neal snapped away, giving her direction as he had before, sending her so many compliments that after a while they started to sound like a record playing the same track over and over again.

Was that what it was like for her? He'd noticed how she deferred his compliments, as if she didn't believe them. Maybe, after years of hearing the same words of praise, they had lost their meaning.

She struck a funny pose, aping for the camera between shots. Jack smiled.

After talking to her last night, he felt as if a weight had been lifted off his shoulders. Well, maybe not lifted, but at least he wasn't the only one carrying it. With his brother, his aunt and now Madison behind his ideas, he had the ammunition he needed to win the battle to save the business and everything important to him.

Madison was the last key he'd needed to propel Cheese Pleese into true success. Energy surged within Jack, along with another feeling that had nothing to do with business.

And everything to do with the woman standing a few feet away. A woman who supported him, who cared about his daughter, his company. He'd thought women like her didn't exist, but now, here she was, standing in his field, cozied up to his best milk makers.

It was a far cry from the first day he'd met her and she'd pronounced his farm smelly and his animals ill-mannered. Since the cows hadn't changed an ounce since Madison had arrived, Jack could only think that maybe she was beginning to like this place.

To like him.

"That's it, sweetie. Now get up closer to that cow. Could you give him a kiss?" Neal said.

Jack didn't bother to correct Neal's gender mistake.

"A kiss?" Madison asked, dubious.

From her position against the fence, Ginny giggled at the prospect.

"Yeah, like you totally love his milk. Thank that little milk machine for his contribution to the dairy industry."

"Uh, okay." Her nose wrinkled and she drew back for a second. Then she seemed to pull a shade over her reservations and slip into smile mode again. While Ginny laughed, Madison bent over, puckered up and gave Clarice a pert peck on the cheek.

Jack choked down a laugh. The pose, he could see from here, was both sexy and endearing. With that on a milk jug, Pleeseman wouldn't have any trouble landing sales in grocery stores.

Particularly among the young, single male population. Hell, she could be responsible for an entirely new drinking regimen among men. All he had to do was paste "Got Madison?" on the label and every male with a beating heart would become a calcium addict.

"Great, great, sweetie," Neal said. "Now scooch in a tiny bit closer, yes, yes, that's it. How 'bout a hug for your new best friend?"

Madison draped her arm around Clarice's neck, despite the bovine's heavy dose of Eau de Farm— instead of Eau de Parfum.

"Okay, how about one more peck on the cheek? Just to be sure we got the shot."

Madison leaned over to do as Neal had asked. Clarice balked, apparently not in the mood for additional snuggling. The three-year-old Jersey backed up quick, knocking into two other cows who were happily chewing their curds, part of the background decorations. The other two let out a moo of indignation, then confused, started heading toward Madison instead of away from her.

Three-inch heels were no match for a mini cow stampede. Madison tried to scramble away from the nine-hundred pound beasts, but they moved forward in mindless panic, slamming into her, just as Jack started shouting and waving his arms, leaping over the split rail fence and into the pasture.

"Madison!" Jack reached out, but she teetered, losing her balance and whispering past his grasp. In slow, awful motion, he watched her topple to the ground—butt first into a freshly made cow patty.

"You okay?" He asked, reaching her side.

She grinned. "Nothing a gallon of Clorox can't fix. Did we work laundry services into the contract?"

Jack laughed. "If we didn't, we will. Here, let me help you—"

"Oh, my goodness! Madison? Is that you, honey?"

Jack and Madison both turned at the sound of the voice. Five feet away stood a tall, willowy woman, dressed in a rainbow colored skirt that hung nearly to her Birkenstock sandals. Tan, muscular arms showed beneath a navy tank top. She wore no makeup, no jewelry, but her hair was the same gold color as Madison's and hung in one long braid down her back, with beads woven in and out of the strands.

"Mother?" Madison scrambled to her feet, ignoring Jack's outstretched hand. She went to brush off the cow residue from the back of her skirt, then thought twice and put down her hands. "What are you doing here?"

This was Madison Worth's *mother*? Jack did a double take and decided, yes, she had to be. Given the identical color of their eyes and their nearly twin heights, this woman was definitely an older version of Madison.

"I told you on the phone that I was coming to visit my daughter." She gestured toward the pasture. "Who appears to have become a dairy farmer when I wasn't looking."

"It's a photo shoot, Mother," Madison replied, regaining her poise and striding across the grassy field as if nothing had happened. "How did you find me?"

"I called Harry." She faced Jack. "He's an old friend of the family," she explained to him, as if Jack had just become one of those, too. "I'm Vivian Worth." She thrust a hand over the railing to him. "Madison's mother."

"Jack Pleeseman, the one responsible for the cows."

She laughed as they shook, the same rich, deep laughter as her daughter. "Madison's never been one for the great outdoors. How in the world did you convince her to do this?"

"I'm *working*, Mother," Madison said, climbing over the fence, heedless of how her skirt rose up to her thighs. Neal arched a brow, clearly considering taking that particular photo, then lowered his camera again when Madison glared at him. "Don't you dare."

He grinned. "*People* would have paid me a nice chunk of change for that one."

"Yeah, just enough to pay your hospital bill after I cracked your skull open with a Jimmy Choo."

Neal laughed good-naturedly, then turned to Jack. "Did you get what you wanted today?"

"Yeah, we're done. Thanks a lot." Neal promised to mail a CD of the two shoots, then packed up his camera and headed back to his car, laughing the whole way there about Madison's tumble into cow patties.

"I'm now a running joke," Madison muttered.

Jack gave her a one-armed hug, ignoring the Eau de Farm she'd picked up from Clarice's pasture deposit. "Hey, doesn't everyone want to be a legend?"

The look on her face told him she could have done without this particular moment of notoriety.

Vivian stepped forward, opened her arms for an embrace, then caught a whiff and changed her mind. Instead, she frowned at the look on her daughter's face. "The least you can do, Madison, is pretend to be happy to see me," Vivian said. "Because I don't intend to go anywhere. Not until you and I have had a chance to catch up."

Madison's Double-Trouble Twice Baked Potatoes

6 large potatoes, baked
1/4 cup butter
2 tablespoons milk
1/2 cup cheddar cheese, shredded
1 teaspoon salt
1/4 teaspoon pepper
Parsley, chopped, for decoration

Not only have you landed in something undesirable, everything you've been avoiding in your life has shown up for a visit. Avoid the hugs and mushy reunion by working on these potatoes instead.

Keep the oven on after you bake the potatoes, bumping it up if need be to 375 degrees. Take the spuds out, slice off the top part of the skin, then scoop out the insides. Mix in a bowl with all ingredients, then return to the potato shells. Sprinkle with extra cheese and parsley to make them all pretty. Hopefully their scrumptious appearance will help you distract your visitors from the cow questions.

Return to the oven for ten to fifteen minutes, long enough to crisp the tops and melt the cheese. Serve with anything that helps you keep your mouth shut and avoid the subject.

CHAPTER TWENTY-FOUR

After taking a hot shower, applying a liberal dose of Chanel No. 5 and double-bagging her Kenneth Cole skirt in Hefty, Madison felt ready to face her mother.

As ready as she could be, considering the circumstances. And the lingering scents.

Madison found Vivian in the kitchen with Harriet, the two of them sitting at the chrome and Formica table, drinking coffee and dipping into a plate filled with cheddar slices and Ritz. "Tell me, what did Elvis say then?" Vivian asked.

"He didn't want to ever perform the hound dog song again. Said he got tired of singing about that silly animal." Harriet leaned forward and lowered her voice. "Personally, I think he's more of a cat person."

Vivian nodded, as if this was all a perfectly ordinary conversation. "Is he here now?"

"Oh no, it's too early for him." Harriet cupped a hand over her mouth, lest the King was listening. "He likes to sleep in. Apparently some things don't change, even in the afterlife."

Vivian laughed, then turned and noticed Madison standing in the doorway. "Why come on in, dear, and pull up a chair. Cheese, crackers?" She raised the plate in her daughter's direction.

"No, thank you." Outside the window, Madison saw Ginny playing on the swing set. In her lap, she held Ella Mae. She swung her legs to and fro, giggling and talking to the doll as she glided toward the sky. Katydid ran by the window, a wide-brimmed Panama hat in her mouth and a frantic Joe following far behind, yelling and waving futilely.

"Honey, you never told me your photo shoots were like that," Vivian said, drawing Madison's attention back. "I would have come to see one a long time ago if I'd known they were such an adventure."

"Normally, I work with people, Mother, not animals."

"Oh, but animals are so much more fun! You can take your career in an entirely new direction with this." Vivian spread her hands, indicating an imaginary billboard. "I can see it now—Madison Worth, the face of pork."

Madison rolled her eyes, deciding the argument wasn't worth the effort. Her mother wouldn't be around long enough to have any input into future career choices. There was no point in explaining that her next job was showing off foundation, not pigs. Instead, Madison crossed the kitchen, poured some coffee into a "Graceland is Great" mug. Her gaze strayed to the stove. What was for dinner tonight? And would it be as good as the incredible fettuccini from the night before?

Or would it be something as tempting as the nachos?

No, no, *no*. She couldn't go down that road. Tonight, she absolutely had to tell Jack that she was leaving. Coop would be here in a few hours with her car. Delaying would only make leaving that much worse.

While her mother and Harriet debated whether the Post Office should have gone with the young Elvis or the old version on the postage stamp, Madison slid into a seat at the kitchen table, silent, cupping her hands around the hot mug. Ginny dashed into the house, Ella Mae in her arms. "Grandma, wanna play Candyland?"

"Sure, sweetie. Just one quick game before I start dinner." Harriet took Ginny's hand, then headed out to the living room.

"She's holding Ella Mae," Vivian said after they had left.

"I know. I'm letting her play with her."

"Why?"

Madison didn't want to tell her mother it was because she saw herself in the little girl, that she had wanted to try to fill the gap in Ginny's maternal life. "She forgot to bring dolls with her when she came to see Jack, so I let her have Ella Mae for now."

Her mother studied her, not saying anything for a long time.

"Why are you here, Mother?" Madison got right to the point rather than beat around banalities. "Really."

"I told you. To see you. It's been so long since we had a good chat."

"I can count on one hand the number of times I've seen you in the last ten years, Mother. Don't tell me you wanted to spend some time with me because you don't do that."

Vivian toyed with a cracker, spinning the Ritz on the smooth tabletop. "I read about what happened at that fashion show, with the chocolate cake. And I thought...well, I thought you might need me."

Ignoring the hint of need and vulnerability in her mother's voice, Madison got to her feet, suddenly angry at this delayed entry into her life. Jack had moved heaven and earth to spend more time with his daughter. He would never have let twenty-nine years go by before building a relationship.

Madison's mother had ditched her almost from the minute she was born. Vivian couldn't expect all would be forgiven simply because she showed up.

"I'm all grown up now," Madison said, "something you might not have noticed. I haven't seen you in more than three years. I didn't need a mother then, I don't need a mother now. I can take care of myself."

Vivian reached for her. "Madison—"

"No, Mother, don't." Madison jerked away from her mother's touch. "Don't try and build a relationship now. We both know you'll be gone again before we get past *hello*."

Madison strode out of the kitchen, leaving her mother with the dead king of rock and roll, who undoubtedly had lower expectations for his beyond-the-grave relationships.

Vivian's Gluing-The-Family-Together Cheesy Crackers

1/2 pound cheddar cheese, shredded
1 1/2 tablespoons butter, melted
Saltines
Paprika

There's nothing like a little appetizer to bring the family together. Keep it simple so you spend less time in the kitchen and more time with those you haven't seen in a while.

Get the broiler roaring. Mix the cheese and butter, then spread over the saltines, being smart enough to put them on a cookie sheet first (who wants to transfer all those little suckers later?). Sprinkle with paprika, then broil till the cheese is melted and gooey—the perfect glue to bring your broken family back together.

CHAPTER TWENTY-FIVE

D inner was a nightmare.

Harriet had insisted they all dine together again. Joe complained and came up with a litany of better ways to spend his time, but his sister insisted. "Joseph Pleeseman, I swear, if you don't sit down at that kitchen table, I will never cook another meal in this house."

He sat.

David opened his mouth to protest, caught one glimpse of Harriet's determination, and sat down, too.

Vivian and Madison sat on one side, Ginny and Jack on the other. At either end sat Aunt Harriet and Joe.

Before them, Harriet had set a veritable feast— roasted chicken, green beans cooked with crispy bacon, and her famous mac and cheese. Madison didn't dare inhale. Surely every breath was a hundred calories. Or more.

"Joseph, you say grace." Harriet bowed her head and laced her fingers together.

Joe scowled, but bent his head, waiting while the rest of the table followed suit. "Lord, thanks for the food and please get my sister off my back while I eat it. Amen."

Harriet pursed her lips, but passed the macaroni anyway.

Madison hovered her fork over the green beans she'd scooped onto her plate, knowing the vegetables were the better, lower calorie choice. The devil on her shoulder—or maybe it was Elvis—whispered the mac and cheese sitting a few inches away would be so much more satisfying.

Beside her, Jack sent her a smile, one that said he was glad she was here.

And depending on her to be here tomorrow.

Guilt gnawed at her, creating a cavern in her stomach. Leaving was the best choice, though. If she stayed even one day longer, she would get too wrapped up in Jack Pleeseman—so wrapped up that her heart would be irretrievably lost to the dairy farmer. If there was one thing Madison could stake money on, it was that she would end up alone and heartbroken at the end.

Dairy farmers didn't settle down with models. And models didn't live among the cows. It was as simple as the fish and the bird allegory. Trying to change such a basic fact would only lead to disappointment.

Besides, hadn't she learned already that love was as shallow as a tube of concealer? She could fool herself into thinking Jack was there because he loved her, but after a day, a week, a month, reality would come knocking at her door.

The emptiness within her expanded. There was only one way, Madison knew from experience, to fill that hole.

Food.

Madison reached for the macaroni.

A second later, she was making her way through a cheese-laden pastafest. As Harriet had promised, the macaroni dish was amazing, so thick with cheese it would have embarrassed the CEO of Kraft. Going back for seconds—something Madison hadn't done in more than fifteen years—sounded like a better idea with every bite.

Plus, keeping her mouth filled with food would keep her from having a conversation with her mother. Talking to Vivian, Madison knew, was about as productive as a hamster on a wheel.

"Oh, dear," Vivian said, the serving spoon from the green beans halfway to her plate.

"What?" Harriet's brow wrinkled with concern. "Is something wrong? Undercooked?"

"Oh, no, everything's wonderful. I was simply thinking of all the children I could feed with a meal like this. So many poor babies are starving on the other side of the world."

"I'll cut a check to the Red Cross," Joe muttered. "Now pass the damned green beans."

Harriet shot her brother a glare. "I agree with you, Vivian. Perhaps we should think of making a corporate donation," at this, she eyed Jack, "to your next philanthropic project."

"Would you?" Vivian said. "You could help so many people."

Her mother was soliciting contributions at the *dinner table*? Vivian might as well call up Jerry Lewis and start broadcasting a telethon from the living room.

Once again, it was abundantly clear to Madison that her mother wasn't here to see her daughter or build a relationship. She was looking for money that would fund her return to the other side of the world.

"Of course we will," Harriet said. "Won't we, Jack? Joe?"

Both men nodded in agreement with Harriet, clearly aware of which side their bread was buttered on—and who was doing the buttering. Madison kept her opinions to herself, dishing up a second helping of macaroni instead. She grabbed a biscuit, slathered on the butter, then added extra gravy to her roast chicken.

"Daddy, can I ask?" Ginny said, putting down her fork and tapping Jack on the arm.

Jack stabbed up some macaroni, glancing at his daughter. "Ask what, honey?"

"If Madison will stay and live with us."

A hush descended over the table. Everyone stopped eating, their gazes swiveling to Madison. She felt them waiting, wondering what she was going to say.

What *was* she going to say? Stay and live…here? It was the same thing Jack had asked her before. She'd said no. Meant no.

Well…more or less.

For a second, the thought of saying yes—and the reaction that would bring to Ginny's face, to the little girl whose life had been such a mirror of Madison's—ran through her. She wanted to say yes, even began to form the letters with her lips, but then pulled the word back before she gave it voice.

Whoa. What was she thinking? Staying was out of the question. Whatever pull she might feel for this place—and these people—would dissipate as soon as she hit the bustling streets of New York and got back to her old life.

Not to mention the new one waiting for her, Great Lash mascara included. By Saturday, she'd be back to her old self, back to the world she knew. The thoughts of staying here would become a distant memory.

But even as she told herself that, she wondered if she would ever forget any of her time here, from the tea with Elvis to the grapes by the lake.

Especially the grapes by the lake.

"Will you?" Ginny asked again, her wide brown eyes filled with hope.

"Uh…" Madison scrambled for an answer. The one she should vocalize—that she was leaving tonight—seemed somehow wrong. Besides, she couldn't simply drop the truth on the table like a twenty-pound Thanksgiving turkey. "Well, Ginny, I live in New York."

"You can live here. We have a extra room," Ginny reasoned.

"My job is in New York."

"Daddy could give you a new job."

Daddy had, in fact, already offered her a job. One that would have been perfect…under different circumstances. And for a different woman.

"I…" She looked around the table, hoping for some help, but no one from the Pleeseman family or her own came to rescue her with a good excuse. "I just can't, Ginny, I'm sorry."

Ginny frowned, not happy with that answer. "But why?"

Oh Lord, how many times had Madison said those same words? *But why are you leaving again? But why can't I come with you?* "Oh, Ginny—" Madison began.

"Madison can't stay," Jack cut in, his voice sharp, "Her life is somewhere else. And that's that."

The words sliced through Madison, severing the connections she'd built around this table as quickly as a chainsaw. Jack had made it clear—she didn't belong here.

And giving anyone false hope about any other outcome was cruel.

Yet when she looked at Ginny's crestfallen face, she wanted to take it all back, to stay right where she was. Move in, take the marketing job…and become a part of the family, sit down at this table and eat with these people—with Jack—every day for the rest of her life.

"Madison never was one for staying still," Vivian cut in, adding a drumstick to her plate. "Takes after her mother that way."

Takes after her mother? How would her mother know anything about who she took after or didn't? Or if she'd been an antsy kid? Madison had spent less time with her mother in the last ten years than she had with her gynecologist.

Jack caught her eye, but Madison looked away before she began to think he truly cared. If she did, leaving tonight would be a hundred times harder.

Through the open window, Madison heard the sound of tires crunching on gravel. Coop, with her car. The last thing she needed to help her get back to New York.

"Excuse me," Madison said, rising and dropping her napkin to the table, the macaroni in her stomach no longer feeling comforting, but more like a lead weight. "I have to go."

Then she left the room, before she let loose twenty-nine years of disappointments on a mother who had just dropped back into her life like a carrier pigeon with a long-overdue message.

"Ain't she a beauty?" Coop said. He stood next to her car, beaming at the four-wheeled artwork, thankfully relatively sober in his blue jumpsuit and grease-stained Red Sox cap. He kept turning the hat around in his hands as he bandied about words like "timing" and "differentials" that Madison didn't understand one bit. "Anyway, this one is definitely one of my masterpieces." He plopped the cap back onto his head.

The silver finish had disappeared beneath a cacophony of color. In the dining room of her Manhattan apartment, she had a hand-painted cloisonné vase from Beijing, with an elaborate five thousand flower design. Here, on her Mercedes, Madison saw a pattern nearly similar, but instead of five-petaled flowers, Coop had painted a jigsaw puzzle of butterflies.

Butterflies. Exquisite winged creatures that seemed ready to take flight, using the quarter panel as a launching pad.

Some were as tiny as a finger, others larger than the palm of her hand. None looked exactly the same as the other and each sported its own unique splash of paint. She took a step forward, running her hand over the smooth, colorful finish, tracing a butterfly with her finger. "They're so individual. Like snowflakes."

"Yep," Coop said, pride puffing his chest out, "just like the car's owner. Different from every other woman in the world."

"Oh, I don't know about that," Madison said.

Coop leaned toward her, removing his grease-stained ball cap. "You're entitled to your opinion, same as those goddamned critics, may they all spend the next ten years with the flames of hell licking at their feet." He cleared his throat, then smiled. "Sorry. Little artist frustration there. Anyway, if you ask me, sometimes, the butterfly can't see how unique it is, till it looks in a mirror." Then he stepped back, waving a hand over the car. "And this is your mirror."

In the Mercedes' colorful exterior, Madison saw another self reflected. One that was wild, free. Fun. It was like looking at who she could be—if she didn't have the Worth name, the expectations of her career and the constraints of her looks hanging over her, like an executioner with a strange sense of humor.

Madison drew herself back to reality. To dollars and cents. "How much do I owe you?"

"Not a thing," Coop said, waving a hand like David Copperfield. "It's all been taken care of."

"Taken care of? But why? By who?"

"Me."

Madison pivoted. Jack stood on the porch, tall and handsome. The setting sun had brushed him with gold, making him seem stronger, more powerful.

And sexy as hell.

Oh, boy. For a butterfly, she sure didn't have much inspiration to fly away. The nectar was just way too attractive.

Coop's Beauty-Takes-Flight Saucy Chicken

2 tablespoons olive oil
4 chicken breasts
salt and pepper
8 ounces tomato sauce
1 tablespoon Italian seasoning
1/2 cup Italian blend cheese, shredded

Let your inner beauty shine, even in a skillet. Brown the chicken breasts in the olive oil, seasoning with salt and pepper on each side. Look at that lovely golden brown color! Mix tomato sauce with Italian seasoning then pour over the chicken breasts. Ah, crimson! It's art in a kitchen.

Cover and cook for 30 minutes or so, until the chicken is done. Don't want that evil salmonella bug ruining your hard created work. Sprinkle on the cheese, then cover again for another five minutes, until it's all melted and gooey. Ignore any of those damned critics who come in and disagree with your presentation. It's your creation, take pride in it, damn it. And if you want to paint on some butterflies with a little Cheez Whiz, hey, be my guest artist.

CHAPTER TWENTY-SIX

Jack came the rest of the way down the stairs, approaching the blonde and the Benz. Coop had clearly outdone himself. Madison's car was almost as beautiful as she was. And the butterfly theme…he couldn't think of a more perfect metaphor for this amazing woman who had brought color to a life that had been stuck in shades of gray for far too long.

Too bad this rainbow had to be temporary.

"Why would you do that?" she asked. "Pay my bill?"

"Because I owe you." Their gazes connected, sending a bolt of lightning down his spine. "I don't mean for the job, I'll still pay for the modeling, like I agreed. I did it because you helped me out, more than you know," Jack said. "Your ideas… they were great. Exactly what I needed to take this company to the next level. Plus, you were a great sport about the cow thing—"

She laughed. "I don't think I had a choice. It was either that, or move in with the herd."

"Hey, my barn door is always open." He grinned.

The words were said as a joke, but Jack wasn't kidding. And yet, something stopped him from coming right out and promising to be Madison's personal Motel 6, leaving the light on, waiting for her to come home.

Yeah, a little something called reality.

"Well, I better go," Coop said, shuffling from foot to foot. "I've got some canvas waiting back in the shop. This baby," at that, he patted the Benz, "has inspired me in a whole new direction." He spread his hands wide, indicating a blank palette. "I see birds. Butterflies. A veritable garden of Eden, painted on the back of a Dodge Durango."

"You did a great job with the car, Coop," Jack said. "How about you do my truck next?"

Coop glanced over at the beat-up, dented pickup. "No can do, Jack. I'm an *artiste*. I have standards, you know." Then he was gone, chugging off in a purple tow truck sporting two newly painted butterflies on the tailgate.

With a truck like that, Jack wasn't so sure Coop could argue standards.

After Coop had pulled out of the driveway, Jack reached out and clasped Madison's hand. She looked so forlorn, so lonely, that he wanted to gather her up into his arms and tell her everything would be okay. "You all right?"

"Of course."

He could see the lie in her eyes. Madison was holding something back. He didn't know what it was, but attributed it to the arrival of her mother and the earlier comment at the dinner table. "Madison, you look more unhappy now than you did when you fell in the manure."

"I'm fine."

Even Jack could tell she was anything but.

"Listen, Aunt Harriet made pie. Let's grab a piece of lemon meringue and sit outside." He pointed to the two Adirondack chairs around the corner of the house. "The day's cooled off and we can talk about the plan for Saturday. And," he continued when she didn't respond, "I can apologize for my daughter. When she wants something, she goes after it. Apparently, she wants you."

What Jack didn't say was whether he wanted Madison too. He did, indeed, want her to stay as much as Ginny did. Maybe more.

However, the one thing Madison Worth had made clear to him was that she didn't fit into his world. Thinking otherwise would only lead him down a path to heartbreak that he'd already taken once before with Alyssa. He didn't need to hitchhike a ride to that destination again.

Yet, a part of him wanted to think that Madison would change her mind. Clearly, that was the part that operated solely on testosterone.

"Can we go for a walk instead?" Madison asked. "Just for a little while, to get away from, well, everyone."

He chuckled. "Believe me, I, of all people, understand the need to put some distance between yourself and your family." He gestured toward the barn. "Let's go check on Ellie and Becky."

She laughed. "Good idea. No one will think to look for me among the cows."

They walked along, a comfortable silence descending between them, the kind that usually happened with people who'd known each other a long time and had developed that unspoken language. Madison may have only arrived on Sunday, yet Jack felt as if she'd lived here for years.

"Did you always want to do this?" she asked when they stepped inside the cool shadows of the barn. They headed down the center aisle, passing the other cows busily eating hay, their tails flicking away the occasional fly. In one of the center stalls, Katydid had curled up and gone to sleep, as if it were perfectly normal to bed down with Clarice.

Jack looked over at Madison and noticed the environment didn't seem to bother her at all. Maybe Pleeseman Dairy Farm had started to grow on her.

"You mean make cheese, milk cows?" He shook his head. "No, that was David's dream. He was the one who took to the farm like a hippo to water. You couldn't get him out of the barn if you paid him. Me, I was the one who always had my head in a book. I was going to *be* something."

"Something more than what your father was?"

He shrugged, reaching forward to scratch Ellie behind the ear. "Yeah. I didn't get too far."

"Why?"

"Because my mother had other plans for me, plans I couldn't run away from, no matter how hard I tried. She left her half of the business to me."

Madison rubbed Ellie's other ear, sending the calf into spoiling heaven. "Maybe she knew something you didn't know."

"Or she was hoping for something. For the longest time, I ignored that inheritance. Worked at a snack food company for a while, climbing the corporate ladder with the other rats. But when Ginny was born, I chucked it all and came back here. All of a sudden, I got it. Family is the most important thing you have. I realized I would be doing my mother's memory a terrible disservice if I walked away from her legacy."

She shook her head, amazed. "I don't know anyone like you, Jack."

"I'm no one special. Just a dairy farmer with a dream for his cheddar." He gave Ellie a final pat, then the two of them started walking again. "What about you? Did you always want to be a model?"

A cow mooed in a nearby pen, another shuffled from foot to foot, boards creaking beneath the weight. Sunlight peeked through the slats of the barn, glinting off the hay.

"It was an accident. You know those legendary stories about actresses being discovered in cafes? Or models being spotted on the street in North Dakota? That was me. I was at a party and Harry was there. He asked me if I'd ever considered modeling, and I hadn't, not really."

"What did you want to be?"

"I'm part of the Worth family, which means work is an option for me. I never had to *be* anything."

"A Paris Hilton clone?"

"It's pretty much par for the course where I come from." She shrugged. "A career isn't a necessity."

"Then why do it?"

They'd reached the back entrance of the barn. The setting sun swept across the acres beyond them, painting the Pleeseman land in shades of yellow. Madison looked out over the property, but her gaze seemed to go to some place in the past.

"I found something before the camera..." She stopped, then started again. "No, I *thought* I found something there that I didn't have at home."

"What were you looking for?"

"We should get back inside." She stepped out of the shadows and into the sun, leaving the barn behind.

"Why do you do that?" he asked.

"Do what?"

"Put up a wall the second anyone tries to get close."

"I don't put up walls." But even as Madison said the words, she knew they were a lie. Boy, was she screwed up. She wanted belonging, and yet everything she did was designed to put space between her and other people. She sighed. "It's part of the business, I guess. In this field, few people are real friends. Not when there's a plum magazine cover to fight for, or a position on the runway to wrangle away."

He arched a brow. "And this is a career that fulfills you?"

"Sure," she said, quickly.

"I saw a different side of you when we were planning that ad campaign." They paused by a tree, Madison leaning against the rough bark. Jack put his hand above her head, coming nearly close enough to kiss her. "You were excited, Madison. Charged up."

She let out a little laugh. "I was nervous as hell that I was going to be responsible for the failure of your business."

"Bull. You're smart, you've got a sense for this. You should have gone to college for marketing. You would have aced it."

Madison pushed away from the tree, heading toward the split rail fence of the pasture. She draped her arms over the hard wood, watching the last few cows head toward the barn as the sun began to set. "Been there, done that, and don't have the mortarboard to show for it."

He looked genuinely surprised. "You didn't finish?"

"No. I stuck to what I know best." She turned away, wrapped her arms around herself. "A job that doesn't require brainpower. Looking pretty."

"You are one of the most beautiful women I have ever met and yet, you have all the self confidence of an envelope. Why is that?"

"Because that's all anyone has ever seen, Jack." She circled her free hand around her face. "This.

The pretty face. It can't possibly come with a brain. I'm like the scarecrow in the *Wizard of Oz*. Filled with nothing but fluff."

"I never said that to you."

"You didn't have to. Everyone else I ever met did." Her voice cracked, the perfect façade of Madison Worth crumbling in those last few words.

"You are more than a pretty face, much more," he said, taking both her hands, trying to get her to look at him. If, as odd as it sounded, this dairy farmer from the Berkshires understood her. That was a dangerous thought, the kind that could make her think of giving it all up to become one with this man, this place. "You just need to have faith in yourself."

"Oh yeah? The one time I had faith, it blew up in my face." She let out a bitter laugh. "Actually, I guess you could say it blew up in Kate Moss's face. I *went* to college, Jack. Worked like hell to get my GED, then signed up for a few marketing classes at NYU. A friend of mine, another model, did the same thing. Janine and I had this brilliant idea of gong into business together, because neither one of us were getting any younger. The need for gray-haired wrinkled old ladies is pretty sparse."

"What happened?"

"Janine got all A's and me, I flunked out."

Jack's brown eyes met hers. "How could that happen? You're a smart woman."

"Not smart enough to know when someone was screwing me behind my back. We worked on a project together, but Janine neglected to put my name on it. She wanted all the credit. She wanted the moment in the sun." Madison shook her head. "That's the problem when you work with a model. She doesn't like to share her cover."

"Then why didn't you fight her? Go to the dean?"

"I did." The memory of that imposing office, the oversized dark cherry furniture, the deep-pile emerald green rug, and most of all, the disbelieving face of the man behind the desk, came to mind. It had been high school all over again, except without the crappy cafeteria food. "You know what he said to me? 'Why waste a degree on such a pretty face?'"

"And you didn't fight back? If there's one thing I've noticed about you, Madison, it's that you don't take anything lying down."

"Jack, I'm a high school dropout who has spent her life doing nothing more complicated than putting on skirts and perfecting my smile. I've quit kidding myself that I could change my life." She shook her head, willing the tears away but they slid down her face all the same. "I'm the quintessential dumb blonde. Never finished high school, not enough brains in her head to be anything but pretty."

"Madison, it's not that you aren't smart, it's not that some dean got mean." He reached up, brushing the hair away from her eyes in a gesture so tender, it made her cry even more. "I bet you're just afraid that if you step out of that box, you'll fail."

"I can't *afford* to fail," she said. "It's not what a Worth does."

"Seems to me being a Worth isn't all that much fun if you aren't allowed to take a chance once in a while. To fall on your face and get back up again."

"The tabloids would have a field day."

He smiled. "Let 'em. You're Madison Worth. You can stand up to me, half the cows in the field and not, to mention, Kitty Dandy. I'd think the *National Enquirer* would be a piece of cake after that." He brought her hands to his lips, giving them a quick kiss before releasing her. "In fact, I can't wait to see what you've got in mind for the wine festival. I know you're going to kick some ass." He chuckled. "Or rather, kick some cow."

Hope and trust shone in Jack's eyes. Madison would rather pose with the two-headed bubble boy in the *National Enquirer* than say the words that would erase that look.

Vivian's Mending-Broken-Fences Easy Breadsticks

2 tubes refrigerated breadstick dough
1/4 cup butter, melted
2 tablespoons parsley, minced
1 clove garlic, minced
1/4 cup Parmesan cheese, grated

You're going to need something tasty to repair this particular bridge. It also has to be quick, because you have a lot of ground to cover before your daughter runs away again. Start by preheating the oven to 425 degrees.

Mix butter, parsley and garlic. While you're trying to make amends, brush the mixture over the breadsticks, then top with Parmesan. You have fifteen minutes to bake these. Enough time to get started on the truth.

CHAPTER TWENTY-SEVEN

Vivian stood in Madison's room later that night, looking at the piles of packed suitcases. Suitcases Madison had packed because it had been easier to stuff her underwear into Louis Vuitton than to finish the conversation with Jack.

In the last few days, Madison had become as wimpy as limp spaghetti.

"What's all this?" Vivian said.

Madison shut the final suitcase with a click. The sound seemed so loud in the quiet of the house. Ginny had gone to bed, as had Harriet. Jack was working in his office, Joe was watching TV and David was out, saying something about a date. "I'm leaving. Tonight."

Her mother looked stricken. "But...I just got here. We've barely had a chance to talk."

"I told you not to come, Mother. But you did anyway." Madison ran a hand through her hair, not caring what the movement did to the curls she'd so carefully done this morning. "You never think about whether it's convenient for me to have a little visit or not."

"*Little visit?* I came here to spend time with you."

Madison threw up her hands. "And since when do you do that? No offense, Mother, but you never spend time with me."

"I do too." Her mother thought for a second, then put a finger up. "What about the time I brought you to Honduras?"

Madison remembered that trip in vivid detail. She'd been seven, on spring break from school, and her mother had thought it would be educational for her to make a pit stop in a rebellion-torn country. Where Madison had stayed had been safe, but so filled with poverty, the problem of helping these people seemed too big for one person, one organization, even one country to solve.

The country had been fascinating and had spurred Madison's love of travel, her thirst to see the rest of the world, something that had been quenched by her modeling career. It had also inspired her to give more to her mother's causes, to send money to things like Oprah's Angel Network and the Red Cross. Still, besides a little Spanish, though, Madison hadn't learned a whole lot about her mother.

"I never saw you," Madison said. "You were busy building huts or stringing fishing poles or something like that. I stayed with some woman I didn't even know." Madison shook her head. "My whole life, I've spent with strangers. Nannies, maids, boarding schools."

"I would have taken you with me more often, but many of the places I go simply aren't safe for children."

"Then why did you have me?" Madison said, the words coming out in a gush of past hurts, a flood so long held back, it seemed to pour out of her, unstoppable. "Why didn't you just give me up for adoption or something? At least then, I could have parents that were home more than six days out of the year."

Vivian looked stunned, as if she had never expected Madison to feel this way. "You grew up with everything you could have asked for. The best schools, the best clothes, the best home."

"*Home?* I didn't have a home, Mother." Madison came across her brush on the vanity table, strode over to the pile of suitcases and tossed it into the first available one. "I lived with nannies in that gigantic, silent mausoleum of Grandfather's. You know him; he worked a million hours a week. Daniel's parents were always off in Europe. You *paid* people to raise me."

"You don't understand, Madison, I had to do what I did."

Madison snorted. "Yeah. Because everyone else in the world was more important to you than your own child."

Vivian took a step back, the words coming at her like a slap. She sank onto the bed, displacing a throw pillow. It tumbled to the floor, landing silently beside her feet. "That was never the case. If we could just talk for a while—"

"I don't have time for this, Mother," Madison said, pulling out the drawers in the vanity, looking for anything she might have missed. But most of all, avoiding that look on her mother's face. "You want to have a little closure or whatever, call a psychologist. I don't need to clean up this particular corner of my life."

Vivian reached for her, but her touch brushed off of her daughter's arm as Madison moved away, stuffing a forgotten Velcro roller into the front pocket of the suitcase. "Oh, Madison, don't."

For a moment, Madison thought of holding back, of heading off this argument at the pass. But it had festered too long to be delayed another moment.

"Don't what? Don't tell you how I really feel?" Madison straightened, one hand on her hip. The box she'd kept all these feelings in for most of her life had been opened and there was no shutting the lid or stuffing it all back in. "Should I keep pretending it's all wonderful and gee, aren't I glad you came to visit me when I'm sitting in the middle of a pile of crap? And, hey, Mom, let's pick up where we left off, if either of us can remember where that was."

"You're angry, honey, and you're completely justified." Vivian reached for her again, but pulled back at the last second, as if she was unsure of her reception.

Tears stung at Madison's·eyes but she refused to shed them. "You're damned right I am."

Vivian drew in a breath, released it. Her shoulders seemed to slump, that perfect Worth posture losing a degree or two. She picked at the comforter, toying with a loose thread. "I came here for a reason, to tell you something. Maybe once I do, you'll understand." She looked up, her gaze connecting with her daughter's. "Maybe…forgive me?"

Madison turned her head away, not wanting to listen, to reopen this wound. She was an adult now, not a child continually asking "why." Nevertheless, the damned tears kept pushing at her eyes, waiting to spill over. "I have to leave."

Yet she didn't reach for her bags, didn't move from her spot by the vanity table.

"Your father was a wonderful man," Vivian began slowly, as if the story was something she had to pull from deep within herself. "His whole life was wrapped up in caring for other people. His family was like that too, you know? They didn't just donate money, they were right there, handing out blankets and bags of rice. That's how the Downey family spent their vacations, with Steve getting his hands right into whatever his parents were doing. He grew up with this compassion, this connection, to the poor of the world. I guess that's what made me fall in love with him, the way he took care of others." She sighed. "Especially the way he took care of me."

Still, Madison kept silent, afraid that if she said anything, she wouldn't be able to stop.

"He would have loved you," her mother went on. "He was so great with kids. Not like me. I'm better with adults. Kids scare the living daylights out of me."

Madison let out a little laugh. "That's something we have in common."

Vivian returned the smile, then sobered. "Then he died, leaving me alone and pregnant in a foreign country."

"How did he die?" Madison asked, vocalizing the one question her mother had never answered. What had happened to her father? What event had stolen one parent from her before she even had her first lungful of air?

Her mother exhaled slowly. When she spoke again, her voice was tinged with years of grief. "We were in Thailand, working in one of the refugee camps. There was an accident on the Mekong River. Three families, all in one little boat, trying to cross the river and get to us." She shook her head, her eyes closing, clearly seeing it all over again. "It was horrible. None of them could swim; the boat didn't have any life preservers. I mean, it's not like there's a Y there, taking the kids out on the diving board."

Madison slipped into the vanity table chair, hit by the images of that day. She'd never imagined that people who drew their lives from a river wouldn't know how to swim.

"Your father, though," Vivian continued, a look of pride taking over her features, "he jumped in, went right into that water, without even thinking."

"Did he save them?"

"Almost all of them," Vivian said. "The other Peace Corps workers helped, too, but in the end, there were three who didn't make it. Two of them were children. We found their bodies a few days later on the banks of the river." Vivian shook her head, the memory even now clearly still vivid and painful. "And the third was Steve."

Madison sat back against the seat. "He died rescuing them?"

"Yeah." Her mother smoothed a hand across the comforter, tears glistening in her eyes.

The same feeling of pride she'd seen on her mother's face bloomed in Madison's chest. Her father wasn't just a name anymore, he was a living, breathing person who had risked his life for strangers. "He was a hero."

Vivian smiled, a soft smile that spoke of the love she'd shared with a man long gone. "Knowing Steve, he would have said he was just doing his job."

How different this image was than the one Madison had crafted in her own mind, built on years of not knowing anything. She'd pictured her father as a distant, rebellious man, based on her grandfather's response to questions and her mother's reticence. But now she saw that maybe Grandfather's refusal to talk about Steven Downey was more out of anger that Steven had left Vivian without a spouse and Madison without a father.

"Why didn't you two ever get married?"

Her mother laughed. "In every other aspect of my life, I'm as untraditional as they come. But when it came to getting married, I wanted to be home, with my family. There always seemed to be something that got in the way of that."

The question that Madison had never asked, sprung forward before she could stop it. "Like getting pregnant with me?"

Vivian reached for her daughter's hand, giving it a squeeze. "You were never in the way, Madison. *Never*." Her eyes misted over, and in their blue depths, Madison saw truth. "Your father and I wanted you, more than you can know. He was so looking forward to seeing you born."

Madison's mind raced over the years, to when she was six, wondering why she didn't have a mother around like all the other kids. When she was twelve and started menstruating and the nanny had to take her to CVS. When she was seventeen and wondering whether to drop out of school because someone had come along and told her she could be on a magazine. "Then why were you never there?" she asked, the words scraping by her throat.

Vivian released a deep breath. "Do you know why I did all this? Worked in other countries, helped all those people? Instead of being with you?" When Madison didn't answer, Vivian went on. "Because Steven asked me to." Her mother rose, crossing to the window, seeming like a smaller version of herself. She wrapped her arms around her body. "The day before your father died, he made me promise two things. First, that I wouldn't let you be raised in the places where we worked, because we had seen too many children die in those awful conditions. He wanted to know that you would always be safe, healthy and cared for. And second…"

"What else?" Madison prodded when her mother didn't finish.

"And second, that before I had you, I would finish the job we started in Thailand. He loved those people, like they were his own. Steven didn't just go in and work in a community, then move on. He connected, he cared. And he was afraid that if he was gone and I left, the work would be forgotten."

"And did you stay?"

"No." Her mother's voice broke on a sob of regret. She pivoted back, tears in her eyes. "I couldn't stay there, not after I lost him. So I left, I broke my promise. I came home to America, and had you, just a few weeks after your father died. You were a little early, maybe because I was such an emotional mess. I was still grieving; I wasn't in any shape to raise a child. Your grandfather told me he'd take care of you. That I should go pull myself together somewhere. So I went. But I couldn't go back to Thailand. I couldn't go back there and see that river, those people. I was angry at them, at the Mekong, even though it wasn't their fault. I was so hurt, so devastated by losing Steven and that loss was so consuming, I…" She sighed. "I went everywhere else in the world but there."

"And after that? Why didn't you come back?"

"Because it never seemed enough." The tears in her mother's eyes multiplied. "None of the children I fed, the crops I helped plant, the homes I helped build, none of it was enough to fill that hole in my heart."

"Wasn't *I* enough?" Madison asked, the words slipping from her in a tight, sad whisper.

"Oh, Madison, you would have been, but I…" she bit her lip, then tried again. "I stayed away too long. It was my fault, for leaving, for not being there to be your mother. And after a while, it just got easier to stay away, than to try and fix all that had gone wrong between us. By the time I came home that first time, you were calling the nannies *Momma*. I'd reach for you and you'd turn away. It wasn't your fault, you were still a baby and to you, I was a stranger, but it tore my heart in two. I couldn't stay, couldn't—"

"Be rejected by the one person who was supposed to love you more than anyone else?" The tears, so long held back, finally burst past Madison's control and slid down her face.

Vivian's gaze met her daughter's. Understanding flowed between them, a connection built by two women who had lost each other, and went off seeking something else to fill that void.

"I never realized," Vivian began. "I never knew you…"

And then, her mother was there, coming to her daughter, drawing her into her arms. For a long time, the embrace felt odd, uncomfortable, and then, Madison inhaled the quiet floral fragrance her mother had worn for thirty years, and her arms stole around her Vivian's waist, her head slipping into the comfort of her mother's shoulder.

Making the first steps at bridging the decades-old divide between them.

A sense of peace, of knowledge, settled into Madison's heart. For so long, she had thought she had been the inadequate one, that her mother was rejecting her. She had never thought that maybe her mother had been as devastated by their lack of connection as Madison was. The tears continued their journey down her face, blurring her vision, soaking into her mother's soft T-shirt.

"I'm sorry, Madison," Vivian said, her voice hoarse. "I know that doesn't even begin to make up for me not being there, for everything I missed. But—"

"But it's a start," Madison finished. "We have time."

Vivian drew back, a watery smile on her tear-stained face, then gathered her daughter close again. "Yeah, we have time." Her mother cupped her chin, her blue eyes now softer with age, the wrinkles around her eyes the unconscious marks of a woman who had never cared much about the signs of age. "It was you, who inspired me to go back there."

"Me? I didn't do anything."

"Oh, but you did. You went to school."

Madison blinked. "How did you know about that?"

"I know about everything, sweetheart." Her mother broke away from her then, lifting an over-sized knitted bag over the floor. From the multi-colored bag, she withdrew a four-inch thick photo album, its pages stuffed to bursting. She laid it on the bed, then opened the cover and began to flip through the pages.

There, between the glossy pages, was Madison's first cover on *Seventeen*. Her first print ad, for Clearasil. A clipping about her contract with a furniture store. Her appearances in *Vogue, Mademoiselle, Self,* even a tiny gossip page item about Madison enrolling at NYU. One of those tidbits the paparazzi loved to unearth and broadcast to the world.

"You saved *everything*?" Madison sank onto the bed, turning page after page.

"Of course. You're my daughter." She sat down beside her. "I was so proud of you, I've always been so proud of you. But when you worked so hard to get your GED and then enrolled in college, I saw you going after what you wanted instead of sticking with the easy road. And I knew I had to do the same."

Madison swallowed. "Yeah, but I dropped out of college."

Her mother waved a hand in dismissal. "You'll go back. Soon as you're done here, I'm sure you'll be right back in school. And then someday, maybe you can come with me, to the village where he died. He's there, Madison, in every hut, every well we dug."

"I'd like that, but I can't."

"Come with me, Madison. Meet the people your father saved. The children are grown now, the parents older, gray-haired. I went back there, just last month, and finally began to finish the job Steven and I started."

Madison shook her head. "Maybelline wants me, Mother. I'm leaving for New York tonight."

Vivian was silent for a long moment. "Is that what you really want?"

"Of course. It's what I've worked for, all these years."

"If that's what makes you feel satisfied and happy," her mother said, "then by all means, do it."

The trouble, though, was that ever since she'd met Jack Pleeseman, Madison wasn't so sure she'd ever be satisfied and happy with her old life ever again.

Madison's Ducking-Out-Early Cheese and Crab Dip

1 10-ounce brick Cheddar cheese, diced
1 8-ounce package American cheese slices (Velveeta can also work)
1/3 cup milk
1/2 cup white wine
Salt and pepper to taste
8 ounces crab meat, flaked

It's time to go—and face the music with a certain dairy farmer whose mere presence has you dreaming of things that can never be. Instead, get busy over the stove so that when he asks you a question, you can lie to the pan instead of him.

Melt the cheese with the milk in a saucepan over low heat. Add remaining ingredients and stir until heated. Serve with crackers—or anything that will keep your mouth too full to talk.

CHAPTER TWENTY-EIGHT

When Madison screwed up her life, she did it with flair. It was nearly midnight and she had yet to leave, though her bags were packed and waiting by the door, nor had she mustered up the courage to tell Jack where she was going.

The closure with her mother was still a surprise, one that Madison returned to every few minutes. Once this deal with Maybelline was done and she could take some time off, she'd fly to Thailand. Get to know her father and her mother.

But for now, she had to concentrate on leaving. A few hours ago, Harry had called again, reminding her of the meeting with Maybelline tomorrow. "You can put the damned cheese behind you and be the million dollar face of make-up," he'd said.

"Do you think they'd reschedule?"

"Are you *insane?* This is Maybelline, Madison, not some rinky-dink two-shade lipstick company. You get your ass into their offices at ten tomorrow morning or they'll find someone else." Harry let out a curse, then inhaled some smoke. "And I'll have to cut you off, too. I can't keep clients who don't want to work."

"I'll be there, Harry," she said, sighing. "You can count on me."

She'd said the same thing to Jack.

Why was she still delaying her departure? The cosmetics contract would be the answer to everything. Steady money, restoration of her reputation, a second chance to achieve everything she had worked so hard to gain.

And yet, a part of Madison wanted to stay just where she was.

Yeah, the part that had been overwhelmed by the not-so-fresh smell of cows, drifting through her open window with the evening breeze.

What model in her right mind chose to stay here with the ravenous goat, the Elvis sightings, and the man who was pulling her in the opposite direction that she wanted to go?

She needed to get out of here, and fast, before she did something really stupid.

Like stayed. For good.

Madison left the last of her bags near the front door, then hesitated before leaving. Part of her wanted the kind of love her mother had had with Steven, a powerful emotion that lingered in the heart for decades. And so, instead of leaving, she turned and headed down the hall to the kitchen, seeking...

A snack? A solution? A repeat of the kitchen sink scene?

Something, anything, to fill that yawning void inside her.

Yet even as she entered the homey room, clearly the heart of this house, she knew that what she sought the most was what she had found for those few minutes in Jack's arms, under the canopy of trees and the dappled afternoon sun.

That feeling of being safe. Protected...

Loved.

"I need more carbs," she muttered to herself, pulling open the refrigerator and looking for something fattening, gooey and filled with the kind of things she normally denied herself. One binge and she'd be fine.

She saw a block of cheese sitting beside a jar of salsa, a few jalapenos. A container of sour cream.

Loaded nachos. Those would do it.

She bypassed the extra ingredients, choosing only the cheddar block. As she had seen Jack do, she shredded some cheese, layering it over a sprinkling of tortilla chips on a plate. "Just nachos and cheese, no extras," she told herself, wrapping the remaining cheese up and putting it back.

But as soon as the plate was in the microwave, her stomach grumbled and she found herself going back to pull out the rest of the fixings, loading up the steaming nachos until the tortilla chips were barely visible beneath the overload of calories.

She was just sinking her mouth into the first one when she heard a sound and turned.

Jack. She swallowed back the joy at the sight of him, as familiar as her own hand, and pretended to be unaffected by his presence. "Oh, it's you," she said. "I was expecting Katydid."

"She doesn't like nachos. She's more of a tin can kind of girl."

Madison laughed. Everything within her wanted Jack, with a side of chips. In the moonlight, it all felt right, as if forever stretched ahead of them.

Unfortunately, forever was coming to a screeching halt as soon as she got in the Benz. If she knew what was good for her, she'd take the plate up to her room and eat alone.

But Madison was tired of feeling alone. Here, in this quirky house, with this man, she'd found something that hadn't been a part of her life, that she couldn't buy, couldn't charge.

Belonging.

Every member of the house, despite the occasional spats she'd seen, belonged to someone else and they had drawn her in as if she, too, was part of the bloodline.

Now, with the new connection with her mother, it seemed as if a circle was closing. It was crazy, really. All the luxury items in the world, the mansions she'd grown up in, none of them made her feel as complete as a little macaroni and cheese and this house had.

Those dinners around the kitchen table, as torturous as they had clearly been for the Pleeseman men, had shown her another side of home, the kind where people traded barbs with the platters. The only time she'd had that had been when she'd been with her cousin Daniel.

After being here, she understood what Daniel was talking about when he spoke about his life with Olivia, a life so unlike the one where they'd both grown up. She wanted more of that. More of the camaraderie and warmth, the food, the people.

And most of all, Jack.

"Join me," she said to him, indicating the empty chair beside her. "I promise to share."

"Beer?" he asked, dipping into the fridge.

Well, hell, she was already stuffing her face with nachos. What was the damage in a beer? "Sure."

He twisted the top off a Coors and laid it in front of her. "Oh, wait. You probably want a glass."

"No, today, I'm an ordinary woman. Which means I'm going to chug it back out of the bottle." He laughed as she did just that, swiping off the bit of foam that lingered on her lips with the back of her hand.

"You surprise me," he said. "And in a good way."

Madison ate another loaded chip, refusing to feel one ounce of guilt. Tomorrow would come soon enough. "Not all your surprises have been good?"

"Well, let's see," he said, twirling his amber bottle on the smooth tabletop. "There was the time I caught my wife in bed with another man. The day she told me she was leaving me for someone with a bigger bank account."

Madison scooped up a chip. Loaded on the sour cream. "I can relate to that," she said. "My last boyfriend decided the maids needed a bonus. Namely him."

"And here I thought giving out a DVD player was a good thank you to the employees."

She laughed, then consumed another chip, the smooth cheese settling against her tongue, igniting her hunger even more. "The funny part is that everyone thought Renaldo and I were made for each other. People were shocked when we broke up."

Jack nodded. "Same for me and Alyssa. We grew up right next door to each other, went to the same school, dated for five years before we got married. It should have been the perfect match."

"Why wasn't it?" She worked another chip into the toppings, but waited to eat it. "That was what I wanted to know with Renaldo. What ingredient were we missing?"

Jack thought a moment, sipping at his beer. "A shared view of the road ahead."

"Yeah, that was it. I wanted to settle down, stay in one place for a while. He was still sowing oats." She grimaced. "All over the south of France."

The thought of Renaldo's betrayal, the shock of it, rippled through Madison once again. She looked at Jack and wondered if he too would someday betray her. Right now, he seemed like a great man. A wonderful father.

But like the ads she saw created every day, what truth was buried beneath the façade? Once again, she told herself she was smart for leaving now, before she got in too deep.

"Isn't it funny," she said, "how what we think is reality is so far from what other people see?"

"And what about you, Madison? Are you real? Or airbrushed?"

Madison dipped her head, avoiding his gaze, a faint blush filling her cheeks. She looked vulnerable, shy.

"I'm a lot of make-up and hairspray," she said quietly. "You wouldn't even recognize me without the Lancôme."

"I beg to differ," Jack said, moving closer, ignoring the instincts that told him to go the other way, the half of his brain that had been down this path before with another woman, one who had broken his heart and shredded the pieces. He knew better, and yet, he wanted Madison all the same.

Maybe it was the optimist in him, the part of Jack that wanted to believe not every woman was like Alyssa. That she had been the anomaly, not the rule.

"I saw something in that *Sports Illustrated* picture." He smiled. "Something besides the bikini."

She grinned. "Breasts?"

"Well, yeah, I would have had to be dead not to notice those." He rubbed his thumb across the back of her hand. "When you look at the camera, there's an honesty there, as if you're putting yourself into that image. I saw that here, I saw it in *Sports Illustrated*."

"Trust me, there was an airbrush involved. What you see of me there, none of it's truly how I look."

"I don't believe you." And he didn't. The woman who had looked that camera in the eye wasn't just modeling. She was exposing her emotions, her passion. It was the same depth he'd seen in her eyes that day at the lake. Yet, he heard her self-deprecating words and wondered if she saw the same thing when she looked at her photos. Did she see past the computer enhancements, down to the woman he had glimpsed?

The woman his heart told him was unlike his ex-wife, unlike any woman he had met. A woman he could trust.

Jack reached up, drifting the back of his hand against her cheek, the velvet of her skin sending fire along his fingers, down his arm. Then he shifted in his chair until they were as close as the nachos on the plate. "You…you are real, Madison. You're more than an image."

She opened her mouth, to protest he was sure, but before she could speak, his mouth was on top of hers, picking up where they'd left off the day before. He kissed her, long and thoroughly, allowing the luxury of exploring her mouth with his own, tasting the sweetness of her, a blend of the muted and sharp notes of cheese and salsa. Then he drew back, cupping her face in his hands, while his pulse hammered in his veins and his gaze connected with her wide blue eyes.

He'd half expected her to shove him away, but Madison Worth, as she had from the moment he'd met her, did the exact opposite of what Jack expected.

She started to cry.

A single tear slipped down her cheek, followed quickly by another and another, leaving shimmery streaks along her flawless face.

Aw, hell. Now he'd done it. "What is it?"

"None of this is real, Jack," she said, getting to her feet. "That kiss wasn't and neither am I. I'm sorry."

Jack's The-Truth-Hurts Broccoli Casserole

2 tablespoons butter
2 tablespoons flour
1 cup milk
1 3-ounce package cream cheese, softened
1/2 cup Cheddar cheese, shredded
2 10-ounce packages frozen broccoli, cooked and drained
1/3 cup Ritz crackers, crushed

Just like eating your broccoli, sometimes you've got to eat—and hear—what you don't want. You knew she was hiding something and now that the truth is out, take your knocks and deal with it.

Preheat the oven to 350 degrees. In a saucepan, melt the butter, then add the flour. When that's well mixed, add the milk gradually. When it boils (just like your temper is about to), stir for one minute, until sauce is thickened. Add the cheese. When melted, stir in the broccoli.

Grease a one-quart casserole, then fill with the broccoli mixture. The sauce covers up the broccoli truth pretty well, just like her pretty exterior kept the whole story from you. Bake for 30 minutes, just long enough for her to walk out of your life for good.

CHAPTER TWENTY-NINE

Jack headed down the hall after Madison. She reached the front door, then stopped suddenly, her hand on the doorknob. The moonlight cascading in through the oval window illuminated a pile of rectangles, small and large, thick and thin. It took him a second before he realized what they were.

Suitcases.

A ball of lead sunk to the bottom of his stomach. He knew, as surely as he knew Becky the cow would get jealous over Big George's affections for Petunia, that those suitcases were a sign of the one thing he'd believed wouldn't happen.

Betrayal.

His concern for her vanished, replaced by a flash of anger. "What the hell is going on?"

She let out a sigh, one that mirrored the pain in her eyes. He refused to feel sorry for her. Five seconds ago, he'd believed in her honesty. Now he saw everything had been a lie.

"We need to talk," she said.

"You're damned right we do."

"I have to leave, Jack."

He'd seen the suitcases but still didn't want to consider the obvious. "Yeah, on Sunday, right?"

"No, now."

"*Now?* But the wine festival is in thirty-six hours. You'll be back for that, right?"

She shook her head, her gaze going away from him and toward something far off. "No. I'm not coming back."

"We had a contract, Madison."

"And Harry is going to fulfill that. He's sending another girl. She should be her in a few hours. She's got experience with this kind of thing. You'll be fine."

Fine. He was anything but fine right now.

"I don't want another model," he said, slamming his hand against the wall, causing her to jump and the wall to shiver. Betrayal sliced through him. What had he expected? That Madison would truly be different? That when he needed her support, she'd be there?

Even if he had to pay her for it.

"She'll do everything you want," Madison insisted. "She'll be perfect for the—"

He wheeled around. "Didn't you hear me? I don't want another model. I want you."

"I can't, Jack. I'm sorry. I have a shot at the Maybelline contract and if I don't go now, I'll miss the meeting in the morning. This is everything I've worked for. Everything I dreamed of."

He eyed her, watching the flicker in her blue eyes. "Is it, Madison? Really?"

"Of course." But she didn't look at him when she said it. She was lying and he knew it. And he didn't care.

"Just walking out on me, right when I need you the most?" He let out a curse. "And maybe I thought there was something more between us than some nachos and a quick lay." The words were as harsh as the raw emotion slicing away at his gut.

"That isn't fair." Something hot stung at her eyes, but she refused to give in to it. It was better this way. For a second, she'd lost herself in his dark brown eyes and opened up, allowing Jack Pleeseman into her heart.

A temporary brain fog, nothing more. She was leaving. She had to remember that. What was she thinking? That she could stay here, marry him and be happy living among the cows and the one-horned goat?

"What was I, anyway, to you?" he said, hurt and anger reflected in his eyes. "A temporary fix until you go back to the men with the limos and the penthouses? It's what I should have expected from the minute I met you."

"What the hell is that supposed to mean?"

He had no time to explain that to her. To run through his past again, with a woman who was going to walk away when he needed her most. "I'm not doing this again," he said, throwing up his hands, striding away from her. "I'm not getting involved with someone who's going to betray me."

He wasn't talking about her. Another woman had done him wrong and Madison was the one taking the brunt of the blame. "I'm not Alyssa," she said. "And I didn't use you for a temporary fix."

"Oh yeah?" He wheeled to face her, the anger clear in his eyes, despite the dark hallway. "Then tell me, Madison, how many real relationships have you had? Ones where you actually opened up and allowed someone into your heart? Where you gave back as much as you got?"

"That's none of your damned business."

"I think it is," he said, moving closer, invading her space, searching her gaze for the truth. "Because I let you into my house. My life. My—" He cut himself off, let out a curse. "You know what you are? A coward."

"*I'm* scared?" She shook her head. "What about you? You're like a clam who refuses to open up. Every time I get a little bit close, you retreat. No wonder you and your father don't agree on the business. You don't talk to anyone, Jack. Not me, not your family."

"I talk."

"Then why don't I know anything about what's going on behind there," she said, pointing at his eyes. "You're more than happy to have sex with me, but when it comes to opening up, you go so far and then you stop."

"You're wrong." Yet even as Jack said the words, he knew she was right. He hadn't been all that open with anyone, not in a long time, maybe not ever. Well, he sure as hell wasn't going to start now.

"You told me I'm afraid," she said. "Well so are you. And you know what you're afraid of?" She didn't wait for his reply, just pushed forward with her Psych 101 lesson in the front hall. "Of putting your trust in anyone. You'd much rather be Jack the Martyr than ask for help."

"I asked for your help, if you remember. With my marketing. With the wine festival. And what are you doing? Walking out on me."

"And you knew this day was going to come, didn't you? You banked on it, like you bank on everyone else to let you down. So you made sure you didn't get too close. Didn't expose too much of Jack Pleeseman. That way, no one gets hurt."

"My business gets hurt."

"Yeah, and I'm sorry for that. But right now, I have to worry about me. About my future."

"Your future could be here, with us."

"*You* are going to be okay. Because if there's one thing you do pour your heart and soul into, Jack, it's this business." She took a step forward, and for a second, her eyes softened, a slight sheen covering the cobalt color. "Because it sure as hell wasn't me."

Then she turned and walked away, grabbing two of the suitcases, carrying them outside and over to the car, loading them into the trunk. If he hadn't been so busy hating her right now, he might have given her a hand.

But Madison was too damned concerned with her own options. So he let her carry them herself, chivalry be damned.

Madison's Distance-Doesn't-Help Macaroni Salad

8 ounces elbow macaroni, cooked and drained
1 cup Cheddar cheese, cubed
1/2 cup celery, diced
1/4 cup green pepper, chopped
1/4 cup onion, chopped
1/2 cup mayonnaise
1/2 teaspoon salt
1/4 teaspoon pepper

No matter how many miles you put between you and that man, it doesn't make you forget him. The solution? Take all the above ingredients, mix well, then dig in with a fork and keep eating until he's a distant memory.

CHAPTER THIRTY

M adison told herself on the long, boring ride to New York City that she had done the right thing. That leaving behind the rolling green hills of the Berkshires—and the one man she had begun to care about—was a far better choice than staying and being the face on a chunk of cheddar.

Maybelline wanted her. That should be enough to make her happy.

But several hours later, as she wound her way through the busy streets of Manhattan to her apartment building, she felt a growing emptiness. She was surrounded by a crowded city of people and yet she felt as lonely and adrift as a castaway.

She shook off those thoughts and pulled into the garage. Give her a few days and she'd be back to her normal self. She'd take off the few pounds she'd gained at Jack's, get back into her normal routine. The fettuccini, nachos and macaroni had already begun to take over her waistline. She could feel it in the snugness of her shorts, the fullness of her breasts.

Penance. She needed penance. She'd camp out at a yoga studio until she'd worked all of it out of her system. All of the calories and all the memories of the man.

Even as she made a plan to lose the weight, another part of her wanted to hold onto those extra pounds. For one thing, she felt healthier, fuller, like she finally knew what food was all about. Not to mention why people indulged in the pleasure. Many, many times.

A few minutes later, Madison was back in her apartment. Home, though it hardly felt like home after the days in the Berkshires. She flicked on the lights, half expecting Katydid or Buster to come running. Nothing. Just the familiar cold emptiness, a style her decorator had called "clean modern" or some such thing. It was clean all right, so clean Madison didn't dare breath for fear of disturbing the air.

She put her makeup bag on the credenza. The rest of the bags could be brought up by the door-man later. There were some advantages to living in a luxury high-rise, after all.

A cozy environment, however, wasn't one of them. Madison sighed and leaned against the wall, the Manolos on her feet feeling as out of place as the art on the walls, the furniture in her rooms.

Jack had been wrong.

She didn't belong here, not in this world. Not anymore. The only trouble was figuring out where she did belong.

Madison crossed the room, flicking on the TV as she went, more for the company than for the news. She wandered into her kitchen. As always, the refrigerator was stocked with the typical Madison menu: fresh fruit, salad greens, Sugar-Free-Jell-O, Evian and nothing else. The cabinet, she already knew, would be filled with pretty much the same.

All the cabinets except one.

Madison grabbed a chair from the quartet around the glass kitchen table, then dragged it over to the refrigerator. She slipped off her pumps, then stood on the leather seat, reaching into the tiny space over the white Whirlpool. Buried in the very back was what she was looking for—one lone box of Kraft Macaroni and Cheese.

This was the one thing Madison knew how to make. It had been the food that had gotten her through the loneliness of her childhood, the only meal she had mastered, an amazing feat considering she had all the cooking skills of a hippo.

The doorman rang the apartment just as Madison was putting a pot of water on the stove. She looked through the video monitor, then called down to let her visitor in. "Cally!" she exclaimed, pulling open the door. "What are you doing here?"

"Wishing you luck for tomorrow." She hoisted a bottle of Dom Perignon. "And celebrating a little."

"Celebrating? But I didn't get the job yet."

"Hey," Cally said, mocking a look of annoyance, "the world does not revolve around Madison Worth, you know."

Madison laughed as they walked down the hall and into the kitchen. She withdrew two champagne flutes from the glass-front cabinet above the mini wine cooler. "What are we celebrating?"

Cally beamed. "I broke up with Robert."

"You did? For good?"

"Yep. I finally realized that I do deserve better."

"Good for you! That's definitely a reason to celebrate."

"Hey, I'll drink to almost anything." Cally grinned, then got to work opening the champagne bottle. The cork popped off, propelled as if by a sonic jet, and pinged off the wooden back of the kitchen chair, leaving a golf-ball sized dent. "Oh, shit, Madison. I'm sorry."

Madison shook her head, holding out the glasses for Cally to fill. "No biggie. I like a little wear on my things."

Cally pressed the back of her free hand against Madison's temples. "Are you feeling all right?"

"Perfect." She smiled. "Well, yeah, I am a little different."

"Ah, the cow boy turned your head for good, did he?"

Madison shrugged, sipping at her champagne.

"You can't lie to me. I've known you way too long."

"It doesn't matter. Jack and I are not together, not anymore." Madison rose, crossing to the stove. She opened the box of pasta and dumped it into the boiling water, stirring it with one of the stainless steel spoons in the white marble holder beside the stove. "Remember, I left on pretty bad terms."

"So? Return on better ones." Cally joined Madison at the stove, watching her swish the tiny elbows back and forth. "What are you making?"

"Comfort in a box." She held up the cardboard container. "Kraft Macaroni and Cheese."

Cally read the nutritional information on the side. "Whoo-hoo. Going for the big guns, huh?"

"It's the only cheese dish I know how to make."

"So you didn't just fall in love with the man, you fell in love with his dairy products, too?"

Madison turned away from the stove, picking up her champagne flute again and swirled the pale liquid around. Lying was pointless. For one, Cally could spot deception on Madison's face from a store aisle away. For another, she was done with lying. It was far too taxing and in the end, all it did was hurt people. "Yeah, I did."

"So what are you going to do about it?"

"Make some macaroni, drink some champagne, and go to bed."

"You're not going to go back there? Fight for what you want?"

"Since when did fighting for what I wanted get me anywhere?"

Cally took a seat at the table, crossed her legs, smoothing an invisible wrinkle out of her slacks. "Do you know why I broke up with Robert?" her voice was quiet, confidential.

Madison shook her head.

"Because I heard your voice on the phone when you talked about this guy and I…" She looked away, then back. "I wanted some of that."

Madison did, too. She wanted Jack, and everything that came with Jack, with an intensity that bordered on pain. She couldn't have him, though, not after what she'd done. So instead here she was, eating boxed macaroni and cheese when the real thing was a few hours away.

Because the opportunity of a lifetime was in New York. Not in the Berkshires.

She returned to the pot, testing the pasta against the side of the pan. It was done, so she busied herself with draining it, then stirring in the rest of the ingredients. She had to settle for adding fat-free instead of regular milk and a light wannabee butter.

"Mad?" Cally asked, laying a touch on her shoulder. "You okay?"

Madison poured the macaroni into a serving bowl, then dug two spoons out of the drawer and turned around. "I saved this box of macaroni and cheese for all this time," she said. "It was crazy, but it was something I needed, kind of like an ex-smoker who keeps that one cigarette in a glass case, to prove he can resist it." Madison sunk into a seat, waiting until Cally had joined her at the table. Together, they each took a spoon and dug in. Part of always telling the truth, she realized, was talking to the people who cared about her. "When I was a kid, my mom was never around. She was always off in one country or another, taking care of other people. I grew up pretty much alone." She drew in a breath, then faced some more reality. "I could blame it all on her, but you know what? I'm a grown-up and I realize that a lot of what I did when I was a kid, especially eating like a horse at a trough, was because I wanted attention. I had this need that I wanted to fill. I guess I did it with food."

"I understand that," Cally said. "Lots of people do those things. For me, it's shoes. Jimmy Choo sure knows the way to my heart."

"Mine too." Madison laughed, took another bite, swallowed, then continued. "All that eating, though, led to weight gain, of course. I was a chubby kid, till I was about fifteen and I realized there was another way to fill myself."

Cally's eyes met hers, understanding and connection running deep. "With men."

"Yeah. But that didn't work either. So I started controlling everything. My house," she swept a hand around the sterile, plain environment, "what I ate. What I looked like. I thought that control would make me happy. But all it did was make me stressed."

Cally chuckled. "Hence, the frequent visits to the spa?"

She smiled. "Those were purely for pleasure. And a tax write-off."

Cally roared with laughter. "I'll have to remember that, come April."

"So now," Madison said, raising a forkful of golden macaroni, "I need to figure out what will make me feel fulfilled. But first, I'm going to finish off this bowl." Not to fill herself, but to prove she could have a little indulgence and still be fine.

"A woman with priorities," Cally said. "Now that I can respect."

Madison was gone and Jack was in a really bad mood. Unfortunately, there weren't enough trees on the property to work this out of his system.

But he chopped wood all the same on Friday morning, avoiding making the decision he knew he was going to have to make.

"What are you doing? Stockpiling for the blizzard of '06?"

Jack turned at the sound of his father's voice. For a second, he could see the age in his father's face, not the normal age that came from more than sixty years on the planet, but the kind of lines that came from loss, from having a dream snatched away, too soon, too young.

Jack didn't mention any of that. Instead, he swung the axe into a piece of oak, splitting the log clearly in half. "Just getting some chores done, Dad."

"I thought you needed to get ready for that shindig tomorrow."

"I will." Jack put another log on the stump, then swung the axe and sent it clearly through the wood.

Out of the corner of his eye, he saw his father shuffle his feet, open his mouth, shut it, then try again. "What are you doing to do now that the princess has flown the coop?"

"I don't know." Chop. The severed pieces landed on the ground with a clunk. "I'll work it out."

"You going to get another girl?"

Jack had already made that phone call, telling Harry not to bother. Madison Worth was the face he wanted on his products, and after this week, no one else would do. He loaded another piece of oak onto the stump. "No."

"Talking to you is like pulling nails out of a pig's ass." Joe cursed. "Impossible."

Jack lowered the axe, swiping the sweat off his brow with one hand. "Who do you think I learned it from?"

Joe scowled. "I talk," he said, unwittingly echoing Jack's words to his brother and to Madison.

"To who? To me? To Aunt Harriet? Because if you do, we sure as hell don't hear you." The axe went up again, came down with one clean stroke.

Joe ran his hand over the nearby pile of newly stacked wood. "To your mother," he said, his voice quiet.

Jack stopped chopping. "What do you mean?"

"Where do you think I go every day? It sure as hell isn't to the proctologist."

Most days, Joe was gone for an hour, sometimes as many as three or four. Jack had never questioned his absence, figuring his father had the right to spend his retirement days as he chose. "You're visiting Mom's grave?"

"No. She isn't there. Not really." Joe let out a breath, then cast his glance over the land that had been in his family for generations. His face grew soft and a small smile spread across his features. "I go to the house. That's where she is. For me."

"The house?" And then, Jack realized what house he meant. The one that was supposed to face the lake, the one where his mother had talked of sitting on the porch, watching the world go by. "The lake house."

"Yeah." Joe shrugged, as if it was nothing. "I feel better when I'm out there, like she's with me."

"But I thought you let that house go, after—"

"I did. For a while." Joe brushed chips of wood off one of the stumps, then sat down, a big man in an oversized Carhartt jacket, his shoulders hunched forward. "But then I started again."

"You started working on the house?" That explained the saw he and Madison had heard that afternoon at the lake.

"I'm not making much progress." Joe held out his hands. "These aren't what they used to be, and neither is this." He pressed one hand to his back. "I'll tell you one thing, Jack, it sucks to get old."

"Why didn't you ask for help? David and I would have pitched in."

Joe lowered his palms to his knees and leaned forward, his face intent. "This is something I have to do myself. Do you understand that?"

Jack looked over the Pleeseman property, his gaze sweeping past the barn, the gift shop, the places that he had invested so much time and energy into in the last few years, because he felt it was his mission to make it all a success. Because this was all part of his family, his heritage. "Yeah, I guess I do."

"Besides, your mother would kill me if I took you away from the business." Joe flicked a shard of wood across the sawdust filled pile. "You were always the one, you know."

"For what?" Jack sat down on the opposite stump, laying the axe on the ground at his feet.

"The one she wanted in charge. When you came back, it took me a while, but I stepped down. Because…" Joe drew in a breath. "That was the way she would have wanted it. She loved this place, more than anything."

Jack felt the words rise up in his throat, begging to be released. "Then why did she leave?"

"Leave?" Joe smiled, shaking his head. "Your mother didn't leave. She went out to see those hoity-toity relatives of hers." He snorted. "She had dreams, like you. Me, I'm the nuts and bolts guy. Your mother, she was the one with the vision."

Jack's mind reached back in time, seeing his mother in the kitchen, the garden, the barn. She'd fostered his love of learning and of thinking forward instead of staying where he was. He'd done that with business. His personal life was another story. "Yeah, Mom was always like that. She could see an entire field of flowers in a single package of seeds."

"Then she'd put me to work making sure it happened." Joe laughed. "I still have nightmares about mulch."

Jack toed at the axe handle. "So what was her vision for the business?"

"She wanted to make this cheese thing work. She used to tell me, "Joe, it's going to be the future of this farm." But I...I disagreed."

Jack thought of the argument he had heard a couple of days before his mother left. Raised voices, such a rarity in his family, coming up through the vents of the house, but not enough that he and David could truly eavesdrop. "About the direction of the company?"

"About me being as stubborn as a jackass. She said she'd do it herself. Because she believed, she trusted. Me, I'm the cautious one. Don't change it, if it ain't broke."

Jack had to bite back a laugh. If there was one phrase that made up his father's guiding principle, that was it. "Did she go there to ask for money? So she could run things her way?"

"Nope." Joe flicked another piece of wood at the pile. He drew in a breath, exhaled it. "You remember your grandparents, right, Jack?"

He'd barely seen them as a child, as if they had sworn off everyone and everything associated with the man who had stolen their daughter's heart. "A little."

"Well, your grandfather... How can I put this?" Joe paused. "Frankly, he was a mean son of a—" He cut himself off. "Let's just say he wouldn't have been at the top of anyone's friends and family list."

Jack nodded, remembering the stern, controlling man who had used his temper like ranch hands used horses—to corral the people in his family into their own designated pens. He'd been full of lectures and not much else. "Yeah, I remember that."

"Your grandma, though, she was like your mom. Sweet as can be. *And* she actually liked me." Joe grinned. "I think."

All Jack could recall about his grandmother was the scent of L'air du Temps, which had wrapped around him in a cloud with every hug, not that there'd been many of those. His grandparents had visited the farm twice, once for David's birth, once for Jack's communion, and both times been out the door within twenty minutes because of Grandfather Kendall.

"Anyway," Jack went on. "Your grandma loved this place, loved your mom. Then one day she called your mom and told her she was leaving your grandpa."

"Mom went out there to help her," Jack said, the light dawning.

"Yeah." Joe looked up at the sky, as if the sun could erase the glimmer of tears in his eyes. "She never made it."

Jack thought back to the details he remembered. "And Grandma stayed where she was."

Joe took a slice of wood and began peeling off the bark, the eye contact avoidance of men talking about a difficult subject. "She had to, Jack. Your grandfather was never the same after Nancy…" Even now, all these years later, the word "died" wouldn't cross his lips. "So she stayed, took care of him, till he passed, too, a few years later."

"Wow." Jack ran a hand through his hair, sending a trickle of wood shavings drifting to the ground. "I never knew that."

"He blamed himself, you know, for what happened to your mom. I think that's what made him sick."

Jack picked up the sliver of a log beside his feet and tossed it onto the growing pile of wood. The information, so long held back, settled a peace around Jack's shoulders. He'd never known why his mother had left, and thought it was because she'd grown to hate the farm life, her family.

But instead she'd been, as she always was, hurrying off to help a person she loved.

"I always thought she was leaving us," Jack admitted to his father, the words coming out in a guttural, thick voice.

Joe looked up, surprised. "You did? Well, hell, she wouldn't do that, Jack. She loved it here."

"But she left all that money, her family, when she left her San Francisco life. She never missed it?"

Joe tossed the stripped sliver of wood into the pile. "You know what she said to me the first time she stepped onto this land?"

"No, what?"

"We were walking right over there," Joe said, pointing at the hill that rolled along the barn, "and she stopped me, even grabbed my arm to be sure I was paying attention. "This is freedom," she said. "Not the money." She loved the land, the animals, all of it. To her, it let her be free to be herself. In her world, appearances are everything. But here, your mom could let down her hair, dance with the dog, chase the goat out of her flowerbeds, and it was all okay. Your mother was a daisy in a field of thistles."

Jack's mind went back a couple dozen years, to the days when his mother had, indeed, done that. She hadn't just danced with the dog, she'd danced with him and David, too, swinging them around the kitchen as she sang along to some Burt Bacharach song on the radio. "She was one of a kind."

"Actually, I think there's more than one woman like her." Joe rose, brushing the chips of wood off his lap. "That New York princess you hired..."

"Madison."

Joe nodded. "Seems to me she looked a lot happier here, with her hair down, petting Ellie and pushing Ginny on the swing than she ever was in those goddamned ridiculous shoes of hers."

"Yeah, well, she had us all fooled." Jack rose and grabbed his axe. "She made it clear she isn't coming back."

"Then go after her. Don't let her slip away." Joe looked out over the acres around them, his gaze going past the farm, in the direction of the lake. "Life's too damned short."

That it was. And, Jack realized as he stood there, on land that had been in his family for generations, that it was high time he quit standing still and began instead to move forward with his life.

"You're right, Dad," Jack said.

His father arched a brow. "I'm right? Now there's a new phrase out of your mouth."

"Hey, don't ruin a perfectly good Hallmark moment."

Joe chuckled. "You going to go see her?"

"First, I have to see another woman," Jack said, slicing the last log in half. "And I need to talk to you about an idea I had."

Harry's Fruity-Decisions Apple Plate

2 Golden Delicious apples, sliced
Assorted cheeses, sliced

What, you think I have time to mess around with some gourmet meal? The clock is ticking, always ticking. Slap the apples and the cheese on a plate, then serve it to someone whose decision making skills seem to have flown the coop.

CHAPTER THIRTY-ONE

Three hours later, Madison left the offices of Maybelline. She stood on the busy Fifth Avenue sidewalk, watching the traffic moving by in a steady, honking stream, and wondered if she'd just made the biggest mistake of her life.

As Harry had predicted, the head honchos at the cosmetics company had taken one look at her and pronounced her the face for the more mature Maybelline user. Harry sat beside her, beaming as if he'd just won ten thousand bonus minutes.

They'd slid a contract across the table for her and Harry to look at. The first thing Madison noticed was the numbers on the first page—more pay than she'd ever made in a year, the kind of dollar signs that even Grandfather Worth would be impressed by.

It was everything she'd ever wanted. Harry handed her a pen, an encouraging smile on his face. "Nothing to quibble about with this one, Madison. It's a good deal, no doubt about it."

She took the Bic from Harry, clicked the top and flipped to the last page, skimming as she went.

The ball tip was poised over the line marked for her name. Her agreement.

"This is the kind of deal models dream about," Harry said. "You'll never have to work another cheese farm again. So sign it, quick, before they think you don't want this."

She didn't "sign it, quick." Instead, she thought of Jack, the way he had poured himself into his business, fulfilling a mission and a challenge set by his mother. Building a legacy, one sale at a time.

Then she thought of Ginny, naming each calf, giving the farm a personality. In her mind, she saw Ginny on the swing, the starched dress and patent leather shoes no longer spotless, scuffed by a day of play with her father.

She thought of Daniel and Olivia, picturing them with their new baby, carving out a life that wasn't built on the Worth wealth, but rather on the passion of lifelong dreams. Traveling that shared road Jack had spoken about.

Then she thought of her apartment in Manhattan. The stark, contemporary décor, so pristine that dust didn't dare cross her threshold. Every inch of those rooms was exquisite perfection—

And yet lonely as hell.

Now, standing on the sidewalk, Madison glanced down at her hand and saw she still held Harry's Bic pen, the point clicked back inside the barrel.

And as unused as a virgin.

"What the hell was that?" Harry shouted, hustling out the doors at Maybelline, his labored breathing speaking of too many Marlboros and not enough lung capacity.

"I'm sorry, Harry. But I'm going…" she paused, then realized she knew exactly where she was headed now, "home."

"Are you nuts? You can't keep people like that waiting." He pointed at the building. "Get back in there and sign the damned thing."

"No."

Harry's face turned crimson. "Have you gone *completely* insane?"

She grinned. "Nope. For the first time in my life, I feel like I'm finally thinking with a clear head. Like I know which road to take."

"Yeah, the one that leads you back inside and upstairs," Harry said, thumbing toward the doors.

She placed a quick kiss on Harry's cheek. "Thanks for everything, Harry."

"Are you leaving me? Leaving this deal on the table?"

She reached in her purse for the keys to her Benz, then thumbed the remote to the butterfly-covered car. "There's always going to be another deal like that one," she said. "But there won't always be another deal like the one waiting for me in the Berkshires."

"You're going to choose *cows* over *Maybelline?*"

"Nope. I'm choosing the man." She looked at her car, and for the first time since Coop had given her the newly finished vehicle, she understood what he meant. The butterfly, Madison now realized, had to do its own work to escape the cocoon. Madison was done with being a caterpillar waiting for someone else to come along and transform her.

"Models," Harry muttered. Then his face softened and he shook his head. "You always were better than this, Madison. But if you ever decide to come back…"

"I know your cell number." She gave him a quick hug, then turned and walked away.

"What am I supposed to do with Maybelline?" Harry said, calling after her.

"Send another girl. Because this one is heading for greener pastures."

Jack's Making-Hard-Choices Cheesy Cauliflower

1 16-ounce bag frozen cauliflower, cooked and drained
1/2 cup mayonnaise
2 teaspoons mustard
3/4 cup Cheddar cheese, shredded
Salt and pepper

If you'd had a crystal ball, maybe you wouldn't have made the choice you were forced to make. But when you're backed into a corner, you do what you have to do.

And then you eat some cheese to make it all easier to take.

Preheat the oven to 375 degrees. Mix all ingredients together, then pour into a greased casserole dish. Bake 15 minutes, or until the cheese is melted and your decisions are a bit easier to swallow.

CHAPTER THIRTY-TWO

The last person Jack expected to see pulling into the Pleeseman driveway on Saturday morning in a multi-colored dust cloud was Madison Worth. Unbidden, joy surged in his chest.

Madison had returned.

Then, just as quickly as it began, the feeling subsided. She may be here, but she was too late.

Madison stepped out of the butterflied car, striding toward him in a light blue suit and matching heels. Something in his heart began to thud and thud hard, like a metal detector pinging on a diamond ring.

Half of him hoped she was back to stay and the other half—the cautious half—said she was here to say goodbye forever because she was jetting off on a round-the-world cosmetics tour. Getting his hopes up would be a futile exercise. He'd had far too much experience with futility lately to want to go there again.

"Hey," she said when she reached him, a soft blush filling her cheeks. It took him a second before he realized the pink tint and quiet word meant she was feeling shy. Of all people, Madison feeling shy.

"Hey yourself." He strode down the stairs, meeting her on the path that led to the house. "How'd it go in New York?"

She paused, and in that interminable wait, it seemed as if she held his heart in her hands. "They offered me the job."

"Great, congratulations," Jack said, trying to work some enthusiasm into his voice. The pessimist in him had been right, damn it.

"And I turned it down."

"You…" Had he heard her right? "You did what?"

Her lips curled up into smile number seven hundred and two, this one a sweet, happy smile that took over her face, adding light to her eyes. "I turned it down, Jack."

"Why?"

"Because I don't want to be the face of Maybelline. Or Revlon. Or Estee Lauder." She met his gaze. "I want to be the face of Cheese Pleese."

Jack looked away, his gaze sweeping over the land, skimming past the barn, the silos, the Cheese Pleese store, a sense of loss descending heavy and deep into his gut. An hour ago, things had been different. Pleeseman Dairy had been in Pleeseman hands. Until today. "You're too late, Madison."

"Too late? But—"

"Go back to New York, Madison," he cut in, his voice sharp. "I don't need you anymore."

"Jack, I know you're mad at me and you have every right to be," she said, moving toward him, her hand extending to his arm. "I should never have left like that. But there's still plenty of time to prepare for the wine—"

"Cheese Pleese isn't going to be at the wine festival. Or anywhere else."

She stopped, stunned. "What do you mean?"

"I mean I gave the company to Kitty." He cursed again at the thought of it, of the younger Dandy sister winning. Undoubtedly, Kitty was holding a party right now, distributing gloat with the champagne.

"Why would you do that?" Madison asked. "You love this company."

He gestured toward a small figure in the distance, walking through the back pasture with David. "I love Ginny more."

And then, it made sense. The pieces slipped into place and Madison knew. "You traded the business for custody." It didn't need to be a question. She already knew the answer.

He lifted one shoulder, then dropped it, as if this was a small thing. But in his eyes, she read the exact opposite. "That was Alyssa's price."

"She sold her daughter for a *business*?" Madison heard her voice rise on the last word, disbelief tinting the syllables.

Jack gestured to Madison to follow him, leading the way up the stairs and onto the porch swing. They sat down, the wooden seat arcing backward with the added weight, then it settled into a regular pattern. For a moment, Madison felt like she was on *The Waltons*, sitting with a beau on the front porch.

Jack stopped the swing, putting his elbows on his knees, his shoulders hunched around him. "If there's one thing that motivates my ex-wife, it's money," he began, his voice quiet and low. "She never wanted to be a mother, never wanted Ginny at all. When she found out she was pregnant, she was going to—" He cut off the words, unable to finish that sentence. He didn't need to. Madison could read the intent in Jack's eyes. "I stopped her, told her I'd raise Ginny myself if I had to. Begged her to give our marriage and what I thought was our child a chance."

Madison turned, watching the dark-haired girl patting a calf, then laughing. The lack of resemblance between her and Jack struck Madison. "Ginny isn't yours?"

Jack studied his hands as if they held the memories he was revisiting. "Alyssa's not big on fidelity either. At the time she got pregnant, she was running around with more than one guy and never knew who Ginny's real father was. But the minute I heard Ginny's heartbeat in the doctor's office," now he looked up at her, sincerity running deep in his brown irises, "she became mine. She became a part of my heart."

Madison couldn't respond. This man was like no other she had ever met. In twenty-nine years of life, she had never met anyone who loved like Jack loved Ginny.

Unconditionally. Without question. Without even the tie of DNA to bind them together. He loved his daughter just because.

Something in Madison's chest began to ache, hard and sharp. She suddenly realized all that she had been denied, all that she had missed out on growing up in the mansion with the butler and the maids. She'd had every single thing a girl could ask for.

But none of the intangibles that created a real family.

Jack had given up all those tangible things for someone he loved. "But the business means so much to you, to your family," she said.

"I know." The words came out in a gust. "Of course, I talked to them before I did this. We had a big family meeting last night, because I knew Alyssa was coming back this morning. When they heard what was at stake, though, they were behind me a hundred and ten percent. To my family, nothing is worth losing Ginny."

"But you gave up your mother's dream, your—"

"My mother is dead, Madison. She's not here to have a dream, not anymore. The sooner I realize that, the better off I am." He cursed. "There are just some things more important than business."

She could see the pain, the loss, etched in his face, in the set of his shoulders. As much as he loved Ginny, it had surely killed him to have to give up the company that had been in generations of his family's hands. It was a legacy, and clearly the knowledge that he had been the one to let it go was killing him.

"But what if you could have both?" Madison said, reaching for him, the touch of comfort sending a surge of something powerful through her. "The business *and* Ginny?"

He snorted. "That would never happen. You don't know my ex-wife."

"No, I don't," Madison admitted. "But I know her kind."

She'd seen women like Alyssa in the face of Janine Turner, who had stolen Madison's grades to cover up for her own failure. She'd seen it dozens of beautiful women she'd met over the years who had been insecure yet as money hungry as squirrels in a nut factory.

Of course, not every model fit in that category. There were some, like Cally, who believed in friendship and treated it like a treasure.

"You can't give up without a fight, Jack." She took his hand in both of hers. He didn't pull away, but he stayed stiff and unyielding. Maybe if he let go, he'd fall apart.

"I can't fight money like that," he said finally, his voice weary with defeat, eyes watery with loss. "You know that better than anyone. When wealth is involved, the little guy loses." Jack let go of one of her hands, reached into his chest pocket and withdrew a sheaf of papers, laying them on the seat between him and Madison. "This was my deal. And if you ask me, I got the better end of the bargain." His gaze went to his daughter, still playing in the distance. His smile became softer, full of obvious love, before he returned his attention to Madison. The smile lingered for just a second. A craving for someone to look at her with that same level of intensity and emotion growled inside her.

The same way Daniel looked at Olivia. Like there was nothing else in the world more important than that person.

Madison decided she wasn't going to wait for that smile to come to her. She was going to bring it to Jack. Because for her, right now, there was nothing more important than helping Jack.

Was that love? Madison shook off the thought. Later, she would deal with those questions.

"There's got to be a way for you to have both. Let me help you, Jack."

He shook his head. "I appreciate all you're trying to do for me—"

"For you and your family."

He reached up and cupped her chin in one hand. "What are you going to do, Madison? Take on Alyssa? Let it go. I may not look it right now, but I'm happy. This will all work out. I can always get another job. But I can't get another Ginny."

"Oh, Jack, don't give up." She pressed her palm over his. "If there's one thing I've learned from these past few days, it's that anything can be changed, if you want it bad enough. There's a way to beat Kitty, I'm sure of it."

He laughed, then gathered her into his arms, pressing a sweet, brief kiss on her lips.

"What was that for?" Madison said.

"For wanting to fight even though the war is already over. I do believe this place has grown on you."

She smiled, her hands seeking his touch again, needing that closeness, needing him. "That's not the only thing that's grown on me."

His smile grew bittersweet, then he rose and stepped away, the porch swing swooping backward, the papers ruffling in the breeze. "Go back to New York, Madison. Go back to your world."

She took in a deep breath. "I don't want to go back to New York or anywhere else. I want to be with you."

He shook his head, refusing to listen. "Don't. You and I both know models don't settle down with dairy farmers. So let's be smart about this and end it now. Before either of us gets in too deep."

Madison looked up at Jack, searching his dark brown eyes. Her gut told her she'd already gotten in too deep. "End it?" Her voice cracked. "Are you quitting on me, too?"

"No. I'm letting you go. I was kidding myself in thinking you were meant for this place. For me. We're from two different worlds. You deserve to be happy in your own world."

"But Jack, I *wasn't* happy there." She stood, then took his hand, holding it tight, hoping to make him understand. "I was happy here."

"I can't make you happy, Madison. I can't make anyone happy." He tugged his hand out of hers and took a step back. "I have to concentrate on Ginny now. Her and the unemployment line."

"I won't let you quit, Jack. I won't let you give up on this place."

"For once in your life, Madison, don't fight me. I want you to go back to your life. Now." He drew in a breath, then hardened his face. "You're fired, Madison."

Then he turned, headed across the driveway, climbing into his truck and pulling away from the house before she could stop him.

Well, hell. If Jack wasn't going to save his own skin then Madison damned well would do it for him.

Madison's Making-A-Plan Cheddar Cheese Bites

1 8-ounce package refrigerated biscuits
¼ cup butter
¼ cup Cheddar cheese, shredded

Call a family meeting because it's time to bring in the troops. Preheat your oven to 400 degrees, then cut the biscuits into quarters so there's plenty to go around. You're going to need sustenance for what's ahead.

Arrange the biscuit pieces in two 8-inch cake pans. Melt the butter, then brush over all the biscuit pieces. Top with Cheddar and then bake for 12-15 minutes. By the time they're golden brown, your plan should be in motion, whether he likes it or not.

Chapter Thirty-Three

Madison sat on the Pleeseman porch, watching Jack's taillights disappear around a corner. The sale papers for the business were still sitting beside her. Knowing she was being nosy, but justifying it as helping Jack, she leafed through them, understanding some of it after years of reading her own contracts. There was a way out of this, she was sure of it. She dug her phone out of her purse and dialed.

She'd vowed on her way back to Massachusetts this morning to change her life. To take control again—assuming she had ever had control. One of the first steps in that journey was to stop running from the truth.

And especially from her grandfather.

"Hello?" The voice was sharp and short, the greeting as familiar as her own hand.

"Grandfather? It's Madison."

"Madison?" In those three syllables, she heard her grandfather's voice soften, nearly crumble. "Where are you?"

"The Berkshires," she said. "I'm working on some...new career options."

"You're not doing the modeling anymore?"

She glanced at the muddled reflection of herself in the silver base of the birdfeeder. "No, I'm not. I'm tired of missing Camelot."

"Camelot? You moving in with the Kennedys or something?"

She laughed. "I was thinking of a dairy farm."

"My hearing's not always so good," Grandfather said. "You didn't just say you were thinking of living on a *dairy farm*, did you?"

"Yes, I did." She gazed at the acres of green surrounding her, the fauna broken up by the red barn, the white house. Even Katydid the goat, who was trotting away from the pasture with a half-chewed burlap sack hanging from her single horn. "I found something here I never found in Boston and New York. Or anywhere else in the world."

Her grandfather was silent for a few seconds. Madison braced herself for the lecture she was sure was coming. "I'm glad, Madison. I want you to be happy."

She waited, but he didn't say anything else. Didn't tell her she was crazy, wasting her life. After a second, it finally hit her that her grandfather was being sincere, that Daniel hadn't been kidding when he'd said Grandfather had changed. "I *am* happy," Madison said. "Very much so." Except for this little problem with Jack, which she'd already started creating a solution for.

"Good."

She wanted to tell him about her conversation with her mother, about the Maybelline meeting and Harry's reaction, but didn't. There would be time for that. Later. Right now, she had a mission and she knew exactly who to ask for assistance. "Grandfather, I know it's been a while since we talked. I'm sorry for that, for avoiding you."

"That's okay," he said. "I'm just glad to hear from you now. It's never too late for family."

Madison hoped that was true, that she wasn't too late, for her family or the Pleeseman family. But most especially for Jack. "I need your help. I need you to call in the cavalry."

Her grandfather chuckled. "What do you think money is for? Tell me how many horses and they'll be there."

Madison looked at the cows grazing in the field, watching as Ginny broke into a run, dashing away from David and toward the porch at the sight of Madison. She smiled, then shared her plan with her Grandfather. Within five minutes, everything was in motion.

By tomorrow, Jack Pleeseman would either be thanking her or suing her for cheddar interference.

He'd been too hard on her. He'd been, in fact, a real jerk. Like a wounded animal, Jack had lashed out at someone who was simply trying to help.

He sat on the hard wooden stool at Casey's Cove bar and nursed a Coors he didn't really want. There were few people here at this hour of the morning.

The only real noise came from the jukebox playing country music, Casey's favorite, and the one thing patrons had to tolerate if the owner was behind the bar.

"You look like a frog up and died on your plate," Casey said, sending a bowl of peanuts sailing down the oak surface toward Jack.

Jack chuckled. "That Conway Twitty isn't helping, either."

"That's not Conway. It's Randy Travis. And he's good for what ails you, whether it be the flu or a broken heart." Casey leaned his elbows on the bar. "Tell me, did some woman do you wrong?"

"No, she tried to do everything right." Jack took a gulp of beer, then laid the bottle back on the bar. "That's the problem."

Casey shrugged, then went back to drying glasses.

"We need to talk." Alyssa's acid voice cut through the air.

The last person Jack wanted to see right now. "I don't want to talk to you, Alyssa. You got the blood you came for. Leave me alone."

"I know you don't want to talk to me. Frankly, I don't blame you. But today…today I saw a man who would do anything for someone he loved. And it got me thinking. About us." She slid onto the stool beside him, wriggling a bit to perch on it without making her pencil skirt ride up. She placed her small, square purse on the bar, then folded her hands over the clasp. "Why did you marry me, Jack?"

Sarcasm waited on his tongue, the kind of sarcasm that came packaged with a divorce, from repeated betrayal. Jack, however, was tired of living with this anger. Life was too short, as his father had said. "Because I loved you," he said simply.

"Did you? Or did you marry me because it was expected? Because we'd known each other for so long?"

He considered that for a long second. "Maybe a little of both," he admitted. "Why did you marry me?"

"Partly both of those reasons, but also because…" she paused, fiddled with the clasp, "because I thought you'd do what I could never do."

He lowered the beer instead of taking another sip. "What was that?"

"Have the courage to leave this place." She waved a hand, indicating not the bar, but a much bigger area.

"We did leave, Alyssa. It wasn't enough for you." He didn't mention her first affair, coming thirteen months after they'd gotten married.

"Leaving this town, these farms, wasn't what I needed," she said, her voice sounding the same as the one he remembered from before. Before the marriage. Before the betrayal. The one he'd grown up with, dated for years and thought he knew as well as his own. "I thought I did, because I hated growing up here. I hated the smell, the work, the cows." She looked to the doorway of Casey's, as if seeing the Dandy Dairy farm. "But most of all, I hated myself.

I hated my glasses. I hated the shape of my body. I hated the color of my hair."

"And you hated me," he added.

She shook her head. "No, I didn't. I loved you. The problem was never you, Jack, it was me. I got contacts, I worked out, I dyed my hair. But it didn't solve the problem." She let out a laugh. "Nothing did. So then, I started to blame you."

"Blame me? What did I do?"

She looked to the ceiling for a moment, and Jack could swear he saw tears in her eyes. "You loved me, you fool. You kept right on doing it, no matter how crappy I was. And all that did was make me feel more guilty, less adequate. So…I started looking for those feelings elsewhere."

He knew she wasn't talking about her membership at the Y. "You cheated on me, out of guilt?"

"And…" she drew in a breath, then faced him, "because I never loved you the way a woman should love the man she married. You deserved more than someone who was with you because she thought you'd be the one to change her life for her."

The truth hung there over the bar, along with the scent of stale beer and old peanuts. His wife had never loved him. It didn't surprise him, but it stung. "Then why did you have Ginny? I mean, if you didn't love me, why did you go through with the pregnancy?"

"It wasn't because you asked me to," she said, surprising Jack. "I saw how excited you got at the first ultrasound. How happy you were. And for a while, I thought maybe if we had a baby, that would solve everything, fix you and me, but especially me. But it didn't. And then, after we got divorced, Ginny became a tool."

"A tool? For what?"

"For staying in touch with you, as twisted as that sounds." She shrugged. "Every time I saw you, I guess I was looking for…" her voice trailed off, her eyes going to his.

"Forgiveness," Jack finished.

Alyssa nodded, mute.

At that moment, Jack could have exacted revenge. He could have lashed out at Alyssa, hurting her as much as she had hurt him over the years. She'd done him wrong, as Randy Travis would say, many times over, and she probably deserved a little payback.

Enough hurt had been dished out for one lifetime. Jack slid off the stool, then crossed to his ex-wife and drew her into a hug.

She stayed stiff for a moment, then let go, dissolving into a puddle of tears on his shoulder. It had been years since either of them had touched. Yet Alyssa felt as familiar as an old pair of jeans. She clutched at his back, buried her head into his shoulder and cried. After a moment, she drew back, apparently realizing the patrons in the bar were staring at them. She resettled herself on the stool, her back stiff and straight, then swiped away the mascara tracks with the back of one hand. "Thank you," she whispered.

"Thank *you*, for giving me Ginny," he said, laying a hand over hers, giving it a squeeze before withdrawing.

She bit her lip, went back to toying with the clasp on her purse. "That's why I came here, Jack, to talk to you about Ginny."

Jack braced himself for the worst. After all he'd given up, the emotional wringer he'd gone through, he couldn't lose Ginny now.

"When I signed the papers yesterday, I wasn't thinking about anything other than hurting you." She let out a dry, bitter laugh. "I wonder if psychologists give bulk discounts?"

He smiled, but still the tension in his gut twisted, waiting for Alyssa to get to the point.

"George doesn't want kids at all," at this, a pained look took over Alyssa's face as if she'd just realized her new husband wasn't the package she'd expected, "and I thought I didn't either, until I finally signed those papers."

Here it came, the rescinding of the deal. Ginny would be gone, off with the queen and the foxes and he'd be left here, alone. He held his breath, unable to speak.

"Could I..." Alyssa began, the words tentative, "could I still see her sometimes?"

He let out a breath of relief. "Of course."

Tears glistened again in her eyes. "I don't want her to think I'm a bad mother. That I don't love her.

It's just that I shouldn't be trying to raise someone else while I'm still figuring myself out."

He could have used the business as leverage, could have insisted that she return ownership of Pleeseman in exchange for seeing her daughter. Jack, however, was done with fighting. He wanted only for his daughter to be happy, for all of them to move forward. "Come by anytime," he said. "You're welcome in our home."

"Thank you." She smiled. For the first time in years, Jack thought Alyssa looked happy. Then she drew in a breath. "There's one more thing, Jack," she said. "I need to talk to you about the business."

With that, the tension that had been eased a moment ago tripled in Jack's gut. He ordered another round, then braced himself for what was coming.

Joe's Making-the-Sale Cheese Samples

Assorted cheese slices, arranged nicely on trays
Harriet's macaroni and cheese, hot and bubbly
2 sexy models, ready to work
1 determined family

That Dandy witch will not win, damn it. Bring all
to the local wine festival, then bust your tail making
the sales that are going to save this company and
everyone's future.

CHAPTER THIRTY-FOUR

Madison shut off the Benz, the engine ceasing without letting out any of the last gasps it had been giving her before Coop's magic touch. She stepped from the luxury car, grabbing a garment bag and a box of supplies from the back.

She moved out of the parking space beside hers, then stepped onto the lush expansive lawn of the town green. Ahead of her, large rectangular tents formed a sea of white ringing a wooden pavilion. A dozen workers were busy readying it for a band. Even though the festival didn't start for another forty-five minutes, it was already filling with people, the fruity scent of wine filling the air, the hum of conversation carrying along the wind.

Madison looked behind her, at the entourage of help now pulling up and piling out of their vehicles, loading themselves up with everything it was going to take to make this event a success.

Alyssa Thurgood was *not* going to get the better of Pleeseman Dairy Farms, Cheese Pleese, or, most of all, Jack Pleeseman.

"You sure you know what you're doing?" Joe asked, coming up to her. In his arms, he held a huge cooler, filled with the cheese scheduled to be put out at the wine festival.

"Yep." Madison gave him a grin. "And if I don't, Cally's here."

The willowy brunette reached her side and smiled at Joe. "Trust us. We're professionals."

Joe grunted, then let out an oomph when Harriet slugged him in the arm. "Things are going to work out just fine," his sister said. "So quit being a grump and help us set up."

The four of them headed across the lawn, into the tent and over to the booth designated for the Pleeseman Dairy Farm. David stepped down from a ladder as they reached him, waving a *Voila!* hand at the banner hanging over their two tables. "What do you think?"

The massive banner was exactly what Grandfather had promised. He'd gone, as usual, with the best digital printer. The colors were crisp; the images Neal had taken the other day sharp and clear. Twelve Days of Christmas, laid out in a collage that seemed to beckon to everyone passing by. If there was anyone who could pull some strings—and pull off a miracle, it was her grandfather. He'd contacted Neal, gotten the pictures and put Madison's verbal design into action.

"My brother's going to kill me for doing this," David said. "But I don't mind. I'm a little brother; I live for annoying him."

Cally came up and grabbed her arm. "Who's that?" she whispered.

"Him? That's David, Jack's brother."

"Jack has a brother who looks like that and you don't tell me? That's it, girlfriend. You're never borrowing my gold Manolos again."

Madison laughed. "How about I introduce you two?"

Cally grinned. "You do and you're forgiven."

Madison made the necessary introductions, then to Cally's clear annoyance, reminded David of an errand he had to run. A few minutes later, David was gone. "He'll be back," Madison assured her.

Cally watched David cross the field, with the same purposeful gait as his brother. "He seems the type. The keeper type, I mean."

Madison laughed, sent Cally off to grab her dress, then started laying out some of the contents of the box onto the table. She set up napkins, paper plates, tiny toothpicks, all bought earlier today in the distinctive Cheese Pleese colors.

"You want some help with that?"

Madison spun around to find her mother standing behind her, hair in a ponytail, a floral print dress adding a little jazz to her look. "Mother! You came."

"You needed my help. Of course I did." Vivian smiled, then gestured behind her. "*And* I brought reinforcements."

Tears welled in Madison's eyes when she saw the pair coming up behind her mother. "Daniel!

Olivia!" She stepped around the table, sweeping her cousin and his wife up into a hug.

"I figured you could use a little extra Worth power," Daniel said. Her cousin stood taller than she did, his blue eyes and dark hair making him stand out in a crowd, without him even trying. "And if you get the urge to throw anything, I'll be here to stop that pitching arm."

"Very funny," she said, but a smile took over her face anyway.

"Make yourself useful," Olivia said, giving her husband a playful jab, "and go lay out the tablecloths and display." He did as his wife requested, stopping first to peck a kiss on top of her brunette curls.

In minutes, the Worths had the table set up. Madison deferred to Olivia's great sense of decorating. Olivia took charge of the table, directing Joe and Harriet to pick some of the wildflowers and berry twigs in a nearby field, then she wove the colorful plants in and out of the cheese arrangements. She varied the heights by tucking boxes under the tablecloth, creating an appetizing array of Cheese Pleese's finest.

"You're incredible," Madison said when Olivia was done.

"I only took the cue from your ideas," Olivia replied. She stepped back, nodded with satisfaction at her display, then waved toward Madison. 'Now it's up to the *piece de resistance* to make the sale."

Madison laughed. "This time, it should be easy to do."

"Why's that?"

"Because I believe in the product." She ran a hand over the Cheese Pleese logo, emblazoned on the shrink-wrap. "In fact, I love it."

Olivia sent Daniel a knowing look. "I'll keep my calendar open."

"For what?"

Olivia grinned. "Why for decorating your wedding cake, of course."

Madison threw up her hands. "Keep that piping bag in the drawer. I'm not getting married."

"Yet," Daniel said.

Madison shook her head. "I'm going to get changed." She wagged a finger at her cousin. "And don't you be renting a reception hall while I'm gone."

She grabbed Cally, then the two of them headed into the restrooms. A few minutes later, they emerged; each dressed in a full-length gown and open toed wedge heels, to allow for easier walking on the grass. Cally wore black, Madison the teal, creating a human blend of the Cheese Pleese company colors.

It was all about image, Madison knew, and she intended to give the company the best possible image.

"You think this is going to work?" Harriet asked her when she reached the table again.

"No," Madison said, deciding truth was the best option. "But we'll never know if we don't try."

"That woman isn't going to like you doing this," Joe said.

"I can handle Kitty," Madison said. "I know exactly what to say to her." Ginny skipped over, done playing in the field, apparently bored with climbing the big rocks a few feet away. "I have something for you, too," Madison said, bending down to Ginny's level.

"You do? What?"

Madison pulled out a bag from under the table, the distinctive rainbow of Toys R Us's logo across the front. She hadn't had time to make this extra stop this afternoon, but did it anyway, just to see the look on Ginny's face. "Open it and see."

Ginny peeked inside, then gasped. "Ella Mae. And lots of new clothes for her. But...but she's yours."

Madison took Ginny's hand. "Now she's yours. Ellie needs to know who she was named after, don't you think?"

Ginny nodded. "I gotta show it to her. When she gets bigger, though. 'Cuz she might try to eat Ella Mae now."

Madison laughed. "When she's bigger then."

Would she be here when the calf had grown? Would she see her become a cow, go on to have calves of her own? She had no intentions of returning to the life she'd left in New York—

But she wasn't sure she was wanted here, in Jack's life. And, if she was, would he still want her a year from now? Ten? When she was no longer Madison Worth the flawless model, but an ordinary woman wearing slippers and mascara smudges?

Would he reject her, as so many other men had, when she let that façade slip?

Later, she'd worry about that and about repairing the damage she'd done when she walked out on Jack. For now, there was a job to do. Madison straightened, laid a hand on Ginny's head for a second, then directed her attention back to the table. "Festival starts in ten minutes," she told everyone. "Are we ready?"

Joe grunted, Harriet gave a thumbs-up and Callie sent her a grin. "Where's David?" Joe asked.

"Bringing back something special," Madison said. "Assuming that, is, that he can find it."

A moment later, the opening to the tent was lifted back and the crowd surged in, heading for the two dozen tables of samples set up throughout the space. The dress was casual, the mood festive thanks to a band that started playing some light jazz at the other end of the tent.

A couple who had already snagged two glasses of chardonnay came up to the Cheese Pleese table. "Never heard of you," the man said, his gaze sweeping over the table as he rubbed at his close-cropped gray beard. His companion already looked bored.

"You will after today," Madison promised. She hoisted a tray of sliced Apple Cinnamon Jack toward the two people, sending a smile with the offering. "Try Cheese Pleese," Madison said, "and you'll be sure to say more, please."

The man raised a dubious brow, selected the thinnest, smallest slice, then popped it into this mouth. Madison knew the instant the flavors hit his palate because a smile spread across his face. He washed it down with a sip of wine, then speared a second piece with a toothpick. After he was done with that, he worked his way through one of each of the other samples. The woman beside him tried a timid bite, then was quickly won over as well. She declared the Apple Cinnamon Jack as her favorite.

"Damned good cheese," the man said. "What store carries this?"

"Almost any grocery near you will be, very soon. Until then, we've got a website," Madison sent a Vanna White hand toward the sign behind her, showing the dot-com address. "Here, take a catalog." She handed him the newly printed document, bearing her image on the front.

"Hey, this is you," he said, tapping at the glossy cover. "You own the place?"

"Nope, I'm just the spokesmodel."

He scoffed. "I bet you don't eat any of this."

Her gaze met his, clear, direct and honest. "Actually, it's my favorite food."

He flipped to the ordering page, then pulled out his billfold and withdrew a credit card. "If I give you an order now, can you get it shipped to me overnight?"

Madison glanced at Joe, who sent her a nod and what she was convinced was a smile. "Certainly. And may I recommend our cheddar? You haven't had mac and cheese until you've had Mac and Cheese Pleese."

Harriet bustled forward, a steaming serving of her macaroni dish at the ready. The man gladly accepted it, nodding as Madison went down the list on the ordering form. Behind him, a number of other people had gathered, sampling from the platters and keeping Harriet busy with macaroni requests. Madison glanced over at Cally, who was just as busy at the other end of the table, flirting with the men, commiserating with the women and all the while, handing out Cheese Pleese samples and order forms.

"What the hell do you think you're doing?"

Madison turned to see a very angry Kitty Dandy standing in front of the crowded Cheese Pleese booth, her arms akimbo, her face a mask of fury. "Selling our product," Madison said, smiling innocently.

"I own this company now," Kitty said. "So you and your little fiancé, wherever he is, better get out of here before I call the police."

"Actually," Madison said, "I had someone look into the paperwork for this deal and surprise, surprise there were a few legal issues that are going to tie it up." She eyed Kitty. "Indefinitely."

Kitty glared at her. "Do you think just because you have money you can do what you want?"

Madison gave her a sweet smile. "Actually, yes."

The Worth wealth, however, had only been the part that expedited the lawyer research. Grandfather had put his personal attorney onto the contract as soon as Madison faxed it over. The contract had neglected to name all three owners, citing only Jack and Joe. Apparently Kitty and Alyssa didn't know that David had been given a percentage of the business a few years ago. Though it probably wasn't enough to stop the sale of the business, it was enough to throw a monkey wrench into the Dandy plans and give the Pleesemans a chance.

When she'd told the family about what she'd learned, their fighting spirit had been ignited. Harriet set to work cooking, Joe to readying the product and David to oversee the details of the booth. Madison had stepped into the job Jack had offered her—heading up the marketing—and found she had fun. The thought of going back to college and finally getting that degree no longer filled her with dread. Instead, it had her charged and ready to drag out the notebooks and number 2's.

"You can't do this," Kitty hissed. "Alyssa will go after Jack with everything she has."

"Everything George has," Madison corrected. "Oh, and you might want to know something else. As of today, George has lost his interest in this particular investment."

"What'd you do? Blackmail him?"

Grandfather had simply called an old rival, invited him over for a glass of Dewar's and put his cards on the table. George had done the same. Unfortunately, George had only had two Jacks while Grandfather had a full house.

"I want the Pleeseman business," Kitty said, taking a step forward, pointing a long bony finger in

Madison's direction. "Then I'll be the biggest dairy producer in the state."

Joe and Harriet moved to flank Madison, with Vivian and Cally bringing up the rear. Daniel and Olivia paused in handing out samples to join the family battalion. "You aren't taking anything away from this family," Joe said to Kitty. "And if you try, we'll have Katydid up your butt so fast, you'll be walking with a limp for the rest of your life."

"Your stupid goat doesn't scare me."

Joe glanced over at his sister. "Harriet, I think it's about time we went to Florida, don't you?"

Harriet nodded. "I hear the weather is really nice in Bonita Springs. In fact, while we're there, we should look up some old neighbors."

"Good idea," Joe said, rubbing his chin. "We can tell him how things are going on the family farm."

"Leave my father out of this," Kitty said. "This is my business now."

"Last I heard your dad owned fifty-one percent," Joe said. "I've known Carl Dandy all my life and if he knew what you were doing, how you were acting, he'd put you over his knee."

"Or worse, out to pasture," Harriet added.

Kitty opened her mouth to speak, the fury still sparking in her eyes. Then she took a second look at the mini army ahead of her and closed her mouth again. She pivoted, then stomped back to the Dandy Dairy booth.

"Do we really have a legal leg to stand on?" Joe asked after she was gone.

"We have one that can be a true pain in the ass to Kitty," Madison admitted. "But with more profit, we can have more to battle her with."

"Well then, everyone better get back to work." Joe slapped a Cheese Pleese ball cap on his head, then tied one of the teal aprons around his waist. He took one of the platters and raised it over his head. "Now, who wants cheese?"

David's What's-Good-for-the-Goose Two-Cheese Dip

2/3 cup blue cheese, crumbled
2/3 cup Cheddar cheese, shredded
1/4 cup sour cream
1 1/2 teaspoons onion, minced
1/2 teaspoon Worcestershire sauce

It's about time these two had someone interfering. If you have to take drastic measures to make him realize a happy ending is just a few miles away, then do it. As his little brother, you're well within your rights.

Combine all ingredients in a bowl, then beat with an electric mixer till smooth and fluffy. Chill, then serve with crackers. Yeah, yeah, no stove involved in this one—

A guy's dream come true.

CHAPTER THIRTY-FIVE

"What do you think you're doing, kidnapping me?" Jack asked, scowling at his brother. David had come into Casey's Cove shortly after Alyssa left, latched onto Jack's arm and dragged him out of the bar, tossing a ten at Casey as they left. They were now sitting inside the pick-up, heading God only knew where.

"You're my brother," David said. "So that doesn't make this kidnapping. It makes it knocking some sense into your damned head."

"Will you at least tell me where we're going?"

David thought a second. "Nope."

"What about why you did this?"

David put a finger to his chin. "Nope again."

"Did I ever tell you what a complete pain in the ass you are?"

"Tell me again in about...one minute." David swung into a parking lot, choked with cars.

"You brought me to the wine festival?"

"Yep."

"Why?"

David grinned again while he wrangled the old pick-up truck into a narrow space at the very back. "You'll see."

Jack grumbled a few curses as they got out and walked toward the big tent. It wasn't until they'd actually stepped inside that Jack realized why he was there.

He stopped. "What is everyone doing here? With…" he paused, rubbed his eyes to be sure he was seeing what he thought he saw, "Madison?"

"Trying to have our cake and eat it, too," David said, then took his brother's arm and guided him through the crowd and over to the tables.

It took a second before Jack realized the crush of people was all centered around one place—the pair of tables reserved for Cheese Pleese. Above them hung a colorful banner that married his and Madison's ideas for promotion.

In the midst of it all, Jack saw Madison, alongside a few people he didn't recognize, plus his family and Vivian Worth, all working hard to fill the multiple requests for samples. Catalogs—since when did he have catalogs?—were being passed through the crowd like teenagers in a mosh pit.

It was insane.

It was amazing.

Jack shouldered his way to the tables, then waited for Madison to finish her spiel and notice him standing there.

"Every product in the Cheese Pleese family is made with natural, wholesome ingredients. You'll find our cheeses to be a cut above the competition, and with an edge," at this she turned on that thousand-watt Madison Worth smile, her eyes hooded slightly by long, black lashes, her chest a tease beneath the V of her teal dress, "that's guaranteed to have you saying "more, please." Again and again and again."

The men outside the booth practically started drooling. She smiled again, this time a softer version of the earlier gesture, then passed them the refilled plate of samples his father had just finished readying.

"I never knew you could make cheese so sexy," Jack said, leaning forward.

She turned, and her eyes lit up with surprise, then delight. "I can make *anything* sexy," she said.

The flirtation sent a thrill through him, reminding him instantly of the kitchen, the lake. If they'd been alone, he would have reminded her, too. In fact, he fully intended to do both, very soon. After all, life was short and Jack was through waiting for the right time to begin his life again. The time was now. And the right woman was right here.

Saving his ass, even when he'd told her not to.

"What are you doing here?" he asked her.

"Rescuing your company." She grinned, then waved behind her. "With a little help from the people who believe in you."

Later, he would tell her that he and Alyssa had worked things out back in the bar, that she'd told him to tear up the agreement and to keep the company as a legacy to their daughter. "That way, it'll be a part of Dandy and Pleeseman," Alyssa had said.

Jack chuckled. "Ginny can have world domination in cheese."

Alyssa wagged a finger at him. "As long as she goes to college first."

He and Alyssa had never had a conversation like that, one where they were on the same page where Ginny was concerned. It gave him hope that all of this would work out.

And that everyone would have a happy ending.

Now, he slipped around the table, grabbed a platter and began distributing slices of cheese on little Cheese Pleese emblazoned napkins. The crowd surged forward, a clear sign that there was success on the horizon for the business. His mother had been right, and so had Madison. Seemed Jack needed to give the women in his life a few thank-you's. "Where did all this come from?"

Madison shrugged, like it was no big deal to pull off this kind of miracle in less than twenty-four hours. "Sometimes being a Worth has its advantages."

He looked at her, really looked at her. This was a woman who had dropped everything, including the chance of a lifetime for her career, to come back here and help him. She could be anywhere in the world right now, doing anything else but handing out cheese and catalogs, and yet she was here. Because she loved him?

He sure hoped so. In that instant, Jack realized Madison was everything he'd ever wanted, wrapped up in one gorgeous package. She challenged him, she supported him, she excited him, but most of all, she clearly loved him.

And he definitely loved her.

"How about being a Pleeseman?" he said, whispering in her ear. "Do you see any advantages to that?"

She opened her mouth to answer, but was interrupted by the MC, who took the stage and tapped on the microphone. "And now," he said, we'll announce the winner of the wine cup, presented by Bacchus himself."

A fat man in a too-small toga and grape leaf crown took the stage. He thanked everyone for coming. "This year's winner of the wine cup," Bacchus said, raising a gold trophy shaped like a wine goblet, "is Berkshire Wineries."

The owner of the company charged up the stairs, accepting his trophy with a long-winded speech that thanked everyone from his kindergarten teacher to his great aunt in Alberquerque. Bacchus ended up giving him a good-natured elbow to get him off the stage.

Bacchus wrapped a meaty fist around the mike. "We have one more award to give out. The Berkshire County Wine Festival's Golden Grape Award for most innovative product." He showed the audience a plaque, decorated with fat grapes in brushed gold. "This goes to Cheese Please, for their incredible Apple Cinnamon Jack cheese." Bacchus cupped a hand over his mouth and leaned closer to the mike.

"And if you haven't had a bite, I suggest you try some now. Just see that pretty little lady over there." He pointed in Madison's direction. "Cheese Pleese, come on up and accept this award."

Joe gestured to Jack to go up. The elder Pleeseman beamed with pride and clapped with all the enthusiastic vigor of a contestant on *Family Feud* as Jack made his way to the dais.

"Thank you," Jack said as the crowd's applause died down. In front of him, he saw Kitty, glaring at him. Ah well. He couldn't win them all over. "I'd especially like to thank my mother, for giving me this dream. My father, brother and aunt for helping to build this company to where it is today. And finally, Madison Worth, for being another daisy in this field of thistles."

He drew in a breath, then looked at the plaque for a moment. None of this, he realized meant a thing if he didn't have Madison by his side. He couldn't imagine walking the land, visiting the new calves, plotting the future of the business, without the woman he loved—and loved with a fierceness he had never experienced before—by his side.

What better way to tell her that, than here, in front of a good chunk of the residents of Berkshire County?

"Some of you might have heard a rumor that I'm engaged to this woman," he said, indicating Madison. "But I never asked her properly, so I'm going to do it here." He grinned, then locked his gaze with hers. "Madison Worth, will you marry me?"

The crowd parted as people turned to see Madison's response. A hush descended over the group, punctuated by the occasional voice calling out, "Say yes!"

A heartbeat passed. Another. Madison looked at him, her mouth open in shock. Then she shut it and he could see, even from here, a tear in her eye.

Before she could say the word he dreaded, and thus, break his heart in public, Jack let out a nervous little laugh. "I forgot the ring," he said. "No wonder she's not answering me. Give me a minute and I'll come back with a better offer." The crowd laughed. Jack hoisted his plaque, then thanked the festival one last time before descending the stairs into a sea of congratulations.

By the time he reached the Cheese Please booth, Madison was gone. Aunt Harriet gave him a pat on the shoulder. "She went out the side exit," his aunt said, pointing.

"Thanks." He glanced over at David and noticed his brother deep in a flirtatious conversation with Madison's friend. He suspected there'd be another model on the dairy farm before long.

"Daddy, are you gonna go get Madison?" Ginny asked. "'Cuz I didn't hear if she said yes."

Jack smiled. "Neither did I. So yes, I'm going to go find her." He ruffled his daughter's hair, then looked down at the doll in her hands. "Can I borrow one of those?" he asked, pointing at the pink bowed elastics holding Ella Mae's hair back.

"Sure, Daddy." Ginny slid it off and gave it to her father.

He pressed a quick kiss to her cheek, then headed out of the tent. He found Madison a minute later, standing by the stacks of empty containers used to transport the wine and other offerings.

"Madison."

She turned at the sound of his voice. Tears welled in her eyes. "Jack, I'm sorry. I—"

He put up a hand to stop her. "Listen, I know I put you on the spot back there and we haven't known each other all that long, so I'll understand if you need some time to think about it. I'm sorry I sprung that on you."

"It doesn't matter how much time you give me," she said. "My answer is no."

"No?" He rocked back on his heels, stunned. "Why?"

"Because when you love someone, they leave you." The tears streamed down her face, leaving sad tracks in the flawless makeup.

This woman had had all the money in the world, but not enough security to make her believe that sometimes, people stayed. He could practically see her putting armor around her heart, despite all she had done for him. It was as if now that the moment of truth was here, and the proposal was publicly on the table, she was retreating. Well, Jack wasn't going to let that happen. "I'm not going anywhere, Madison."

"Yes you will. Someday, Jack, you'll get tired of his," she swept a hand over her body, "and you'll leave."

Jack reached over, grabbed an empty paper sack off the pile beside them and thrust it up against Madison's chest. "Sorry. I still love you." He grinned. "And might I add, you look mighty sexy in brown."

She pushed the bag away. "Don't."

"Don't what? Don't try to talk you out of something completely crazy? I love you, Madison. And you want to keep pushing me away—"

"Before you do it to me." Madison wanted so badly to trust in Jack. But the scars built up over years of abandonment chafed beneath the rocket of emotions running through her. She loved him, but she was so afraid of letting him love her back.

She'd spent so many years in a world of facades, the lines between was real and what was just for show had become blurred.

He cupped her face, his touch so gentle she wanted to cry. "I won't do that to you. I love you. I love, in fact, everything about you. The way you laugh, the way you fight," he grinned, "but most especially, the way you smile." He took a step closer, tracing the line of her lips with his finger. "You have a thousand different smiles, Madison Worth. When you're happy, you get these little dimples right here," he brushed along the edge of her cheek. "When you're laughing, your smile reaches all the way to your eyes. And when you're satisfied," at that, the rumbling began in Madison's veins, "your smile makes me feel like I'm the only one in the world you're looking at."

Madison looked into Jack's eyes, reading honesty in the deep chocolate color. "You really noticed all that?"

"Uh-huh. And a few other things, like your brains. Your determination. Your willingness to go to any lengths for the people you love."

Jack hadn't mentioned a single thing that had to do with her looks. He had noticed what was inside her, the person who lay just beneath the veneer of foundation and self-curling mascara. He saw her... and he loved her all the same.

She glanced at the tent and thought of all that had happened today. Madison Worth, who'd once been thought of as nothing more than a pretty face, had gone in, taken charge and handled it. There'd been no cake throwing, no nervous breakdowns. She'd done it.

The knowledge that she could be responsible for her own destiny, that *she* was the one who could fill that cavern inside her gut, hit her square in the chest. She'd searched for years for the thing that would make her feel whole—indulging in everything from food to men.

When the answer was already inside her. Well, duh.

The fear that had trembled in her gut when he'd proposed to her a moment ago melted away. For the first time in her life, Madison felt as if the control was in her hands, the decisions all her own. Jack Pleeseman loved her. Really loved *her*, not her looks, not her wealth, not her name.

And she loved him.

"So how 'bout it?" he asked, dropped to one knee and held out the tiny ribbon that had bound Ella Mae's hair. "Will you marry me? Everyone's waiting for your answer. Especially me."

"First," she said, affecting a stern look, nearly biting her cheek to keep the smile contained, "I think you should know how I feel about you."

His face fell and he lowered his hand to his side.

"You are one of the most stubborn men I have ever met in my life—"

"Hey, the pot shouldn't call the kettle black, you know."

She grinned, bending down to him. "I'm not stubborn. I'm determined, remember?"

He chuckled. "That was just me putting a nice spin on your attitude."

She gave him a light jab in the arm. "You drive me crazy."

"In a good way?"

"In the best way," she said. Oh, how she wanted to kiss him, to wrap herself in his arms and let the world drop away. But first, she had to finish what she wanted to tell him. "Second, I want you to know I don't need you."

He looked confused. "And how is that a good thing?"

She smiled, feeling the joy of independence, of power over her future, take root in her chest. "It means I'm not with you because I expect you to fulfill me. I'm with you now and I'll be with you for a million tomorrows simply because I love you. I don't need you to fill what's in here," she put a hand over her gut, "because that's my job. In the last two days, I've realized fulfillment is in my hands. And you," her smile widened, "are the cheese on top of the nachos."

He grinned. "I thought it was icing on the cake."

She laughed. "Not on the Pleeseman farm, it's not." Then, Madison stopped waiting for what she wanted and stood up, grabbing Jack's hand and then sliding into his arms. Why had she feared this so much? Once she allowed herself to truly feel and embrace love, she didn't feel afraid, she felt empowered. "I love you. I love Ginny. I even love the damned cows."

"Well, good, because Clarice was feeling a little left out. She's sensitive, you know."

Madison laughed. "If you don't mind a slightly spoiled—"

He arched a brow, kidding her. "Slightly?"

"You better watch yourself, or you'll be the next one kissing Clarice."

He made a motion of zipping his lips.

"If you don't mind a slightly spoiled heiress moving into your life, then my answer is yes."

He beamed, then took her left hand in his and slid the elastic onto her finger. The pink bow didn't twinkle, didn't sparkle. But it shone in Madison's heart, which was all that counted. "I promise, there'll be something nicer later."

She curled herself against him, laying her head on his shoulder. "This is perfect, Jack. Everything I ever wanted."

Above them, a boom announced the start of the fireworks show that capped off the festival. The rocket exploded into a shower of blue stars, seeming to rain down on them.

"I have one condition before I marry you," Jack said, his voice a tease.

"Mmm," she said, enjoying the moment. "What's that?"

"You have to promise me that you'll wear that leopard print bikini on a regular basis. Like to breakfast. Lunch. Dinner. And especially dessert."

"Oh, I'll wear that bikini," she teased, dancing her fingers up his shirt, "in places and ways you can't even begin to imagine."

A low, hungry sound escaped Jack's throat. He leaned over and kissed her, his lips on Madison's so much sweeter than ever before. She wrapped her arms around his neck, returning the kiss, tasting, memorizing, loving this man who had captured her heart. Above them, the fireworks continued, beating out a rhythm of explosions that echoed the ones between the heiress and the dairy farmer.

After a long moment, she pulled back, slipping in against him so they could both watch the grand finale. "I have a condition of my own," she said.

"Trust me, you can have anything you want, if you ask me when you're wearing animal print."

She laughed. "Good. Because I want a hot tub. A girl needs something to relax her muscles after a hard day with the cows."

Jack slid his hand down the silky dress, along her hips, her thighs. Desire quickened in his veins. "Let's go home, Mrs. Pleeseman, and I'll show you a way to relax."

"I have the feeling we won't be relaxing at all." She smiled up at him. "Tell me, are there nachos involved in this plan of yours?"

"Oh, yeah," he murmured. "Cheese is a wonderful aphrodisiac."

"I'll alert the *New England Journal of Medicine*," she said, tipping her lips up to his, a breath away from kissing him again. "Later."

As the grand finale of fireworks let loose above them in a rapid explosion of color, Madison Worth and Jack Pleeseman got busy giving the words "more please" a whole new meaning. From somewhere in the distance, they heard a distinctive baa.

Katydid, coming to join the party. Madison laughed. If there was one thing she knew for sure, marrying Jack was going to be a hell of an adventure.

Excerpt from

The Bride Wore Chocolate
Book One in the *Sweet and Savory Novel Series*

Candace Woodrow stared at the gooey, sunken mess inverting onto itself like there was a Hoover under the table. "This was supposed to be a groom's cake, not a pancake."

Rebecca poked at the chocolate failure. "Did you cook it long enough?"

"I thought I did," Candace said. "I lost track of time because Trifecta needed to go out."

"I've seen you with that dog." Maria wagged a finger at her. "Taking a three-legged dog for a walk is a comedy of errors." She gave an indulgent smile to Candace's shelter-rescued mutt, dozing in the front part of the shop, separated from the kitchen by a glass door. "We still love ya, Trifecta, even if you are a living tripod."

Candace laughed. The best thing about working with her friends every day was the laughter. Without them, she swore she'd have gone crazy planning her wedding.

Two years ago, the three of them had started Gift Baskets to Die For in the basement of Candace's Dorchester duplex. Within a year, their food-themed baskets had hit it big with the corporations in Boston, allowing them to open a storefront in a quaint building not far from Faneuil Hall Marketplace. Business had been brisk enough to pay both the rent and decent salaries for all of them.

Candace's life was settled, secure. On an even, planned keel. She was twenty-seven, three weeks from being married, and her life was chugging along on the path she'd laid out.

Everything was perfect—except the cake.

"Maybe the eggs were spoiled," Candace said. "I mean, look at this thing. It's an overgrown hockey puck."

"It's a sign." Maria nodded and her shoulder-length chestnut curls shook in emphasis. "Yep. Definitely a sign."

Rebecca shushed her. "Will you stop with that? This is Candace's wedding we're talking about. Don't make her more nervous than she already is." She took another look at the cake. "I think you just underbaked it. Besides, this was a trial run. We'll make another one before the wedding."

"What if it *is* a sign?" Candace threw up her hands. "Look at all that's gone wrong with my wedding. The DJ I booked had a heart attack—"

"He said the wheelchair won't stop him from spinning CDs," Rebecca pointed out.

"If he doesn't electrocute himself with the IV drip," Maria added.

"And then last week Father Kenny ran off with the church secretary."

"Who turned out to be a Daniel, not a Danielle like we all thought." Maria grabbed a raspberry thumbprint cookie from the Tupperware container on the counter and took a bite. Maria Pagliano's method of dieting involved buying the latest issues of *Cosmo, Glamour* and *Woman's World*, picking and choosing the parts she liked from their diets of the month, then chucking the whole thing on weekends.

"Don't forget the fire at the dress shop. I still can't believe the store burned to the ground, and with your dress inside." Rebecca twisted a scrunchie around her straight brown hair, creating a jaunty ponytail. On Rebecca Hamilton, almost any hairstyle looked good. She had one of those long, delicate faces made for Cover Girl. "It was kind of heroic, though, how that cute fireman kept you from going in after it. He saved your life."

"I would have rather he saved my dress," Candace muttered. "At least I have insurance. But I still need to find another dress. I can't get that particular one anymore and even if I could, there's not enough time to order it."

"You haven't bought one yet?" Maria's jaw dropped. "But Candace, the wedding's only three weeks away."

Since Candace had said "I will" to Barry, it had been one disaster after another. If she put stock in things like signs, she'd have called off the wedding months ago. But she didn't believe in any of that. The disasters encompassed a string of bad luck, no more. Marrying Barry was the right choice. When she'd weighed the options, Barry had come out high on the good idea side. She'd looked at her upcoming wedding as she had every major move in her life, with careful research, planning and analysis.

Only once had she stepped out of that box. A long time ago. Ever since then, Candace had subscribed to the "more control is better" life mantra. That was what made Barry perfect for her. They matched like plaid and stripes.

On her marrying Barry list the pros had far outweighed any cons. Now if Murphy's Law would just see that too.

Candace sighed. "Between the business and all those last-minute glitches, I haven't had time to find another dress."

Rebecca looped her arm through Candace's. "Tonight we're going dress shopping, and then we'll get good and drunk because tomorrow is Sunday, our day off, and we don't have a single delivery due on Monday."

Of the three of them, Rebecca's status as the oldest by four months had made her the unofficial decision maker. She was also the thinnest and the only one who came equipped with both an iron will and a Blackwell-worthy fashion sense. And, as the sole married one, the wisest when it came to matters of weddings and bridal gowns.

"Wow. An instant vacation." Maria grabbed a second cookie and finished it off in two bites. "I hope the bar is well stocked."

Rebecca gave her a wry look. "You mean you hope the bartender is well built."

"Yeah, that, too." Maria smiled. "But if he doesn't know how to make a killer margarita, what good are looks?"

Candace laughed. She picked up the cake disaster and threw it into the trash, then dropped the spring-form pan in the sink to soak. The bell over the shop door jangled and a second later, an enormous backpack wrangled through the door into the kitchen.

"Grandma?"

Candace's petite grandmother twirled around, spinning the king-size bag in the kitchen with an ease that belied her age—and nearly took out the Cuisinart on the side counter. "I'm making a pit stop," Grandma Woodrow said, swiping at her brow. The bag dwarfed her, and made her seem even smaller and thinner. "Lord, it's hot out there for June."

"What are you doing with that thing?"

"Hiking. What else would you need a backpack for? George is taking me hiking next month along the Appalachian Trail. I'm following the Paul Revere Trail today so I can break it in." Grandma lowered the dark green bag to the floor, slipping her arms out of the metal frame. She tugged off her Red Sox ball cap and fluffed up her short gray hair, using the toaster for a mirror.

Grandma was seventy-six but told everyone she was fifty-eight. Even Candace fell for the age lie once in a while and forgot her grandmother had been collecting social security for more than a decade. She'd inherited Grandma's hazel eyes and the long blond hair she'd had in her youth, but not Grandma's wild, adventurous personality. "When are you going to get old like other self-respecting retirees?"

Her grandmother waved her hand in dismissal. "Never. Old equals dead. Besides, I'd have to buy a rocking chair and I don't even like to rock." She grinned and gave Candace a wink. "Unless I'm rocking with George, of course."

"Stop! Too much information." Candace poured a tall glass of lemonade from the refrigerator and handed it to her grandmother, then pushed the container of cookies across the counter. Grandma scooped up three. Candace smiled. Grandma never could resist any of the shop's baked goodies. Every evening after work, Candace brought home a few cookies and dropped them off at her grandmother's apartment before going to her own half of the duplex they shared.

Six years ago, Candace had moved in at her grandmother's suggestion, to help save money. And, Grandma Woodrow had added, to look after her because she was getting up there in years. Candace suspected the real, unspoken reason hit a little closer to home. Grandma, who had more energy than Carrot Top on steroids, missed the echoes of other people in the house.

Candace's father, Grandma's only child, had headed for a permanent tan in Florida years earlier, making occasional seasonal visits on his way up to his summer lake cottage in New Hampshire. Candace's mother, who seemed to be trying to break Elizabeth Taylor's husband record, was always away on one honeymoon or another.

That left just Candace and Grandma Woodrow. Truth be told, Candace liked it that way, despite Grandma's habit of offering quirky advice on everything from buying watermelon—look for one that thumps when you smack it—to kissing men—look for one that doesn't smack you when you thump him.

"So, what are you girls cooking up today?" Grandma asked.

Rebecca gestured toward the trashcan. "A groom's cake. But it refused to stay up. Maybe we should have added some Viagra to the mix."

Grandma shook half a cookie at Candace. "It's a sign."

"I just undercooked it. It's not a sign of anything." Candace recovered the cookies and put them away.

Grandma's face took on a stricken look. She pouted.

"Okay, two more. We need these for orders." She peeled back the lid and held out the container. Grandma grabbed four before Candace snapped the top shut again.

"I'm an old woman," she said. "You have to indulge me."

Candace laughed. "You're only old when it's convenient."

Grandma ignored her. "Are you sure Barry is your soul mate?"

Too often, they retreaded this familiar ground. Candace wanted the wedding to be over, so all of them would stop quizzing her. "Grandma, you know

I don't believe in signs or soul mates or harbingers of evil. You meet a guy who doesn't have any outrageous fetishes or a criminal record, you marry him and you hope you can hang on for a few years before the lawyers start dividing the toys."

"What about romance? True love? Undying devotion?"

"That only happens in Meg Ryan movies. Not in my life."

Across the room, Maria and Rebecca kept mute. As the maid and matron of honor, they supported Candace marrying Barry, but both still held this deep-seated belief in love at first sight, a statistical improbability according to the article Candace had read in *Newsweek* last month.

Candace knew her friends didn't quite agree with her numerical analysis of her future. The other two lived life on the right side of their brains. Rebecca had settled down, now married and with a three-year-old. Maria had a new love of her life on a regular basis. Right now, it was David, a cute gynecologist who'd moved into Maria's condo last month and pledged his undying devotion with a pearl necklace and one-half the rent.

Candace considered herself too levelheaded to get caught up in that wine and roses stuff. At three years from turning thirty, she told herself she needed to give up on the Cinderella fantasy.

Besides, any woman who had mice for best friends was probably legally insane anyway.

ABOUT THE AUTHOR

New York Times and *USA Today* bestselling author Shirley Jump spends her days writing romance and women's fiction to feed her shoe addiction and avoid cleaning the toilets. She cleverly finds writing time by feeding her kids junk food, allowing them to dress in the clothes they find on the floor and encouraging the dogs to double as vacuum cleaners. Visit her website at *www.ShirleyJump.com*, follow her on Facebook at www.facebook.com/shirleyjump.author or follow her Twitter at www.twitter.com/shirleyjump.

Made in the USA
Middletown, DE
08 January 2015